To the Ends of the Earth
The Last Journey of Lewis & Clark

By
Frances Hunter

Blind Rabbit Press
Austin, Texas

Publishers Cataloging in Publication Data
Hunter, Frances.
     To the ends of the earth : the last journey of Lewis and Clark / Frances Hunter.
       p. cm.

     ISBN 0-9777636-2-5
      1. Lewis and Clark Expedition (1804-1806)—Fiction.
2. Lewis, Meriwether, 1774-1809—Fiction. 3. Clark, William, 1770-1838—Fiction. 4. York, ca. 1775-ca. 1815—Fiction.
5. Natchez Trace—Fiction. 6. Saint Louis (Mo.)—Fiction.
I. Title.

917.804/2—dc22   2006921431

Printed in the United States of America

For Mom and Dad

Honored Parents

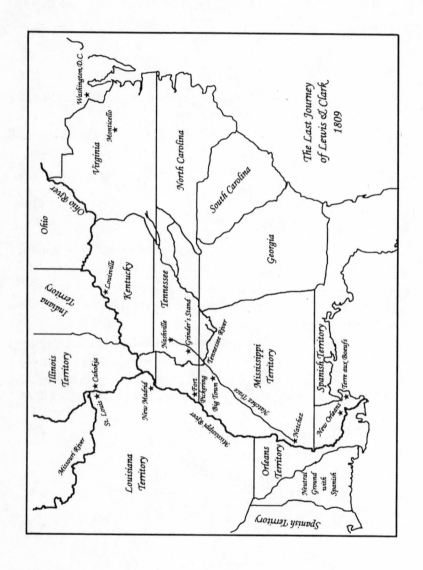

The Last Journey
of Lewis & Clark
1809

Washington, D.C.

Monticello

Virginia

Ohio River

Ohio

North Carolina

South Carolina

Georgia

Indiana Territory

Illinois Territory

Kentucky

Louisville

Tennessee

Nashville

Grinder's Stand

Tennessee River

Mississippi Territory

Spanish Territory

Terre aux Boeufs

St. Louis

Cahokia

Missouri River

Louisiana Territory

New Madrid

Mississippi River

Fort Pickering

Big Town

Natchez Trace

Natchez

New Orleans

Orleans Territory

Neutral Ground with Spanish

Spanish Territory

It was an unusual summer for wolves. In the dark, quiet hours of the night, they crept into the streets of St. Louis and scavenged for garbage in the gutters, driving the pigs away. Padding on silent paws, they slipped into yards and gardens, and the bolder ones even ventured up onto front porches. In the morning, women and slaves woke to find pens broken into and rabbits and chickens snatched away, with scraps of fur and feathers in their place. As the summer wore on, men coming home late from the riverfront or the tavern began to carry walking sticks to defend themselves, just in case.

Later in July, it rained. That discouraged the wolves somehow. They disappeared from the steaming backstreets and alleys of town and slithered back into the vast wilderness. People began to breathe a little easier at night. The pigs reclaimed the gutters, and men lingered longer at the taverns. Women relaxed. Their chickens were safe.

But in the vast, dark, wild land beyond the feeble lamps and sputtering torches of town, the wolves waited. Travelers saw them skulking about on back roads and Indian trails. At night, the air was full of yearning howls. The people of St. Louis shut their doors against the noise and shivered in their beds, praying for more rain.

Chapter 1
Lewis

Cahokia, Illinois Territory
July 29, 1809

Meriwether Lewis buried his face deeper into the pillow, his tongue furred with rum and sleep. He felt easy and content. Soon, it would be time to get up, get the pirogues loaded, get on the river. That endless ribbon of shimmering water, under a deep blue sky. He would walk on the bluffs today, with his spyglass and his notebook. Take the dog. Don't forget to borrow the good compass from Clark—

Soft fingers traced a trail down his back. Lewis started awake. Slowly, the room resolved itself into a collection of familiar objects. A curtained window, washbasin, chair. Oh, yes, Pinsoneau's Inn. He always roomed here when he came across the river to do business.

"Gov'ner? Didn't ye say ye needed to be somewhere at eight o'clock?"

Lewis raised up on his elbow and turned to look at the girl lying beside him. Blonde, big gray eyes, a riot of curly hair.

"Yes," he said thickly. "So I did." He glanced at the window and saw that the afternoon had come and gone, and the sky was already darkening into night. "Lord, have I been out all this time?"

The girl giggled and traced small circles on his forearm with her finger. "You were tired." Memories came back to him of soft white thighs, and heels digging into the back of his legs. For the kind of girl she was, she was really rather good-looking. But God help him, he couldn't remember her name.

Lewis shook off her hand and sat up, trying to hold back an avalanche of shame. He'd sworn to himself he would hold his liquor this time, and stay away from the waterfront tarts. Swinging his legs off the bed, he got up and started hunting for his clothes. Damned if I don't break my own promises, he thought. Mr. Jefferson was right. I'll make a politician yet.

"Are you goin' to meet another trader, love?" The girl's pale eyes followed him around the room.

"No. That's all done." He found his shirt on the floor and pulled it on over his head, then yanked on his breeches. At least that was one aspect of the trip he didn't have to feel guilty about. Cahokia was the jumping-off point for shipping goods from the West down the Mississippi River and up the Ohio, for delivery to the big eastern merchant houses. The St. Louis Missouri River Fur Company was counting on him to negotiate a good deal. A couple of months ago, the newly minted company had sent a flotilla of flatboats up the Missouri River, supposedly on an official military expedition. Secretly, the company partners were praying that the flatboats would return in the fall with a cargo of animal pelts, which the Cahokia traders would transform into cash.

As usual, he played his part to perfection. A little grin and gab, and the traders fell right into his hands. Smiling, nodding, fawning. Everybody wanted to do a favor for the young hero governor. In his heart, he knew they only showed him respect because they thought he could make them a lot of money.

He fastened his waistcoat, then wrapped his neck cloth around his neck, snugging it nice and tight in the latest fashion. His stomach tightened along with the necktie. If the fur company didn't succeed, he'd have nothing to his name but acres of worthless wilderness land and a mountain of debt. Fur was the only way to make money in this miserable hole—

But he mustn't think about it right now. He had a friend to meet. He plucked his crisp blue coat off the back of the chair, dug in the pocket, and pulled out the crumpled note. He'd found it stuck in his door when he returned to his room that afternoon with...the unnamed woman who was now occupying his bed.

An old friend wishes to see you—at Brady's tonight—8 o'clock.

Lewis sat down on the edge of the bed and pulled on his shiny black hussar's boots. He stood up and eased into the blue coat, feeling it slide snugly over his shoulders. His fingers flew down the two rows of brass buttons on the front. He ran a tortoiseshell comb through his hair and picked up his beaver hat: shiny, blue-black, brim perfectly rolled. When donned at a rakish angle, the hat created just the right effect.

He checked his appearance in a small silvered looking-glass hanging on the wall.

His Excellency, Meriwether Lewis, Governor of the Territory of Upper Louisiana. At least he looked the part. It occurred to him that a man's clothes were like a suit of armor: a better, stronger image of yourself that stood between you and the world. Of course, the theory fell apart when you considered that Mr. Jefferson went around in an old corduroy vest and house slippers. Mr. Jefferson didn't need armor.

The girl lay on the bed, watching him. "Do you want me to wait for you, Gov'ner?"

Mary? Sally? Sarah? "No. That won't be necessary. I'll be out late."

She smiled and smoothed the bedsheets around herself. "I don't mind."

"No, you'd better run along. No rush. Just take your leave whenever you're ready." He had the impulse to lean over and kiss her, but he pushed it away. Instead, he grabbed his walking stick, hurried to the door, and stepped out into the muddy street.

The evening air smelled fresh from the summer rain, and the riverfront was cooler and less stifling than before. Unfortunately, the improvement didn't reach beneath the surface. The brief shower had turned the dusty streets of Cahokia into an ankle-deep soup of rotting garbage and animal filth. Lewis walked nimbly, taking care not to lose his footing in the foul-smelling sludge.

In the fading light to the west, he noticed the sudden illumination of lamps on the opposite side of the river. The sight made a dull pain start behind his eyes. St. Louis was the seat of government of the Territory of Upper Louisiana. According to Mr. Jefferson, the governorship was his reward for successfully leading the Corps of Discovery to the Pacific Ocean and back.

Lewis snorted. Who in his right mind would want the job? The United States had gained control of the vast territory just a few years before, but it was in name only. He'd arrived there last spring to assume his post and found the citizens in a virtual civil war over land grants and Indian trading rights.

But he had to give himself credit for one thing. His attempts to set things right—you can trade here, you can't trap there—had succeeded admirably in uniting a divided populace. They all agreed to a man that their new governor was an ignorant ass.

The trouble, he reflected, was that in his mind he was still a soldier. Though he had resigned his captain's commission when he accepted the governorship, it wasn't easy to give up his military habits. He still kept his hair in the close-cropped style prescribed by military regulations, and his posture was still ramrod straight. And when he gave orders, he still expected them to be obeyed.

He was not a soldier anymore.

Lewis sighed. Maybe it would help if he got a wife. Clark said it did wonders for a man's morale, and God knew, he could use a little encouragement. He couldn't help thinking that a couple of years ago, his hair had been dark and curly. Now it was going gray, though he was not yet thirty-five. He sometimes wondered if it would be white by the time he left the governor's post.

Approaching Brady's tavern, Lewis stopped for a moment and turned the walking stick in his hands. The incidents of the dinner hour must not be repeated. His meeting with the traders had gone so well that conviviality reigned, and the wine and rum flowed as free as the wide Missouri. He'd ended up thoroughly soused. The next thing he knew, he'd woken up in bed with...

"Elizabeth," he whispered.

He put his shoulders back. The unpleasantness of this afternoon was behind him. He would not get drunk again tonight. He paused at the door to stomp mud off his boots.

"Oy! Gov'ner!"

"Evening, Tom." Lewis took off his black beaver hat, ducked his head, and stepped through the narrow doorway into the cool darkness of the tavern. The place reeked of the comforting smells of hard liquor, tobacco smoke, and men's sweat. Tom Brady rushed up to him, his florid face beaming.

"Gov'ner Lewis! An honor, sar! Yer looking fine, ye are!" The big Irishman grabbed his hand and wrung it heartily.

"Easy, Brady, you'll have it off." Lewis smiled and extricated his hand from Brady's powerful grip. "How have you been? Business is good, I see."

Brady nodded and grinned at the dozen or so men who crowded around crude wooden tables in the sputtering light of oil lamps, drinking and laughing over their card games. "Always good in the summer, sar. A stiff drink makes ye immune from the muskeetors."

"I'll remember that, Brady." Lewis handed Brady his hat and walking stick and shrugged out of his coat. His white linen shirt stuck to his body in the humid air. "I'm supposed to meet a fellow here, but I don't think he's arrived."

"The gen'lman's here, sar." Brady thumbed toward the back room. "He wanted to speak to yeh in private."

"Oh. All right." The smell of the liquor and the sight of so many men drinking made his throat ache. Lewis swallowed. "Why don't you give me a yard of flannel, Brady?"

To his chagrin, Brady's smile faded a bit. The way people talked around here, it was obvious Brady had already heard about what happened this afternoon. There was nothing to do but brazen it out. "Just one. What the hell. It's a special occasion."

"Very good, sar."

"Don't forget the egg." His stomach clenching, Lewis stood drumming his fingers while Brady prepared the concoction of beer, sugar, molasses, dried pumpkin, and rum. After what seemed like an eternity of stirring, Brady cracked in an egg, finished it off with a hot iron, and handed him the still-steaming tankard.

"Thank you, Tom." He took a sip and let the warm sweet liquid burn a trickle down his throat. Just one, he thought. So help me God.

Lewis paid Brady for the drink and moved away, eager to avoid the concern in the man's eyes. He slipped through the dark passageway to the room where his visitor was waiting.

In the dim light, a man sat at a table, reading by the light of a small lamp he was pushing around the table to illuminate different parts of his text. Across the back of his chair hung the greatcoat of a general of the army. When the man raised his eyes to acknowledge Lewis's presence, his identity was unmistakable.

Lewis drew in a breath. He heard his own voice blurt in amazement, "General Wilkinson."

Rolling up his papers, Wilkinson leapt to his feet and strode across the room, his arms outstretched. "Governor!" He clasped Lewis's hand. "It's a great honor to see you, sir!"

"To see me?" Lewis said, stunned. The last person he'd expected to find here tonight was James Wilkinson, the commanding general of the United States Army. "General, I must admit I'm surprised."

"Don't be," Wilkinson said. "When I heard you were also in Cahokia, I thought, what serendipity! It's rare that I get the chance to sit down and talk with a young man of such promise."

"Your opinion is in the minority these days, General. I'm afraid I'm not the most popular politician in the territory right now."

"No?" Wilkinson raised his eyebrows. "Well, I can't imagine why not. You'd think these bumpkins would appreciate a man of your rugged qualities. Scientist—explorer—bona fide hero of the West—"

"You flatter me, General."

"Well, perhaps." Wilkinson chuckled as if they had just shared a very funny joke. "Come sit down, Lewis, and indulge an old man in conversation."

Lewis hesitated. He well remembered the last time he had seen James Wilkinson. It was two years ago in a Virginia courtroom, where the general had been in the witness box, stammering and sweating as the chief witness in the trial of Aaron Burr. Lewis had attended the trial for Mr. Jefferson, and he remembered every implausible detail that he'd reported back to the president. Wilkinson had seemed to know an awful lot about Burr's mad plan to attack Mexico and form a new fiefdom out of Spanish territory and the states west of the Alleghenies.

Like most people, Lewis came away believing that, far from being a disinterested witness, Wilkinson was one of Burr's fellow conspirators. The jury thought so too, for they acquitted Burr of treason and left him to live out his life in exile. Wilkinson, on the other hand, went back to his command—with Mr. Jefferson's blessing, of course. Politics was indeed a strange business.

Curious, Lewis took the chair across from Wilkinson and placed his tankard on the table, careful not to make a ring on the general's papers. Wilkinson smiled at him. "So, how are you finding the governorship?"

"A challenge." Lewis sighed. "There are many competing interests, and it's impossible to please them all—well, I daresay you know all about it. You held the job before I did."

"Indeed." Wilkinson leaned forward with a wink. "Tell me—is official Washington as helpful as ever?"

"If by helpful you mean not at all, I suppose so," Lewis said. "Frankly, General, I don't think President Madison knows a thing about what I'm facing out here. The traders fight with the trappers, the trappers fight with the Indians...and they expect me to get things under control, without money *or* authority."

"A familiar tale." Wilkinson's brow furrowed with concern. "To be honest, I'm in the same boat in my position. The British are knocking at the door, and here I am—the commanding general of the Army, for God's sake!— valiantly trying to defend the West, and all I get from Washington are silly instructions and insane demands." He cleared his throat. "And truly, how soon they forget. It's tragic the way your countrymen have treated you. A man such as yourself, mistreated and abused...your exploits forgotten, your immense contribution ignored—"

"General, please." If there was anything Lewis hated being reminded of, it was his own apparent fall from grace. "Why dwell on things you can do nothing about?"

"Well, if *you* are not angry about it, then *I* am, sir!" Wilkinson smacked the table with his hand. "President Madison cares nothing for your fame. To him, your entire expedition—what do you call it, you're so clever with names—the Corps of Volunteers for Northwestern Discovery? Only the greatest feat of exploration ever attempted on this continent—" He paused in mid-sentence and fixed Lewis with a disconcerting look. "Well, in Madison's petty mind, it was a colossal waste of money."

"That's because he doesn't understand what we discovered. When the expedition journals are published, he'll see that it wasn't a waste—"

"But that's not the point!" Wilkinson cut him off. "The point is, Madison has no *vision* for what this country could be! But you do, Lewis, and so do I."

Lewis looked at him in wonderment. Wilkinson never changed, either in appearance or in his fanciful ideas. Though past fifty, the general resembled an overgrown elf, his face naturally merry, his white hair frizzed, his nose reddened from claret. But Wilkinson was anything but harmless. Just ask Aaron Burr. Under the lilting brows and broad, open forehead were the small black eyes of a snake.

"This country is in a pickle, Lewis." Wilkinson's breath came faster. "Our beloved president, the esteemed Jefferson, is retired and forgotten now. You no longer have your patron, and I no longer have my mainstay." A glow of rage returned to his cheeks. "And in his place is that *pygmy*, Madison, who is intent on speeding the country to ruin."

"Well, there's little to be done about that, either," Lewis said. "He was fairly elected, and we must represent the interests of the West to his administration as best we can."

"Oh, Governor," Wilkinson said. "Surely you don't think that's *all* that can be done."

Lewis lifted a corner of his mouth. Whatever Wilkinson was up to, it was bound to be amusing. "So what are you proposing?"

"An empire," Wilkinson whispered.

Lewis's eyes widened, and he swallowed hard. He suddenly realized that this was no idle conversation—it was the beginning of a conspiracy. "My God, is this how it started with Aaron Burr?"

Wilkinson's eyes gleamed. "Aaron Burr, that aspiring Caesar? Not in your league, Governor. Burr was merely a pretender. You are the real thing, sir."

Lewis's heart began to hammer in his chest. "Wilkinson, what in God's name are you talking about?"

"I'm talking about...an empire." Wilkinson's breath wheezed as he grappled with his papers and unrolled a map onto the grease-stained table. Lewis recognized it immediately as a copy of one drawn by William Clark during the expedition, outlining the various rivers and landforms of the West. The map was as familiar to him as the back of his own hand. He looked at it numbly as Wilkinson said: "You and William Clark know this land better than any white men alive, because you traveled through it, didn't you? The British aren't a factor out there yet, except on the Pacific Coast. And the Spanish? Well, God knows I can take care of them."

Wilkinson chuckled and continued, "So how about a little 'expedition', so to speak? You and Clark together again, leading a handpicked force of your own men! You'd have the full backing of the army, of course. Imagine it—hundreds of miles of beautiful, rich land, yours for the taking! Why, after you'd taken what you wanted of Upper Louisiana, you could go all the way to Santa Fe. Or even Mexico! And there would be nothing Madison could do to stop you."

His eyes danced as he stared down at the map. "Think of it, Lewis. You shouldn't have to spend your life begging for the allegiance of smelly Frenchmen in tawdry riverfront towns! For God's sake, if there were any justice in this world, you'd have riches and glory already. Join me, and you'll be a king—*El Jefe* of your own domain! You and your best friend Clark, on the golden throne of the Montezumas!" He panted, struggling for breath. "It's what you've always wanted. It's what you deserve. And it's what you will get—with my help, naturally."

Lewis's tongue felt wooden in his mouth. This conversation, this very meeting, was a disaster. He willed himself to be calm. "Very generous. But pray, General...what do *you* expect to get out of all this?"

"Besides the money?" Wilkinson blinked in confusion. "Why, I will head up the army, of course."

Lewis gripped the edge of the table. By God, in his mind he was still a soldier. "And which army were you intending to use, General?" He leaned forward, his voice growing heated. "We hear things up here too, sir. Tell me, will we march with the poor sick fellows at Terre aux Boeufs? Those self-same troops you have quartered in the meanest poverty? Your army that is now starving to death at New Orleans, under your watch?"

"You shouldn't believe everything you hear, Governor."

Lewis got to his feet. "General, you are insane."

"I hardly think so." Wilkinson shrugged. "See here, Lewis, all I want is for you to have the wealth and recognition that your ungrateful country has denied you. You must admit it's a tempting offer! Why don't you at least discuss it with your friend Clark? That's how you make all your decisions, isn't it? By putting your heads together?"

"Clark!" Lewis exclaimed. "Frankly, General, I'm amazed at your gall. Why, if William Clark knew I was even in the same room with you, there'd be the devil to pay. After what you did to his brother—"

"What *I* did? For God's sake, is he still mad about that?" Wilkinson fumed. "That was years ago! What happened to that idiot was unavoidable! He assumed the risks—"

"You destroyed George Rogers Clark." Lewis said, his voice shaking. "The man was a hero. He had nothing left when you got through with him—"

"George Rogers Clark was a fool," Wilkinson snapped. "He was eternally drunk, and full of design. Little better than a barbarian, really. He couldn't understand the first thing about confidentiality. I do hope his brother's a little smarter."

"And Aaron Burr? He had trouble with confidentiality, too, I suppose! That's why you sold him out on the witness stand! I was there, remember? I saw it! You branded him a traitor in front of the whole country—"

"Well, Burr *was* a traitor," Wilkinson said. "All I did was tell the truth."

"The truth?" Lewis laughed. "Your testimony in the Burr trial was the most preposterous thing I ever heard. You were in on the goddamn conspiracy! You ought to be in exile right next to him—or the insane asylum, I can't decide which."

"There's not a shred of evidence connecting me with the incidents you describe," Wilkinson said, glaring. "Spare me the righteous indignation, Governor, and let's talk business. You told me yourself, the government of the United States has denied you both money and authority. I'm offering you both. This little expedition promises to be very rewarding—for *all* of us."

Lewis stared. His heart was pounding so hard he was afraid it would burst out of his chest. "Why me, General?" he asked. "Why in God's name would you think I would act against the United States?"

"Don't you see?" Wilkinson's expression softened. "You'd be doing the United States a favor. They bought the Louisiana Territory, but you know as well as I do they'll never be able to hold it, at least not with an imbecile like Madison in charge. Better to have you on their western border than the

Spanish, or God forbid, the British, eh? As a patriot, I would think you'd jump at the chance to do well by your country, while doing well by yourself." He smiled. "Have I misjudged you, then?"

Lewis pointed his finger in the pink, amiable face. It was all he could do to keep from trembling. "Wilkinson," he said, "you are a liar, a traitor and a maniac. And you have misjudged me badly, if you think I would join you on the path of treason."

"Easy," Wilkinson warned. "You're letting your temper get the better of you."

"I would never betray my country, General."

"Oh?" Wilkinson said, still smiling. "But you would betray the public trust, I suppose."

Lewis gulped. "What the hell are you talking about?"

"Tut, Lewis! You've been in the wilderness too long. Be civilized," Wilkinson said. "I know all about the new venture—what's it called? The St. Louis Missouri River Fur Company? Rather a grandiose name—did you think of it?"

Lewis's jaw worked. "How do you know about that?"

"Oh, I still have a few friends in St. Louis," Wilkinson said. "You're very clever, Governor. A silent partner in what could be the biggest fur trading operation in history! I understand you've already sent an expedition up the Missouri River to get things started. If all goes well, the profits to you and your friends will be—well, beyond imagination, really." His eyes sparkled as he raised his hands off the table and waved them in dramatic fashion. "Flatboats coming down the river, piled to the sky with the most valuable pelts—"

"You don't know what you're talking about."

"Oh please, it's a little late to play the outraged maiden, don't you think?" Wilkinson laughed scornfully. "I know, I know, you're a government official. And it would be a conflict of interest, wouldn't it? You'd never use your position to enrich yourself—oh heavens, no." He smirked at Lewis across the table. "So what *are* you doing here in Cahokia? Surely not meeting with the big trading companies—working out the details to turn all those pelts into a pot of gold in the eastern markets?"

Wilkinson leaned back in his chair and folded his hands across his portly belly. "My, my, Lewis. How sneaky you are! Using your official position for personal gain! Now what do you suppose our dear Mr. Madison and the good old War Department would have to say about that?"

Lewis took a swallow from his tankard, feeling the burning warmth and the bitter aftertaste on his tongue. Fury and fear battled inside him. The general's sources were good, all right, but what a scoundrel like Wilkinson could never understand was that he wasn't in it for the money. God knew he needed the cash. But what he really cared about was the future of his country, the opening of the West, the building of a new American—

Empire.

He clenched his fists. On a tide of rage, he said, "I don't know what kind of game you think you're playing, General, but I'm not interested. The President and the War Department will hear about a *lot* of things—including the conversation we've had here tonight."

For the first time, a hint of fear darted through Wilkinson's eyes. "You are famed for your keen intelligence, Governor. I trust you will use it and keep your mouth shut."

"*I will not.*" Lewis leaned across the table and stared into Wilkinson's small black eyes. "General, you have cut your own throat. At last, the government in Washington is going to see you for what you really are. And I assure you, it will give me the greatest pleasure of my life to be the one to *bring you down.*"

Wilkinson's face was no longer affable and smiling. "You disappoint me, sir. But then, you always were an incomparable rascal." Then his eyes narrowed, and his gaze turned venomous. "You have no proof of this conversation. It will be your word against mine. If you go to the administration with a story like this, they'll all think you're mad."

When Lewis didn't look away, Wilkinson added: "If you act against me, you will wish you had never been born."

"So be it then." Lewis downed the last of his drink and slammed the tankard down on the table. "The next time I see you, sir, I trust you'll be in irons. Good night." He got up and walked out.

In the crowded outer room of the tavern, Lewis motioned Brady for his hat and coat. His shirt was soaked with sweat. His legs were shaking so badly he was afraid they wouldn't hold him up.

He held onto Brady's shoulder to steady himself as the Irishman helped him on with his coat. Brady gave him a crosswise look and said softly, "Gov'ner, some men ought not to drink."

He was anything but drunk, but Lewis didn't bother to correct Brady's false impression. He had to get out, to get home, right away.

"Wait, Gov'ner!" Brady caught him at the door and handed him his walking stick. "For the wolves, sar."

Lewis looked at the stick, looked at Brady, and laughed. It was going to take more than a stick to defend himself against the black beasts skulking about in this long night.

Chapter 2
Clark

St. Louis, Louisiana Territory
July 30, 1809

The drumbeat sounded a savage warning.

Just for a moment, William Clark put aside the strange, sad letter from home and closed his eyes, listening to the pulsing of the tom-tom. *Get up*, it said. Go help. Do something. Get the rifle, fix bayonets. *Charge!*

The drum pounded in his throat and his temple and deep inside his chest. Brother's in trouble, William. Got to help George—

He swallowed and blinked his eyes. There was no drumming of course, just his own foolish heart, thrumming the tocsin of the latest family crisis back home in Kentucky. There was no battle to join, just the mundane surroundings of Masonic Lodge Number 111, corner of Second and Walnut in the city of St. Louis, founded last year by His Worshipful Master Meriwether Lewis.

From his vantage point in a cushioned wingback chair at one of the writing tables, Clark considered that an unimaginative man might easily mistake the Masonic Lodge for a billiard parlor. Which, in fact, it was. His friend Lewis had not yet gotten around to raising the funds to transform it into a gathering place for high-minded men with service on their minds. In the meantime, the place was redolent with the smells of chalk, tobacco smoke, and whiskey, and dominated by the soft laughter of men gathered around a wooden table covered with green felt cloth.

Clark realized he had slumped down in the chair, almost as if he wanted to hide. He hitched himself into a more dignified position and plucked the letter back off the table. It was from his brother Jonathan. He let his eyes roam again over the painful words.

Dear Brother,

I receiv'd yr affectionate letter of the 5th May and was exceedingly gratified to hear that you and yr wife and son are all in tolerably good health. How do things drive on with your position? I believe you will shew yourself to a very great advantage.

Praise from Jonathan meant a lot to him—his brother was a substantial man of affairs back in Louisville. It pleased him that Jonathan recognized and appreciated the challenges of his job in the Louisiana Territory. Two jobs, actually: Superintendent of Indian Affairs and Brigadier General of the territorial militia. He was challenged every day in every part of his knowledge and experience, and he loved it.

As I know yr desire always to hear all the particulars of our situation here in Louisville it is with heavy heart that I write of the most recent misfortunes of our brother George.

Last week George was alone at his cabin when he took ill. The doctor thinks he had another stroke. Or perhaps he was drunk. You will readily suppose that both could be true.

A glass of brandy sat on the table in front of Clark, untouched. Ordinarily he enjoyed a good dram, but today its sweet, sour scent made his stomach flop over. How many times had he watched George pick up a jug and race the whiskey to the bottom, seeking drunken oblivion from his pain?

Somehow he fell into the fireplace.

Clark let his finger stroke his upper lip and read over the sentence again, as if repetition would lessen the horror. It did not.

He lay there for sometime and like to have burned his leg off.

Still staring at Jonathan's familiar script, Clark dug in his coat for his pipe. Something to do with his hands, his mouth, his lungs might help. His earliest memories of his big, red-headed brother flashed through his mind. Eighteen years his senior, George was always the best rider, the best marksman, the best dancer, and for damn sure the best talker among six brothers and four sisters. When he was little, Clark had wanted to be exactly like him.

I fear that is not the worst of it. The burns on his leg were so bad as to endues the flesh to become mortified and the doctor had to take it clean off.

Clark placed the letter face down on the writing table and fumbled with the pipe. He took out his tobacco pouch and started to sprinkle some dark flakes into the bowl, but managed only to scatter it over the table. Irritated with himself, he shoved the pipe and tobacco back inside his coat. Years ago, he had been George's protector. If only somebody had been there to help George, like he used to be—

It will not Surprise you to learn that bro George bore the unhappy incident with forti-tude. He hired a fife and drum to stand outside the window and play military airs for two hours while the surgeon did the business.

Clark laughed hoarsely. Lord, that was vintage George!

He now stays with sister Lucy and I doubt he will ever again return to his cabin.

Clark felt a lump rise in his throat. When had George ceased to be the swashbuckling hero of his memories and become simply a problem to be dealt with? Humiliations had gamboled through his brother's life like spring fawns. For years, Clark had nourished a small hope his big brother might fool them all, the way he had bamboozled the British and Indians in his gallant, fighting youth. That he might yet regain his former powers and emerge once more still standing. Still unconquered.

Now, George would never stand again.

He may have felt that catastrophe though it was, it was no less than what has already been done to him. His life has bred in him a dark and turrible resentment, that he has trusted and been betrayed, the victim of a savage ruthless power.

Clark sighed and folded the letter. He stared bleakly at the men playing billiards and enjoying their afternoon whiskey. If they had ever known in the first place, it was likely that none of them remembered the things that George had done in the West during the Revolution. George had chased out the British and whipped the Indians everywhere from Kentucky to Detroit. The Indians, out of fear and respect, referred to him as the First Man Living, the Great and Invincible Long Knife.

Surely the name still meant something. George Rogers Clark, the conqueror of the Northwest Territory. The man who had added Ohio, Indiana, Illinois, and the lands all the way to the Great Lakes to the map of the United States. But it was all so long ago, and so much had happened since then. Nobody cared about the ways in which George had been betrayed by others, and even less about the ways in which he'd betrayed himself.

His memory pricked him: something his mother had once said. He too would be a hero, she promised, because he and George were twins, born eighteen years apart.

She spoke true. They looked just alike, the same person at two different ages. Both were tall and strapping, with huge chests, blue eyes, and flaming red hair tied back into a thick queue. With his thirty-ninth birthday just two days away, he noticed his hairline creeping back just a bit, and a fan of fine lines crinkling at the down-turned corners of each eye. Just like George.

He swallowed. Once he'd loved being compared to his brother. Now, the thought sickened him. Lord, please don't ever let me look in the mirror and see myself desperate—alone—defeated—

Clark tapped the table twice, decisively. George was in Louisville and surrounded by family. It was no use fretting about him, much less entertaining gloomy thoughts about himself. He hadn't gone all the way to the Pacific Ocean, or won the hand of his beautiful wife, or gotten his two jobs in the most promising town in the West, by moping around a billiard hall.

The floorboards creaked, and the men at the billiard table called greetings to a fellow Mason seeking refuge from the steaming streets. "Afternoon, boys," the man sang out as he stood in the doorway and scraped muck from his boots. "Better put away them cues and knock off the dirty jokes. The Gov'ner's back in town."

Clark got to his feet quickly, sipped the brandy, made a face. He grabbed his hat and headed for the door. The office of his best friend, Governor Meriwether Lewis, was right across the street. He wanted to hear the latest from Cahokia. Without a doubt, Lewis had news that would take his mind off his troubles.

Chapter 3

Lewis

St. Louis, Louisiana Territory
July 30, 1809

S*ir,*

I feel compelled to relate to you an incident that occurred in Cahokia yesterday evening, the
29ᵗʰ inst. I had a most extraordinary conversation with Genl. J.W., who made me the
object of a most perfidious and treasonous proposal—

Lewis crossed out the last phrase and wrote:

who proposed to me the most astonishing and treasonable plot

He crossed it out again and wrote:

who endeavored to gain my assistance in a heinous conspiracy

Lewis lifted up his pen and stared at the wet ink bleeding across the paper.
Then he wadded the letter into a ball and threw it on the floor with all his
other crumpled drafts. Seething with frustration, he pushed himself back
from his desk and stared around his cluttered office. There were hundreds of
matters in here that needed his attention. Bills, petitions, problems. Instead,
he was spending his time on *this—*

Angrily, Lewis pursed his lips and deposited a plug of snuff with a loud
ping into the spittoon near his desk. His dog, a large black Newfoundland,
raised his head from the floor near the fireplace and snorted. "Remind me to
burn these papers, Seaman," Lewis told the dog. He rubbed his forehead
with ink-stained hands. When it came right down to it, there was no simple
way to accuse the commanding general of the Army of treason.

Lewis pulled another piece of foolscap towards him and picked up his pen,
then put it down again. "God, what will they think of me in Washington?" he
asked Seaman. Madison's new Secretary of War, William Eustis, was known
to be a humorless fellow. Clark went so far as to call Eustis a cheap Yankee
peddler. How in the world could he explain to such a man what had passed
between him and Wilkinson last night? In the harshness of the written word,
the general's proposal seemed even more vile and bizarre than when he'd

delivered it in person. Lewis could well imagine Secretary Eustis reading his claims and thinking he'd gone insane; he wasn't even sure it was safe to entrust the letter to the vagaries of the weekly post.

In any case, the tale certainly wasn't going to enhance his own shaky reputation. Ever since last night, he'd had the terrible sensation of being...

"A marked man," he said to the dog. "Seaman, I am a marked man."

Sleepily, Seaman got to his feet and lumbered over to rest his heavy head on Lewis's knee. Grateful for the distraction, Lewis rubbed Seaman's ears and petted his muzzle while the dog whined with silent pleasure. One thing he liked about Seaman was that the dog never fretted about the future, unless it was to wonder what kind of meat was on the menu at the Eagle Tavern that night.

"This is an absurd predicament." He smoothed the dog's broad brow. "I need to talk to Clark before I do anything else. I won't have to convince him that this conversation really took place. Unfortunately, he's already acquainted with the general and his schemes."

He corked his ink bottle, shook Seaman's head off his knee, and gathered the discarded papers into a pile. In truth, William Clark was the man he always relied on when he needed advice. During the journey to the Pacific, they had shared everything: the burden of decision-making, the day-to-day discipline of the men, the responsibility for the Expedition's success. Even after they returned, it had been hard to break the habit of shared command. Though Lewis was His Excellency the Governor in St. Louis, he shared most government decisions with Clark. The only thing he made it a point not to share was the blame when things went wrong.

Not that his friend needed protecting. The man was as brave as Caesar. He'd first met William Clark in 1795. Clark was twenty-five, the lieutenant in charge of the Chosen Rifles, a company of elite sharpshooters in General Anthony Wayne's army. Lewis was a twenty-one year old ensign who had been assigned to Clark's company not because he was a great rifleman, but because he was a troublemaker. After a drunken fight, his last commanding officer had brought him up on charges. "Mad Anthony" Wayne acquitted Lewis, but he also made it clear that the Chosen Rifles was his last chance.

William Clark had given him that chance, and he'd made the most of it. Years later, when he was Thomas Jefferson's private secretary and Mr. Jefferson tapped him to lead the expedition to the Pacific Ocean, he'd finally been able to return the favor. He'd chosen William Clark as his co-commander on the greatest adventure of their lives.

"Well, Seaman," he said, poking the discarded papers into the fire, "I sure as hell could use his advice now. We'll send word 'round to his house—"

He heard the rapping of footsteps across the wooden planks outside the door. Seaman lifted his head from his paws and got up to greet the visitor.

"Clark! I was just thinking of you, friend. Come in, I have some rather important business to discuss."

"Hi, Meriwether." Clark held his hands out for Seaman to have a sniff. "Damn, why in blazes are you burnin' papers on a day like today? It's hotter out there than a billygoat's ass in a pepper patch."

Lewis laughed, both at the saying and the way it sounded in Clark's resonant bluegrass accent. But Clark gave his own joke only a fleeting smile. He was a big-hearted man whose moods were evident on his face. Right now, he looked so grave Lewis felt alarmed. *Surely Wilkinson hasn't gotten to him already—*

Clark shrugged out of his square-tailed blue coat and folded it across a chair, then took off his broad-brimmed black hat and sat down opposite Lewis's desk. "So, tell me all about this important business. How does it go in Cahokia?" He ran a finger around the edge of his wilted cravat and managed a wry smile, one that still didn't reach his eyes. "Are we gonna be rich come fall?"

It took Lewis a moment to remember his meeting with the fur traders, the reason he'd gone to Cahokia in the first place. "It went fine," he said. "Just as I hoped."

"I figured you could talk 'em into it," Clark said. "Those trading companies have got their tongues hanging out for more merchandise. We'll make it worth their while."

"I just hope we end up with some furs to sell," Lewis said. He picked up a quill pen and used it to make random scratch marks on his ink blotter. Wilkinson had threatened to expose his investment in the St. Louis Missouri River Fur Company, to make the whole venture sound corrupt and scheming. Clark had also put a hefty sum into the enterprise. Lewis's anxiety ratcheted up another level. "I confess I wonder what's happening out there with our boys on the river. They've got to make it up the Missouri first, and then all the way back. Past the Sioux and Arikaras both ways. Damn river pirates!"

He glanced up, expecting Clark to agree. But Clark wasn't even looking at him. He sat jiggling one leg and staring at the limp curtains hanging in the open window.

"Clark...what is it?"

Clark leaned forward and sighed. "Sorry, Lewis." He reached over and pulled his coat off the chair, and found a letter tucked inside. "I got a letter from home today. Bad news about George."

Lord, is there ever any other kind? Lewis accepted the letter without comment. Like every Virginia boy, he'd grown up knowing about the amazing exploits of George Rogers Clark in the Revolutionary War. Later, when he'd become fast friends with William, he'd learned of George's equally spectacular fall into financial and personal ruin.

He skimmed quickly over the painful words detailing the latest disaster. When he finished reading, he took his time folding up the letter. "Poor devil. Clark, I'm heartily sorry." He wished he could avoid the next words, but he forced himself to say, "I can spare you, you know, if you need to go to Kentucky."

Clark nodded and swallowed. "My sister's looking after him. I can't leave right now, I've got too much work here. Maybe later in the fall." He looked at the motionless curtains, then at Seaman dozing next to Lewis's chair, then at the letter lying on the desk. Finally he said, "I don't really want to go all that bad."

Lewis understood at once that it pained Clark to admit it. He remembered a gray October day in 1803, when he had tied up at a isolated cabin near the Falls of the Ohio across from Louisville. Clark was living there with George at the time, getting ready to take up his role as co-captain of the Corps of Discovery. Even old and drunk, George had still seemed capable of sudden violence. Lewis recalled how gently Clark had spoken to his brother, and how the old man had responded with the feral disinterest of an ancient wildcat.

Lewis shifted uncomfortably. He never knew what to say about George. He pushed the letter back across the desk. "Coincidentally, I was thinking of your brother last night. His name came up in an interesting conversation at Brady's tavern in Cahokia."

Clark's eyes narrowed. "That's good to hear. I hope the folks were raising a toast to the man who put this country on the map."

Lewis said carefully, "Actually, it had to do with James Wilkinson. I was, ah, trying to recall what had happened in the old days, with your brother and the general..."

Blue lightning flashed through Clark's eyes. "That goddamn plan to take over New Orleans? Lord, are people still flapping their gums over that?"

"Well, yes—"

Clark's face colored. "My brother wasn't any traitor, Lewis!"

"I know." Lewis longed for a drink.

Flushed, Clark leaned forward, tapping his a finger on the table to accentuate his points. "Lewis, in this 'interesting conversation' you heard, did anybody think to mention that my brother never got paid for his Revolutionary service? Not a goddamn dime! George ran the entire western campaign on his own credit, and when the time came to compensate him, Virginia and the United States dumped him on his ass. He was flat-broke. Worse! He owed twelve thousand dollars out of his own pockets."

Lewis's stomach twisted. He thought about the fur company, and his own debts.

"Is it any wonder he felt like the world owed him something?" Clark demanded. "I can't say as I blame him."

"It's understandable, to a point," Lewis said. "There's no doubt he'd been ill-treated—"

"Maybe so," Clark said. "So when he had the opportunity to get some of the glory back, he took it. Lord, back in '93 everybody in Kentucky had their eyes on New Orleans. With the Spanish controlling the Mississippi, nobody could get their goods to market. The West was strangling! If we could just get hold of the lower Mississippi—"

"Which we finally did, thanks to Mr. Jefferson," Lewis put in.

"Which we *finally* did, *ten years later*," Clark said pointedly. "Well, George was never the type to wait for the politicians. My brother could talk anybody into anything. He rounded up hundreds of Kentucky men. They were all ready to go stormin' down the river and take New Orleans! Trouble was, the U.S. government wasn't interested. So George said he'd renounce his citizenship, take Kentucky out of the Union, and command the force in the name of the French. Can you picture that? The United States of Kentucky, allied with France?"

He sagged back in his chair and pulled at his jaw, and sighed. "I gotta admit, it was the goddamnedest fool plan I've ever heard."

Lewis stammered, "Clark, about James Wilkinson—"

"He was part of it, Lewis." Clark shook his head. "I swear to God he cooked up the idea in the first place. When George talks about it—when he's drunk enough to face it, that is—he's told me as much. In those days, Wilkinson was a merchant, traveling back and forth from Kentucky to the Spanish territory. Somehow he could get into New Orleans when no one else could. He gave George all kinds of information about the city's defenses, and told him all about how he'd be the chieftain of the West, with land and money beyond imagination..."

Clark closed his eyes for a long moment, then gave Lewis a sardonic smile. "Meriwether, I'm sorry for runnin' on. I guess the news from home got to me pretty bad. To make a long story short, the plan fell apart before it even got going. Overnight, everybody in Kentucky suddenly knew what George was planning to do. And shortly after that, James Wilkinson settled up his own debts—thousands of dollars worth, paid off in Spanish gold —and went back in the Army."

"Where he is our beloved commanding general today," Lewis said. "You think Wilkinson sold your brother out to the Spanish?"

"I know he did," Clark said bitterly. "But proving it is something else again, especially when you have only the testimony of a ruined man. George was a leper after that. He couldn't pay his debts, couldn't find work. Lord knows no respectable woman would have anything to do with him. So he became a goddamn drunk." Clark dragged a hand across his face. "But he wasn't a traitor, Lewis. I'm telling you. He wasn't."

"Clark, I know." Lewis squirmed in his chair, his insides churning. How was he supposed to say the words? *Want to hear a good joke, Clark? Wilkinson's back, and this time he wants you and me, instead of brother George—*

"You know why I don't want to go home, Lewis?" Clark asked, his voice raw with emotion. "It's not because of the pity, though Lord knows I hate the thought of seeing him, finally beaten." The muscles in his jaw twitched. "It's because I'm scared. I'm scared to death that somehow, someway, I'll end up like that."

"That won't ever happen, Clark," Lewis said, with more assurance than he felt. He stared at the fireplace, where his attempts to write to Secretary Eustis had burned to embers. What had Wilkinson said? *You and Clark, on the golden throne of the Montezumas!*

Clark blew air slowly out between his lips, then smiled. "Well, enough of this fiddle-faddle. Doesn't do any good to beat a dead horse. I still want to hear all about your meetings in Cahokia. Any chance you'd like to continue our conversation on the way over to my house? Or you already got plans for supper?"

"Just whatever's on the menu at the Eagle Tavern, right, Seaman?" The dog looked up and let his tongue loll out of his mouth, causing both men to laugh.

"Well, Julia's learnin' her way around the kitchen yet, but I guarantee the company'll be a sight prettier than you'll find at the tavern, and there'll be no more sad talk from me."

"Then I accept with pleasure." Lewis grinned and shoved himself back from his desk. He slipped on his coat and gathered up his hat and walking stick. As he watched Clark shrug back into his blue coat, he felt a sudden surge of anger. Why should a good man like Clark have to be dragged into this mess?

The streets of the town were still a steaming quagmire after yesterday's rain, and the muck pulled at their boots as they headed up Walnut Street past the Masonic Hall. Seaman pranced along, stopping to sniff a pig that was wallowing in the undrained street. Lewis didn't wait for him. Any dog that could make it to the Pacific Ocean and back could certainly find his way around St. Louis. The entire city was only three blocks deep; in truth, it was scarcely more than a village.

The Eagle Tavern stood at the corner of Walnut and Main Street. It had once been a government house; in fact, Lewis had represented Mr. Jefferson there five years earlier at the ceremony marking the transfer of the Louisiana Territory to the United States. Since then, a man named William Christy had bought the place and refurbished it into a tavern as fine as any this side of Philadelphia.

Some of the men playing cards on the gallery out front waved as they passed, and big William Christy came out on the porch. "Gov'ner Lewis! General Clark! Can I interest you in some good whiskey and some supper this evenin'?"

"Not this time, Christy," Lewis called back. "I might stop by later, though."

"Shepherd's pie! And wafers with pink cream!" Christy bawled.

"My wife's cookin'!" Clark hollered. "You can't compete with that, Christy!" He inclined his head and said to Lewis: "Still time to change your mind."

Lewis crinkled his eyes in a smile. "No. Mr. Christy might be a better chef than the fair Miss Julia, but a home-cooked meal in the bosom of your family is a far more tempting offer."

Clark grinned and they continued up Main Street. If you didn't look too close, Lewis thought, St. Louis possessed a certain charm. The whitewashed houses that rose step by step against the hillside sparkled in the sunshine, and the crumbling old Spanish citadel at the crest of the hill looked mysterious and exotic. But up close, the illusion fell away. Goats, pigs, and dogs wandered through narrow lanes littered with refuse of every description, and the houses crowded close to the narrow streets. After having spent so much of his life in open country, Lewis found the closeness oppressive.

As they neared Clark's house at the corner of Spruce and Main, Seaman raced ahead, his black tail waving like a plume, and charged into the garden. "Seaman!" Lewis called, but it was too late. The dog had already bowled into one of Clark's slaves, who was down on his hands and knees pulling up vegetables.

" Hey, Seaman!" The man grabbed the dog and rubbed behind his ears, laughing. "How you doin', you old hound?" The dog responded by lapping his face with a huge, dripping tongue.

"Sorry, York. I tried to warn you," Lewis said as he watched York tussle with the dog. Working in the late afternoon sun, York was shirtless except for an old waistcoat, which stretched across broad shoulders to reveal rippling muscles and skin as black as a buffalo. Like Seaman, York had gone with his master in the Corps of Discovery, all the way to the Pacific Ocean and back. York's exotic black skin had amazed Indians all across the American continent.

Seaman gamboled around York's feet as he got up and wiped the slobber off his face. "Evening, Cap'n," he said to Clark, then held up a cabbage head he'd just pulled from the garden. "Evening, Cap'n Lewis. I hope you like cabbage, sir, 'cause we got plenty of it. We been eatin' on it for weeks and no end in sight."

"Isn't it always the way," Lewis said. "If only one could grow beef haunches and sugar cakes as easily as one can grow cabbage, the world would be a better place."

York laughed, then asked Clark, "Cap'n, you want I should help ye get dressed for dinner, or'd you rather I kept on workin' out here?"

"Workin' out here," Clark said. With the toe of his boot, he pointed silently to a weed encroaching on the walk between rows of summer vegetables. "And get those cabbages back to the kitchen. Don't keep Miss Julia waitin'."

York shifted his shoulders and a look of tension passed between them. Lewis flinched inwardly. The trouble between Clark and York reminded him of why he preferred to employ paid servants rather than rely on slaves. It made things a lot less complicated. If a servant grew surly or refused to work, he could be discharged. The problem of York could not be so easily solved.

York had been Clark's property virtually all his life. The two men had grown up together and were bound to one another in a thousand ways, not only as master and servant but by shared decades of home and family. But going on the Expedition had soured York on his daily routine as a St. Louis slave, and in the three years since they'd returned, he'd become downright sullen.

Clark had tried everything: threatening York, hiring him out, punishing him, putting him in jail. That spring, the friction between them had built into an explosion. Clark had flown into a rage and beaten York within an inch of life. He'd even talked about selling York if things didn't improve. Lewis hoped it didn't come to that. He missed the easy companionship between the two men, and he knew Clark well enough to know that after his anger died down, he would regret such an action forever.

Leaving York digging savagely at the weed, they walked through the garden up to the little house. A variety of vegetables took up the bulk of the yard, but the edges were given over to flowers and herbs. The house itself was whitewashed wood, with galleries on all sides to provide sheltered workspaces and a pleasant place to sit on warm nights. Two stone chimneys, one on each side, gave the house a unique profile, but they were both quiet tonight. Only the kitchen hearth out back poured hickory smoke today.

Lewis followed Clark onto the piazza, Seaman trotting close on their heels. Clark swung open the front door. "Julia! I brought Meriwether home for supper, so put another cup of water in the soup, all right?"

The only answer was a piercing wail. In the sitting room, three of Clark's slaves were gathered in great consternation. It was abundantly clear that young Meriwether Lewis Clark was not happy about something. A middle-aged woman named Nancy was trying to quiet the squalling baby boy, while a young woman and an old man stood around offering advice.

"Here, lemme see 'im," the young woman said. "What you wanna do is rub his gums wit' a piece a' wet cotton. That worked real good wit' my Tom."

"Rub his gums?" Nancy exclaimed. "Lord, Easter, I'd lose a finger."

"Might help if he had a leather strap to bite on," the old man suggested. "Them teeth wanna cut through. Got to chew their way out."

"Well, maybe," Nancy said. "Get it for me, will you, Pa? Nothin' too dirty—"

"I never thought I'd see the day when it took three people to comfort a crying babe," Clark complained. The slaves jumped at the sound of his voice.

"Easter, go on out to the kitchen and tell Miss Julia I'm home, then help her get supper on the table. Scipio, go fetch that strap and bring it here, then get outside and help York."

The two slaves hurried to obey. Nancy jiggled the baby on her lap and looked up at Clark. "Sorry, General, but Massa Lew's just crazy with these teeth! Been givin' us fits all day."

"Have you tried dosing him with chamomile?" Lewis asked. "I understand it can provide relief in these cases."

"No, Governor, but if you think it might help, I'll sure try it."

"The problem is, he's getting too much attention." Clark leaned down and caressed Lew's whorl of reddish hair. The baby wailed even louder. "My momma used to give us an apple wedge, maybe that'd help—"

The door from the outside kitchen banged open and Julia Clark hurried in, looking hot and harassed. She went to her husband and gave him a quick kiss, then held a wooden spoon up to his mouth. "Here, taste this and tell me if it seems done."

"All right, but I don't know what I'm tastin' for." Clark licked the spoon and rolled his tongue around. He looked at Julia and guessed, "Blueberry cobbler?"

"Is that what it tastes like?" Julia shrieked. She took the spoon and licked it herself. "Oh, for heaven's sake." She flounced her dress in frustration, then colored with embarrassment when she noticed Lewis standing there.

Lewis smiled. Clark's wife was a wonder to him. Julia Hancock Clark had grown up in one of the finest mansions in Fincastle County, Virginia, and she was still struggling with the challenges of domestic life out here in the hinterlands. Clark had rhapsodized and mooned about the charms of Julia Hancock all the way across the continent, and the second they got back to civilization he'd made a beeline for Fincastle to claim her.

There was no doubt Julia Clark was sweet and charming, with pretty chestnut hair and big brown eyes, but Lewis had to admit that he'd been a little puzzled as to what all the fuss was about. To him, she seemed a mere child, still reedy and unfinished at seventeen. But to Clark, she was everything he'd ever wanted. He'd never seen a grown man so smitten.

Julia lowered her eyes and shyly tucked a stray curl of dark hair up into her cap. "I'm afraid you caught me in my day dress, Meriwether. I've been working so hard on supper I forgot the time."

"Not at all, madam," Lewis said. "I do hope I'm not imposing."

"Of course not! You're always welcome. Will says you're our messmate."

Julia giggled and looked at Clark. "We're having something really special, by the way, so I hope you're good and hungry. It's going to be the best supper I've ever made."

"Good," Lewis said. "Seaman and I are starving."

"Oh, Meriwether, why'd you have to bring that dirty old dog?" Julia wrinkled her nose at Seaman, who was sprawled on the floor by the front door. "All he does is pester everybody."

"Seaman and I are inseparable, madam! We go everywhere together."

"Fine, but don't you dare feed him scraps from my table." Julia glanced at the clock with wide eyes. "Oh! I have to get dressed. Supper will be ready any minute. Nancy—"

Still clutching the wailing baby, the slave rose and hurried back to Julia's bedroom to lay out her clothes. Julia kissed Clark on the cheek and rushed after her, calling over her shoulder, "Will, don't you go anywhere—it's almost ready, I swear—"

When Julia was out of earshot, Lewis whispered, "So if it isn't blueberry cobbler, what is it?"

Clark gazed after his wife and shrugged. "Must be roast beef."

They laughed, and Clark's face took on an expression of such fondness that Lewis found himself unexpectedly touched. He didn't envy his friend, exactly, but the sight of Clark and Julia together always made him feel a little wistful. His own romances never seemed to work out. More and more, he felt doomed to be one of those rusty old bachelors you saw playing cards at the tavern on Sunday afternoon.

He fidgeted with a small tasseled doily on the arm of the chair that Nancy had just vacated. Clark was getting used to having such frilly things around. His friend had a lot of responsibilities now, and a lot of troubles, too. Telling him about Wilkinson would just add to the burden —

"Clark, I really need to talk to you."

"Fine," Clark said. "I'm sorry you caught me in such a disagreeable mood today, Lewis. After supper, we'll have a good talk. "

Lewis smiled and nodded. "After supper, then."

Once Julia finally got the meal on the table, the evening passed in pleasant conversation. Julia recovered from the embarrassment of the roast beef and rattled on happily about the latest town gossip as she stuffed mashed potatoes into the baby. Shaking off the bad news about George, Clark was soon regaling everyone with his jokes. He reminded his wife to take time to eat her own supper, saying, "You know, Julia, a good commander never asks his men to suffer hardships when he won't do it himself."

Julia giggled and looked down the table at Lewis. "Meriwether ate it. He didn't complain."

"Meriwether will eat anything," Clark said. "Even dogs."

Lewis smiled dreamily. "On the trail of an evening, I always did enjoy a good dog stew. Present company excepted, of course, Seaman." He ignored Julia's frown and fed Seaman the last piece of blueberry roast beef off his plate. "If properly prepared in the Nez Perce style, dog can be a most agreeable food."

"That's horrible," Julia said. "How did you stand it?"

"I enjoyed it every bit as much as my namesake there is enjoying his potatoes." Lewis said. "Wasn't it Falstaff who said, 'Let the sky rain potatoes; let it thunder to the tune of Green Sleeves...'"

Julia smiled and finished the quote. "'...Let there come a tempest of provocation, I will shelter me here.' The Merry Wives of Windsor, I believe!"

"Yes, you're quite right." Looking at her happy, innocent face, Lewis felt suddenly heavy-hearted. "Madam, I'm afraid I have to borrow your husband for a little while. We have something to discuss."

"All right." Julia rang the bell for Nancy and Easter to come clear the dishes. Clark wiped his mouth on his napkin and pushed himself away from the table. He nodded at Lewis, then jerked his head down to the far end of the house. "Let's go in your room and have a smoke."

Lewis followed him down the hall. It amused him that Clark still referred to the room as his. Last year, when Clark and Julia and their retinue of servants had arrived from Virginia, the two men had entertained the foolish idea that they would all live in the house together—he at one end, and the Clarks at the other. It took about a week for them all to realize there was one bachelor too many in the house. He'd moved his office to a building on Second Street and rented a room from the trader Pierre Choteau, but in some ways this house was still his home—the only place in town where he didn't feel lonely. *Let there come a tempest of provocation, I will shelter me here.*

In the room that had once been his, Clark now kept an office, with large comfortable chairs that were good for a long talk. Lewis gratefully accepted Clark's offer of tobacco and filled his pipe. Seaman lay down at his feet. Clark positioned his chair so he could rest his feet on a buffalo robe he'd spread out on the floor. The two men puffed silently for a long minute.

The sensation of sweet tobacco smoke filling his lungs made Lewis feel a little calmer, but when he looked up and saw the worry in Clark's expression, his tension flooded back. He swallowed and cleared his throat.

"Clark, when James Wilkinson approached your brother all those years ago, with the Kentucky scheme—"

Clark looked at him sharply. "Damn it, Lewis, are you still on about that? I told you before, George never betrayed this country."

"*I know.*" Lewis took his pipe out of his mouth and leaned forward. "The only reason I bring it up, is that I don't think General Wilkinson—"

"I don't want to hear it," Clark said. "Whatever you heard, discount it. As far as I'm concerned, that bastard can rot in hell for what he did to my family."

"Well, I'm sure he will, eventually. But you should know that—"

"Lewis, I'm tellin' you—"

A sudden noise at the door made them both jump. Julia stuck her head in, her delicate forehead shiny with sweat. "Will, I'm sorry to interrupt, but could you watch Lew while the girls and I get things cleaned up? I promise he won't be fussy and awful."

"Don't make promises you can't keep." Clark smiled. "Sure, I'll take the little man boy."

Julia put the baby in his arms and hurried off to supervise the kitchen. Clark grinned. Lewis knew that Clark had always dreamed of being a father, and he'd never seen anyone more thrilled than the day Meriwether Lewis Clark arrived in the world. Clark delighted in his son's antics and assumed that everyone else was equally fascinated.

Clark put the baby down on the buffalo robe, hunted in his pocket for a flask, and winked at Lewis. "I'm gonna give him a whiskey rub."

Lewis sat with his long legs stretched out in front of him, watching as Clark poured a few drops of whiskey into his palm and gently rubbed it over the baby's body. It amazed him how Clark's big rough hands could be so tender with this boy. *Could that ever be me, with a son of my own?* he wondered. *Maybe someday.* But he couldn't imagine it.

Clark held the baby in his hands, the tiny feet dancing on the buffalo robe, and looked at his son intently. "I'll never let anything happen to you or your momma," Clark whispered. "You're gonna grow up strong, and proud to be a Clark."

Lewis almost choked. God, how could he tell Clark what had happened? It was unthinkable that this man, his wife and son could be dragged into Wilkinson's treachery. *He'll wind up like his brother, branded forever as a traitor—*

Julia came in and threw herself down in a chair, blowing a dark curl of hair off her forehead. Clark looked up at her and said, "Julia, I reckon I owe you an apology."

"What for, Will?"

Clark studied the baby's face. "I'm afraid our son is getting a mite homely."

"Will! How can you say that? Lew is a beautiful baby! He's the prettiest baby in St. Louis."

"Naw, he's a Clark through and through. His hair's getting redder by the day."

"I don't mind it," Julia said, stifling a yawn. "I think red hair is becoming on a man."

Ordinarily, Lewis would have enjoyed their little argument, but couldn't bring himself to laugh. A grim tangle of thoughts crowded into his mind. He glanced up only when he noticed Julia looking at him with puzzled concern.

"Meriwether," she said, "did you and Will finish your talk?"

Clark looked at him, a question reflected in his eyes. Lewis hesitated, then made a decision. He would handle Wilkinson on his own. God willing, Clark wouldn't find out about it until he exposed Wilkinson to the world as a traitorous rascal, once and for all.

"Yes," he said. "It was nothing, really. Nothing at all."

Chapter 4

Clark

When he heard the sound of the cart outside and the accented Creole voices of his visitors, Clark tied a freshly laundered white cravat around his neck and shrugged into his dark jacket. He felt a trifle foolish. He'd just checked his thermometer—the mahogany cased beauty was one of his prized possessions—and discovered that the temperature had already hit ninety-two degrees. By noon, it would be soaring to the century mark. Not for the first time, Clark wondered who had decided that a gentleman had to dress like he lived in London or Paree, instead of a damned oven like St. Louis in the summertime.

He greeted his visitors and led them back to the office. In spite of feeling like a stuffed sausage in his suit, he was glad he was well dressed. Charles Gratiot was almost as much of a fashion plate as Meriwether Lewis, and as for Nicholas Jarrot, the trader looked elegant even in buckskins. If you wanted to do business with these Frenchies, you couldn't be caught sitting around in your drawers

"Gentlemen, can I offer you anything? Is it too early for a mint julep?"

"Maybe later, General," Jarrot said. "Right now, I'm more interested in your advice."

Gratiot and Jarrot had come to him to talk about Tecumseh, the Shawnee chief who had allied himself with the British and was trying to unite all the tribes west of the Appalachians against the Americans. Clark was Indian superintendent now, and he commanded the territory's militia, but he knew that a British-backed Indian uprising could overrun St. Louis and devastate the fur trade. Understandably, Gratiot and Jarrot were worried about their investments.

In the end, Clark promised to write to Governor William Henry Harrison in the Indiana Territory and coordinate a plan for defense of the river towns in case of a general Indian attack. He had faith in his ability to talk peace with the Indians of the lower Missouri, but when it came to Tecumseh, Harrison was the expert.

As he walked Gratiot and Jarrot to the door, he assured them, "I'm going over to Governor Lewis's office right now. We'll discuss it. His approach has kept the Osages quiet in these parts, and he'll have good ideas about this, too. Nobody wants to see river trade grow more than Governor Lewis." *Lord yes,* Clark thought. *We're both invested in that fur company up to our eyeballs.*

To Clark's surprise, Gratiot and Jarrot exchanged uneasy glances. Gratiot cleared his throat, started to say something, then gave Jarrot a Gallic shrug. Jarrot smirked and said, "Governor Lewis is business-minded, it's true. In fact, he seems to be keeping half the taverns in St. Louis in prosperity."

Clark swallowed hard, but he kept his temper under control. "Gentlemen, there's three things you've gotta understand about Americans. We never go anywhere without a Kentucky rifle, a deck o' cards, and a bottle of whiskey." He grinned and put a hand on each man's shoulder. "Not to worry. I've known Meriwether Lewis since we were both pups. He could drink us all under the table and then get up and out-fight, out-shoot, and out-think the three of us put together."

The Creoles laughed as Gratiot's servant brought his cart around, and Clark thought he had been successful in putting the joke over. He kept a cheerful expression on his face until the horse clip-clopped away down Main Street.

After they left, Clark chewed over the conversation in his mind: the trouble with the Indians, and especially the last remark about Lewis. Any criticism of his friend rankled him. He remembered the first time he ever laid eyes on Lewis, not long after the Battle of Fallen Timbers. Clark had seen at once that the twenty-one-year-old Virginian was one tall, opinionated, hard-drinking, hard-fighting, cocky sonofabitch. They got along famously.

To hell with it, Clark decided. *Maybe we ain't boys any more, but if a couple of Frenchies can't see that a man as tightly wound as Lewis needs to let down once in a while, then let them try being governor of this territory for a while.*

He shut the door and walked to the back of the house. "York, I'll be with the Governor. I should be home for supper. You tell Miss Julia, hear?"

"Yessir, Cap'n!" York said with exaggerated good cheer. Clark shot him a warning look and headed down Main Street.

The street was alive with people on foot; sometimes, it seemed that everyone in St. Louis spent half the day jostling up and down the city's principal thoroughfare. All the stores fronted Main Street, and French Creoles and brash Americans came together daily to hustle for their fortunes. Negroes of all descriptions—dark and light, slave and free—carried on their own trade with wheedling street hawkers touting a variety of produce and goods just unloaded from riverboats. Something was always happening, and Clark enjoyed the constant buzz. He didn't even mind dodging the dogs, hogs, mud puddles, and wagons and carts dragging merchandise through the streets.

He had to admit he did mind the smell, especially on a day like today. The still air reeked of horse manure, household garbage, and burning oak and hickory from cook fires. More people were pouring into St. Louis every day, and the practices that had suited a French river outpost weren't working too well for a growing center of American trade. He'd have to talk to Lewis about it.

Clark could hear the click-clack of billiards from the open door of the Masonic Hall. He passed by and entered the palisade around the building where Lewis had his office. Glad to get out of the sun, he stepped onto the piazza and let himself in.

Before he even entered the room he caught the familiar haranguing voice of the Territorial Secretary, Frederick Bates. "The difficulties with which I am forced to contend are *intolerable!*" the young Virginian was shouting, as if he were addressing a crowd of a thousand people. "For the life of me, I cannot understand *why* you *refuse* to allow me to do my job!"

Clark grimaced as he slipped unseen into the office and took up a place leaning against a bookshelf. Bates didn't even seem to notice he had joined them. Clark's heart sank when he saw the flush on Bates's jowls and the wild look in his eyes. The Secretary appeared to be even more exercised than usual.

Frederick Bates was a handsome man—or at least Julia said so. Just past thirty, he always dressed in the latest fashion and wore his brown hair tousled so elaborately that Clark thought he looked like a frightened owl. Like Lewis, Bates came from a fine old Virginia family and was one of the best-educated men in town. But unlike Lewis, Bates was better suited to the life of a scholar than a frontiersman. With a doughy body and soft, almost feminine hands, he would have been out of place shouldering a rifle, paddling a canoe, or trekking through a mountain pass.

"It is the right of our American citizens to hunt, yet you refused to allow me to issue sufficient hunting licenses—"

"And *yet*, you did it anyway," Lewis said, cleaning his pipe with an attitude of supreme boredom. "Leading to innumerable problems."

Bates pursed his lips in pious disapproval. "It is the God-given right of our American citizens to settle on this land, yet you insist on preserving it so that a few fur traders—*and their investors*—can enrich themselves! I cannot sit by while you turn a blind eye and a deaf ear to the piteous cries of the people of this territory! I will be their champion, even if I must stand alone!"

He stood up and wagged a plump finger in Lewis's face. "You have used me badly, sir! The law states *explicitly* what my duties are! You have stripped me of my powers—*you* have assigned them to General Clark, against the written statutes of this government—"

Clark cleared his throat and shifted his weight. Bates whipped his head around in surprise. Clark said in a low voice, "Bates, be reasonable."

Bates ignored him and turned back to Lewis, leaning across his desk so that the two men were almost nose-to-nose. "You cannot hide behind General Clark's muscle forever, Governor."

Lewis laid down his pipe and raised his gaze to meet Bates. His dark grey eyes were almost black with anger. Clark flinched. The storm was coming. The lightning was about to hit the ground.

With pompous indignation, Bates yelled, "What am I supposed to tell the *people*, when in their suffering, they turn to me for help? By God, I will act my *conscience*, sir—"

Lewis sprang forward, slamming his palm down on his desk so hard it sounded like a gunshot. "I don't give a good *goddamn* what you do, Bates! Just so long as you do it someplace else!"

Lewis came around the desk. It was his turn to point his finger in Bates's face. "Bates, you are without doubt the most *useless* creature that God ever put on this earth! You come in here, three times a week, puling and whining about your trivial problems—a three-year-old *girl* would be a more capable deputy than you have been—"

Bates spluttered, his face purple. Lewis didn't give him a chance to speak.

"What's worse, you know *nothing* of loyalty!" Lewis shouted. "You have schemed to undermine me to my superiors in Washington—"

Bates shook his head. "You are greatly mistaken! If I have written to Washington, it was only to express my opinions about what is going on in this territory!"

"So you admit it, then!" Lewis backed Bates up to the door. "Well, you just keep on writing to Washington! Just keep on countermanding my orders!

Do your worst, Bates! So help me, if it is your desire to bring our relationship to an open rupture, you have done an admirable job."

"It has only ever been my desire to do the job I was appointed to." Bates's paunch quivered under his waistcoat. "*Someone* in this territory has to look out for the interests of the *people*. And I shall continue to do so!"

"Well, take your own course, Bates. God knows you will anyway."

"I shall!" Bates turned on his heel, red-faced. Glaring at Clark, he said, "I'll leave you two to talk about me." He jerked the door open and slammed it shut behind him.

Lewis paced the room. When he raised his hand to the back of his neck, Clark saw it was trembling.

"Good thing you didn't have your tomahawk with you," Clark said. "Or Frederick Bates would've lost that pretty fluffy hair of his just now."

Lewis ran his hand through his hair. "I fear I am ruined, Clark."

"Because of Bates? Naw, Lewis, if somebody got ruined every time that dandy had a temper tantrum, there wouldn't be a man standing in St. Louis."

Lewis slumped behind his desk. Hands still shaking, he picked up a letter and thrust it into Clark's hands. "No. Well, maybe, I don't know. Bates—other people—are *conspiring* against me—"

Alarmed, Clark unfolded the letter. It bore the official seal of the War Department. He glanced at the last page. The signature of William Eustis, the Secretary of War.

Sir:

After the sum of seven thousand dollars had been advanced on the Bills drawn by your Excellency on account of your Contract with the St. Louis Missouri Fur Company for conveying the Mandan Chief to his Village; and after this Department had been advised that "for this purpose the Company was bound to raise, organize, arm, & equip at their own expense one hundred and forty Volunteers and to furnish whatever might be deemed necessary for the Expedition, or to insure its success"—it was not expected that any further advances or any further agency would be required on the part of the United States.

Seven thousand dollars was considered as competent to effect the object. Your Excellency will not therefore be surprised that your Bill of the 13th of May last drawn in favor of M.P. Chouteau for five hundred dollars for the purchase of Tobacco, Powder, &c. intended as Presents for the Indians, through which this expedition was to pass and to insure its Success, has not been honored.

"They're denying the voucher for the presents?"

Lewis nodded. "It gets worse."

Clark skimmed the rest of the letter. Eustis's tone was scathing:

... it has been usual to advise the Government of the United States when expenditures for a considerable amount are contemplated in the Territorial Governments ...

...a military expedition to a point and purpose not designated...it is thought the Government might, without injury to the public interests, have been consulted...

... it cannot be considered as having the sanction of the Government of the United States...

... another Bill of Your Excellency's ... has not been protected, there being no appropriation of this Department applicable to such an object...

The final line made Clark's heart skip a beat.

... the President has been consulted and the observations herein have his approval.

For a long moment, Clark was stunned into silence. All of the officials out in the territories—Lewis, Clark, William Henry Harrison over in Indiana, even Bates—wrote vouchers for what they needed, and sent the bills to the War Department. It was the only way they could do business, when an exchange of letters with Washington could take months.

Clark shook his head. "If Eustis is going to start second-guessing every expenditure we've made, and hold us personally responsible, well, then—"

He stood up. "Goddamnit, nothing ever changes. This is the same old song they pulled on my brother! They send men like you or me or George out here to take care of business in the West—'Go to it, boys! Find out what's out there for your country, and whip up on those Indians!' Then, when you do it, they expect you to answer to some little pork-eater in Washington who never set foot off a paved street—"

"They think I have done something wrong, Clark. They think I have been *dishonorable.*" Lewis's voice sounded hollow. "As God is my witness, Clark, I have done nothing dishonest. Every expenditure I have made, I have always accompanied with an explanation. I have never received a penny of public money for myself. Never!"

"Lewis, I know. You're *too* honest, that's your trouble." Clark studied his friend's face. "You know, the fur expedition has already been gone three months. It's way too late to call 'em back.. With any luck, they'll get past the Sioux and find a lot of rich new country. We'll finally be making some money, which we deserve, by the way. There's no shame in that."

Lewis took the letter from Clark and read the first few lines, his lips moving, his eyes black and intense. "Clark, this letter was mailed July fifteenth. It's almost a month old. I have nothing to fight them but my *word*—"

He turned his head away, his jaw clenched. "How could he have gotten to them so quickly?" He dropped his head and stared down at the scarred surface of the desk. "He *couldn't* have... Did he somehow *know* this was going to happen? *My God*—I should have acted already, but how—"

"Who are you talking about, Lewis?" Clark said. "Bates? By God, if he's behind this, he'll answer to me."

Lewis clenched his hands into fists, then straightened up. "Forget Bates. This has gone beyond Bates. And Clark, I appreciate everything you've said, but you're not in trouble. This is my fight, not yours."

"Oh, no, you don't." Clark sat back down, across from Lewis. "We'll fight this together, just the way we always have." He tapped the desktop, thinking fast. "Number one, you've got to write to Eustis, today. Lots of people have had their vouchers questioned and it's all come out right. Odds are, Eustis isn't really out to get you—he's just stupid. So we'll let him know what's what. Lewis, I'll help you write the letter."

Lewis set his jaw. The old defiance came back into his eyes. "It's all right, Clark. I know what to say." He pulled out a sheaf of fresh paper and began to sharpen his quill. His hand trembling slightly, he bent over the paper and started to write, the pen scratching away in a rhythm Clark knew as well as Lewis's own voice. "Oh yes, Clark, they will hear from me—on a *number* of subjects. But trying to straighten out this mess through the mail won't do it. I must go to Washington in person, right away."

Clark came around the desk and looked over Lewis's shoulder.

Sir

Yours of the 15th July is now before me, the feelings it excites are truly painful...

Lewis looked up at him. "By God, Clark, I'll fight 'em. They won't take me down if I can do anything about it. But remember, it doesn't really matter what they say about me. No one can ever sever my devotion to my country. They won't make a Burr out of me."

"That's crazy, Lewis. Nobody would ever think that," Clark said. "Look, I'll go to Washington with you."

"No." Lewis said. "I will go *alone*."

He sounded so adamant that Clark rocked back a step. In all the years of their association, Lewis had never given him an order. This sounded an awful lot like one. Lewis softened his expression and said, "Clark, somebody needs to stay and control Bates."

Clark nodded and chose to let the tense moment pass. "That's a tall order, Gov'ner. Lewis, what I'm trying to tell you is that I'll do anything you need. Anything that might help."

Lewis nodded, his face drawn and tight. "I know, Clark. I know."

Chapter 5
Wilkinson

New Orleans, Orleans Territory
August 27, 1809

James Wilkinson impatiently brushed away a bee that was buzzing around his face. He'd been away too long. The army quartered him in a galleried plantation home in the American quarter of New Orleans, just outside the *Vieux Carré*, and the place showed the effects of his absence. Most vexing, the garden was overgrown and badly in need of tending. He touched his tongue to the corner of his mouth, raised himself on his toes, and gently cut away a scuppernong vine that strayed errantly across the garden wall.

"Good Lord! How can you bear to live in this climate?" Captain House wailed, fanning himself with his felt *chapeau bras* as he sprawled on a stone bench under a tree. Beads of sweat trickled down from his widow's peak of dark hair, making him look even more dissipated than usual. "I tell you, General, human beings weren't meant for conditions like this."

Winded, Wilkinson rocked back on his heels and mopped his face with a handkerchief. It was his own fault things were in such disarray. The unseasonable heat wasn't helping matters any, and neither was Captain House's whining.

House was a royal pain, but there were two reasons why he kept him on his personal payroll. First, House loved to talk—particularly if the topic was sordid alehouse gossip. Second, House traveled up and down the Mississippi River frequently carrying dispatches, and he was acquainted with many young officers who did the same thing.

House was a one-man rumor mill, and that made him indispensable. With his spartan constitution and wagging tongue, a rumor started in New Orleans could be a scandal in St. Louis a week later, and a shopworn fact in Prairie du Chien the week after that.

Wilkinson craned his neck for a better view of a pearly cluster of grapes, just beginning to ripen. "Is that fungus I see?" he murmured. "No, it can't be—just a trick of the light—"

"For God's sake, let's go to Maspero's," House begged. He mopped his handsome face with a handkerchief and pulled violently at the stiff collar of his blue uniform coat. "If I don't get something cold to drink, I'll die."

Wilkinson put down his garden shears. "House, use your head. I asked you here so we could talk in confidence, not shout our business to the common mob."

"But it must be a hundred degrees." House yanked open a few collar buttons and resumed fanning himself.

"So—" Wilkinson bent down to examine a small bed of delicate lavender obedients. "—what news do you have of our impulsive young friend in St. Louis?"

House mused a while, rubbing sweat from his jaw. "Well...not much. He's drinking a lot."

"That's hardly news." Wilkinson pulled up a weed. "Anyone would drink a lot in that dreadful job. I held it myself, remember?"

"No, I mean he's drinking to excess, even by St. Louis standards. I'd say he qualifies as a stumbling sot."

"In public?"

"God, yes," House said. "He's a regular at every tavern in the city. He gets positively pickled. Half the time his servant has to carry him home."

"Well, that's promising, but it's hardly grounds for recall. I need more."

House pondered a moment. "He's broke," he said slowly. "By Jove, he's worse than broke! He's in arrears up to his arse."

"Give me details."

House cursed under his breath and smacked a mosquito, leaving a thin smear of blood on the side of his neck. "Well, he's invested heavily in land, and as you know, the prices in St. Louis have gone into the cesspool. I imagine he's been rather stung."

"You imagine?" Wilkinson turned around to face him, eyebrows arched. "House, what do I pay you for?"

House lifted his shoulders in a sweaty shrug and said in a casual tone, "Then there's his little problem with Secretary of War Eustis."

Wilkinson stopped clipping and got to his feet. A smile spread across his face. "Are you holding out on me? Is that what you're doing, my boy?"

House grinned. "Actually, General, I'm praying for an assignment out of New Orleans. The army camp at Terre aux Boeufs is the ninth circle of hell. God, you can smell it from here! Poor sick devils lying in their own filth—"

"Enough!" Wilkinson said. "That's my affair, not yours. What of Lewis's 'problem' with Eustis?"

"Well, it seems that Eustis has disallowed a very large voucher the Governor wrote on his own authority, to the tune of over five hundred dollars. It concerned some aspect of this fur-trading scheme he's trying to pull off. And this isn't the only voucher dear old Eustis has denied," House continued. "As far as official Washington is concerned, Lewis has been cut off. Columbia's tit has run dry."

"By God, I've had my own problems with Eustis, but all is forgiven!" Wilkinson clapped House on the shoulder. "His miserly majesty might turn out to be my best friend after all."

"There's more." House leaned forward. "Some people say that since he got his whipping from Eustis, Lewis has gone clean out of his head. He's been fighting with everybody—acting like a veritable madman. I got a letter from my friend Bates the other day, and he's just beside himself at the way he's been treated by the Governor."

Wilkinson paced about the garden. "Such good fortune—and so unexpected!" he exulted. "House, here's what I want you to do. Understand me, now. It's critical that no one believe a word Lewis says."

House nodded and Wilkinson continued, "You'll get your traveling papers, as requested. I want you to go upriver. Tell the same tale to anybody who will listen. Governor Lewis is a drunk, he's in debt, he's been refused by the War Department. He disports himself with harlots. Tell them he's in trouble for pilfering from the public purse. Tell them he's mad."

"All that?" House guffawed. "Good Lord! Nobody'll believe it! Why don't I just tell them he's the devil himself?"

"The devil? No." Wilkinson's eyes gleamed. "But before I'm done, he'll know he's in hell." He rummaged in his pocket and tossed House a gold dollar. "There's a lot more where that came from! Now go and get your drink, my boy. You've earned it."

Chapter 6

Lewis

St. Louis, ~~Missouri~~ Territory
September 2, 1809

(handwritten note: Louisiana)

The late afternoon sky was heavy with iron-gray clouds. An occasional fat droplet sputtered down and splattered the street, but Lewis knew it wouldn't rain. There wasn't enough lift in the atmosphere. Clouds lay over the city like a wet blanket, holding the heat close to the ground and stifling any hint of a breeze.

Lewis stopped on the corner of Main and Market to wait for his servant to catch up. John Pernia was a droll little fellow of about thirty, who had been his personal assistant for over a year. According to his own fanciful account, he was the son of a lovely black woman and the wastrel heir of prominent French Creole family in New Orleans. Lewis didn't know if it was true, but he did know that Pernia made a hell of a hangover remedy out of chicory coffee.

"We must hurry, Pernia. The tailor's shop closes at five o'clock, and the fellow's a Catholic. He doesn't open on Sunday."

"Sorry, Governor." Pernia gasped for air, practically running to keep up. "You walk too fast for me, sir."

"Your dissolute life has made you most unfit, Pernia," Lewis said, without a trace of a smile. "If we don't get there on time, you won't have anything decent to wear in the Federal City. You want to look nice while you watch me get pilloried by Secretary Eustis, don't you?"

"Of course, sir," Pernia panted. "But your legs are so much longer than mine, you'd gone half a block before I even—"

"Which is precisely the problem, Pernia." Lewis took Pernia's arm and steered him down Market Street. "If you could only grow a few inches and gain fifty pounds, I wouldn't have to get my clothes taken in at all. You could wear them 'as is.'"

"My apologies, sir. I'll endeavor to do that."

Lewis laughed in spite of himself. All of these last minute details had him on edge. This morning, he'd taken Seaman and gone on a ramble out west of the city. He'd felt desperate to escape the squalid air of St. Louis and to concentrate on anything except his trip to Washington City the day after tomorrow. He covered a good eight miles, gathering plants and flowers along the way, before his nagging conscience forced him to turn home again. The fresh air calmed him and the blessed quiet helped him think, but now he was a little sorry he'd gone. His body ached and he had a touch of a sore throat.

He slowed down a little to let Pernia catch his breath as they approached the tailor's shop.

"Are you looking forward to visiting all the ladies of New Orleans while we wait for a ship to the Federal City? I certainly am," Pernia said.

"If the ladies of New Orleans are anything like the ladies of Virginia or St. Louis, I haven't a chance."

Pernia grinned. "They're *nothing* like the ladies of Virginia or St. Louis!"

"Well, I'm looking forward to it very much then."

They reached the door of the tailor's shop. Lewis pulled out his watch and checked it: just before five. The thin-lipped tailor, Trottier, was moving around inside.

Lewis pulled open the door. With all the woolen cloth, the place reeked like a damp sheep. "Evening, Trottier. I've come to pick up the coat and breeches you altered for my servant."

"Of course." Trottier went in the back and rummaged around for a while. Finally he came back with several shirts, a black waistcoat and white wool breeches, neatly folded. He placed them on the counter and said, "That will be seven dollars..."

"Fine, put it on my account." Lewis moved to pick up the clothes.

"...*cash*," Trottier finished.

Lewis looked at him in surprise. "I don't have seven dollars cash on me."

"Well...you can pick them up when you do, Governor." Trottier fixed him with a blank stare.

"But I'm leaving the territory on Monday," Lewis said, astonished. "Pernia has to have something to wear on the trip."

Trottier shrugged. "They'll be waiting for you when you get back, then."

"Trottier, you've always done business on credit. You do it all the time."

"With certain customers," Trottier said. "Governor, *excuse moi*, but I can't extend you credit anymore. With all these rumors going around—"

"What rumors?" Lewis demanded. Pernia shifted uncomfortably beside him. "If you have something to say, let's just clear it up right now—"

"I have nothing to say. But all the same, I will require cash."

Lewis spluttered. "Well, I suppose you can just keep the damn things, for all I care."

"Very well." Trottier nodded and calmly put the clothes under the counter. Pernia took hold of Lewis' arm. "Governor, we should go."

"*Indeed.*" Lewis's face was crimson. He started for the door, then turned to glare back at Trottier. "I *am* good for it, you know."

"I'm sure you are, Governor," Trottier replied, bored. He turned away before Lewis was even out of the shop.

"Can you *believe* that, Pernia?" Lewis exclaimed as the two men made their way back up Market Street, headed to Lewis's room at Pierre Choteau's. "The sonofabitch wouldn't extend me seven dollars credit! He knows I'm good for it! I've always paid him in the past!"

His mind reeled. He didn't know why Trottier would have behaved the way he did unless he'd gotten wind of his troubles with the War Department. Surely Clark wouldn't have let it slip. That left—

"*Bates.*" Lewis clenched his teeth. There was no doubt the pompous twit had heard about the disputed vouchers by now. Perhaps the crisis wasn't Wilkinson's doing at all.

He was still mulling it over in his mind as they turned the corner onto Main and started up to the small log building he shared with a number of Choteau's other renters. Lewis noticed a knot of men gathered out in the street.

"Lewis!" One man separated himself from the pack. It was Monsieur Papin, the man who supplied the government of St. Louis with building materials. "Governor, you owe me five hundred livres for one hundred and fifty pounds of nails!"

Before Papin could continue, a young man named Peter Provenchere shoved him aside. "Governor, I know you're leaving the territory." Provenchere grabbed at Lewis's sleeve. "You owe me eighteen dollars and fifty cents, for translating the territorial laws from English to French. Remember?"

Provenchere was interrupted by Matigue Macarty, the town blacksmith. "Lewis, you're forty-two dollars in arrears," he said. "Remember those pigs of iron you ordered in June, for bullets for the Territorial Militia? When do I get my money?"

"Yes, Governor, I must request immediate payment—"

"Yeah, when are you going to pay us?" Papin roared.

"You'll all be paid, you'll all get your money." Lewis struggled to stay calm. "That's the whole reason I'm going to Washington. I have to explain these vouchers to the War Department."

" How do we know you'll ever come back? I want my money *now*, Lewis!"

"Well, you'll have to take my word for it—"

"Your word?" Papin snorted. "I don't trust your word any more than the War Department does!"

Lewis's hands balled into fists. "What else can I give you?" he shouted. "I have no idea why the War Department rejected my vouchers! I don't have the money, goddamnit—"

"*Governor.*" Pierre Choteau stepped off the piazza. The sound of his voice caused them all to fall silent. Choteau glared at the other men and made a gesture with his hand, flicking them away. He put his hand on Lewis's shoulder and guided him up toward the house.

Lewis's heart pounded. Along with his half-brother Auguste, Pierre Choteau was one of the most powerful men in St. Louis. His acumen as a trader and his diplomatic skill with the Indians was legendary. In addition to being his landlord, Choteau was one of the biggest investors in the St. Louis Missouri River Fur Company.

When they were out of earshot, Choteau turned him around and fixed him with his cold black eyes. "Meriwether," he said through his teeth, "what kind of trouble have you gotten us into?"

Lewis gulped. "It's...it's not irreparable, sir," he said. "I have only to go and lay out the situation for Secretary Eustis. I'm sure he'll understand. I'm *sure* he will."

"He must." Choteau's fingers dug into Lewis's shoulder, the force belying the softness of his voice. "Meriwether, I advanced the Fur Company goods worth in excess of five hundred dollars. I have every expectation of being paid."

"And you will be." Lewis's voice crept up a register. "I...I will talk to him, sir. I'll explain everything. I flatter myself that *all* the disputed drafts will be honored."

"I don't care about these other petty debts," Choteau said. "My concern is for *my* investment."

Lewis found it difficult to speak and even harder to look Choteau in the face. "I'm confident everything will turn out all right."

"Good," Choteau said. "I'll see you when you get back, then." He clapped Lewis on the shoulder, rather roughly. Then he turned away and swept into the street, gathering the other men about him. Papin looked over his shoulder and sneered. Still squabbling, the men allowed Choteau to herd them away.

Lewis's legs shook. He wrenched open the door and held onto the doorframe, almost staggering. Once inside the safety of his room, he slumped behind his desk, accidentally scattering the leaves and flowers he'd collected on his morning walk onto the floor. Pernia put a cup of tea in front of him and began to sweep up the mess without comment.

"Just leave them, I still want them." Lewis put his head in his hands and closed his eyes. "Pernia, this has been the worst day of my life."

"Governor, I'm sorry for that scene back there. Those men were inexcusably rude."

Lewis didn't answer. He felt the unmistakable sensation of fever gnawing at the edge of his brain. The humiliation was almost intolerable. In his heart, he knew Bates couldn't pull off something like this—

Wilkinson—Oh God, it's started already—

"Governor, a letter came for you this morning, while you were out." Pernia placed a sealed letter on the desk, then went to tend to his chores.

The handwriting on the envelope was familiar. Still shaking, Lewis ripped the letter open and started to read. The precise, spidery calligraphy of Thomas Jefferson spun across the page.

Lewis had known Jefferson all his life. The president's refuge, Monticello, was just a few miles from his late father's farm in Albemarle County, Virginia. Over the years, as Lewis grew from an adventurous, independent boy into a tough soldier and competent officer, Jefferson had kept a fatherly eye on him.

Following Jefferson's election to the presidency of the United States, Lewis had been astonished to receive a letter from his old neighbor, offering him the post of personal secretary to the president. He'd accepted, of course, and the position had turned out to be much more than copying letters and running errands. Jefferson had personally trained him in the scientific methods he would need to lead the Corps of Discovery.

Jefferson opened the letter with some chatty news, then got down to business:

I regret I must press you further about the publication of your book, based on the journals you kept on your voyage to the Pacific Ocean. I am very often applied to know when

*your work will begin to appear; and I have so long promised copies to my literary corre-
spondents in France, that I am almost bankrupt in their eyes.*

*I shall be very happy to receive from yourself information of your expectation on this
subject. Everybody is impatient for it. It is astonishing that I get not one word from you—*

Lewis sighed heavily and shoved the letter aside. Pernia looked up from his
workbench, where he was blacking Lewis's boots. "Bad news, sir?"

Lewis rubbed his aching forehead. "Mr. Jefferson's going off about the
journals again. I hardly have time to write a book, with everything that's
going on here."

"Governor, I'm worried about you. You don't look well."

"After what happened today, I feel like a shadow," Lewis said. "Pernia,
we're in deep trouble. These men are expecting their money, and the
President's expecting his book. And I don't have either one."

"What are we going to do, Governor?"

"I'll tell you what we're going to do." Lewis opened the desk drawer and
started hunting through it. "We're going to go to Washington, and we're
going to straighten *everything* out. Then we're going to Philadelphia, and we're
going to *write the damn book*. If my assumptions are correct, it'll sell a thousand
copies, making us rich as Midas."

Pernia nodded encouragingly.

"But first," Lewis said, digging through the drawer, "...we're going to take
the last ten dollars we've got..." he held up a tattered banknote—"...and we're
going to go to Christy's..."—he stood up, slamming the drawer shut—"...and
we're going to get roaring drunk."

"Hear, hear!" Pernia said with a grin. "I'll get your coat."

William Christy's Eagle Tavern was where all the prominent gentlemen of St.
Louis came to relax. The tavern was located in the old Spanish Governor's
Palace, and Christy prided himself on maintaining the palatial atmosphere.
On Saturday nights, men who spent all week on sedate and serious business
tossed off their sobriety and crowded around the polished wooden tables for
cards and conversation, eating their dinner off china plates and pouring their
whiskey from crystal decanters. The huge mahogany bar, brought piece by
piece from the East, gleamed under the lamps.

It was always a festive time, but tonight the atmosphere in the taproom
was positively electric. It was always something to see when Governor Lewis
decided to put on a show.

About fifty men were crowded into the room, laughing and shouting. "You tell 'em, Governor, you tell 'em!" someone yelled from the front of a crowd, which squeezed around the bar to get the round of free drinks Lewis had just bought for the house.

Standing on the big mahogany bar, Lewis swigged from his glass of grog and hollered, "You *bet* I'll tell 'em!" He raised his glass and yelled over the growing din. "Since personal business compels me to leave this fair city—"

"Don't forget us little people back home, Governor!" Monsieur Papin shouted.

"Oh, how could I?" Lewis laughed. "These past two years have been the most enjoyable of my life! I'll be thinking of you every moment, I assure you—"

At his feet, Pernia pounded the bar in helpless laughter, tears rolling down his face. Next to Pernia, Cadet Choteau, Pierre Choteau's twenty-year old son, blew beer out his nose.

"But before I make my reluctant journey eastward—"

"Sort of the Expedition in reverse, eh, Lewis?" Papin yelled, slapping his knee.

"Very like it! No easy route here either." Lewis grinned. "As I depart this wonderful place, perhaps never to return—"

"Don't get our hopes up!" laughed a man named Peter Dupree, who happened to be Secretary Bates's assistant.

"So glad you spoke up, sir," Lewis said. "For there can be no doubt, in all the great sentimentality of this occasion, the man I'll miss most in the *whole territory* is that tireless whelp, Secretary Bates."

Howls of shocked laughter rose from the crowd. Someone yanked Dupree's chair back and dumped him unceremoniously onto the polished floor. Standing near the taproom door, William Christy craned his neck and frowned.

"So allow me to propose a toast to that man who has done *so much* for the government of Upper Louisiana," Lewis said, waiting for them all to get their glasses ready. "To Frederick Bates!" he shouted, raising his glass. "The most unending ass on *either* side of the Mississippi!"

"To Frederick Bates!" his friends in the crowd roared. Lewis tipped his glass back and emptied it down his throat, then held it down for Pernia to refill with more grog. The room resounded with grumbles and cheers. In the corner, the French traders Nicholas Jarrot and Charles Gratiot exchanged disgusted glances.

"And lest I forget," Lewis continued, pausing to wipe his mouth on his lace cuff, "the good gentleman who is the inspiration for my latest ramble...of course I mean Secretary Useless...er, Eustis—"

As the crowd howled, Lewis held his glass high and shouted, "Yes, a toast to Secretary Eustis! The *cheapest* sonofabitch ever to disgrace, I mean, *grace* the Federal City! Good health!"

"Good health to Eustis!" men shouted. Laughing, Pernia clutched at the bar to keep from sliding onto the floor.

"And *last*, but assuredly not *least*," Lewis brayed, grabbing the bottle of rum out of Pernia's hand, "I would be remiss if I did not recognize another man to whom I owe *so much*—I am speaking, of course, of my illustrious predecessor, General James Wilkinson—"

The noise level in the room rose to a deafening clamor. Christy started pushing his way toward the bar. In the corner, Jarrot and Gratiot got up and left, their faces grim.

"Absent in war, malcontented in peace, a discredit to his country and his countrymen—"

"Lewis—" Christy shouted, but his voice was lost in the din.

"Drink up, everybody! To James Wilkinson!" Lewis raised his glass in his fist. "May he burn in hell—and not take me with him!"

"To Wilkinson!" the cry went up. Lewis grinned. Damned if he wasn't invincible. He would whip the bastards, all of them at once, if he had to. He drained the bottle and hurled it against the wall, sending shattered glass everywhere.

The room dissolved in a riotous clamor of yelling, pushing and shoving. Turkey legs and cards were trampled underfoot in the crowd of laughing, swearing men. Near the door, someone threw a fist—

Christy shoved men aside and fought his way the bar, face flushed with anger. He shouted up at Lewis, "For God's sake, Governor, this isn't a bleedin' disorderly house! Things are getting broken! Ten dollars isn't going to cover this!"

Lewis jumped down, almost falling against Pernia and Cadet Choteau. He laughed recklessly. "Would you like me to write you a voucher, Christy?"

"I'll send you a bloody bill," Christy said. "Criminy, man—pull yourself together! And you—" he turned to Pernia. "Why don't you make yourself useful, you worthless bibber, and go find a carriage to take you and your master home?"

Chastised, Pernia lurched out to look for a drayman. Sensing the fun was over for tonight, the crowd began to break up. Men got their coats and hats and headed for home, back to their families, mindful of early church services tomorrow.

Cadet Choteau grabbed Lewis by the elbow. "Governor Lewis! You're not really going home, are you? We could go to the alehouse down the street—"

"No," Lewis struggled to make his tongue form the right words. "I'm going home to my room. It's my home for one more night, anyway."

"But we will see you back in St. Louis, won't we, sir? You *are* coming back, aren't you?"

"I don't know." Surprised by his own blurting voice, Lewis said quickly, "Of *course* you'll see me back. I owe your father money, remember?"

Cadet tried to laugh, but ended up in embarrassed silence. Christy cursed under his breath and surveyed the damage to his taproom.

After a few minutes, Pernia reappeared in the doorway. Avoiding Christy's glare, Lewis followed him out over a litter of broken glass and upturned dinner plates. Out in the street, a dark carriage waited to carry him home.

Chapter 7

Clark

St. Louis, Louisiana Territory
September 3, 1809

Clark lit his pipe, sat back in his chair and took a long, firm puff. He held the smoke in his mouth a few seconds, then let it drift out again into the room. A light rain beat against the glass. Nothing like a rainy Sunday afternoon, he thought, for a quiet talk and a little peace-making.

He checked the clock. *Damn, where's Bates?* Clark tapped out his pipe and wandered out of his office into the parlor, where he found York lounging in a straight chair by the front door.

"Any sign of Secretary Bates? He was supposed to be here at half-past one. Now it's almost two o'clock."

The front steps creaked, followed by a sharp rap on the door. "That'll be him now," York said. He jumped up and pulled open the door with a big smile. "Good afternoon, Secretary Bates! Oh, and you too, Mr. Dupree!"

Frederick Bates and Peter Dupree stood dripping in the entryway, wiping the mud off their boots. York bustled around them, made small talk about the rain, and took their hats and umbrellas. Clark was disappointed to see that Bates had brought his little assistant with him. Dupree's quick movements, small gleaming eyes, and pointed face reminded Clark of a weasel.

"Bates, how d'ye do this afternoon? Dupree, it's an unexpected pleasure."

"I brought Mr. Dupree as a witness to our conversation," Bates said. "I believe he may also have something to contribute."

"Well, that's fine by me," Clark said. "I guess now we know where we stand. York, why don't you make some coffee? Or would you fellows like something stronger? You look like you could use a little pick-me-up." It was true. Bates was dead pale, and pursing his lips together with such force they were almost blue.

Bates shook his head. "I doubt we'll be staying long enough to have anything, General Clark."

"Aw, Bates, don't be that way," Clark said. "York, fix three shots of Kentucky rye. We'll be in the back."

Clark led the men back to his office. "Have a seat, boys, make yourselves at home." Dupree sat down, looking everywhere but at Clark, finally settling his gaze on the painted Shoshone elk hide on the wall. Bates appeared reluctant to take a chair, but finally sat down at Clark's repeated urging.

"Bates," Clark began, "There's been a great deal of bad blood between Governor Lewis and yourself, and no one regrets that more than I do. You fellows are both good men who care a great deal about this territory, and I know you both want the best."

Bates looked at Dupree, his blue eyes bulging. As if in reply, Dupree raised his narrow eyebrows at Bates. The corners of Bates' mouth twitched and his jaw came forward. But he said nothing.

This new, silent Bates worried Clark, but he pressed on. "So, what I was figurin', Lewis is goin' out of town tomorrow, and God knows when he'll be back. I think it would mean a lot to the people here in St. Louis and out in the territory to know that you parted on speaking terms."

At last the color rose back into Bates's face, and his voice rang out in the stentorian tones that Clark had expected all along. "General Clark, I must tender to you my *astonishment*, nay, my *admiration*, that you can address your proposal to me with a straight face! Either you are even more naïve and impudent than I had previously imagined, or you have truly missed your calling on the stage."

Clark felt his face flush hot all the way to his scalp. Just then, York came in with a tray and three shots of Kentucky whiskey. As York withdrew, Clark said, "Bates, I asked you to call on me because I want to patch things up among all of us. Now, I just want to say that as far as I'm concerned, there're no apologies necessary, we're all a bunch of hot-tempered fellows. I don't know what cause you've got to come into my home so lathered up—"

"What cause? What *cause*, sir?" Bates bellowed with such force that spittle flew from his mouth and landed on Clark's desk. Clark heard the baby start to wail out in the parlor.

"I will ask *you* to explain *what cause!* You invite me here to represent yourself as *my* friend? How can you expect me to separate you from Governor Lewis? You, who have trodden the ups and downs of life with him, while he has at last made it clear, *in front of the entire city*, that he holds for me only the most hearty contempt?"

"Bates, what in God's name are you talking about?" Clark kept his own voice low and steady. "First off, what you're saying just ain't so. You and Lewis have had rough words, it's true, but in private, not on the street corner."

Dupree jumped in. "You obviously weren't at Christy's tavern last night."

"No, I wasn't," Clark said. "For pity's sake, if there's something you fellows are busting to get off your chests, let's have it out."

Dupree babbled, "Well, Secretary Bates wasn't there, but I was, and I can tell you that Lewis was drunk as an emperor. He was bragging and swaggering like a common quayside layabout."

"Oh, Lordy." Clark sat back in his chair, his face stinging with embarrassment. *Lewis, you promised, the last time—*

"And the things he said!" Dupree rattled on. "First, he called the Secretary the most unending—"

"That's enough, Dupree!" Bates shouted. Dupree cringed in his chair and fell silent. Bates turned on Clark. "If you want to know what happened at Christy's last night, why don't you ask *your friend?* You are so anxious to make *peace* between us, sir, perhaps you might get a clearer picture of the task you've set for yourself!"

Clark's face was burning. His thoughts scattered away from him. For a moment, he didn't trust himself to speak. "Bates, I'll do just that. This is probably all a big misunderstanding. I'll talk to him—"

"General Clark, it is immaterial to me what you do, for Governor Lewis has insulted me for the last time." Bates stood up and wagged his finger in Clark's face. "I am a man of *pacific* temperament, but I have been pushed to the limit, to beyond the limit, of *human endurance*, sir! If we cannot settle our differences like gentlemen—which Governor Lewis most assuredly is *not*—then we will settle it with pistols at ten paces!"

Clark's gut cramped. "Bates, no. Not a duel. Blazes, let's not let this foolishness turn into a tragedy."

"As usual, you argue for his *convenience*, rather than his *honor*, of which he has none." Bates snapped his fingers at Dupree. "I will have satisfaction, General—one way or another. Good *day*."

With that, Bates swept out of Clark's office, Dupree scuttling after. Clark yelled, "York, help the gentlemen out, would you?"

He noticed the shot of Kentucky rye before him on the desk. He threw it down his throat, then let his head fall forward into his hands. *Congratulations, man, that was some peace talk. Lord, Meriwether, what have you done?*

Julia came to the door. "Will, is everything all right?"

"Everything's fine, honey."

"All that yelling," Julia said. "It scared Lew. To tell you the truth, it scared me too. Secretary Bates looked so angry." She studied him, catching her lower lip in her teeth. "You look terrible."

Clark managed to laugh. "Don't worry, I'll live." He got to his feet. "Julia, I've got to go see Meriwether and help him get ready to go on his trip. We've got a whole lot to talk about, so don't wait supper for me."

He changed into his rain gear—old hat, army coat, high-topped boots. York handed him an umbrella and lantern on his way out the door. As he slogged down Main Street, he barely noticed the mud sucking at his boots and the rivers of filth flowing down to the public landing from the narrow, gutterless side streets. He was too busy rehearsing what he was going to say to Lewis. *When you decided to burn all your bridges on your way out of St. Louis, Meriwether, I wish to hell you'd warned me.*

By the time Clark got to Choteau's, he was ready to have it out with Lewis. Several men were lounging on the piazza, smoking and watching the rain. The door to Lewis's room was shut. Clark put down his umbrella, scraped the mud off his boots, and knocked on the door.

"Damn you, Lewis, you'd better not be out cattin' around," he hollered.

"I'm here," Lewis's voice sounded faint. "For God's sake, Clark, come in out of the rain."

Clark came in, shaking the rain off his hat and umbrella. Seaman got up to greet him, tail wagging. Clark let him out onto the porch. "Go watch the rain, dog." He turned back to the room, saying, "Lewis, you've really soured the milk this time. You picked a dilly of a time to tell off Bates—"

He stopped, blinked, and gulped for air. He had never seen such a mess in his life.

Lewis's things were everywhere. His bed was buried under a mountain of coats, pants, vests, and underwear. On the desk, books, letters, and their journals from the Expedition were jumbled in no particular order, with a tomahawk and an officer's sword balanced precariously on top. Botanical specimens lay strewn all over the floor.

Lewis stood by the bed, cursing under his breath and trying to cram more papers into an already overstuffed portfolio. A large trunk lay open on the floor, empty except for a large mounted magpie, staring sightlessly up at the ceiling. Seemingly satisfied, Lewis tied the portfolio shut and threw it in the trunk, breaking off the magpie's tail in the process.

Lewis grabbed the magpie out of the trunk. "Damn," he muttered. "That was supposed to be for Jefferson." He threw it in the corner and turned to his desk, where he began to rummage through more papers. The tomahawk crashed onto the floor, narrowly missing his foot.

"Caesar's ghost," Clark said. "Lewis, what the hell are you doing?"

"What does it look like I'm doing, Clark? I'm packing." He shoved past Clark to the other side of the little room and crouched on the floor, where he began rolling up the skin of a large bull buffalo. "You need to move, Clark, you're standing on it."

"Lewis." Clark hunkered down beside him. "Just hold up a minute. Stop what you're doing, right now."

Lewis stared at him for a long moment. He looked dreadful; his unshaven face was as pale as his bleached linen shirt and the skin under his eyes looked so dark that for a moment Clark thought he must have been in a fistfight. His dark eyes looked glazed, the lids reddened.

"That must have been a hell of a toot you went on last night."

Lewis turned his gaze away. He passed his hand over his eyes and swallowed, his jaw muscles working.

A wave of dread washed over Clark. He pulled Lewis to his feet and steered him to his desk chair, clearing off three hats and a beautiful sea otter skin. Lewis slumped in the chair and began to shuffle through a pile of letters, as if buried in the stack was something that would solve all his problems. His hands were shaking.

Clark gritted his teeth. "Settle down, now," he commanded. To give Lewis a chance to collect himself, he got busy cleaning up the mess. He scraped the books and papers off the desk and began to sort them out. The Expedition journals and notebooks he placed carefully in the bottom of the trunk. A stack of personal letters, he tied up with string and put next to Lewis's pistol case, as something he might want to have easily to hand. He pulled open the portfolio and began to repack it, neater—

"Where's Pernia? Shouldn't he be here helping you with all this?"

Lewis shrugged, not looking at him. "I don't know where he is. I haven't seen him since this morning. He said something about having to go say good-bye to a girl." He laughed. "No such problems for me."

"I can't imagine why not, Lewis," Clark said. "What woman doesn't dream of a scene like this?"

Clark was immediately sorry he'd said it. Lewis looked hurt, then turned away from him, staring past him at the corner of the room. Clark followed his gaze but saw nothing of interest.

Lewis choked, "Last night was the *last time*, Clark. I swear to you, I'm through with drinking. You've been too good a friend to me. It was never my intention to cause you any pain."

"Well, the pain's gonna be yours if Frederick Bates has anything to say about it," Clark said. "What'd you say last night, anyway? Bates was at my house just now, fit to be tied."

"Bates at your house on a Sunday? That's nothing short of a desecration." Lewis pulled at his collar and curled his lip with annoyance. "To be honest, I don't remember what I said about him. Whatever it was, I hope it was damned insulting."

"I expect it was, seein' as he's threatening to kill you. You may have to duel him on your way out of town."

"Bates challenge *me?*" Lewis jumped to his feet, his face flushed. "Well, that suits me fine! There's nothing I'd like better than to settle things with that puppy once and for all." He paced the room, trampling dried leaves and flowers under his feet. "If he so much as *tries* to interfere with me again, I will put him in the ground, Clark. In the ground!"

Lewis pointed an imaginary pistol at Clark's forehead and mimed pulling the trigger. Standing there watching Lewis pretend to shoot Frederick Bates, Clark could not escape a memory, many memories, flashes of disastrous times with George he'd done his best to put out of his mind.

"Lewis..." he said. "Bates ain't worth it. You gotta try to be...philosophical." He felt lost. He had never known how to get through to George, and had no idea now how to get through to Lewis. "Some things are just a part of life. St. Louis and Bates...just go together, somehow. They're like horseshit and flies. You just can't have one without the other."

A heartbeat passed, then two. Lewis burst out laughing. He slumped at his desk and buried his face in his hands. "Clark, you have a way with words. Don't ever let anybody tell you different." He wiped his eyes on his cuffs and seemed finally to come to himself.

Relieved, Clark cleared away some of the clutter on the bed and sat down opposite Lewis. "Meriwether, what's goin' on? You've got yourself in a right state."

"I know, Clark." Lewis pushed his sweaty hair off his forehead. "I'm ashamed. I apologize for my lack of self-control."

"It's all right," Clark said. "I know you're worried about Eustis. But Lewis, I'm telling you, they can't hold you over a barrel on those vouchers. You can back up everything you've done. And then, when you get that straightened out, you can spend Christmas with your mother."

Lewis smiled a little. "Christmas at Locust Hill is always..." he began, then broke off. "But my mother—God, what will she think of me? If she feels I have brought disgrace—"

Lewis choked and turned away from him, his chest heaving. Clark felt horrified. He'd never seen Lewis shed so much as a tear before. He forced himself to sound calm.

"That's just it," he said. "You won't be in disgrace. You can have a good rest in Virginia. You can visit with Mr. Jefferson, I'm sure he'd love to see you. And, then, you can go to Philadelphia and finish our book."

Lewis laughed, a strange, painful laugh. "Oh, yes, *Mr. Jefferson*," he repeated. "And the book! I *will finish* the book."

"You'll finish the book," Clark said. "And it'll sell like a house a-fire. And by the time you get back here, all those furs will be rolling down the river, and our money right along with it. You just watch yourself, Lewis." He grinned. "A man could get rich in this country if he wasn't careful."

Lewis didn't return the smile. His head twitched once and his eyes darted over Clark's shoulder into the corner of the room.

"You're jumpy as a cat, man," Clark said. "What do you think you see?"

"Nothing. Forgive me." Slowly, Lewis began to shuffle through his papers again. Clark stood up. Lewis was prodigiously strong, and Clark dreaded the thoughts of trying to restrain him. Thankfully, Lewis found what he was looking within a minute.

"Clark, there is something I must ask you to do for me."

"You know it. Anything."

Lewis thrust a paper into his hand. "This is my power of attorney. I had it drawn up yesterday. I want you to sell the land I got from the Expedition and use the money to pay off my creditors."

Clark moaned. "Lewis, I can't sell your land. That's your farm, that's your dream. You've told me a thousand times what you're going to build out there, how you're going to settle your mother and your brothers, bring the whole family together again."

"I know. But that's not going to happen, at least not now," Lewis said. "Clark, I'm broke. I'm worse than broke—I'm in debt."

He got up and resumed the grim, haunted pacing. "Pay Pierre Choteau first, for God's sake. It's all down in my account book. Pay Papin, and that blasted tailor. And Christy, I owe him money, including the bill from last night. And pay yourself, I owe you at least a hundred dollars. And—"

"Lewis," Clark interrupted. "I don't want to do this. "

" Clark, I'm begging you to do it. It's the only way," Lewis said. "I have no other means by which to pay these people. Really, I have nothing. Even the money I've invested in the fur company is borrowed. I don't have a penny that's really mine."

"It can't be as bad as all that," Clark said. "How much have you borrowed, man?"

Lewis sank down in his chair again and opened his hands. "I don't know exactly. I've been trying to tally it up. Somewhere around four thousand dollars."

Clark gaped at him, speechless. He'd known Lewis had borrowed some money, but he'd had no idea his friend owed such an astronomical sum.

"And that's just my private debts," Lewis said. "That's not to mention my other government vouchers. I must have six thousand dollars outstanding with the government, at least. I signed another voucher just the other day for more money for the fur company, to use if they need to hire some Indian warriors to help get past the Sioux. If Eustis won't pay it—" He stared up at Clark. "Clark, I'm reduced to poverty. I'm a pauper."

He looked bleakly around the room. "I'll take everything with me that I care about. Sell the rest. I know it's a lot to ask. I won't blame you if you don't want to do it."

Clark shook his head. "It's not that. I just *hate* to do it, that's all. I still think in a few months, this mess will all be over, and you'll wish you had your things back."

"If I do, it will be my own fault, and a good lesson to me," Lewis said with strained bravado. "You know me, Clark. I have always put too much store by *things*. Besides, we're going to get rich, remember? I'll buy all new things, and come back in style, with enough silk for ten new dresses for your lovely little wife." He held out his hand to Clark. "Are we agreed, then?"

Reluctantly, Clark took his hand, and they shook. "Of course, Lewis. I'll do whatever you think best."

"Thank you," Lewis said. He seemed to take in the clutter for the first time. "Well," he said at last. "It looks as if we have our work cut out for us, and no sign of Pernia! I suppose he's had great success with his lady."

"Who can blame him? I expect she's a hell of a lot better lookin' than you are," Clark said. "C'mon, let's get to work."

Pernia finally showed up about nine o'clock. Clark and Lewis had finished packing the two big trunks an hour ago, with Clark doing most of the packing and Lewis rearranging the items according to various theories of what he would need to keep handy for his journey. After they had finished, Clark persuaded Lewis to lie down and rest. His friend refused to take the bed, insisting that he was more comfortable on the floor on his buffalo robe. Clark let Seaman back in to keep Lewis company, then wilted into a chair and sat with his legs stretched out, utterly spent.

When Pernia came in, Clark pulled the little Creole aside. "Take care of him, Pernia. He's had a hard day." He glanced at Lewis and whispered, "Come get me if he's this bad off in the morning. You two can't go down-river with him like this."

Pernia nodded, looking scared. Lewis said sharply from the floor, "There's nothing that can stop me from going. I'll be fine."

"All right, then," Clark said, sounding more certain than he felt. "I'll see you boys in the morning."

At least it had quit raining, but the walk back to his house seemed darker than ever. His lantern barely illuminated his way through the dark, muddy streets. Further down toward the landing, he could hear faint whoops of drunken trappers and boatmen, taking their chances gambling or enjoying the company of the riverfront bawds.

He kept thinking of brother George. When he was twenty-six, he had resigned a captain's commission in the Army because George needed help. He had poured out jugs of good, valuable whiskey to keep it away from George. He had traveled four thousand miles, he once estimated, to try to settle the tangle of George's debts and obligations. He had bankrupted himself trying to keep his brother's creditors at bay. He had spent sleepless nights listening to George rave about the treachery of James Wilkinson, who destroyed him, and the ingratitude of the people of Virginia and Kentucky, for whom he'd risked everything. George had given them their safety, given them their lives, given them their country and gotten nothing in return.

Well, except that ceremonial sword the Virginia legislature had sent him that one year. George had kicked it to pieces and thrown it in the Ohio River.

Tonight had been like that. Like the worst nights with George.

Clark's legs felt heavy. The little house on Main and Spruce never looked so good as when he finally hauled himself up on the front porch and let himself in. York had waited up for him, dozing in the chair by the front door. York helped him off with the dirty boots and took the hat, the umbrella, the lantern, the old coat.

"Fix you somethin' warm to eat, Cap'n? Or a drink?"

Clark shook his head. His stomach hurt. "In the morning, York. You get off to bed now."

He went to his bedroom in his stocking feet. Julia was sleeping on her side, her long brown braided hair lying next to her on the pillow. In the cradle next to the bed, the baby stretched his chubby arms in a tiny, innocent dream.

He stripped down to his shirt, bent over Lew's cradle and brushed his son's forehead in the barest kiss, then slipped into bed. Julia moved over, into his arms.

"Will," she murmured against his chest. "How was Meriwether?"

Clark tightened his arms around her. "Lonely. I wish I was going with him." He stroked her little braid, brought it up to his lips and kissed it.

"I'm glad you're not," Julia said. "Lew fussed at dinner. He wanted his daddy." She settled against him and put her head on his chest. "I love you, Will."

"I love you, too, sweetheart." Clark felt numb with gratitude. He cleared his throat and said, "Hush, now. It's been a long day."

He expected to lie awake all night, but it had been a very long day. In the quiet safety of that place, with his wife and his son right beside him, he found sleep.

Chapter 8
Wilkinson

New Orleans, Orleans Territory
September 4, 1809

Wilkinson was panting by the time he reached the stately brick home on Chartres Street in the French Quarter. He hustled through the elaborate ironwork gate and let it swing shut behind him with a loud clang. He rounded a small sculpture of a cherub spouting water in the courtyard and was halfway up the steps to the veranda before he noticed a portly man with dark hair and aristocratic features, leaning against the balustrade.

The man took out his pocket watch, flicked it open, and made a show of studying it. He looked up at Wilkinson, bemused irritation in his slanting, cat-like eyes.

"Don Diego, a thousand pardons," Wilkinson said. "I was unavoidably detained by an administrative matter. I am mortified to have kept you waiting so long."

"I was beginning to think you weren't coming," said Don Diego Morphy. "*You* were the one who called this meeting, remember?"

"Of course." Wilkinson bowed in apology and did his best to look contrite. He could see already that the new Spanish consul wasn't going to be easy to get along with. He understood Morphy was half-Spanish and half-Irish—a lethal combination for the temperament.

"Well, now that you're here, do come in," Morphy said, a little too politely. He ushered Wilkinson inside and led him to the sitting room, where there was a small table laden with a serving platter of delicious-looking sweets and cakes. Wilkinson's stomach growled. It had been a long time since breakfast.

"*Sientese, por favor.*" Morphy gestured to a pair of elegant brocaded chairs on either side of the table. Wilkinson heaved himself into one of them and waited while Morphy's servant poured the coffee.

He glanced around the handsomely appointed room. One thing you had to say for the Spanish, was they kept their ministers in style. Sitting here with

Morphy made him feel a little nostalgic. It was just a few years ago that he'd stood in the splendid office of José Vidal, Morphy's predecessor, and given up everything he knew about his erstwhile friend, Aaron Burr.

Burr really was quite something, Wilkinson mused, sipping his coffee. So dynamic and ambitious...he really seemed to *believe* that he could build a vast empire in the South, with the western United States thrown in for good measure! It was a shame they hadn't pulled it off, but Burr had simply become too reckless. Wilkinson still felt bad about revealing their little conspiracy, and certainly Burr must have felt betrayed during his desperate attempt to flee the country, when he realized that his old friend Wilkinson was no longer his co-conspirator, but his pursuer. But what other course could he have taken? If he hadn't moved first, the fool would have sunk him.

They're all the same, aren't they? Wilkinson thought. *All but one, that is.*

Lewis alone had refused him. Who would have dreamed that that climber, Meriwether Lewis, would turn down a chance to become an emperor? *Maybe I should have approached Clark first,* Wilkinson thought. Years ago in Kentucky, George Rogers Clark had come over to his side like a blushing maiden to the marriage bed, for all his rough bluster. Perhaps his younger brother would have been receptive as well—

Morphy interrupted his thoughts. "General Wilkinson, I understand congratulations are in order."

"What? Oh, yes! My dear Celeste." Wilkinson smiled. He'd forgotten; the Spanish inevitably started every business conversation with small talk. "After having lost my beloved Ann, I feel truly blessed to have found her. The wedding will be in March."

"My most sincere felicitations," Morphy said. "Mademoiselle Trudeau is a lovely woman. I wish you both happiness."

"Thank you, Don Diego." Wilkinson plucked a cake off the platter. "Are you enjoying New Orleans, sir?"

"Yes, it's a very interesting city," Morphy replied. "So French, and yet now so overrun by Americans. And of course—" he scooped some sugar into his coffee—" my government hasn't given up hope that it may one day be Spanish again."

Wilkinson relaxed. In his experience, you could never go wrong by banking on Spanish greed. Ever since their archenemy Napoleon sold the Louisiana Territory to Jefferson for a sordid consideration back in 1803, the Spanish had been wild to get that particular jewel back in their crown. Although Spain controlled the entire southwestern portion of the continent, they were still smarting over their Paradise Lost.

"Don Diego, you know I have always been a friend of Spanish aspirations in this part of the country—"

"So my predecessors inform me." Morphy took a bite of cake.

Wilkinson smiled. The best thing about the Spanish was that they understood the value of information—and of having their own man at the head of the United States military. Why, just a few years ago, the Spanish had paid him $12,000 for information about a certain American scientific expedition in the territory west of the Mississippi. He'd urged them to intercept and stop the Expedition, torture the captains for information, take their maps, and...

He chuckled to himself. *And here we are talking about Lewis and Clark again!* If the Spanish had pulled it off, he and Morphy wouldn't have much to talk about today, would they?

"Well, Don Diego, you know I have always tried to warn you about my own government's licentiousness, when it comes to gobbling up the Western lands. But the reason I requested this meeting is to warn you about an even graver threat than American ambitions to the dominions of Spain on this continent."

"A danger worse than the vandals in Washington?" Morphy raised an eyebrow. "The mere thought sets me trembling, General."

"As well you should." Wilkinson pressed on. "I am speaking, of course, of those two rascals now in charge of Upper Louisiana, Meriwether Lewis and William Clark."

"Lewis and Clark?" Morphy repeated. "What possible threat could they be? They are mere administrators. I doubt they do more than carry out the directives of President Madison."

"That's where you're wrong, *Señor!*" Wilkinson said fervently. "I have come into the possession of some intelligence—evidence of a *plot*—"

Morphy rolled his eyes. "This is beginning to sound familiar."

"Ignore me at your own peril, sir!" Wilkinson leapt to his feet. "This is far more serious than the threat posed by Aaron Burr! If successful, the plot of which I speak will destabilize the entire territory west of the Mississippi! It will break Madison's hold on Louisiana! And it could deliver these lands into the hands of Spain—perhaps permanently—if you are prepared to take advantage of it."

He had Morphy's attention now. "What exactly *is* the plot, General?"

"Lewis and Clark are raising an army of adventurers." Wilkinson paced around the parlor. "You have to understand, these men are gods to every layabout rogue on the frontier! They have secured the allegiance of hundreds of Kentucky riflemen—and at least that number of Indians! The Osages, the Iowas—even some of the Cherokees—"

"What are you saying, General? That Lewis and Clark have broken with the United States government?"

"That's exactly what I'm saying. With St. Louis as their base, and at the head of an army of the most lawless brigands the world has seen since the Middle Ages, Lewis and Clark will take Upper Louisiana by force."

"But that's insane," Morphy blurted. "Even if they were able to—"

"And their ambitions don't stop there! Oh no, sir!" Wilkinson interrupted. He bent close to Morphy, who was now perched on the edge of his chair. "These blackguards will stop nowhere short of Santa Fe!"

Morphy looked appalled. He gulped some coffee and asked, "What do you know of these men, sir?"

"Lewis and Clark? Blackhearted villains, the pair of them." Wilkinson waved a hand. "Their ravening ambition consumes all, like the fire of Prometheus. Arrogant devils, convinced they are nothing less than divine."

"But, General—no, let me finish." Morphy frowned as Wilkinson tried to interrupt him again. "Even if Lewis and Clark *are* able to wrest control of Upper Louisiana from the United States—which will be no easy task—and even if they *do* somehow make it to Santa Fe—which by my lights, is impossible—how can they possibly hope to hold it all?"

"Well, that's just it, Don Diego." Wilkinson sat down with a little smile and tented his fingers in front of his mouth. "They can't."

Morphy looked at him in silence. Then a light appeared in his eyes, and he too smiled. "General, I think I finally understand you," he said. "Lewis and Clark will take Upper Louisiana from the United States...and then Spain will take it from Lewis and Clark."

"*Exactamente*, Don Diego."

"But General," Morphy said, "doesn't this put *you* in a rather difficult position? After all, when Lewis and Clark begin their agitation, won't you, as the commanding general of the United States Army, be expected to respond?"

"No doubt," Wilkinson said. "In fact, I'm already planning to move my troops upriver."

"Then you have also informed Washington of this plot?"

"Oh no." Wilkinson smiled. "Secretary Eustis knows nothing of what I've shared with you today. He thinks I'm moving the troops to Natchez because they need a more salubrious climate." It was a small lie; in fact, his men were dying of yellow fever at such an alarming rate that Eustis had ordered him to remove them from New Orleans. "But a position higher on the Mississippi will be all the more convenient for our purposes, sir."

"You will be there to meet them." Morphy's lips twitched. "You will intercept Lewis and Clark's army, when they come down the Missouri en route to Santa Fe."

"Precisely," Wilkinson said. He felt an excitement that was almost indecent. "But Don Diego, surely you must understand that if I am to repel the intentions of Lewis and Clark—*and* to ensure that Upper Louisiana is subsequently occupied by Spanish forces—I will need some resources, sir."

"How much?"

Wilkinson took a breath. "One hundred thousand dollars."

The Spanish consul's shoulders sagged. He looked at Wilkinson with round-eyed incredulity. "Well, General, you are a bold man, I'll give you that."

"Come now, Don Diego," Wilkinson said. "If you are able to take Upper Louisiana for yourselves, the services I can render will be priceless."

"Let me get this straight," Morphy said. "If the Spanish government provides you with...*resources*, "—he couldn't bring himself to say the amount—"—you will crush the rebellion of Lewis and Clark...and then stand aside while Spain occupies the Western Territories?"

"Yes," Wilkinson said. "That is what I am offering to do."

"Won't you be hung as a traitor?"

"You're presuming I intend to return to the United States," Wilkinson purred. "My allegiance is to Spain. Surely I've proved that."

"General..." Morphy let out a nervous little laugh. "You have surprised me today. I need to consult with my government about this offer you've described to me. They will be most intrigued, I'm sure."

"I thought they might be." Wilkinson patted his mouth with a napkin. Although Morphy had promised nothing, he could tell by the expression on the Spaniard's face that he was already dreaming about what his country could do with the vast, rich land of Upper Louisiana restored to her dominion. "I'm afraid I must take my leave now, sir. My duties with the army are so very pressing—"

"Of course." Morphy rose. "General, you are a true friend of Spain. I will write to Havana at once. We'll discuss the matter of...resources."

"*Muy bien*, Don Diego. And when you decide, please send me a letter by courier. You can't trust the post these days, you know." Wilkinson winked and made his way to the door. "*Adios*, my dear friend."

Wilkinson's mind buzzed pleasantly as he made his way back down Chartres Street. The meeting could hardly have gone better. Why, the poor fellow was eating out of his hand!

How do you like that, Governor Lewis? he chuckled as he ducked into Maspero's for a drink. *Who's on the golden throne now?*

Chapter 9
York

St. Louis, Louisiana Territory
September 4, 1809

York rolled out of bed at first light that morning, hoping to get a jump on the heat he knew was coming. He fixed himself a cold breakfast of bread and butter, and a bowl of cabbage and potatoes left over from the night before. The captain must have heard him moving around, because he joined York in the half-light of dawn, coming to the kitchen in his nightshirt, with a pair of old breeches pulled on for decency.

Clark sat down heavily at the table with his eyes closed. York stoked up the cook fire and put on some coffee, buttered up some more bread, and dished up more cabbage and potatoes.

"Go ahead and eat, Cap'n. Coffee'll be ready directly."

Clark pushed his mussed hair away from his face and took a few bites of the cabbage and potatoes. York poured the coffee and then sat down opposite Clark, wanting to finish up his own breakfast before things got too busy. He had always preferred to start off the day like this, whether in camp or at home, just him and Massa Billy. It was better than serving at the dining table in the house; it was almost like he and the captain were just old friends. Sometimes he forgot that they weren't. Forgot his place.

And then, Billy would remind him.

"York, take the wagon on over to Governor Lewis's and get those trunks of his down to the levee before it gets too hot."

Last night's rain had opened up new holes on Main Street. York's wagon got stuck in one of them, and the horses stubbornly refused to pull as York tried to heave the wheel out of the mire. By the time he finally got the wagon over to Lewis's room, he found Lewis standing on the front porch, resplendent in a wide-brimmed black hat, bottle-green frock coat, buff-colored waistcoat, high white cravat, and tight white pantaloons tucked into shining black hussar's boots.

York jumped down from the wagon. "Cap'n Lewis, you lookin' good, sir!" He'd heard about the captain's carrying on, and was glad to see that Lewis was none the worse for wear.

Lewis smiled. "I'm leaving with all flags flying, York." He turned back to the doorway of his room and called, "Pernia! York's here for the trunks. You go ahead and help him. Seaman and I going to walk up and meet General Clark."

Flies and mosquitoes buzzed around the steaming mud puddles in front of the boarding house, and York felt sweat trickling down his back. His shirt and breeches were already clinging to his body, damp and uncomfortable. "You sure about that walking, Cap'n?" York asked. "You wait, I can take you in the wagon." But he wasn't surprised when Lewis shook his head, *no*. It was obvious that he wanted the people of St. Louis to see him leave in style.

Pernia emerged, also looking dapper in a black coat and red waistcoat. He caught York's eye and winked.

York curled his lip. Pernia always looked down on him, because he was a slave and Pernia was free. As far as York could tell, Pernia spent every spare minute and every penny of his salary on whiskey and whores. But that didn't stop him from strutting around like a goddamn peacock!

York knew about fine clothes—tending to Clark's wardrobe was one of his jobs—so he also noticed the carefully mended patches on Pernia's lapel and sleeve, the stain on the lace cuff, and how the breeches were not quite as white as they were meant to be. His eyes flicked back to Pernia's face. The Creole had seen his appraisal and resented it. But then Pernia smiled and ran the few steps to Lewis. Fussing over the captain in French, he straightened Lewis's necktie and bent down to give his boots one last polish.

York knew better than to count on any help with the heavy work from Pernia, so he went ahead and loaded the wagon, carrying out two full trunks and one smaller portmanteau. "These trunks feel like they have rocks in 'em, Cap'n!"

"Mostly just government papers," Lewis said. "I'm going to have to leave most of my plant and mineral specimens." He nodded at his servant. "Pernia, I'll see you at the levee. General Clark and I will be along." He whistled at Seaman and set off down Main in the direction of Clark's house.

Pernia went back in the room and got his carpetbag, then clambered up on the wagon beside York. York clicked his tongue at the horses. "Gee!" Slowly, the beasts began to pull, the wheels of the wagon creaking as they got free of the mud.

"Nice to see the Captain full a' ginger this morning." York said.

"Or something." Pernia shrugged. "At least this morning he can walk and talk. An improvement over yesterday."

York winced. "You're a fine one to talk, boy, the way you drink. 'Sides, you better watch your mouth, talkin' that way about your master."

"He's not my *master*," Pernia snapped. "I'm a free man."

"Well, the man who pays you then," York said. "You oughta show him some respect."

"Respect? How touching, York. You're such a good darky. Really, I should look to you as an example." Pernia smiled. "If and when Lewis pays me, then I will be happy to show my respect, just before giving my notice. That's the only reason I'm going on this trip. The Governor owes me two hundred and forty dollars in back wages."

York raised his eyebrows. That was a lot of money. When he thought about what he could do with two hundred and forty dollars! He allowed himself to fantasize about walking up to Clark and handing him a bag of gold, enough to buy his way free! Pernia's money would get him about halfway there—

"And then, as soon as I collect, I'm through with him," Pernia was saying. "I hope he pays me off in New Orleans. The home of the most beautiful, bewitching women in the world!" He glanced at York. "Oh, sorry, York. I forgot. The only way *you'll* ever see New Orleans is if you're on the auction block!"

York gritted his teeth. He longed to punch Pernia in his smirking face. Instead, he spoke to the horses, urging them to make the turn on to Pine so they could get headed back in the right direction.

Pernia elbowed him. "You know, it's really quite an honor for me to ride with you. The travellingest nigger of all time! The Great York! Canoe paddler, buffalo hunter, mountain climber...boot black, tomato gardener, scrubber of chamber pots..."

"Shut up, Pernia," York said darkly. Involuntarily, he pulled up on the horses' reins, bringing the animals to a dead stop in the middle of the intersection. Angry with himself, he persuaded the animals to move again. They joined the other wagons crowding Market.

At the intersection with Main, Pernia pointed up the street. "There they are."

York sat up straighter when he saw them and shaded his eyes from the sun to get a better look. Lewis and Clark were walking together down Main

Street. Captain Lewis was tipping his hat gallantly to everyone they passed. Clark strode along beside him. In his elegant brown suit, high-topped boots, and beaver felt hat, he looked seven feet tall.

York wiped the sweat off his forehead with his sleeve. "Man, they *own* this town this mornin'."

Pernia sang so quietly that only York could hear him.

You're the man that I adore, handsome Willie-o!
You're the man that I adore, handsome Willie-o!
Come a-tripping down the stairs, tie up your yellow hair
And bid a last farewell to handsome Willie-o!

Disgusted, York clucked his tongue again, moving the horses on until he found a spot to pull off near the drop-off to the river. St. Louis had no wharf, only a steep, unpaved road leading down to a wide beach onto which the boats and barges pulled up and loaded. "Pernia, shut your damn smart mouth," he snapped. He swung himself down, secured the horses, and began putting the blocks under the wheels to keep the wagon from rolling. Pernia climbed down and lounged against the wagon.

"You shouldn't talk to me that way, York," Pernia said. "Remember the slave code. You wouldn't want your master to whip you again for your bad attitude."

York swung the portmanteau down from the wagon and threw it on the ground at Pernia's feet. "You so damn proud of bein' free! What d'ye ever do with it, or any of your wages, except drink and whore around the riverfront?"

"So you disapprove of me?" Pernia laughed. "That's right; you're a married man. But where is your wife? Back in Louisville, or whatever hick town it is you and your master are from? Well, no matter. Since you're the marrying kind, I suppose next time I see you, you'll have a St. Louis wife. After all—" Pernia altered his French accent, mocking York's Kentucky cadences—"You gawta make some more little pickaninnies for de Cap'n!"

"You goin' in the water, boy!" York lunged at Pernia and grabbed at his shirtfront. Pernia dove under his arm, almost losing his balance on the muddy slope. York caught him by a handful of neckcloth, brought back his hand to deliver a slap on the chops—

"York!" Clark's voice cut through the air. Before he knew it, Clark had stepped between them, taken an iron grip on his raised arm, and was holding him and Pernia apart.

"For heaven's sake! What's the matter with you?" Clark exclaimed. His face was red; he didn't like fighting. York knew what Massa Billy wanted— the old happy, laughing York, smiling all the time. "I'm surprised at you, York," Clark scolded him. "Now, you got a job to do. You get Cap'n Lewis's things on the boat, you hear? Hop to!"

Very deliberately, he turned his back on York to resume talking to Lewis. Captain Lewis was standing with his hands behind his back, his head slightly tilted, observing everything the way he always did, taking in the whole scene at the levee, himself and Pernia just a tiny part of everything he saw.

Pernia had rushed to Lewis's side to brush non-existent dust off his coat. "Most inspiring, sir," Pernia was saying. "Really, you are the king of this town this morning."

Lewis ignored Pernia and spoke to Clark, his voice loud, almost boastful. "I can be at the Federal City in a matter of a few weeks only, assuming I can get a ship promptly from New Orleans. I am quite sure the President will be very interested in what I have to say." York wasn't sure whom Lewis was trying to impress; obviously, Captain Clark knew all about his travel plans.

York started hauling the baggage down to the waiting barge. He hated the idea of Captain Lewis going off on this long trip, with no one to look after him but that trashy little snake, Pernia.

By the time he finished with the baggage, his back ached, and he was so slick with sweat he felt as if he might slide out of his clothes. Back at the wagon, the horses were steaming. Seaman had crawled under the wagon, his tongue dripping on the ground. Even the captains, talking with each other softly now, showed the effects of the heat. Clark ran his finger under the edge of his cravat and held it away from his neck. Lewis gulped air through his mouth, his face pale and shiny. York leaned against the wagon and fanned himself with his hat.

Lewis gave him a nod. "Thank you, York."

"My pleasure, sir." It was just like Captain Lewis to notice when you needed something, even if it was just a kind word.

"Oh, Clark!" Lewis said. "I almost forgot. You haven't said anything about Seaman this morning." He whistled and called the panting dog back to his side. "Do you notice anything different about him?"

Clark petted Seaman's ears. "Well, he ain't no cleaner." Clark sniffed the air. "Don't smell no better." He shook his head. "Naw, Lewis, I can't say as I do."

Lewis looked disappointed. York helped Clark out. "His collar, Cap'n."

"Oh, you got him a collar! Well, let's have a look." Clark knelt down and examined the dog's new finery. "It's engraved." He shaded the collar with his hand and read aloud, "The greatest traveler of my species. My name is Seaman, the dog of Meriwether Lewis..." Clark looked up at Lewis and laughed, then finished reading, "...whom I accompanied to the Pacific ocean through the interior of the continent of North America." He stood up, shaking his head. "Well, ain't that something, Lewis. I don't see how old Seaman could have gotten along without it."

York chuckled to himself and shook his head. Captain Lewis tickled him— spending his time and money dreaming up something like a fancy collar for the dog. Lewis needed a son about as bad as anyone he had ever seen. Maybe he'd bring a wife back with him from Virginia this time—

Pernia sidled up to York and nudged him while the captains joked with each other. "How do you like that, York?" he whispered. "Maybe your master could order a collar like that for you. 'I am York, the travellingest of my species—"

York wheeled on Pernia, fist clenched. "I'll knock you on your ass, boy!"

Clark barked, "York, what's gotten into you! I'm gonna send you home, you don't behave!"

Lewis mouthed his servant's name and frowned at Pernia's contrite expression. "Leave York alone, Pernia. He's hot and tired. You go ahead and board, I'll be along in a minute."

Pernia obeyed immediately, heading down the hill without a backward glance. "Be good, Pernia," Clark called. "Take good care of your master." Pernia waved up at Clark and gave him a little salute. York smiled inwardly. He knew how much Clark's choice of words must have rankled.

The boatmen were calling for all passengers to board. Clark turned back to Lewis, his jaw set. York noticed him swallow twice before speaking.

"Now, you write to me, Lewis."

"Of course," Lewis assured him. "I'll write to you from Fort Pickering, if not before. I'll keep you apprised of all my adventures."

Clark reached out and gripped Lewis's forearm in the traditional military handshake.

"Stand your ground, Lewis," Clark said. "Everything will come right."

"I know." Lewis crinkled his eyes in a defiant little smile. "I'll whip 'em all, and come back with flying colors. Take care of yourself, Clark."

For a long moment, York didn't think Clark was going to let go of Captain Lewis's arm. But finally, he spread his fingers and stepped back. Lewis strode down the steep bank, splashed out to the barge, and boarded. He turned around and faced them and the city and waved as jauntily as if he were leaving town in triumph. It could almost have been three years ago, leaving for Washington to report on the magnificent success of the Expedition.

Except this time, there were no cheering crowds, just him and Massa Billy, and Billy's jaw clenched so hard that it was a wonder he didn't break a tooth.

Clark and York walked along the cliff that overlooked the river, keeping pace with the boat as the boatmen poled it away from the levee and struggled to find the current that would float their passengers and cargo down the Mississippi.

"Just don't seem right, Massa Billy, the cap'n going off without us," York said, as the barge disappeared around one of the river's great bends. "Wish we was goin' with him."

Clark nodded, his arms still folded tight across his chest, and said, "Go get the wagon." For another moment, he studied the river. Then Clark released his body with a great sigh, and started back into town, alone.

Chapter 10
Lewis

They rounded a bend in the river and St. Louis slid out of sight. Lewis shook his head, trying to clear it, as the morning sun beat down on him. The fever was biting into his brain.

Like an apparition in some dreadful nightmare, the trees on the other side of the river began to swim in and out of focus, first advancing, then receding. Before he could grab onto something, his knees went out from under him and he fell hard onto the deck of the barge.

He lay on his side on the rough planks, moaning. Seaman whined and licked at his face. One of the boatmen, a rough-looking chap with yellow hair, glanced over at him and laughed roughly. Catching the attention of his fellows, he inclined his head towards Lewis and muttered, "All hail his Excellency the Governor—king of the drunks."

Lewis didn't have the strength to protest. He was sick, very sick, and it had been all he could do to act normal this morning in front of Clark and the others. The performance had exhausted the last bit of energy he had.

Pernia came running from the other end of the barge, where he'd been busy securing the baggage. "Governor!" he cried. "*Mon Dieu!* What's the matter?"

"Malarial ague," Lewis said haltingly. "It's flared up again." He was shivering like a leaf in the wind; the sunlight itself seemed to be the source of the pain. "Pernia, please...bring me some water."

"Of course! *Pour le bien de Dieu*, let me move you out of the sun."

With difficulty, Pernia dragged him under the wooden canopy that sheltered the boatmen, passengers and baggage from sun and rain. He propped Lewis up against a barrel of flour and ran to dip some cool water out of the river.

Pouring sweat, Lewis dragged off his cravat and struggled to remove his green coat. He felt robbed of his senses. He'd had the ague off and on for years, but never this bad, not that he could remember. "Pernia," he called, "get my medicine chest, will you? It's in the big black trunk, right on top...you know what it looks like..."

Pernia rushed back with a bucket and a dipper of water, then ran to fetch the medicine chest. Lewis held the dipper in shaky hands and gulped down a couple of mouthfuls. His stomach cramped. He gagged and spit up a little onto his waistcoat, but forced himself to keep the rest down. Pernia came back with the chest and helped him out of his coat, laying it carefully over the top of the barrel.

With trembling fingers, Lewis pried open the medicine chest and hunted through his myriad collection of medicinal herbs and pills. Finally, he found a small bottle of milky liquid labeled *Laudanum*.

"All right, Pernia, this helped the other day." He handed the bottle to the little Creole. "Put thirty drops of this into a spoon...I would do it myself, but my hands are a bit unsteady..."

Pernia uncorked the bottle and measured out the required dose. The medicine smelled strongly of alcohol. Lewis took the spoon and gulped it down, blanching at the foul taste.

"There, that'll make it better..." Lewis leaned his head back against the barrel and gave Pernia a weak, glassy-eyed smile. He fumbled with the buttons on his waistcoat. "You know, this heat is terrible...it shouldn't be this hot in September..."

"Governor, maybe we ought to turn back," Pernia said. "You're ill, sir. We could hail a boat going back to St. Louis, and wait to leave until you're well again—"

"*No.*" Lewis shut his eyes against the glare of the sun. "I can't turn back, Pernia. I've tarried too long already. I should've left a month ago. As it is, he'll be ready...he'll be waiting..."

"Who, Governor?" Pernia mopped Lewis's forehead with his discarded cravat. "Secretary Eustis? Why, you can make short work of him."

Lewis didn't answer. Behind his eyelids, an odd illusion was taking shape. The gentle rocking of the boat on the river reminded him of being on the back of a horse. He was riding on a gray horse through an endless forest...mist was rising from the cool forest floor, and dark twisted trees were growing up all around him...Pernia was also on horseback, and Seaman was running by his side...but they weren't alone—

Lewis jerked back into consciousness and stared around him. Pernia was bending over him, his brow furrowed with concern. A short distance away, Seaman lay in the shade, panting. But he knew when he turned his head, he would see it.

The other creature was there, too.

It took the form of a black wolf. It sat on the deck grinning at him, its black lips skinned back over yellowed teeth, its slick greasy fur gleaming blue-black in the sun. It licked its lips with its enormous tongue and looked at him with small, gray, evil eyes.

"Damn." He felt a stab of despair. "The sonofabitch followed me."

"Who, Governor?" Pernia lifted his head, his eyes darting around at the boatmen and fellow passengers. "Who are you talking about?"

Lewis didn't answer. He knew Pernia couldn't see it. Nobody but himself could see the black wolf, not even Seaman. The creature had been dogging his steps for weeks. It was with him all the time now—in the streets of St. Louis, in the Masonic hall, in the alley outside the tavern. God, it had even been in the room with him and Clark last night!

Somehow, it always knew the worst possible time to appear. When he was sick, when he was weak, when he was scared.

"Oh, he's very clever," he mumbled to himself. "And *bold*...so very bold..."

"Governor," Pernia wiped Lewis's forehead again. "I really wish you'd let us turn back—"

"We can't, Pernia." Lewis tore his eyes away from the black wolf and focused them on Pernia. He grabbed his servant's wrist and gripped it hard. "Pernia...you've got to help me now. Please...I need you. Help me, Pernia."

"Of course," Pernia said, watching the river.

Exhausted and aching, Lewis closed his eyes and waited for the medicine to take effect. The barge bobbed gently as the current of the river lapped against its sides. The yellow-haired boatman looked in their direction and said something to his mate, and they both laughed. Out in the sun, the black wolf drooled and grinned.

"It's a long trip ahead," Lewis mumbled. "But don't worry. We'll make it, Pernia."

Despite the heat, Pernia shivered. "I'm not worried," he said.

Chapter 11
Wilkinson

Terre aux Boeufs, Orleans Territory
September 10, 1809

Four ragged lines of men in shabby blue coats stood strung out over a mile of tall prairie grass. Flies rose in clouds over the plain, and swarms of mosquitoes whined around the men and raised welts on their hands and faces. The stream of murmured obscenities swelled into one indistinguishable rumble, a long low chorus of misery. The men sweated and swore in the noonday sun. They had been standing for hours.

Towards the front of the column, a private staggered out of line and fell on his face, his musket flipping in a lazy arc into the mud. His comrades glanced at him indifferently. No one moved. Every soldier there knew what would happen if he stepped out of line, and nobody was willing to risk the lash.

On a small rise above the steaming, stinking plain, James Wilkinson sat on his fine horse, enjoying the sight of the United States Army arrayed before him. Was there any more cheerful sight than the pageantry of an army on the march? Guidons flapping in the breeze, muskets swaying on strong young shoulders...soon he would hear the thrilling cadence of thousands of tramping feet...

But as usual, something wasn't right. "Colonel!" he cried to one of his officers. He stabbed an accusatory finger in the direction of the fallen private. "Revive that man and get him back into the line. If he can't stand up, send him to the sick wagons. If he's malingering, whip him!"

The colonel muttered his assent and spurred his horse through the swampy grass, the horse's hooves sending little clots of mud flying into the air. Wilkinson sniffed, satisfied to see the man jerked to his feet and shoved back into the line.

He looked up and down the column. Now all was ready.

He paused, savoring the moment. The heat and the stench bothered him not a bit; after all, it was a soldier's lot to suffer for his country. With the wind ruffling his hair, he felt an odd sensation of coolness and grace. The dramatic tension was all but unbearable. When he could stand it no longer, he drew his general's sword from its scabbard and thrust it high in the air.

"FORWARD! HO!"

At his command, like a long blue serpent, the two thousand men of the United States Army began to inch slowly forward. He saw lean, starved faces break out into grins, and some of the troops sent up a feeble cheer. Down the column, knock-kneed, hollow-cheeked men laughed and slapped each other on the back. He found their happiness touching. They were headed upriver to New Orleans, where ships were waiting—ships bound for Natchez.

Overcome by sentiment, Wilkinson watched as the shabby blue column straggled past him. He sat erect in the saddle, knowing how the sight of their commander would inspire the men. Resplendent in a bright red coat with golden braid—a uniform of his own design—and perched upon a leopard-skin saddle cloth with dangling claws, he looked every inch the commanding general. And oh, how the men responded! As each brigade passed, they turned and gave him a snappy salute!

Wilkinson dug his gold spurs into his horse's flanks and turned to ride alongside the line, eager to share in his soldiers' rowdy good cheer. At the rear of the column, a long train of hospital wagons creaked into motion, its reeking, suffering human cargo screaming with each bump and jolt. It was a pity he'd have to leave those poor devils in the hospital in New Orleans.

In retrospect, perhaps Terre aux Boeufs hadn't been the best place for an army camp. When the men weren't complaining about flies and mosquitoes, they were crying about alligators and snakes; if they weren't lamenting the scorching heat, they were grousing about the drenching rain. A full sixty percent of the army was on the sick list. To his annoyance, his chief surgeon had the temerity to claim that the rations were rotten, and the men weren't getting enough food.

Wilkinson fumed. He'd made a lucrative deal with a contractor in New Orleans to provide the army with stores—and, well, he couldn't be expected to supervise everything personally, could he? "Steady on, boys," he urged as the ragged line limped forward. He turned in the saddle and bleated at the wagon masters: "Close it up, damn you!"

Over the inspiring sound of the fife-and-drum corps tootling "A Soldier's Farewell," Wilkinson reined his horse and turned his attention to the rolled-up copy of the *Louisiana Gazette* he had bought in the city this morning. Napoleon's doings on the Danube were all the news—with the Austrians defeated, Bonaparte seemed to be contemplating his next target. Wilkinson shuddered. Gads, he hoped it wasn't Spain!

Smoothing the paper over his gleaming saddle horn, he scanned down the page and suddenly drew in his breath. Buried beneath the story about Napoleon's victory at Wagram, a small item caught his eye:

GOV'R LEWIS IN N.O. EN ROUTE TO FEDERAL CITY

Gov'r Meriwether Lewis of Upper Louisiana will pass through Orleans on his way to Washington City. He will be expected to remain in New Orleans for one week, and from hence embarque by ship to Baltimore. Gentlemen wishing to see the famed leader of the late voyage to the Pacific Ocean during his stay in the city are encouraged to apply at the home of the Hon. Julien Poydras in Faubourg deClouet.

"Blast!" Wilkinson smacked the paper and muttered under his breath. "This Lewis really is a troublesome gnat! First he dawdles when I want him to move...then when I want him to tarry, he comes on! Doubtless Morphy hasn't even written to his *patrón* in Havana yet!"

He pulled at his upper lip, the wheels cranking frantically in his head. What was Lewis up to? Surely he wouldn't be such a fool as to come through New Orleans! *He'd have to know I'd be waiting for him...*

*But...*he stopped to consider. Lewis had contacts in the Federal City, too, and he must have heard that Eustis had ordered the army to Natchez. He was no doubt hoping to sneak past him when he was busy on the march...or perhaps he had other, more sinister reasons for coming...

"That dim-witted cock-robin!" Wilkinson crumpled the *Gazette* in his hands. "He thinks he can *confront* me here!" He tossed the wadded paper into the grass. "Well, he best think again! Only a fool would let himself be taken that easily."

His mind worked voraciously, spinning through various possibilities. "I know what to do," he muttered to himself. "If he dares to show his face in this town, in *my* town, I will expose him. I'll arrest him as a traitor *on the spot!* It will spoil things with Morphy—but no matter. I can seek my fortune another time. It would be worth the price, just to see Lewis fall."

His excitement returned, and spots of color dotted his cheeks. It was a real game now. Red-faced, he spurred his horse and rode to the front of the column, splashing over the swampy ground. The men in the van watched him with incurious, yellowed eyes, wondering what General Wilkinson had to be so exercised about.

Chapter 12
Clark

St. Louis, Louisiana Territory
September 25, 1809

It was high noon when Clark burst out of the military briefing at the fortress-like mansion of Auguste Choteau feeling as if he had just been liberated from a British hulk ship. Before he left, Lewis had signed an executive order transferring much of his power to Clark. Now Clark found his days eaten up in endless meetings. The interested parties always seemed to find a thousand details to quibble about and a thousand reasons to avoid making any decisions. He was beginning to understand why Lewis had been so short-tempered and overwhelmed in this job.

He crossed Main Street, heading for the Eagle Tavern. Christy had propped the doors and windows open to take advantage of any breeze, and men lounged on the piazza, some playing cards, some just talking easily with one another. From inside, the inviting sounds of men's laughter and friendly arguments drifted out into the street. Clark checked the board outside: chicken on a string, with green corn pudding and apple cake. His stomach growled. After a steady diet of Julia's experiments, it sounded wonderful. He could already smell the chicken twirling on the tavern room's hearth, roasting to perfection.

Clark sprang up on the piazza. He had no use for town gossip, but he couldn't help catching snatches of the conversation now underway.

"Probably just corned out of his mind. You know, they didn't carry liquor on the Expedition, that's the only reason they made it—"

"I heard Lewis was crazy as a loon, they ended up lashing him to the baggage—"

"Shut up, man! That's General Clark!"

The men stopped talking. Clark knew most of them. A couple of them had the guts to acknowledge him before they looked away.

"It's always the cowardly dogs who sit up on the porch and bark the loudest." Clark paused long enough to see the color draining out of their faces. "Any of you work up the brass to bite, you know where to find me." He shouldered a young man out of his way and entered the cool darkness of the tavern.

Square-headed William Christy spotted him and motioned him over with a grin. "Hey, General, where you been keepin' yourself? I'd about given you up for dead."

Clark smiled and shook his old friend's hand. "I've found someone prettier to spend my evenings with. 'Sides, seems like I've been given up for dead before, 'bout three years ago when we came straggling into St. Louis looking like a bunch of Robinson Crusoes."

"Not me!" Christy said. "I always knew you'd make it. What a day that was! Remember that party we had that night, and you and Lewis still in your buckskins?" Christy sobered and leaned over the bar in a confidential manner. "Have you heard anything from Lewis, then?"

Clark shook his head. "No, but it's early yet. Only three weeks. I never saw the beat of this city, Christy. More damn gossip than at a ladies' tea party."

"Well, a river town runs on rumors." Christy took Clark's hat for him, his shrewd eyes passing over Clark's face in a quick study. "It's not like you to take it personal, Bill."

Clark rolled his shoulders back to loosen them. "Blazes, does it show? Tell you somethin' funny, Christy—"

"Let me get your dinner going and get you something to drink," Christy said. He began to bustle around with his brandy bottle and his spice jars.

"Listen, Christy, I was gonna tell you, my son is getting' his teeth in now, and it's the damnedest thing—"

Clark heard someone say the name *Lewis* and turned his head, distracted from his story. Christy was pouring an alarming amount of sugar into the glass and uncorking a bottle of white wine.

Clark's back stiffened. Men were eating, drinking, crystal and china clattering. But now that he listened, all he heard was Lewis...skipped town...Lewis...staggering drunk...Lewis... Lewis... Lewis...just plain *crazy*—

Clark felt the hair rise on the back of his neck. He pulled at his cravat. "Why is it so goddamn hot in here, Christy?" he heard himself snap.

Christy blinked in surprise, then plunked the glass down on the bar in front of him. "A finishing touch of raspberry vinegar! Go ahead, Bill, tell me what you think."

Clark picked up the glass and took a sip. The sweetness spread across his tongue a few seconds before the liquor warmed his chest. "Good Lord, Christy." He shook his head. There wasn't a more honest, better man in St. Louis than Meriwether Lewis. It was like someone was conspiring against Lewis, to make sure he could never come back—

He sensed someone beside him at the bar and glanced over. Bulging blue eyes, beautiful fluffy hair, double-breasted striped waistcoat with brass buttons, paunch.

Lord spare me, Clark thought. *If this day gets any better, I'll break a leg next.*

"General Clark," Secretary Bates said. "I might have known that the only place I would run into you is at the tavern. I see you so seldom these days. Pray, what is the news from the Louisiana Territory?"

"Bates, your sarcasm ain't necessary," Clark said. "I've just been doin' my job—"

"Your job, sir?" Bates looked down his long nose at Clark. "Unless there have been changes to the statutes of which I have not been informed, your appointment is as general of the militia and superintendent of Indian affairs. In other words, my subordinate."

Clark's jaw worked. Christy looked on with wary interest while Bates continued, "Tell me, General, when were you going to advise me of the new trading licenses you granted out at Fort Osage last week?"

"You know damn well that Governor Lewis ceded that power to me before he left—"

"Which he had no right to do!"

"I don't answer to you, Bates. I answer to Governor Lewis, and I will carry out his wishes."

"I am the acting governor of this territory!" Bates exclaimed. "You will clear your decisions through me, General Clark. I must *insist* that you do so! I will not suffer your interference in my duty!"

Clark opened his hands. "Bates, you and I both know that Governor Lewis signed an order. Whether you like it or not, it's legal. Now, I'm sorry you ain't the biggest toad in the puddle right now, but cool off, for pity's sake."

"General, I will not be placated by your rustic buffoonery!"

With sudden violence, Clark slammed his glass on the bar and straightened up. "That's quite enough, Freddy," he said. "Tell me, is it your fine hand I see behind all this buzzle about the Governor?"

Incensed, Bates reached inside his coat and closed his fingers around his pistol.

"I ain't armed with anything except my wits," Clark said. "Tell you what, Fred. I'll make it a fair fight and use only half."

"*That* is an impudent stupidity, even for you, General." Bates shook with anger. "If Governor Lewis's reputation is destroyed in this city, he has accomplished the task without any assistance from me. It is *I* who have been ill-used by you and your friend. I would not stoop to your level. I have taken the high road. I have stepped a *high* and a *proud* path!"

"Well, while you're stepping that high and proud path, why don't you step it on outta here, Fred. You're spoilin' my dinner."

The tavern had fallen silent. Everyone was watching them now. Clark felt sweat trickling through his hair down the back of his neck.

From behind the bar, Christy said, "Gentlemen, I'll not have this. Not in my establishment."

Clark felt sick. He looked Bates up and down. The pudgy secretary looked as if he were about to have a stroke. "I'll leave, Christy." Clark picked up his drink, took one last swallow, and grabbed his hat. He knew his face was red. *Stupid—*

He was glad to get out into the sunlight. The air outside was hot and laden with putrid city smells, but he pulled it into his lungs anyway, trying to slow his breathing. He was beginning to understand how just being in the same room with Bates could provoke Lewis to the point of brawling. *How does he put up with it? Is it like this every damn day?*

He couldn't stop chewing over the rest of the gossip in his mind. Part of him feared there was truth in it. That night in his room before he'd left for New Orleans, Lewis had behaved like he didn't have all his buttons. And anybody could see that his playacting at the levee had been pure bluff; Clark had seen far more desperation than defiance in his friend's face. Now, with all these strange rumors going around, he didn't know what to think.

Meriwether, I wish to hell you'd write...

The worst part about his argument with Bates was that he'd left in such a hurry, he hadn't gotten any dinner. There was nothing for it but to go home and risk eating whatever Julia put on the table.

As Clark approached his house, steeling himself for whatever might be waiting for him in the larder, he saw a big yellow dun horse tied up outside. He didn't recognize the animal, but he did notice the standard issue army saddle. The horse looked well cared-for but winded; its nose was buried in a pile of hay.

The soldier that belonged to the horse lounged on his front steps, resting on his elbows as he gazed at the people walking on the street. Clark saw at once that he wasn't one of his militia boys, but a U.S. army regular with a sergeant's red epaulet. He looked young and was covered with dust from top to toe.

The boy finally noticed him. His eyes widened and he scrambled off the porch, arranging his tall, gangly body into a crisp salute.

"At ease, Sergeant." Clark looked the boy over and was pleased to note that although his uniform was dirty, at least he'd taken the time to wash his face and hands. "What brings you to my house on such a warm afternoon?"

With a broad twang, the boy began: "General Clark, sir, I got a letter for you—" He paused, cocked his head and squinted. "You *are* General Clark, ain't yeh?"

Clark suppressed a smile. "Yes, I'm Clark. And who might you be?"

"I'm Sergeant John Thomas, from Fort Pickerin'," the boy said. "Cap'n Russell sent me."

"You've come a long way, Sergeant," Clark said. "You say you got a letter for me?"

"Yessir," Thomas said. He reached a big-knuckled hand into his knapsack and carefully pulled out a letter. "I got orders to put it directly in your hand, sir," he said. With a relieved expression, he added, "Which I done, sir."

Clark's heart leapt. The handwriting and seal on the letter were Lewis's. "Come in, Sergeant. Let's get out of this heat." He took the steps two at a time and motioned Thomas into the parlor, where Julia was curled up in a chair by the window darning one of his shirts.

"Julia, what do you mean letting this poor boy set out in the sun? Least you could do was let him wait inside."

"I asked him to, but he said he was too dirty." Julia put her sewing aside. "Besides, he didn't want to talk to anybody but you." She smiled at Thomas, who removed his round hat and made a futile attempt to smooth his fair, sweat-soaked hair.

"Well, see if you can't come up with some lemonade, or something," Clark said. "And if you got anything layin' around in the kitchen, put a plate aside, 'cause I ain't had dinner yet."

Julia hurried out to the kitchen. Clark noticed Thomas looking after her and said, "Take my advice, Sergeant, you got a choice between settin' outside in the sun or settin' inside with a pretty girl, take the latter. Now come on back to the office."

Thomas goggled around the house as he followed him to the back room.

"You know, sir, I ain't never been in a general's house afore."

"Well, I hope it ain't too much of a disappointment." Clark hunted in his desk for something to slit open the letter.

"Oh, no sir. H'its right nice." Thomas assured him. He settled onto one hip, warming up for the soldier's favorite pastime, complaining. "Now you take Fort Pickerin'—that ain't no palace, sir. 'Cept for the 'skeeters, that is. We got 'skeeters so big and fat you kin tie a string around 'em and use 'em for a—"

Clark eyeballed Thomas. "Son, you from Kentucky?"

"No, sir, Tennessee. Neighbors, I reckon."

"Well, I been in St. Louis too long, I must be out of practice. I thought I could recognize Kentucky bull a mile away."

Thomas grinned, revealing a mouthful of horsey teeth. "Tennessee boys ain't too shabby at prevaricatin', sir."

"I can see that." Clark found his knife and settled himself behind his desk. "Rest yourself a minute, Sergeant, while I read this letter. I might have a reply for you to take back."

Thomas nodded and busied himself studying the painted elk skin hanging on the wall. Clark carefully slipped his knife under the wax seal of the letter and broke it.

> *Ft Pickering*
> *Chickesaw Bluffs, Tennessee*
> *September 16th 09*

> *To his Excellency Genl. Wm. Clark*
> *Saint Louis*

> *Dear Clark,*
>
> *I transmit this letter to you by the trusted hand of Sgt. Thos., and hope it finds you in the best of health &c.*
>
> *I arrived at this place yesterday in a state of some indisposition, having been much exhausted from the heat of the climate and from a recurrent affliction of the ague, which has thus far resisted even my most rigorous attempts to eradicate it. My affliction has caused me great inconvenience and no small concern, owing to my anxiety to get on, but for other reasons as well.*
>
> *My purposes in going to Washington City are well known to you. But Clark, there is one thing I have not told you. Pray be assured you have earned my trust in every respect. My act was not due to any want of confidence, but rather my desire to keep you from being*

drawn into a situation which I feared could only injure your perfect happiness.

Clark, when I told you that there were persons conspiring to ruin and destroy me, it was not mere exaggeration; I regret to say it is all too real. While I was on the boat en route to this place, and most unwell, my svt. Pernia, having overheard a conversation among the boatmen, became much allarmed, fearing they had violent intentions towards me, and had designed to kill me before I reached New Orlns. &c.

Accordingly, we disembarked at New Madrid, where I took the liberty of making my last will and testament, a copy of which I deposited with Mr. Trinchard of that city. In any case, I bequeath all my estate, after my private debts are paid, to my Mother, Lucy Marks. I trust you will see to it that this is handled properly should it be necessary.

Clark, the outcome of this contest is most uncertain, and it is fair you should know that the forces arrayed against me are very strong. I know not how it shall end, or where, but I am determined to stand and fight at the price of my own fortune or even my own life, which I would not consider too dear a price to pay to defeat those who are the enemies of liberty.

But I admit I suffer considerable unease about the fate of the journals and papers relative to our voyage to the Pacific Ocean, which are currently under the protection of Capt. Russell, the commander of this place. I wish I had been forthcoming with you from the start, but as it cannot now be helped, I once again call on you for your help and counsel, which I need more now than ever in my life.

Clark I beg you to come on as quick as you can. Under any other circumstances I would never importune you to leave your family, or to place the govt. in the hands of that idiot Bates, but it may mean more than my life. Do not take one of the regular packet boats that travel between N. O. and St. Louis; travel only with persons who are known to you. I will tell you more when I see you.

I am confident I will soon be well, but am compelled to linger here a few days whilst I recover my health. I am determined to proceed on at the earliest date. I trust no one now and I beg you tell no one Clark. It is my great hope that you will join me as soon as is practicably possible. Send word if you cannot, but for god's sake come on if you can

Your sincere and unalterable friend and Obt. Servt.—
MERIWETHER LEWIS.

Clark read the letter over several times. His mouth felt dry. He glanced up at Sergeant Thomas, who was standing with his hands behind his back, staring with intense curiosity at his collection of Indian ceremonial pipes.

"Thomas," Clark said, "Did you talk to Governor Lewis at Fort Pickering?"

"Yessir." Thomas nodded.

"How'd he seem?" Clark was careful to keep his face neutral; he'd get better information if the boy didn't think he wanted him to tell it one way or another.

"Well...he...he weren't tip-top, sir. The heat had got to him somethin' fierce. They had to carry him off the boat on a litter."

Clark's eyes narrowed. "So he was sick?"

"Yessir," Thomas said. "He was a mite poorly when I saw him. Couldn't keep nothin' on his stomach, sir."

"Was he drunk?"

Clark studied Thomas's face while the boy hesitated. Finally, he stammered, "I couldn't rightly say, sir."

Clark sighed. Thomas's reaction told him all he needed to know. He glanced at the letter again and asked, "Was he out of his head?"

Thomas looked surprised. "No, sir, not by a long chalk! If you're askin' me if the Governor was in his senses, I'd have to say yessir, he was. Sick an' all, that man knew *exactly* what he was doin'."

Clark smiled a little. He felt a tiny bit of weight lift off his shoulders. For the first time, he noticed that Thomas looked bone-weary as well as filthy from the dust of the trail. "How long you been in the saddle, son?"

"Eight days, sir. I left Fort Pickerin' directly after the Gov'ner give me the letter."

"And you came straight here?"

"Yessir. Only stopped to rest my horse."

"Good man." Clark clapped Thomas on the shoulder. "Tell you what. You go on out to Fort Bellefontaine, and they'll give you a place to rest and wash up, and food for you and your horse. And I'll write a letter to Captain Russell, lettin' him know how much I appreciate what you done."

Thomas grinned and gripped Clark's outstretched hand. "Much obliged, sir!" he said, then remembered his duty. "Any message for me to take back, sir?"

"No, Sergeant, I'll give the Governor my reply when I see him." Clark yelled for York. "York, ride with the Sergeant out to the fort, and see he's well taken care of."

York nodded and went to saddle up. Julia hurried in with a couple of glasses of lemonade. "Sorry it took so long. I was—"

"It's all right, ma'am, I was just leavin'." Thomas drained his glass in a gulp. He looked at Julia for a moment with the same curiosity he had the Indian pipes. Then he turned to Clark, saluted, and showed himself out.

Clark sat down and pulled a piece of paper towards him, then looked at

Julia for a long moment. She put his glass of in front of him and sat down on a stool near his chair.

"Will...is everything all right?" She instinctively reached for his hand.

Clark held his wife's tiny fingers in his own. "No, darlin'," he said. "Meriwether's in some trouble. I'm gonna have to go."

"Oh, Will, why?" Julia moaned. "What kind of trouble?"

"I can't tell you that," Clark said. *Even if I knew.* Reading Lewis's letter, he was beginning to have his suspicions. He hoped he was wrong, for the mere thought of it made a hard, bitter feeling grow in his gut.

"Do you have to go all the way to Washington City?" Julia asked. "Will, you'll be away all winter!"

"I guess I'll go as far as I have to go to put things right." He stroked her fingers. "Julia, I'm going to write to brother Jonathan. I'll ask him to come fetch you and Lew and the rest of the family, and take you with him to Louisville. You can close up the house and winter over with Jonathan and Sarah. I'll be takin' York with me."

Julia looked at him with tears in her eyes. But she didn't cry, and she didn't argue. Clark supposed she knew him well enough by now to know when his mind was set on something. She understood what his friendship with Lewis meant to him, and had never questioned it.

"Julia, I don't want to go any more than you want me to, but he needs me for somethin', and I have to help him. I owe that man a lot."

Clark watched her go, then dipped his quill in ink and started scratching out a letter to Jonathan. In a strange way, he felt better. To a man of action, there was nothing worse than sitting around at home wondering what was going on. Now, it was resolved. He had a job to do.

"Lewis, you hang on," he muttered to himself as his pen flew across the paper. He almost smiled. "Don't you worry 'bout them sonsofbitches. I'm comin' as fast as I can."

Chapter 13
Wilkinson

New Orleans, Orleans Territory
September 26, 1809

Every autumn in New Orleans, the local plantation owners threw a lavish ball to celebrate the end of summer. With the onset of cooler weather, the terrifying threat of yellow fever began to fade, and the *élite* of the city were eager to pull down their mosquito nets and kick up their heels as only the French knew how to do.

Wilkinson was excited. This year's *fête* was at the garish plantation home of Robert Gautier Montreuil, one of the richest men in the parish. Montreuil's mansion in the Bywater was nothing short of fabulous. He'd spared no expense, importing the best Persian rugs and crystal chandeliers from Europe to furnish his pleasure palace and impress his friends.

It was a vulgar display, really—but Wilkinson loved it. He loved the carriages and the music, the wonderful wine, the rich food, and most of all the ladies with their feathers and glittering jewels. Riding up to Montreuil's pillared portico in a hired coach, he felt wistful that he might ever have to leave this place.

"Oh, James!" Celeste clutched his arm and breathed into his ear. "Isn't it marvelous!"

"It's lovely, yes...but everything looks cheap and tawdry next to you, my dear."

Celeste rewarded him with a shy glance and a giggle. Montreuil's black liveryman rushed up and helped Wilkinson steer his considerable bulk out of the carriage. In turn, he took Celeste's dainty gloved hand and helped her down onto the drive. She really did look fetching tonight. Her cheeks glowed pink, and her soft blond curls shone in the light of the blazing lamps.

"Good evening, General!" Montreuil called from the door. "And bless me, you've brought your lovely *fiancée*, Madamoiselle Trudeau!" He put his hand on his chest and staggered theatrically. "I'm not sure I can bear so much beauty in the form of one woman."

Celeste blushed madly. *"Monsieur* Montreuil, you flatter me too much! I am only—"

"Nonsense." Montreuil kissed her hand. "There is no such thing as too much flattery. Wouldn't you agree, General?"

"Wholeheartedly, sir." With a friendly nod, Wilkinson escorted Celeste past Montreuil and into the glittering front hall. He was pleased to see all of the best people here tonight—and himself among them. Yes, there could be no doubt he'd *arrived* in this town. If the French didn't care for American manners, at least they appreciated American might. All the genteel *chevaliers* from the top rung of the city's society greeted him effusively. He glowed with vitality as they gathered round, pressing him with their weak French handshakes, kissing his cheeks, offering congratulations to him and Celeste...

Flustered by all the attention, Celeste looked both thrilled and embarrassed. She touched his arm and whispered, "James, I can't bear this crush. I'm going to go join the ladies." Wilkinson smiled paternally as she squeezed his hand and slipped into the ladies' parlor.

He wove his way through the crowd towards a long table at the back of the hall, where servants in fancy dress were pouring wine like water, filling glasses with burgundy and bordeaux so fast that wine slopped onto the floor. Snagging a glass of Montreuil's best Bordeaux, he started for the gaming tables. He was intercepted by a tall, elegant negro in a cutaway coat and white silk cravat, carrying a gleaming salver with a note resting on it.

"General Wilkinson, pardon the interruption, *si vous plaît,*" the negro said in perfect French-accented English. "A gentleman at the door sends his compliments, and says he wishes to see you."

Wilkinson had to laugh. It never ceased to amaze him how darky servants in Orleans had better manners than the finest gentlemen back home in Philadelphia. He plucked the note off the tray and unfolded it.

Back from my travels—must see you—Captain House.

"Blast it! Now?" Wilkinson moaned out loud.

"Shall I tell him you are not available, sir?"

"No," Wilkinson sighed. "I'll see him." He pushed his way back through the cluster of people in the great hall. House had some nerve coming here tonight—and wasn't it just the luck? One of the few occasions when he finally had the chance to enjoy himself—

When Wilkinson burst out onto the portico and saw House leaning against one of the pillars, his annoyance immediately turned to concern. His protégé looked terrible. His face was drawn and wan, his jaw shadowed.

"House, what in God's name is the matter?" Wilkinson hissed. He dragged the younger man into a magnolia grove, out of earshot of the other guests. "Couldn't this have waited until morning?"

"General..." House rolled sick eyes toward him. "I passed the army on my way down from Fort Adams. I expected to find you with them, actually."

"Personal business detained me in the city. What's your problem, House? Have you any news?"

"News? General, those boats are way too crowded. Half the troops are down with dysentery...they're regular hellships. The men are dying!"

"That's none of your business! I pay you for information, not to tell me how to do my job."

"I know, but God, they were piling them in heaps on the decks, weighting them down with—"

"House!" Wilkinson cracked him across the face, knocking his *chapeau bras* askew. "You're babbling, sir! You're jabbering about things you know nothing about! And I won't have it!"

As he'd hoped, the blow calmed House down. He straightened up at once. "Forgive me...I don't know what I was thinking. My apologies...sir."

"Never mind. It's *done*." Wilkinson was determined that House would remember his place; he'd paid him far too much money for his services over the years to ever let him forget it. He pursed his lips. "Well, Captain, as long as you're here, you might as well tell me what you've been up to for the last month. What do you hear of our nettlesome friend from St. Louis?"

A faint bit of color came back to House's pale cheeks. "Plenty. As you probably know by now, he's headed downriver. And from what I hear, he's a total shambles."

"Do tell." Wilkinson pressed close.

"Well, the fine gents of St. Louis have washed their hands of him, from what I gather. When everybody found out that Eustis refused his vouchers, the moneylenders descended on him like a flock of vultures. Apparently it disordered his brain. I hear he went on quite a spree before he left the city."

"Good work, House! I do hope he made an appalling spectacle of himself."

"Quite," House confirmed. "But since he quit St. Louis, I confess my information's been a bit spotty. You know those two riverboat fellows you hired to watch him? It seems he got away from them."

"No! How in blazes did he do that?"

"Either he's a great actor, or he really is damn crazy," House said. "He collapsed on the boat, and his nigger had him carried off at New Madrid, along with all his things. They say he kept sniveling about his journals."

Wilkinson frowned. "House, this is *too* convenient! You don't suppose he's really gone mad, do you?"

"Having never clapped eyes on the gentleman, I really couldn't say." House shrugged. "It could have been pure trickery, for aught anyone knows. Your men decided they couldn't dally about without raising suspicions, so they moved on without him."

"Damn it!" Wilkinson rolled his eyes to the heavens. "Can't those French dolts even follow simple instructions? It's no wonder Napoleon lost Louisiana." He peered at House, his breath coming in shallow gasps. "Tell me you've had news since then! Where is he? How close?"

"While your men were standing around holding their cocks, your able adversary slipped away downriver," House said. "From what I hear, he's moved in bag and baggage at Fort Pickering, where he's been living on Captain Russell's charity and sucking on the whisky bottle as if it were mother's milk."

"For how long?"

"At least a week, maybe longer."

"What? Just sitting there? With all his papers?" Wilkinson paced around and stared off into the darkness. "Egad! What deviltry is this? What could he possibly be waiting for?"

It was clear that House either didn't know or didn't care, because he just shrugged. Wilkinson felt exasperated. The good captain was fine for carrying tales and spreading gossip, but he needed somebody who could control the situation on the field. He thought desperately for a moment, then a broad smile spread across his face as an idea came to him.

It was nothing short of genius. If things worked out—why, he might be able to save the deal with Don Diego Morphy after all!

"House, come 'round to my house first thing in the morning. I need you to carry a message to somebody who could be of great help to us."

"Who?" House asked.

"I just hired him in July—to be honest, his name escapes me at the moment. He's the federal agent at the Chickasaw Agency."

"Oh God!" House moaned. "Don't make me go all the way up there! I can't stand traveling that road."

"What, the Trace? It's a lot better than it used to be. I ought to know, I built the damn thing." Wilkinson glanced back towards Montreuil's house; if he didn't return to the party soon, people would start wondering where he'd gotten off to. "Besides, you have only to get to Natchez, then have a fast courier ride it up to the Chickasaw Agency. But you'll need to hurry."

"General, I'm exhausted," House protested. "Surely you don't mean I should leave right away—"

"I most certainly do," Wilkinson said. "Stop complaining, House! It's devilish important. The reputations of some very important men are on the line...and a great deal of money, too."

A spark of interest returned to House's eyes. "Very well, General," he sighed. "I'll see you in the morning, then."

"Good. I'll expect you early." Without another word, Wilkinson left House under the magnolia trees and returned to the ball. As he'd feared, they'd missed him. The ladies and gentlemen had already been seated for dinner; Montreuil's darky waiters were hustling around serving the *consommé*. With a small bow, Wilkinson slipped into his place at the table next to Celeste.

Celeste gave him a relieved smile. "James, where have you been? I was getting worried."

"No need, my dear." He patted her hand. Glancing around at the curious faces turned in his direction, he sensed a unique opportunity to outdo House at his own game. He cleared his throat. "I've just received some very sad news about an old friend."

"What is it?" Celeste leaned close. Madame Montreuil and her husband were listening as well.

"Well, I'm sure you know the gentleman by reputation," Wilkinson said. "It's Meriwether Lewis, actually. The young man who led Mr. Jefferson's expedition to the Pacific Ocean, a few years back."

"Oh yes, isn't he supposed to be visiting us in a week or two?" Montreuil asked. "I thought I'd go 'round and see him while he's in the city. I do hope he's brought his dog—I've always been interested to see such a remarkable animal." A few people seated nearby chuckled appreciatively.

"I doubt he'll be coming after all, *Monsieur*," Wilkinson said. "It pains me to say it, but I understand the young man has become quite deranged in his mind. The pox, I'm afraid. It's scrambled his brains. They say he caught it from the Indian squaws on his late trip out west—"

A few gasps went up around the table. Celeste's face turned even pinker than usual. Montreuil's eyes darted towards his wife. "General, remember the ladies."

Ignoring him, Wilkinson plowed on: "It's a great tragedy, really. To see such promise, cut short by disease and madness." As he watched the shocked looks and whispers spread around the table, he dropped his spoon into his *consommé* bowl, splashing the tablecloth and drawing everyone's attention.

"My God—" he looked around at all their astonished faces. "You don't suppose Clark...? I mean to say, the captains shared *everything* on that trip. The same tent, the same women—"

"General, please!" Montreuil looked affronted. "This isn't an army camp, sir! We are in mixed company here."

"Forgive me," Wilkinson murmured. "It's just...a little hard to take in, really. To think it might afflict them both...well, the mere thought is almost unbearable. And Clark with that pretty young bride of his too! Tut..."

Blandly, he turned his attention to his soup. Montreuil scowled at him, but the rest of the revelers continued to talk and whisper. Celeste fanned herself and gave Madame Montreuil an embarrassed smile.

Wilkinson chuckled behind his soupspoon as Montreuil labored mightily to change the subject to something less sordid. The way these people talked, and with the connections they had, the rumor would reach the East within weeks. Wouldn't Secretary Eustis be interested to hear about it! And the President—why, it would be gossip over Jimmy Madison's punch bowl in no time!

"James," Celeste whispered in his ear. He turned to look at her soft, gentle face. "I'm so sorry to hear about your friend."

It was all he could do to put on a sad expression. He took her hand in his and gazed into her wide blue eyes. "It happens, my dear."

Chapter 14
Lewis

Fort Pickering, Tennessee
September 26, 1809

Lewis sat by the window and watched the dust drifting in the sunlight. His body was shaking from the exertion of sitting upright, but at least he was clean and dressed. Even more important, he felt clear and calm in his mind. After what seemed like an endless nightmare, all his faculties had returned to him.

On the small desk was a book bound in red morocco leather. He pulled it toward him, opened it to a blank page, and dipped his quill in the inkpot. His hand was steady. He began to write.

Tues Sept 26th Ft. Pickering

I have been ten days in this place, very unwell. Fever took hold in such a way that I was not myself ... suffered the most bizarre delusions I have ever experienced. Fever broke a few days ago, but still very weak. Today has been the first day I have been able to rise and dress myself.

I am afraid I did not comport myself well with Capt. Russell upon my arrival here. I shrink to think of him witnessing such a scene. I am much mortified, cannot imagine what he must think of me.

Regrettably, Pernia has proved himself to be of little account to me here. He's a city man to the core, and is useless away from St. L. I should discharge him if I did not need help for the enterprise I am about to undertake.

He paused, dipped his quill again, and continued:

I believe the black wolf has quit me for now. I do hope that's the last I see of that beast for a while.

He was interrupted by a creak at the door. Captain Russell pushed it open and stuck his head in, letting a blinding shaft of sunlight fall across the floor. Lewis could barely make out Russell's features, silhouetted against the brightness. He blinked and turned his head away.

"Governor!" Russell took a cautious step into the room. "Why, it's good to see you up, sir."

"Good morning, Captain Russell. I'm happy to say I'm much improved this morning." Lewis let the journal fall shut and squinted his eyes against the sunlight. "Would you mind closing the door, please?"

"Of course." Russell pushed it shut behind him. He walked over to the desk and stood with his hands clasped behind his back, looking down at Lewis. Gilbert Russell was a trim, austere man of medium height, a few years his senior. A couple of years before the Expedition, Lewis had served with Russell for a short time, and knew him to be a rather prim fellow—which no doubt explained why he was wearing such a reserved and disapproving expression now.

Lewis sighed. He must look a sight, with his unkempt hair and ten-day growth of beard. "Captain..." he began, "I want to say how much I appreciate...how you've taken all this."

Russell shrugged and focused his round gray eyes on a spot of dirt on the window. "Well, Lewis, I daresay I would've done the same for any fellow officer, in your condition."

"Still...I...I really have no excuse, sir. I let the liquor get the better of me. It's a weakness of mine." He swallowed, clenching his hand around the quill. "Which I am *determined* to conquer."

Russell gave him a curt nod. "I'm heartily glad to hear it, sir. For pity's sake, I was afraid for a while we were going to lose you." He paused uncomfortably. "Governor, may I ask when are you planning to move on?"

Lewis smiled in spite of himself; it wasn't the first time in his life he'd outstayed his welcome. "As soon as I can, sir," he said. "Now that my health is improving, I'll endeavor to regain my strength as rapidly as possible. I hope to leave the day after tomorrow."

Russell's concerned look caught him off guard. "So soon? Governor, please don't go until you're sure you're fully recovered. You're welcome to stay here as long as you need."

Lewis swallowed. It seemed like a long time since anyone had treated him with anything approaching simple kindness or respect. "Thank you, Captain," he said. "But I have duties to attend to. In fact, I thought I'd take a short ramble this morning, and start getting my strength back up. No doubt the fresh air would do me good."

Russell gave him a tight smile and held the door open for him. As Lewis made his way across the room on unsteady legs, he happened to glance into a shaving glass that was hanging on the wall. What he saw stunned him. He hardly recognized the pale, haunted spectre that stared back at him. His skin was ghostly white, and his cheeks had hollowed to the point that his teeth were protruding. Shaggy hair hung in his eyes, and ten days' worth of patchy beard straggled along his jaw. His eyes seemed to be staring out of dark caves in his skull.

"Good God," he said to Russell. "No wonder you were worried."

He stepped out into the bright sunlight, eyes watering in the glare. The heat had broken—thanks to a merciful God—and the air felt cool and crisp.

It seemed like a lifetime ago, but he'd served at Fort Pickering once, as a lieutenant in the First Infantry. The fort looked exactly the same as it had then. Barracks, blockhouses, storage buildings, and men clustered behind a high log palisade, a rough little world of a few thousand square feet. Back then, the cramped confines of the fort's log walls had seemed like a prison, and his duties had been stultifying, a long chain of routine tasks that kept him from the exciting adventures he longed for. Now the snug huts and solid log stockade seemed like the most beautiful thing he'd ever seen. He slowly made his way around the palisade, ignoring the curious stares of the Fort Pickering soldiers. Just breathing the fresh air drew vitality back into his body. To his great relief, he didn't see the black wolf anywhere.

"I'll be fine," he muttered to himself, clutching onto the upright logs for support. "A few good meals and a couple of night's rest. I'll be good as new."

He rounded a corner of the stockade and saw Pernia a short distance away in the open yard, boiling shirts in a wash kettle. Pernia looked tired and sour. A couple of idle soldiers lounged in the door of the barracks nearby, thinking up ways to bedevil him.

"What kine'a monkey you reckon he *is*?" one of them said loudly.

"Pete," the other replied, "I believe that there is what you'd call an *amalgamation*. It's what you get when you cross a polecat with a French poodle."

Their crude laughter rang out across the yard. Pernia muttered a curse in French and made an obscene gesture at the soldiers, which only added to their amusement. He wiped sweat off his brow and poked at the steaming laundry savagely with a stick.

When they caught sight of Lewis, the soldiers straightened up and backed off. With open-mouthed stares, they withdrew into their barracks and stood looking out at him, whispering between themselves.

Pernia glanced up and saw him. "Governor!" he shouted. Still clutching the stick, he raced over and took Lewis's arm. "Sir, I'm so very pleased to see you. Thank God, oh, thank God you're getting better!"

Lewis smiled weakly. "I believe I'm finally on the mend."

He refrained from adding *No thanks to you*. In truth, he was becoming less enamored of the little Creole all the time. When Pernia had realized they were being pursued on the barge from St. Louis, he'd flown into such a panic that Lewis feared he might throw his papers overboard in his haste to get off the boat. Lewis had been so sick at New Madrid he could hardly remember anything that had happened there, but he did recall that Pernia's main concern had been his own safety, rather than helping him or protecting the baggage. In fact, he had the distinct impression that Pernia would have taken what little money he had and abandoned him to his fate, were he not so terrified of the consequences.

"*Mon Dieu*, but you need a shave and a haircut!" Pernia exclaimed, helping Lewis over to a stump. "I'll get my razor, and some soap! I'll have you looking fine in no time, Governor! Then we can get out of this wilderness!"

"That's fine, Pernia. " Lewis sat down, already weary of Pernia's fawning. It amused him that Pernia thought of a place like Fort Pickering, a bustling army post on one of the busiest waterways in the country, as "the wilderness." The man wouldn't have lasted two minutes on the Expedition. He had real doubts that Pernia was going to be able to handle the course of action he was now contemplating.

But it couldn't be helped—at least not until Clark got there. He sent up a silent prayer that Clark would be coming on in the next couple of weeks. Surely he'd gotten his letter by now—

"Governor, now that you're back in your senses, there's something I need to talk to you about," Pernia said anxiously, turning the stick over in his hands.

"What is it, Pernia?"

"Governor, being in your service has enriched my life in countless ways," Pernia said. "But New Orleans is the place of my birth...and when we get there, I'm afraid I'm going to have to sever my employment with you."

Lewis gazed at him and tried to hide the anger rising in his chest. "Pray, what brought this on?"

"Well...it's just...those men..."

"What men? Those men on the boat?"

"Yes." Pernia looked into Lewis's eyes. "Governor, I signed on to be your valet. I didn't sign on to die for you."

"Well, hell, Pernia, who asked you to? I assure you, you're perfectly safe."

"Still, if it's all the same, I'll just stay in New Orleans, thank you very much," Pernia said. "And Governor, I'd like my two-hundred and forty dollars."

"Pernia, where have you been? You of all people should know I don't have it."

"Well..." Pernia set his jaw. "I'm not going on with you to the Federal City, so I guess you'll have to come up with it."

"Well, that's a *wonderful* idea, Pernia. Let me just pull it out of my ass here." Lewis reached behind himself and pretended to do so, then made a great show of counting out imaginary bank notes in the air. "Two-hundred, two-twenty, two-forty. There you go! You and Pierre Choteau."

Pernia's face flushed. "Dammit, I'm not a slave—"

Lewis glared back. "That's for damn sure. You're not worth that much. You've been useless as far as I'm concerned." He looked the Creole up and down. "And I have some news for you, Pernia. We're not going to New Orleans."

Pernia paled. "What?"

"You heard me," Lewis said. "In fact, we were *never* going to New Orleans."

"W- Why not?" Pernia's lips trembled.

"It's not safe," Lewis said. "No matter what you think, I *do* care about your worthless hide. You know those rascals on the boat you were so worried about? Well, the man that hired them lives in New Orleans, and he's waiting for me there. If I try to go through that city, I'll never make it out alive. Then you'll *never* get your money."

Pernia goggled at him. "So you *lied* to me?"

"I lied to everybody, Pernia," Lewis said. "I even lied to Clark. I had to. I couldn't let anybody know where we were going."

Pernia's face screwed up like he was going to cry. "Well, where *are* we going, exactly?"

"We're going overland," Lewis said. "We're going to take the road that runs down to the Chickasaw Agency, then go to Nashville by way of the Chickasaw Trace. And from thence into Virginia, and our destination."

"No!" Pernia shrieked. "Governor, that's insane! I can't go over the Chickasaw Trace! People die on that road—"

"Keep your voice down, goddamnit!" Lewis rasped. His pulse quickened and his heart pounded; this conversation was exhausting him. "Don't be a coward, man," he said in a quieter voice. "Sometimes you have to stand up on your hind legs, you know?"

But Pernia refused to be consoled. "I can't believe you tricked me! All I want is my money. All I want is what you owe me!"

Lewis said with forced calm, "Well, if you feel that way about it, I'll just leave you here, and you can get along the best you can."

Pernia's face flushed with rage. For a terrible moment, Lewis was afraid he was going to do something reckless. He raised the stick in his hand and was poised to strike. Lewis didn't flinch. He just stared at Pernia with a look that said, *You will not hit me, and if you do, I won't be able to save you from the consequences.*

Pernia seemed to realize this, too, because his body sagged in defeat. He'd started to lower his arm when Seaman leapt out of nowhere, growling and nipping his hand. Pernia yelled and dropped the stick in the dirt.

"Goddamn vicious dog!" he shouted. In his anger, he smacked Seaman hard on the muzzle. The dog was on him in an instant.

"No, Seaman!" Aghast, Lewis lunged forward and grabbed a handful of black fur at the base of Seaman's neck. Pernia screamed as Seaman snarled and growled, his sharp teeth inches from Pernia's throat. Struggling to hold on, Lewis couldn't believe that Pernia would do such a foolish thing. Seaman would kill him—

Mustering all his strength, he towed Seaman backward, both of them tumbling into the dirt. Pernia dragged himself away, kicking and crying. Lewis knelt in the dirt and held onto him, gasping, repeating over and over, "No, Seaman. No, boy. No."

Finally, the dog calmed himself, but he still stood vigilant, his furry body tense, his big brown eyes fixed on Pernia. After a while the dog permitted Lewis to pet his head. He noticed that Seaman had dried blood on his muzzle, which meant either that there was good hunting around Fort Pickering, or that the mess cook had been feeding him meat scraps. He was just glad it wasn't Pernia's blood.

After making sure there was no officer in sight, one of the soldiers who'd been watching them from the barracks sauntered over. "You boys all right?" he asked. "That was some gittin' upstairs right then."

Lewis glared; he might not be at his best, but he wouldn't let it be forgotten he was the governor of a territory and a former captain in the army. "Private," he said, "Help this man up, and take him to my quarters. And watch your smart mouth."

Chastised, the soldier pulled Pernia to his feet. "I'm sorry, Governor," Pernia sniffled. "I'm sorry. I don't know what got into me. You saved my life...of course, I'll help you—"

"Pernia!" Lewis said sharply. "Never mind that now. Go lie down a while—I'll be in directly. Believe me. Everything is going to be *all right.*"

Pernia gave a hysterical little giggle. "Of course it is!" He allowed the soldier to steer him away back toward the huts, his feet weaving in the dust.

Lewis released Seaman from his grasp when Pernia was out of sight, but the dog didn't move away. He petted Seaman's head again, then leaned against him and rubbed Seaman's neck, fingering his silver collar.

"Dog, next to Clark, you're the best goddamn friend I have," he said, his mouth against the dog's fur. "And don't you worry. It'll happen just like I said. You wait and see."

With some effort, he got to his feet and limped back towards his hut. He prayed things would be easier from here on out. *If I have to endure another scene like this, Wilkinson might as well bury me right now.*

Chapter 15
Clark

St. Louis, Louisiana Territory
September 28, 1809

At long last, the heat broke. The sun came up in a spectacular scarlet salute to the front that had blown through St. Louis yesterday afternoon. A cool breeze caressed the city as if to apologize for its inexcusable lateness.

Clark barely noticed the change. He was too busy getting ready to leave. It had taken two days to get his government affairs and personal business arranged, a day longer than he'd hoped. As it was, he'd had to turn over a mountain of paperwork to Frederick Bates late yesterday afternoon. He'd expected Bates to gloat over the chance to run the territory his own way, but the territorial secretary had been cold and preoccupied.

Not that I give a damn, Clark reflected. He stood in front of the mirror and smoothed his hair. He reached behind him, plucked his old Wayne's Legion coat off the bed and shrugged into it. It pulled tight across his shoulders.

He turned around to face York, who was taking everything out of Clark's portmanteau and repacking it. Julia had insisted yesterday that she wanted to pack Clark's trunk for the trip, and Clark hadn't had the heart to refuse her. But York was too much of a perfectionist to let Julia's well-intentioned efforts stand. He knew exactly how his master liked his things arranged.

"York, this damn coat shrunk up on me," Clark said.

York continued with his folding and packing without looking up. "Cap'n, I know you set a lotta store by that old Army coat, but could be you done grown in the last fifteen years."

Clark laughed. "Maybe Julia's a better cook than I thought." He sat on the edge of the bed and let York help him on with his boots. There was a tight, vibrating feeling in his chest that he recognized as anxiousness. *Time to go—*

He wandered out of the bedroom to find Julia, only to see her talking to someone at the front door. "My husband is just about to leave town, Mister Dupree," Julia was saying. "I'm not sure he has time—"

Clark wondered what on earth Bates's assistant could want with him this morning. "Julia," he said. "It's all right. York's not quite ready."

Peter Dupree sidled in, his small black eyes cast glittering with anticipation.

"Morning, Dupree," Clark said. "Your boss gonna set off fireworks tonight to celebrate my departure?"

Dupree laughed shortly, then drew himself up with a self-important air and extended an envelope. "I have the honor of delivering to you a message from Secretary Bates. He asked me to wait for a reply."

"Honor, eh?" With a scowl, Clark took the letter from Dupree, pulled out his dirk, and used it to break the seal. Dupree's eyes widened at the sight of the half-foot long gleaming blade. Clark resheathed the knife, unfolded the letter, and read:

Sir:

When a man has been injured, it is incumbent upon him to seek redress. Doubtless you understand me. The conduct of Governor Lewis towards myself has injured both my feelings and character; I have been insulted in the presence of this entire City, and my ability to do my duty has been trammeled.

I therefore call upon you as a Gentleman and a Soldier to present this note to Governor Lewis, as you are presently journeying to join with him, that upon his return to St. Louis Governor Lewis and myself might meet. I must insist on this Challenge in order to wipe off any Odium I might have received by his Ungentlemanly conduct. I further call upon you to give me a satisfactory answer immediately without Equivocation and prior to your own Departure from this City.

FREDERICK BATES.

Clark felt himself flush all the way to the roots of his hair. That Bates would even dare to bother him with his vain, childish games at a time like this! Goddamn, it was just like that little animal to try to hang the specter of a duel over Lewis's head now, when he couldn't fight back!

For a moment, he was so angry that his eyes wouldn't even focus. When they finally did, they fell upon Dupree, who had fallen back a few steps and was watching him with his weasel eyes.

"May I take back your reply?" Dupree asked. "Any idea of the weapons the Governor might choose? Secretary Bates will want to practice."

Clark advanced on him. He tore the letter in two and slapped the pieces on Dupree's chest. The little man scrambled to catch them before they fell to the floor.

Clark's voice sounded harsh and rasping, even to himself. "Tell him the challenge is *not* accepted!"

Dupree gaped at Clark. "How can I tell him that? Aren't you even going to tell Lewis? I can't go back and give him this!" He clutched the torn letter, crumpling it in sweaty hands.

With supreme effort, Clark stilled his body, taking the time for a couple of deep breaths. Then he fixed Dupree with a fatherly smile. Dupree relaxed a little. Clark almost felt sorry for him. He put his arm around Dupree's shoulders and steered him back towards the front door at a slow walk. "You're right, Dupree. I should give a reply. It's only right." He opened the front door. Outside, Scipio, Clark's elderly groomsman, was rigging up the wagon to take him and York to the landing. "Now, I don't have time to write a letter, so you're gonna have to remember what I say, all right?"

Dupree nodded, all but salivating in his eagerness to be on his way and tell Bates all about the results of their latest mischief.

"You listenin' real good, now?" Clark asked.

When Dupree continued to nod, Clark grabbed him by the shoulders, spun him around, and planted his boot firmly on the seat of Dupree's pants, propelling him off the front porch. Yelling in disbelief, Dupree skidded into the mud and sprawled face down in one of the many puddles of pig shit that festooned Main Street.

"Be sure and tell him!" Clark yelled. He slammed the door so hard that the china shook in the cabinet. The baby sent up a rousing wail.

Julia stared at him with huge eyes, her mouth a perfect round O. "Will!" she exclaimed. "What on earth was that about?" She ran to the window and looked out. Dupree picked himself up out of the slop, shaking himself off with a look of shock and humiliation. A small knot of people stood watching, pointing at Dupree and at the house with astonished, animated gestures.

Clark drew her away from the window and into his arms. "Just some government business, honey." He kissed her on the cheek. "Nothin' for you to worry about."

"I do worry—when you—"

"Forget about it," Clark murmured. He pulled her against his body and held her there, his hands spread across her back. Julia stammered into silence and turned her face up to his. He kissed her mouth, a long, warm, gentle kiss.

Julia's arms stole upwards; he could feel her little hands on the back of his neck. She clutched at his queue, pulling some of his hair loose. He put his mouth against her neck. Her knees went weak on him. Somewhere, he was aware of York going out the door with the portmanteau...

"Julia." Clark set her down on her feet and took half a step back, patting her on the shoulders. "I can't get all het up, or I'll never get out the door." He tipped her chin up and kissed her again, lightly this time. "My brother will be here in a couple of weeks to fetch you and Lew to Louisville. The time'll go by fast, you'll see."

He let his eyes roam over her face. On the Expedition, when he was tired or lonely or worried, he calmed himself by turning his thoughts to this girl, her hair and her eyes and her sweet smile. He would do that again on this trip—

Abruptly, his self-control slipped a notch. "I love you, Julia. You know I don't want to—"

"Don't say it. You have to go. I understand." Bravely, she stepped out of his embrace. She scooped up the baby and brought Lew over. Clark took his son in his arms.

"Aw, my little man-boy. Don't you know how much your daddy's gonna miss you?"

York craned his neck inside the door. Massa Billy was still saying goodbye to his family. The scene had been going on for a quarter hour. Billy had laid off Miss Julia and started in with a new round of hugs and kisses for the baby. Father, mother, and child were all in tears.

York felt his gorge rising and turned away, clomping off the porch and back down to the wagon for the fifth time. He felt like taking a swing at somebody, but there was nobody there but old Scipio, waiting to take them to the landing. York walked around the horses, checking their rigging, jerking it tighter, angry enough that one of the beasts rolled its ears and eyes in fear.

"Sorry, Dobbin," York said, ashamed. He petted the horse's neck, trying to send the rage out through his hand and rub it away on the horse's coarse hair.

"York," Scipio said, "I knows what you thinkin', and it don't do no good to torture yourself, boy."

"I can't help it." York gestured toward the house. "Look at him! He loves that little gal and that baby so much! He don't want to leave 'em, even to go after Cap'n Lewis! It's tearin' him up inside."

York made a fist, then let it go. "He *knows* how it feels. So why won't he let me go back to Kentucky? Why can't he understand that I feel just the same about my Lilely as he does about Miss Julia?" The sick feeling expanded again in his chest. "Scipio, I don't even know my kids. I'm just a stranger to 'em."

Scipio shrugged and looked away, watching the carts and people pass by. York didn't really expect an answer. He hadn't known the old slave long—Scipio was a present to the Clarks from Miss Julia's father—but he had known him long enough to see the whipping scars on his back. The scars were old. Scipio had quit trying a long time ago. *Dear God,* York thought, *please don't let that ever be me.*

Finally, Clark came out of the house, followed by Julia holding the baby. "York, we ready to go?"

"Just a minute, Cap'n." York composed his face in a smile — Massa Billy liked smiling faces— then stepped up on the porch and fixed Clark's hair back into a neat queue. He straightened the front of the old campaign coat. "Now we ready."

Julia raised little Lew's chubby hand and waved it. "Bye-bye, daddy."

Clark and York mounted the wagon, Clark wiping his eyes on the cuff of his shirt. Glancing at York, he said roughly, "Got a damn cinder in my eye." As the wagon started to roll, Clark turned around and waved at Julia, not facing front again until the little house at Spruce and Main was out of sight.

Clark didn't speak again until they got to the landing. "Take good care of Miss Julia, Scipio," he told the old man.

York took the baggage down to a keelboat already laden with sweet-smelling tobacco on its way to New Orleans. Clark brought down their Kentucky rifles. Being on the river seemed to bring him back to himself. As for York, things felt right to him again for the first time since Captain Lewis had left without them. As the boatmen pushed off, Clark and York set their faces down river without looking back.

Chapter 16
Wilkinson

New Orleans, Orleans Territory
September 28, 1809

Wilkinson followed an elegant mulatto servant into the Spanish consul's house on Chartres Street. Left to his own devices with a plate of iced lemon cookies, he helped himself, then heaved himself into a brocaded chair. But he couldn't relax. Instead of plotting his approach to Don Diego, he found himself thinking of Captain House. He hoped the fool had made it up to Natchez with his letters, or the whole plan would be sunk.

The Spaniard soon joined him, and Wilkinson forced his racing thoughts aside to endure a round of coffee and a lengthy discussion of the health of Señora Morphy. Finally, he straightened up, discreetly brushing the cookie crumbs off the front of his uniform. "Don Diego, not to let business intrude, but—I suppose you are anxious for news of the rebellion of Lewis and Clark?"

"Of course," Morphy said. "From Havana, I regret to say, Governor Salcedo wants more proof of their villainy before committing the resources of which we spoke."

Wilkinson sat back in amazement. "As a true Spanish patriot, I can only shake my head. If Lewis and Clark were marching through the streets of Santa Fe, I suppose then your government might heed my warnings!" Morphy started to bristle, but Wilkinson stopped him with a hand. "No matter, Don Diego! The situation has changed dramatically since last we spoke." He leaned closer. "I have very reliable sources in St. Louis. They inform me that Lewis and Clark have had a falling-out, and Lewis has left the city!"

"*¿Verdad?*" Morphy said, taking a sip of coffee. "So the rebellion is off, then?"

"That's difficult to say," Wilkinson said. "I still intend to move my troops upriver to Natchez, with a detachment sent to St. Louis, just as a precaution.

Lewis, as you may know, is the brains of the pair, but Clark...well, he fancies himself quite the *generalissimo*. Nothing he might do would surprise me." He leaned closer still and confided: "Delusions of personal omnipotence and grandeur, you know. Mental instability runs in that family...if his depraved ambitions are anything like his brother's..."

Morphy cleared his throat. "Well, it sounds as if you have your hands full, General."

"Indeed!" Wilkinson exclaimed. "But I didn't come here to burden you with talk of Clark. I can deal with that red-headed scoundrel when and if the time comes. No, sir! I came here because of a most extraordinary development!"

"Which is?"

"Don't you see?" Wilkinson cried. "Meriwether Lewis is a man without a country! He has broken with Madison, and now with Clark! He is now alone, friendless on the river—and, I might add, with custody of all of his papers. Journals, field notes, maps—every scrap of paper from the late Western journey is in his possession!"

Morphy looked interested at last. He got up and paced the braided rug, stroking his chin. Wilkinson watched him, his heart pounding with anticipation. "So what you're saying..." Morphy said, "...is that it's over for Captain Merry in your country."

"I imagine he's feeling very lonely, yes." Wilkinson suppressed a smile over Morphy's mangling of Lewis's name—like most Spaniards, Morphy seemed to think the governor's name was Lewis Merry Wether, which had a rather jaunty air about it, didn't it? "Lonely, but not without resources. He's still in possession of his unparalleled knowledge of the western territory, and that treasure chest of papers. Data of incomparable strategic value to any country that controls it."

Morphy pursed his lips, then shook his head, remembering something. "A man like Lewis would be extremely useful to my government. But I have heard from several people that the pox has gotten into his brain. If so, I can't imagine he would live long enough to be of much value."

"What!" Wilkinson's eyes widened in surprise. *Sometimes, I amaze even myself.* "You know what I think of Lewis, Don Diego—he's a rascal, though and through. But I can hardly give credence to such a tale of debauchery. Doubtless, it is an outrageous canard. Mercy! How *do* such rumors get started?"

Morphy continued to pace, stroking his chin with maddening indecisiveness. *Careful, now,* Wilkinson reminded himself. *Press the suit too ardently, and the maiden will run.*

"I have men who even now have instructions to intercept Lewis and bring him to me in Natchez, where I will be traveling with the army," Wilkinson said. "I think I can persuade him to come over to the Crown."

Morphy stopped pacing. "And if he proves troublesome?"

Wilkinson lifted his shoulders, then let them drop. "In any event, I will take the papers. And my men can take care of Lewis. I assure you, he wouldn't be the first traveler ever to meet an unfortunate end on the Natchez Trace."

Don Diego paled, and for a moment Wilkinson was afraid he had gone too far. The Spanish consul groped for his chair and sat down on the edge of the seat, drumming his fingers against the chair's exquisitely carved arm.

"This can't wait for a letter from Havana," Wilkinson said, his voice soft but urgent. "We have to decide today whether to act on this information, or let the opportunity slip away forever. Lewis is on the move. Doubtless he'll run to Jefferson—if he doesn't flee the country altogether, like Burr did. In either case, the papers will be beyond our reach forever." It was time to bring it home. "Where there is no peril in the fight, there is no glory in the triumph, Don Diego."

Morphy turned to Wilkinson with a cynical smile. "*El Cid.* But Señora Morphy could tell you, General, I am not a romantic."

Wilkinson inched closer. "There is one more thing that may make a difference in your thinking. A trifle, really. I almost hesitate to mention it to a man of sophistication such as yourself, but some of your superiors in Havana may find it interesting."

"Don't keep me in suspense, General."

"I happen to know that on their late voyage to the Pacific Ocean, Lewis and Clark discovered interesting mineral deposits in the vicinity of the upper Missouri River. This information has been held back for fear of starting a rush on the field—which the American government hopes to keep for itself. Lewis has the only map. The location was quite remote, as you can imagine. A man could wander in those badlands forever without ever finding it again."

"Mineral deposits?" Morphy demanded. "Say what you mean!"

"Why, gold, of course. What else?" It was a fiction, of course; there was no such mine and no such map. But he hoped Morphy would find the temptation irresistible.

"Gold! Who knows of this?"

"Very few," Wilkinson said. "It is a carefully guarded secret. I myself only saw the map once, in Jefferson's office, and to my knowledge it has never been copied. Only Jefferson, Lewis, Clark, and myself know of its existence. And now you, of course."

Don Diego sat up straighter and blinked several times, as if trying to clear his head. *Not a romantic, perhaps, but still a Spaniard, with the same unnatural desire for that yellow ore as all the rest of them!* He could see the calculations taking place behind Morphy's pensive façade.

But Morphy surprised him. With a steely look, he said, "Surely you do not mistake us any longer for wild-eyed gold seekers."

Wilkinson raised his eyebrows. "Not at all. Besides, how can I criticize others for something I do myself?"

Morphy gave him a thin-lipped smile. "I must admit these items you have mentioned would be worth a great deal to my government."

"The Crown has always dealt equitably with me in such matters. Fair pay for good service, in other words."

Morphy stood up. "I will have to write to Havana, of course. But I feel justified in authorizing you to go ahead. If you can deliver Merry's papers as you say you can—the journals, the notes, and the maps—I am quite certain that my government would recognize your service handsomely."

"I would be prepared to do it for eighty thousand dollars," Wilkinson felt a sheen of sweat beading under his uniform. "And I will need some operating expenses, naturally."

Morphy stared at him with a strange glint in his eyes. "Sixty thousand dollars. Cash on delivery—in Havana."

Wilkinson laughed loudly. "You're a robber, Don Diego!"

"With a bonus, then...if you can bring in Lewis Merry Wether himself."

Wilkinson laughed again, stood up, and took Morphy's extended hand. "Done and done." Breathlessly, he added, "You'll understand if I don't stay. I don't have a moment to lose in getting up to Natchez."

"I look forward to the successful outcome of your mission."

Bursting out through the courtyard, Wilkinson could barely contain his glee. When he ducked around the corner on Barracks Street, it erupted. Other pedestrians stared at the sight of James Wilkinson dancing a little jig, but he didn't give a tittle what they thought. By Jove, with any luck, his man was with Lewis already. A little giggle escaped his lips. *Sixty thousand dollars!* As he hurried along, he crooned to himself. "Run, Lewis, run! You can't hide from me!"

Chapter 17
Lewis

Pigeon Roost Road, Tennessee
September 29, 1809

(From the journal of Meriwether Lewis)

> *Friday Sept 29th*
> *This morning we bid a final adieu to Fort Pickering. Asked Capt. R to tell no one but Genl. Clark of my intended route. He wished to know the reason, which I would not give him, but after arguing with me at length, he agreed to respect my wishes.*
> *Through the most serendipitous good fortune, I have acquired another traveling companion. His name is Major James Neelly, and he arrived at Fort Pickering at a most convenient time. Majr. Neelly serves as the Federal Agent to the Chickasaw Nation and is well acquainted with the Chickasaw Trace, having traveled it frequently in the course of his employment. He has agreed to escort us all the way to Nashville.*
> *I regret the circumstance which compels me to make this journey when not entirely healthy, but having taken a good dose of medicine this morning, I feel myself tolerably well and am determined to proceed on. The situation is one of the greatest exigency, and further delay would be unpardonable on my part. With luck I will reach Washington City on or about the 25th of Oct. proximo.*
> *Not knowing the intent of Clark, I have decided not to wait for him, but I am certain he will overtake me on the Trace, at which time I will be free to abandon secrecy and take him into my full confidence about my reasons for this journey.*

Lewis wiped a trickle of sweat off his forehead. The morning's crisp air had given way to a balmy afternoon. Above him, a tangled canopy of trees stretched overhead, some of them already beginning to drop great red and gold leaves that crumbled to powder under the packhorses' heavy hooves. Seaman trotted by his side, his tail waving like a black plume. Behind him, keeping his distance, Pernia rode alone in sullen silence.

Lewis was shaky and tired, but being on the move again lifted a tremendous weight off his heart. Dressed in his green traveling coat, he looked like himself again, though his shirt collar felt loose and the coat hung on his shoulders.

His persuasive gifts had also returned, and not a moment too soon. Before they'd left the fort, he'd managed to blarney Captain Russell into lending him two Army horses, and a hundred dollars cash on top of that. In his pocket was a copy of the promissory note he'd written out for Russell that morning. He took it out of his pocket and looked at it: he'd promised Russell "the total sum of $379.58, payable on or before January 1, 1810." There wasn't a chance in hell he'd be able to pay it, but what choice did he have? He needed money for expenses and transportation for himself and Pernia.

He hadn't spoken to Pernia about what had happened between them at Fort Pickering. He tried to give his servant the benefit of the doubt, but he couldn't overlook what Pernia had done. The man had threatened him, and for a black man to threaten a white man was a crime which normally exacted the strictest penalty. The merciful thing to do would be to discharge Pernia the minute they got to Nashville or some other civilized place, where he would have a reasonable chance of getting along.

He glanced behind him and pulled up long enough to let the little Creole catch up with him.

"How do you like this road, Pernia?"

Pernia barely seemed to hear him. He started at a noise in the brush and stared uneasily at the trees.

"Governor," he said in a hoarse voice, "What are those birds?"

"I believe they're pigeons, Pernia," Lewis said patiently. "Seaman has already caught three."

Pernia curled his lip at the mention of the dog's name. "But...there's so many of them."

Lewis nodded and turned his gaze upwards, where the limbs were creaking and groaning under the weight of hundreds of birds. "Looks like we'd do well to put on our hats."

Some distance ahead, Major Neelly had stopped and dismounted again. He cupped his hands around his mouth and called back to them, "Tree down."

Pernia groaned under his breath. "*Jésus-Christ*, not another one! Is that all he knows how to say?"

Lewis fixed Pernia with a weary, warning look. "While you're getting out my hat, do me a favor and hunt up my medicine chest, will you? I'm feeling a bit peaked." He turned his horse and set off at a slow trot, taking care to avoid a knee-high stump in the center of the road.

In fact, he was feeling worse than peaked. He'd tried to tell himself that his limbs ached only because he hadn't been on horseback since he'd left St. Louis, but as the afternoon wore on, he knew it was more serious than that. The fever was coming back. The laudanum he'd dosed himself with that morning was already losing its effect.

When he reached Neelly and dismounted, the federal agent was standing with his arms at his sides, staring with silent disgust at an enormous maple that had toppled across the path.

"Big 'un," he said.

Lewis didn't know what to think of his new traveling companion. According to Captain Russell, Neelly had once been a major in the Tennessee volunteer militia, but his appearance was anything but military. He wore a frayed sack coat, badly-mended trousers and a battered felt hat that was so faded it was impossible to tell what color it might once have been. For such a stout, burly fellow, Neelly was uncommonly shy. By Lewis's count, he'd barely stammered out two words since they met, and he rarely looked him in the eye. Still, Neelly seemed competent in the saddle, and he knew the road. That was good enough for his purposes.

"I'm sure we can overcome a downed tree, Major," Lewis said. "We'll just take some of the load off the horses and go 'round through the woods. Hell, I've made a lot bigger portages than that in my time."

"Yeah, but it's my responsibility to keep this road clear." Neelly rubbed his graying beard, kicked at the trunk and broke off a limb or two. "Have ta round up a crew and send 'em back here when we get to the Chickasaw Agency."

Neelly looked so unhappy at the prospect that Lewis felt compelled to suggest alternatives. "I should think Captain Russell could be prevailed upon to send a squad of men from Fort Pickering. It's certainly in the Army's interest to keep the road clear as well."

At this suggestion, Neelly's face turned even gloomier. "Dang, it'll be a cold day in hell before I'd get any help from them so'jers."

"Well, you are the government's representative out here, aren't you, Major? Don't they give you an appropriation for this sort of thing?"

Neelly's hangdog gaze rested on him for a moment, then his eyes darted away. "Hell, on what the government gives me, I can't even afford a decent house for my family, let alone do my job."

Lewis felt himself grow hot. "God Almighty, you too? I swear, Neelly, those bastards in Washington don't have the first clue about how things work out here."

"Naw, that's for sure."

"They send you out here and say, 'Lewis, straighten out the land claims.' 'Lewis, make friends with the Indians.' 'Lewis, build up the fur trade.' They pull your strings like a goddamn puppet, and then, when you don't jump and caper the way they want—" he clenched his hand into a fist. "Then, goddamnit, they crush you."

Neelly cleared his throat. "Is that what they done to you, Governor?"

"No. Not yet. But they've sure as hell tried." Lewis gulped; he had trouble swallowing his anguish. "You see this trunk here?" He pointed to his packhorse. "It's stuffed to the gills with nothing but paperwork. Vouchers, bills, notes of every description. Payments I made—*for legitimate government business, no less*—that the government now refuses to honor."

He paced off a little ways, staring into the woods. "I swear to God, Neelly," he said, his voice rising, "Every expenditure I ever made, I accompanied with an explanation! Every penny of public money I ever spent, I can account for!"

"I believe you, Governor," Neelly said. "But when they get down on you like that, there's not much you can do about it, I reckon."

"You think not, eh? Oh, I'll do something about it, all right." Lewis knew he was letting himself get too worked up, but he couldn't seem to stop. "Neelly, I'm telling you, if this country falls to rack and ruin at the hands of some lunatic, it won't be because they weren't warned. It won't be because nobody had the balls to stand up and tell Jimmy Madison what's what."

Neelly was twisting the reins of his horse in his hands and squirming with discomfort. Lewis didn't blame him. Like himself, Neelly had to cavil to some pinhead in Washington for his federal job. "Who knows, Neelly—maybe I'll lose. Maybe they won't even give me the chance to speak my piece, and that'll just be it for the grand and exciting career of Meriwether Lewis. But all I know is, if I get the chance, I'm going to tell 'em."

Pernia came up, slumping and sullen. Without a word, he slid out of the saddle and handed Lewis his hat and his bottle of laudanum. Lewis didn't bother with a spoon this time; he just uncorked it and took a gulp. Neelly's eyes widened. Lewis handed the bottle back to Pernia, who replaced it in his saddle bag.

"All right, fellas," Neelly said. "We'll go back about a hundred yards to where the road ain't so sunk down, then we'll lead the horses up and around.

Stick close, and pull yer hats down real low, 'cause them pigeons are fierce."

Lewis laughed, and Pernia managed a grimace. They mounted up and doubled back. At a place where the steep bank of the sunken road sloped up more gradually, they climbed down from the saddle and led their horses into the woods. The day was already waning, and the late afternoon sun cast strange, shifting shadows on the ground.

Lewis stopped suddenly, feeling a presence in the woods. A chill came over him. Up ahead, Neelly was stepping along stolidly, Seaman at his heels. His dog had taken a shine to Neelly, which further recommended him, in Lewis's opinion.

No, the animal he sensed in the woods wasn't Seaman. It was the black wolf. On it came, staring, its gray eyes rolling, its great tongue lolling out of the yellow jaws. It waited for him at a distance, and it stopped when he stopped, and moved when he moved. It slipped around the trunks of the trees like quicksilver, a greasy phantasm weaving in and out of his sight.

But it was always there. He knew it was with him, even when he couldn't see it. It had claimed him so many years ago, when he was just a boy, and he had hated it then, just as he hated it now. How many times had he prayed to be rid of the beast? How many times had he thought it had left him for good?

Coming up from behind, Pernia noticed his stricken expression and tried some of his old solicitude. "Governor, are you ill? Do you need to take a rest?"

"No. I'm fine." With his eyes fixed on the wolf, he wondered for a moment what was going on back in St. Louis. How was Clark? Had he gotten off yet? Was he coming at all?

With great force of will, he shook the image of the black wolf out of his mind. "For God's sake, Pernia, let's go on."

Chapter 18
Julia

St. Louis, Louisiana Territory
September 30, 1809

Julia knit her eyebrows and squinted at her embroidery. It seemed like she'd missed some stitches somehow. Despite her best efforts, the yellow star she was trying to make on the baby's linen smock looked fuzzy and undefined.

"Well, Lew," she sighed, "I hope you don't mind wearing a big dandelion on your chest."

Lew gurgled and crawled around on the buffalo robe at her feet. He seemed intent on something near the fireplace. Julia had noticed lately that whenever he got near a table or chair, he'd try to pull himself up. Before you knew it, he would take his first step. It saddened her that Will was going to miss it.

The truth was, Will was what made St. Louis her home, and without him, this frontier river town was just another lonely place. She plucked the skirt of her white day-dress and let her thoughts wander back to the home where she grew up, in the green, rolling hills of Virginia. Santillane. Her father would be on horseback, bossing the slaves in the tobacco fields...her mother would be in the sitting room, with one of her sisters perhaps...they would be reading, or writing letters, or playing on the piano...

She put her embroidery aside and scooped Lew up from the rug. "Let's not sit around being lonely. Let's do something fun! You know that set of Shakespeare your daddy gave us? I'm going to read you a story out of *Twelfth Night*. It's all about disguises, and love, and madness. There's a character in it who's just like Meriwether! You'll love it."

She was carrying Lew to the bookshelf when she heard a commotion outside. She looked out the window. Main Street was full of people. Some were running, while others stood in small groups, talking in urgent voices. The town was "all abuzzle," as Will would say.

Julia noticed some of the men outside pointing at their house. She felt a moment of fear, wondering if it were on fire. She hadn't smelled smoke—

Just then, Nancy and Scipio came in the back door from outside. Julia had known Nancy her entire life; the plump, pretty slave had nursed her as a baby and been her body servant ever since. Old Scipio, the groomsman, was Nancy's father. When Julia and Will had married, her father had given them both slaves as a wedding present.

To Julia's astonishment, they were half-carrying, half-dragging Easter through the back door. The young woman was sobbing. Easter was about Julia's age and had a baby boy of her own named Tom; she was squeezing him so hard he was purple-faced and crying. As soon as she was safely inside, Easter collapsed on the floor, spilling her basket of cabbages everywhere.

"What in heaven's name?" Julia gasped.

"Miss Julia," Scipio said, "There's a whole flock of gentlemens outside, askin' for Massa Will. When I told 'em he ain't to home, they got right fractious about it."

"Why?" Julia asked. "What do they want with Will?"

"The whole town gone crazy, Miss Julia," Easter sobbed. "I done gone to the market, like you said. But nobody was sellin' anything today. There were all these folks there with guns. And they was sayin' the most terrible things — *crazy* talk—"

"What did they say? Easter, tell me now. I promise I'll believe you. And I won't get mad."

"They was sayin'—" Shaking with fear, Easter paused to wipe her eyes on her skirt. "They was sayin' that Massa Will and Gov'ner Lewis had gone and left the city, and that they done raise an army of wild Indians! They say Massa Will and Gov'ner Lewis gonna seize this city for themselves!" She started sobbing anew. "Then they say if Massa Will and Gov'ner Lewis try an' come back...oh, Miss Julia..."

"What, Easter? What'd they say?"

"They say they gonna be shot down like dogs!" Easter pressed her hands to her face and wailed.

Julia stared at her in numb disbelief. "That's the most absurd thing I ever heard." But even as she spoke, she could hear horses galloping down Main Street, and a man's voice shouting, "Arm yourselves! It's treason!"

A terrible fear took hold of her. Will had only set out two days ago; he couldn't be too far down the river. What if he heard about what was happening in St. Louis? He would turn back immediately. When he came back into town, he wouldn't have any idea what these men were intending. And he'd be shot. It was as simple as that.

Julia's mind reeled. Someone had to go downriver and warn Will! She couldn't let him walk into an ambush!

Her mind grasped at the one person in authority who might be able to help her. He wasn't exactly Will's friend, but it was worth a try. "Easter," she said with forced calm, "Get ahold of yourself, now. No one's going to shoot the General. This is all foolishness, and I'll straighten it out. Nancy, lay out my blue cloak and my good bonnet, the one with the plume. I'm going downtown to see Secretary Bates. Scipio, you're going with me."

The servants exchanged glances full of worry and doubt, but at the same time, they seemed grateful for some direction. Julia put Lew in his crib. He pulled himself up and looked at them all curiously. He had no idea his daddy was in terrible trouble.

Julia hurried down Main Street, with Scipio laboring along behind. Before she left, she'd told Nancy and Easter to bolt the door and not open it for anyone. The crowd of men outside their house had dispersed, but now and then she saw a rifleman riding toward the barns on the west side of town.

Julia jumped over a broken harness lying in the street and stopped in front of Robidoux's bakery to wait for Scipio to catch up. She had to remind herself that the old groomsman was almost seventy years old. As she stared at each passing rider, her eye fell on a handbill that was pinned to the wooden fence in front of the bakery.

The handbill had Will's name on it. She tore it off the fence and read:

In justice to the Citizens of this Territory
I denounce to the world
MERIWETHER LEWIS,
Governor of the Territory of Upper Louisiana,
as a Prevaricating and Ignoble SCOUNDREL, POLTROON, and
LIAR,
and furthermore denounce
WILLIAM CLARK,
General of the Militia of this Territory,
For exhibiting
BASE and VILLAINOUS behavior
in every way beneath the notice of a gentleman.

This information is presented so that
the People of St. Louis
may know the character of these men
and act accordingly.

The handbill was signed:

A VIRGINIAN.

"Oh!" Julia's gloved hand flew to her cheek. "This is outrageous! Who on earth would do such a thing?"

Scipio stood by her side, panting. "What's it say, Miss Julia?"

"Terrible, stupid things…about Governor Lewis and the General!" She threw the handbill away, then noticed that another one was posted on the wall of the blacksmith's shop across the street. She raced across, tore it down and threw it in the gutter. To her horror, she saw that the same handbill papered every fence and hitching post along Main Street. "Come on, Scipio —let's hurry!"

Pulling Scipio by the arm, Julia ran all the way to the government building on Walnut and Second Street. She left Scipio wheezing on the piazza and rushed into the building. It seemed awfully bold to be visiting the government offices by herself, but she had no choice. She stood just inside the doorway and collected herself, trying to think of what to say to Mr. Bates. To her great relief, he was in his office; she could hear his booming Virginia drawl all the way down the hall.

"I will tell you one thing—I am entirely prepared to risk the consequences!" Bates was shouting. Someone in the room with him murmured his agreement; it must be Peter Dupree. Bates's voice went on: "That *I* should have to be subordinate to that silly coxcomb, and that bull-faced barbarian, galls me no end, sir!"

Julia drew in a breath. Surely he couldn't be talking about Meriwether, and her darling Will! She hurried to the door of Bates's office. He had his chair turned away and was absorbed in reading something. All she could see was his fluffy hair.

Peter Dupree hovered over Bates's chair. He glanced up and noticed her standing in the doorway. Dupree stiffened at the sight of her, and Julia felt her face grow hot. The last time she'd seen him, he'd been covered in pig manure, lying in the gutter outside their house where Will had kicked him. Dupree cleared his throat and said, "Secretary Bates—"

Bates ignored him. "I have taken the liberty of writing a letter to the President," he continued. "Outlining—*in detail*—*my* efforts to hold this territory together in the face of their remorseless knavery!" Bates scanned the paper in his hand. "To wit—"

"Secretary Bates!" Dupree shouted.

Bates cracked the paper down. "*What*, sir? I really must object to your constant interruptions!"

"But, sir, you have a visitor."

Bates whirled around in his chair. His blue eyes grew round when he saw Julia standing timidly in the doorway.

Bates's lips worked in surprise for a moment. "Mrs. Clark," he said in a strained and formal voice. "*Do* come in." He nodded to Dupree, who was mopping sweat off his forehead. forehead. "You may leave us."

With elaborate courtesy, Dupree withdrew into an anteroom and shut the door behind him. Bates gestured Julia to a chair. "Mrs. Clark," he said, "How may I be of service?"

"Secretary Bates," Julia burst out, "The whole town's gone crazy. People are saying the most terrible things about my husband—"

"I assure you, the government of this territory gives no credence to these ridiculous rumors of an attack on this city," Bates said. "Frankly, Madam, I do not believe Governor Lewis and General Clark could *possibly* have planned such an operation under my nose. In fact, I am sure of it."

Julia felt a flood of relief. Finally, she'd found somebody who was on her side. "But, Mr. Bates, some people seem to believe it, and I'm scared that—"

"Some people are gullible fools, Mrs. Clark. If I were you, I would not concern myself with the sort of person who would believe the idle claptrap that is bandied about in taverns and slave quarters."

"Yes, but as you know, General Clark isn't in the city," Julia said. Bates looked so impatient, she was afraid he'd show her out before she even had a chance to ask for his help. "He went downriver to find Governor Lewis—"

Bates's lip curled, but she pressed on. "And Mr. Bates, I'm terribly afraid he'll hear about these rumors and come back, and with people all worked up the way they are, my husband won't know what's going on, and he'll be hurt."

Bates studied his fingernails. "And pray tell, Madam, what do you expect the government of Upper Louisiana to do about it?"

"Well—" Julia stammered, "I thought maybe you could send a man—"

"Send a man?" Bates said. His handsome face grew red. He pressed his hands down on his desk and stood up. "Send a man?" he repeated, his voice rising to a shout. "Madam, I cannot *spare* a man! There's not a *penny* in the public treasury!" He leaned toward her. "And do you know *why*?"

"Well, I—"

Cutting her off, Bates thundered: "Governor Lewis has *spent it all!* On the ill-conceived schemes that he, and *your husband*—"—he shook a plump finger in her face—"—have dreamed up to *enrich* themselves at the expense of the good people of this territory!" His eyes bulged with contempt. "No, I cannot send a man!"

"But Mr. Bates, I believe my husband could be in real danger!"

"If General Clark *is* in danger, which I *doubt*," Bates said, "that is General Clark's private affair, Madam, and not the responsibility of the government of Upper Louisiana." He paused to dab some sweat off his upper lip with a silk handkerchief. "Besides, if something *were* to happen to him and Governor Lewis, it would be just like the pair of them to skip out and leave *me* holding the bag."

Julia stared at him. She felt tears puddling in her eyes and scolded herself; she wasn't going to cry in front of this nincompoop. She rose to leave. "I'm sorry, Mr. Bates. I'm afraid I've taken up too much of your time."

"Mrs. Clark," Bates said in a more conciliatory tone, as he walked her to the door. "If I hear anything of the General, I promise I will let you know. In the meantime, I suggest you go home and attend to your domestic duties. I feel quite sure that's what General Clark would want."

With his hand on the small of her back, he pushed her out. "Good *day*."

Julia stumbled out onto the piazza. Scipio was sitting on the steps, trying to catch his breath. He struggled to his feet when he saw her. "What'd he say, Miss Julia?"

"Oh, Scipio!" Julia clenched her fists in frustration and disbelief. "That man wouldn't *help* me!" She took his arm and started them back toward home. If there were anyone else—if she could only find—

"What we gonna do, Miss Julia?" Scipio asked.

A thought came into her head that made her tremble. It seemed like a terribly risky thing to do. But she couldn't stand by and let Will walk into danger, when she had any power to stop it. She loved him too much for that.

"Well, if nobody will help me, I'll have to help myself," she said. "Scipio, I'm going to have to go downriver after the General."

"Oh, no ma'am," Scipio moaned. "Miss Julia, it ain't safe! Maybe it'd be better if we send for yo' father."

Scipio had been her father's slave for most of his life; Julia supposed he thought Colonel Hancock could do anything. "Scipio, my father's in Virginia, and we're in St. Louis!"

Scipio racked his brain, grasped at another argument. "Miss Julia, Massa Will done send for his brother befo' he left! Mister Jonathan be comin' most any day!"

"Scipio, Mister Jonathan probably hasn't even left Kentucky yet. It'll take him weeks to get here!" Frantically, she dug into her small reticule. "Look, I'm going to give you a pass and some money. I want you to go down to the landing, and buy passage for you and me on the next packet boat. Will's only been gone two days! We're sure to catch up with him."

"Miss Julia, I just don't know." Scipio looked at her. "It seem awful dangerous to me. An' you wit' the baby and all. I'm not sure Massa Will would want—"

"*Master Will's not here*," Julia said. She could no longer fight back her tears. "Scipio, I can't just sit around here and do nothing, when people are saying they're going to shoot my husband! There's nobody else! I have to go." She pressed a pass and a banknote into his old black hand. "Nancy and Easter can look after Lew for me. Now go and do as I say."

When Scipio still seemed reluctant, Julia almost screamed, "Are you going to help me or not? Go now!"

"Yes'm. I can see you's set on it." Without another word, he turned and ambled down Second Street. Julia watched him turn east on Market, toward the landing.

She turned in the other direction and ran back toward home. The streets were full of agitated people. At Auguste Choteau's fortress, the servants were boarding up the windows. Outside Christy's, a young officer was yelling at the top of his lungs, telling a large crowd of armed men that he'd taken charge of the city's defenses. "I want you to know General Wilkinson has put his troops on high alert," he shouted. "So if we need it, he can send a whole goddamn battalion up here from Natchez!"

Julia shoved her way through the crowd. By the time she reached home, tears were streaming down her cheeks. Nancy and Easter looked shocked when she told them what she was planning to do, but they could see it was useless to try to dissuade her. Nancy went to pack some things for Scipio, while Easter got busy laying out Julia's traveling clothes.

Disturbed by his mother's tears, Lew grumbled and fussed. Julia kissed him and pressed him close to her chest. "Don't cry, darling," she whispered. "I won't let anything happen to your daddy. And don't worry. Mama's only going to be gone a few days."

Chapter 19
Clark

Clark and York set up their camp some distance away from the boatmen. The keelboat had pulled in for repairs again; another damn sawyer, a floating stray log, had smacked the front of the boat. Clark felt maddened by the delay. At the rate they were going, it would take two weeks just to get to Fort Pickering. Hell, on the Expedition, he'd sometimes covered 35 miles a day on foot. He and York could be halfway there if they'd just *walked*.

York went off hunting for their supper. Clark was squatting by the fire, slowly feeding it with small sticks, when he heard a commotion down by the boat. A fleet of five Indian canoes had pulled up on the sand spit near the keelboat. Clark watched as a dozen Shawnee piled out and began to parley with the boatmen. He banked his cook fire and headed down to the beach to get a better look.

The Shawnees were selling catfish, big ugly things that made Clark's mouth water. Hot fried fish for supper would go a long way towards cheering him up. The canoes were big ugly things too—dugouts, not the beautiful carved bark canoes the Shawnees sometimes used. He ran his hand over the prow of one of the canoes. Hollowed from a single poplar log, it was weathered silver and smaller than the others—only about 20 feet. He pushed down, testing his weight on the small craft. He'd been piloting canoes since he was a boy and making them for almost as long. In his judgment, this little boat was tight and fast—just right for two men in a hurry.

One of the Shawnees staggered against him, then grunted. Clark was unclear on whether the Indian had just given him a challenge or an apology, but he opened his hands and smiled to show there was no offense. The Indian grinned back, friendly and feeling no pain. Clark was almost knocked over by the reek of whiskey. It wasn't just the man's breath. The stuff was coming out of his pores.

Clark thumped the boat and said, "Good canoe," while swinging his right hand out flat from his heart. In the sign language used by the Indians, that meant, "level with the heart." He held up both hands and struck them past each other. "You trade?"

The Indian raised his eyebrows and signed back, interested. Fire. Water.

Clark frowned, concentrating on remembering his signs. He shook his head, then held his closed fist in front of his neck and twisted his wrist down. "I don't have it."

The Shawnee turned away, and for a moment Clark felt a little sad. He'd spent a lot of time since they'd left St. Louis brooding on the problems of his hard-drinking brother and his best friend. For the Indians, whiskey was even worse—no better than poison. But he knew if he had it, he'd trade it in a minute for that canoe.

He trotted back up the hill, where York was building up the fire again. He had a big possum slung over his shoulder. Clark began to rummage through the portmanteau, taking out some of his clothes and spreading them on the ground.

York cautioned, "Cap'n, them's some of your best things."

"You and I might think so, but he ain't too impressed." Clark nodded at the Shawnee, who had followed behind and was making a great show of being bored with the merchandise. Clark peered back in the trunk, saw what he was looking for, and pulled it out for the Indian's perusal.

York winced in genuine pain. "No, Cap'n, not that one."

Clark ignored him. York got all his hand-me-downs, and Clark knew he'd had his eye on the double-breasted waistcoat with the silver embroidery ever since he'd bought it in Washington three years ago. Just a couple of months back, when he'd worn it to a ball in St. Louis, York had made a point of saying, "Them big lapels is out of fashion, Cap'n. You oughta buy somethin' more stylish."

The flickering flames of the campfire danced over the fine silver thread. The Shawnee moved forward and touched the fabric. Clark handed the vest to him, concealing his satisfaction. "Go ahead," he motioned. "Try it on."

He knew he'd made the deal, but the Indian drove a hard bargain. In addition to the vest, the Shawnee ended up with Clark's old hat, a shirt, and all of the coffee Clark had brought for the trip.

But he had his canoe.

He awoke very early the next morning, well before first light. The campfire had long since sputtered away to nothing, and the air was heavy and still.

Clark sat up and watched York sleeping for a moment. The Indians' camp was quiet, while the Frenchmen were still asleep on the keelboat. A thick fog had settled over the river.

He rubbed the sleep out of his eyes and, taking care not to stumble in the darkness, went down to the sand spit and found a place to sit near the water. He looked at the blanket of gray mist covering the river, but he wasn't really seeing it. In his mind's eye, he saw instead the fog hovering in the giant, tangled trees along the Columbia River as the Expedition took their canoes through the river channels, coming ever closer to the Pacific Ocean they were so anxious to see. He could almost feel their heavy dugouts quiver in awe of the rough tidewater.

When they'd finally reached the great Pacific, he and Lewis had walked alone a short distance, leaving the men behind to whoop out their pleasure in the achievement. From a towering basalt cliff, they'd stood together in their ragged buckskins, drizzle dripping off their beards, watching enormous waves crash against the rocky shoreline. Clark's heart was so full he couldn't even speak. He would never forget the way Lewis faced down the great ocean with a challenging stare, as if to say *I made it, you sonofabitch.* Then he'd given Clark that defiant, crinkle-eyed smile, and a slow, satisfied nod.

Sunrise was subtle with the fog still lying across the river. The Shawnees got up and pushed off in their canoes, as silent as great fish. If they saw him sitting there watching them, they didn't acknowledge him, not even his friend in the silver vest. Within a few minutes, it was as if they had never existed.

Clark pulled his new canoe a few feet further up the sand spit and then went to wake York. Together they loaded up. York got the fire going again and fried what was left of the Indian's catfish. The French boatmen were stirring, but in no hurry; they knew their captain wouldn't let them push off until the fog had burned away. York licked his fingers and pointed down at the keelboat with a fishbone. "Ain't gonna be sorry to leave them fellas behind."

Clark stripped off every last garment he'd worn down river from St. Louis and packed them away with the rest of his good clothes. He dressed in the most worn cotton shirt he'd brought, and his oldest breeches, which he left open at the knees for comfort. He tied a bandana around his head and another around his neck. They both rubbed possum grease on their hands to try to protect them from the beating they would take today, working the paddles. Neither of them had moccasins to wear, so they just went barefoot; no point in getting a good pair of boots wet.

"We gonna hurt tonight, Cap'n!" York stretched one arm across his chest, then the other. "City life done made us both soft."

Clark studied the river. The mist was white now, and he could see the rays of the sun refracted through its tiny droplets. "What d'ye say, York? Can you see the river?"

"Cap'n, I can see all the way to Fort Pickerin'!"

They shoved the canoe into the water and got in, testing the water with the paddles. Clark felt a light southerly breeze touch his body, and suddenly the sun blazed through the fog, illuminating the entire vista of the Mississippi. In that moment, the titanic flow gleamed in front of him like a silver highway.

He had everything he needed: a strong back, decent weather, and a little luck. "Let's go, York!"

They found the current. He could feel York's power behind him. A flock of pelicans took off across their path, soaring free into the sky with their wings spread wider than a man was tall.

York sang out, "Cap'n, you done me wrong! That was *my* vest!"

Clark grinned. "I'll buy you a brand-new one from the best tailor in New Orleans, you rascal! That's a promise."

"Cap'n, I'm gonna hold you to that!"

The sun spread over the great river flowing beneath them. Clark could feel the cool, sweet splash from their paddles on his arms. A thousand dragonflies buzzed and bubbled across the water in their wake. He dug deep, found his rhythm with York and felt the calm greatness of the Mississippi, and proceeded on to find his friend.

Chapter 20
Neelly

October 3, 1809
Big Town, Chickasaw Agency, Mississippi Territory

N eelly watched the letter from General Wilkinson burn, the last lines disappearing first in the clay ashtray.

Burn this letter

The flames licked over the note, consuming his instructions.

Be ready to adapt to changing circumstances

Which were? Lewis had gotten bad sick again yesterday, about an hour out of camp past the Tallahatchie River. Pale—sweat running down his face and into his collar—he'd ridden his horse into a briar hedge, gone plumb crazy, ripped that pretty bottle-green coat all to hell in the thorns—

Five hundred dollars plus a stake in the mine out West

Jesus, Neelly thought, if Wilkinson came through on his end of the deal, then his luck would have changed forever. He bet his wife would even come back to him. It was just so hard to believe it could really happen to *him*—

You shall make a full report to me in Natchez

How? He knew better than to write anything down, but Governor Lewis talked so fancy, you could hardly make out what he was saying half the time, let alone remember it. At one point, he'd gone on for some time about how Secretary Eustis "lacked the organs necessary for generation." Neelly guessed Lewis must have noticed that he looked puzzled, because he finally barked at him, "Balls, Neelly! I mean he doesn't have any balls!"

Escort Governor Lewis to Nashville

They'd had to stop several times for Lewis to stumble into the woods to be sick. He insisted on priming his pistol, eyes darting over the path and the woods. Neelly pleaded with him to put it away. Lewis snapped, "And leave myself defenseless against that sonofabitch?" If the Governor could get that jumpy at the idea that Wilkinson was following him, what would he do to Neelly if he somehow discovered that he *worked* for the General?

Neelly stood up and walked out of the office, not bothering to lock up. He had nothing worth stealing. Here in Big Town, he was surrounded by over three hundred Indian cabins and thousands of natives, and even the meanest of them had more than he did. Most of them were farmers, growing corn and tobacco or raising apples and plums. The rest of them were hunters, supplying skins to traders at Fort Pickering. In his short time as the Chickasaw agent, Neelly hadn't been able to help noticing that the Indians seemed quite capable of getting along without his services. In fact, he didn't think they'd even noticed that he'd been gone from Big Town for over a week.

Neelly pulled out a plug of tobacco and chomped, staring at the little house that served as his quarters as federal agent. Pernia sat on the broken front step, and the big black dog, Seaman, lay across the front door. Pernia was picking up little sticks and pebbles and lobbing them into the dirt in front of him. Occasionally, he turned around and threw one at Seaman's rear end. The dog bared its teeth but didn't move from his post at the door. Neelly could see that the man and the dog loathed each other, though both served the same master.

Neelly didn't know what he was going to do. What if Lewis couldn't go on to Nashville? Wilkinson expected results. *Come on, Gov'ner, I need that five hundred dollars.*

He walked up to Pernia. "Any change?"

"How should I know?" Pernia replied.

Neelly shifted his tobacco to the other side of his mouth. "No offense meant." Curious, he asked Pernia, "Are all the negroes in New Orleans as tetchy as you?"

Pernia groaned and turned away, holding his head. "Please don't talk to me."

"Now you sound like my wife."

Pernia threw up his hands. "*Sacre bleu!* Deliver me." He got up and started to walk away. "Where is that goddamn Willie-o anyway?"

"Who's Willie-o?" Neelly said.

"William Clark, *brichon*," Pernia said. "The Governor sent for him before we left Fort Pickering."

"Oh," Neelly said. He turned away from Pernia, trying to conceal a shiver of anticipation. He hoped it wasn't true. Over the past few days, Lewis had talked often of "my friend Clark." To hear Lewis tell it, the man was superhuman. Neelly let his tongue turn the plug of tobacco round in his cheek and sent a brown juicy stream splashing onto the ground. Maybe he would go into town and have a drink or a bite to eat. He could have a word with some of the Chickasaw leaders about recruiting a road crew to go clear those logs that had fallen across the road near the pigeon roost.

As Neelly headed into town, he saw a familiar figure waiting just ahead. The man was tall, lean, and dressed in the plain black coat and hat of a Methodist circuit preacher. Leaning against an oak tree, he looked relaxed. As if he had all the time in the world.

Neelly's gut clenched. Now he understood what "changing circumstances" meant—he should have known that Wilkinson wouldn't give him five hundred dollars for providing a simple escort! It couldn't be a coincidence that Tom Runion was here, now!

Runion strolled forward, pinning Neelly in place with his eyes. Neelly squirmed. He hated himself for being such a coward, but Runion's physical appearance unnerved him. Though he couldn't have been over forty-five, Runion looked as old as the hills. The man was so fair-haired and light complexioned that he might be mistaken for an angel, if it weren't for those eyes. They were an icy blue, with the opaque gaze that he'd seen in the faces of wolves and big cats, but never on any other mortal man.

Neelly found himself stammering. "I guess you—you're Reverend Runion today." Tom Runion wasn't really a minister, of course. Neelly didn't think Runion believed in God, or any of the usual substitutes men used, like law, or work, or property. Runion was a bounty hunter and a slave catcher. He couldn't prove it, but he'd always suspected Runion was also a prolific horse thief, and a hired gun.

Runion showed his teeth in a fair approximation of a regular human smile, though the expression didn't reach the remarkable eyes. "I reckoned to walk in love on my way down to Big Town today, Neelly."

Neelly shivered. "I hate it when you quote Scripture."

"Got a guilty conscience?" Runion laughed. "Be not corrupted in silver and gold, my friend. No, be redeemed in the precious blood of the lamb." He shifted his weight, putting Neelly in mind of a panther about to pounce. "So, where is our lamb? I had an interesting message from that lard-assed, whoreson brother in New Orleans who pays us."

"Up at my place," Neelly said. "He got sick on the road yesterday. And you shouldn't talk about the General the way you do." Neelly sighed deeply and looked at his boots. "So what's the plan? What'd he tell *you* we're supposed to do?" Neelly wondered how much money Wilkinson had offered to pay Runion, and if he'd told Runion about the other fabulous prize.

Runion smiled. "Fat Guts says that we're to take the lamb to Natchez. Says he's got a trunk full of papers he'll pay cash money for."

"Natchez!" Neelly goggled at him. "He won't go, Runion! He's bound and determined to go to Nashville." He turned the problem over in his mind, remembering something that Silas Dinsmore, his predecessor at the Chickasaw Agency, had told him before he left. "That assassins trick—is that why you're here?"

"Oh, did Dinsmore tell you about that?" Runion said. "I wouldn't've thought he had the balls to mention it."

"Organs of generation," Neelly said.

"What?"

"That's the scientific term for balls."

"Jesus, Neelly," Runion said with disgust. "Anyway, we never got a chance to try it. That little whelp Burr was too smart to come over the Trace. But Fat Guts says he used it back in Kentucky on some British lord, and it worked like a charm. He's convinced it'll work this time, too. I already brought another man in on this—Junior Squyers, you know him?"

Neelly nodded, feeling morose. Squyres was a simpleton who hung around the Agency. Just a few weeks ago, Neelly had caught him standing in the woods with his pants down around his ankles, watching some little Indian girls hanging out wash. He'd yelled at Squyers and told him he would shoot him if he ever found him doing anything like that again. Squyres hadn't seemed to take his threat very seriously. Neelly guessed he wouldn't either, if he had Tom Runion on his side.

"The way it's supposed to work, according to our friend Fat Guts, is that me and Squyres'll ride outta the woods, yellin' like banshees, to assassinate the lamb—"

Neelly wished to God that Runion would stop calling Lewis the lamb.

"—and you'll ride in and save him. He'll be real scared. When you tell him you're gonna take him to Natchez, instead a' Nashville where all the bad guys are waitin' for him, he'll be so grateful, Fat Guts says he'll eat right outta your hand."

Neelly dug his toe in the dirt, thinking. If there was one thing he'd learned about Lewis in the past three days, it was that he was awfully unpredictable. "I ain't sure that'll work, Runion," he said. "Governor Lewis ain't no British lord."

"Of course it won't work!" Runion snarled. "Fat Guts lives in a world of his own, man. That's somethin' you better learn if you want to make your livin' off him. Didn't you say the lamb was sick? Well, that's good. We'll go ahead and kidnap him tonight, and ride hell for leather for Natchez, along with those papers Fat Guts has his cock up for. If he resists, we'll kill him. Simple as that."

Neelly's mind went blank. He managed to say, "B-but Runion, he-he's got a n-nigger with him."

"Christ, we'll just kill the nigger. What's the matter with you? Ain't you had enough of being diddled by the government? Here's our chance to finally get some of the gingerbread for ourselves!" He bared all his teeth. "You don't have to do anything, granny. Just stand aside and let me do the work."

Neelly found his best federal agent tone. "Reverend Runion, we work for the General, and I've gotta insist we at least try things his way. Maybe just scarin' the lamb, I-I mean the Gov'ner, will work. You know, the General's letters said he wanted Lewis brought in alive. At least mine did."

Runion sighed. "Yeah, so did mine. He even said there'd be a bonus for it." Runion kicked a stone away and watched it roll towards the oak tree. "I don't think he really meant it, though." Runion noticed a small ant hill at their feet, and for a few seconds Neelly watched as he kicked it over and set about to kill every last ant, his feet seeking out and crushing their bodies as they ran frantically out of their ruined mound.

"Look, let's just try it, that's all I'm saying," Neelly told him, then heard himself say, "We can always kill him later."

Runion shrugged. "Shit, all right. We'll try it your way. Squyres'll like it. What the hell, it might even be fun."

Chapter 21
Lewis

Big Town, Chickasaw Agency, Mississippi Territory
October 3, 1809

The pain was making him simple, that was all there was to it.
Lewis lay on the floor on his buffalo robe and tried to breathe. It won't
help to panic, he told himself. If he forced himself to lie quiet, if he just
waited patiently enough, the medicine would take effect and everything
would be all right.

He pushed his sweaty hair off his forehead and swallowed convulsively.
On the way down from Chickasaw Bluffs, he'd had a relapse. By the time
they reached here yesterday afternoon, he'd been on the verge of collapse.
He had never before experienced the fear of not being in control of his own
body. All the potions in his medicine chest had proven useless in defeating
this fever; all the herbs and remedies he could think of did nothing to stop
the tremors that wracked his body; all the mental determination he had was
not enough to drive the black wolf from his mind.

The one thing, the only thing that helped, was laudanum.

Laudanum was opium, diluted with alcohol. It was good for pain; it helped
him sleep. It helped control his diarrhea. Without it, he couldn't get a
moment's peace or rest. But all the same, he despised himself for the
weakness that had led him to it, and for the frantic, desperate craving he felt
when he went too long without its comforting effects. He'd started taking it
back in St. Louis, to calm his stomach and relieve the symptoms of his
malaria. Now he'd been on it for months, taking ever-increasing dosages,
worried that it was robbing him of his vitality. But if he tried to do without,
he felt even more miserable.

But with it...ah, with it came blessed relief and a return of his familiar
strength. With it, he could bear to contemplate the future. In fact, his
predicament was starting to seem rather funny. The hilarity of sitting down
with Madison, of seeing the little midget gape in open-mouthed indignation

when he heard Wilkinson was back to his old tricks...Walking into the grand front hallway of Monticello and telling Jefferson that his confidence in Wilkinson had been horribly misplaced...

"And then," he chuckled to himself, "I'll tell him I haven't written a line of his goddamn book! Lord, that'll be the cherry on the cake!"

His uncontrollable giggles dissolved into a series of painful hiccups. His stomach lurched. He gripped the buffalo pelt and forcibly calmed himself. Clark would be coming on any day now. It wouldn't be near as funny when he told Clark that the book he'd supposedly been working on for years was only a fantasy. He'd promised he'd write the narrative of the Expedition based on their journals, and he'd let Clark think he had the manuscript almost completed. Clark was counting on the book to bring them a lot of money.

What the hell will he say when he realizes I lied to him? Lewis had seen Clark furious and disappointed many times...but never with him. He could hardly blame Clark if he washed his hands of him altogether, though he knew Clark wouldn't. It wasn't in his friend to give up on people. Clark had wasted years of his life and almost bankrupted himself trying to help George out of financial ruin; Lewis doubted a little thing like lying would be able to drive him away.

"Truly," he said, "I don't deserve such a loyal friend."

"You can say that again," Pernia huffed, struggling in the door. Seaman muscled his way in after, almost knocking Pernia off his feet. "Without a doubt, this is the most godforsaken place yet. We're surrounded by savages."

"No worse than St. Louis," Lewis said. "Frankly, I'd rather be in a hole with a thousand fire-breathing Chickasaws than in that snakepit."

Pernia grunted scornfully. "Sir, if you'll forgive me for saying, you've really outdone yourself this time."

"No offense taken," Lewis said. He was starting to feel better; that sense of wild, buoyant euphoria was creeping up on him. Thank God, the laudanum had worked again. He'd be able to get through the night, and possibly tomorrow he'd be rid of the fever. A man had to hope.

"Pernia," he said, rubbing Seaman's ears, "What do these Chickasaws eat, anyway? I'm half-famished."

"Who knows? Probably white men, or dogs. Either would be fine with me."

Lewis laughed. "Help me up, for Christ's sake. Let's go find our boisterous friend the Chickasaw agent and see what we can get for board around here.

Hopefully with some strong libation to go along with it."

"Governor, you amaze me. I don't understand how you can carry on like you do. If you were a lesser man, your habits would kill you."

"People always say that about liquor," Lewis said, after a long, haunted moment. "What they don't understand is that sometimes it's the only thing that keeps you going."

"Well, it won't be me who gets the big funeral, anyway." Pernia took Lewis's arm and dragged him to his feet. "Come on, Governor. We're in the biggest Indian town I ever saw. Surely we can find someplace to get drunk."

The sun was setting over Big Town, but far from settling down to rest, the Chickasaws were abuzz with activity. Smoke from ovens and cookfires drifted over the camp, heavy with the smells of hot corn, hominy and roasting meat. Women carried baskets of apples in from the orchards, and children and dogs scampered across their path. If not for Seaman's imposing appearance, few people would have bothered to stop and look them over. White men were commonplace in Big Town; as for blacks, many Chickasaws kept negro slaves themselves. They were accustomed to a constant parade of soldiers, traders and fortune-seekers crowding into their settlement, and they accepted the newcomers with peaceful, albeit grudging, hospitality.

Lewis and Pernia spotted Neelly standing under a large oak, deep in conversation with a man dressed in the dark vestments of a minister. When he caught sight of Neelly's companion, Pernia stopped short and fell back a step. The man was extraordinary-looking; he was so fair of complexion that light seemed to radiate from his hair and eyes.

"What's the matter?" Lewis asked. "Are you worried that preacher will put the fear of God into you?" To his astonishment, Seaman also backed up, then trotted off in the other direction.

"No..." Pernia said. "But that's a mighty strange-looking fellow, Governor."

"He does look a bit odd," Lewis said. "No doubt it helps him in his trade. People are awfully gullible, Pernia. They're always eager to believe there's a divine answer to all their problems. Unfortunately, I don't think prayer is going to help me with Secretary Eustis." He looked the preacher over. "But hell, if this gent can put in a good word with God for me, it sure can't hurt."

He strode up. "Evening, Neelly. And to you also, sir."

Neelly jumped and nearly inhaled his plug of tobacco. "Governor—good Lord, sir, sick as you were, I thought you were down for the night."

"Well, I'm feeling a bit rejuvenated after my rest," Lewis said. "Pernia and I were going to scare up some supper. Why don't you invite your friend the minister to eat with us?"

Neelly swiveled his head to look at the preacher, who was regarding Lewis with intense interest. Neelly's mouth opened and closed like a whiskered fish. Finally, he stammered, "He's...well, actually, he was just goin'."

"No, I wasn't," said the preacher, sticking out his hand. "I'd be honored, sir. The Reverend Tom Runion."

"Pleased to meet you, Reverend. Meriwether Lewis, lately the governor of Upper Louisiana."

Runion's ice-blue eyes popped. "Surely you ain't *the* Meriwether Lewis?"

Lewis smiled. "I sincerely hope there is not more than one, sir."

"Well, this is a real occasion!" Runion said. "I never dreamed when I came to do God's work in this humble place, I would stumble upon the great explorer of the West! What in blazes brings you to Big Town?"

Lewis inclined his head toward Neelly, who was standing stock-still with his mouth gaping open. "This good gentleman, actually. I'm traveling to Nashville, and he was kind enough to show me the way."

"Well, I have *long* tried to show Brother Neelly the way, so I am glad he has some idea of how to follow the path!" Runion grinned, laying a benevolent hand on Neelly's shoulder. Neelly's mouth finally clapped shut. "Yes, let us sit down together, and share the Lord's bounty! And the lion shall lie down with the lamb."

"You flatter me, sir," Lewis said. "Where can one get a decent meal in this place?"

"We can eat at the table of the woman named Emahota. Nice, clean Chickasaw lady—runs a little place for the wearied traveler. She ain't no Christian, but she's a bang-up cook."

They started off, Runion leading the way. As they walked along, he expounded, "'He that eateth, eateth to the Lord, for he giveth God thanks.' Romans 14:6. D'ya know your scripture, sir?"

"No, I'm afraid that is one subject I have sorely neglected," Lewis said. "Reverend, I spent some time in Georgia as a child. I think I detect that cadence in your speech."

"Yes, I am from that fair place, the original home of the Chickasaws." Runion swept his hand before him expansively. "I ride my little boat on the great tide of His divine will. I have traveled far and wide in the service of my Master."

"I know what you mean." Lewis sighed. If he had a divine master, his name was Thomas Jefferson. Jefferson was skeptical about religion in all its forms, and thought reason and common sense should be sufficient to govern the passions of men. Presuming they had any, that is.

Jefferson would certainly find this fellow to be an interesting specimen. "What brand of Christianity are you selling, Reverend?" he asked.

Runion looked offended. "There ain't no selling involved, sir! In the Methodist faith, we trust in Christ alone for salvation! I have turned away from mammon, and He has taken away my sins, yes, even *mine*, and saved me from the law of sin and death."

They reached the home of Emahota, who operated a small tavern in a hut beside her cabin. Pernia looked at the food on other people's plates with a queasy expression, but he was too hungry to complain. When Pernia sat down at the table with them, a shocked look came over Runion's pale features.

"You don't mind, do you, Reverend? My servant eats with me all the time."

"All God's children," Runion murmured, fixing Pernia with an empty, icy gaze. The little Creole shuddered and inched his chair closer to Lewis's.

There was the small matter of payment. Neely was piss-poor and could barely keep body and soul together; Lewis had learned that during their ride down from Chickasaw Bluffs. The Reverend's black frock coat was thread-bare; he certainly wasn't getting fat doing the Lord's work. Lewis dug in his pocket and came up with some of the specie he'd managed to flimflam out of Captain Russell. "Gentlemen, allow me."

Neely smiled a little and said, "Thankee." Runion grinned broadly. "You're a reg'lar good Samaritan, sir!" Pernia just cocked his head and sighed.

Emahota was a handsome Chickasaw woman, about fifty years old, with two long, coal-black braids that hung over her shoulders. She silently took Lewis's money and placed before each of them a plate of fried pork and steaming cracked corn she called *tafulla*. Lewis caught her arm and handed her some more money. "Darlin', bring us some beer."

Emahota smiled and moved off. Neely looked at him, agog. "Governor, you're sick! I don't think you oughter! Remember what Cap'n Russell said—"

"I don't give a tinker's damn what Captain Russell said. I'll tell you one thing, Neely, I'm not going to go all the way to Nashville on creek water. I'll never make it."

Everyone but Pernia tore into their meals as Emahota returned with four enormous tankards of home-brewed beer. The *tafulla* tasted strong and ashy, but the meat was hot and dripping with juices, and it seemed to Lewis the best meal he'd ever had in his life.

"Reverend," he said, "Are you going to perform a service here? I should like to see that very much."

At that moment, Neely choked on a bit of pork; Runion had to stop eating and pound him on the back. "No, sir, I ain't preachin' tonight. I'm just here ministerin' to the sick, in body and in soul."

"Pity." Lewis took a large swallow of beer. "So do you heal people? Cast out demons and such?"

"I endeavor mightily to do so!" Runion said, his eyes popping. "I've seen the Holy Spirit move people. I've seen men and women fall on the ground, shakin' with sheer delight in the presence of the Almighty God. At my last revival, a man came forward, crawlin' on his knees and barkin' like a dog. But I infused him with the power of the Holy Spirit, and he was cleansed of his sins."

Pernia stopped picking at his food and snorted. "Sounds like hypnotism to me."

"No!" Runion glared at Pernia, his eyes ablaze with anger. "This ain't devil power! It's the rapture of the spirit when God enters the body and casts out your demons!"

Pernia curled his lip, which angered Runion further. "Listen, little fella," he growled, leaning forward to stare at Pernia, "I pray we will all one day know the sweet anguish of the soul, when it turns away from the filthy corruption of the flesh, and embraces the pure ecstasy of the divine."

Pernia started to say something about the unlikelihood of that happening to him, but Lewis quickly interrupted. "Reverend, you are no doubt a persuasive man in the meeting house. How I wish I could take you back East with me! Barking and shaking, eh? What a sensation that would cause at Christchurch in Albemarle!"

Runion gave a tight smile, and the angry moment passed. For a crazy moment Lewis considered talking to the Reverend about the black wolf, but he quickly came to his senses. In all likelihood, the man was a charlatan; his credentials as a preacher were probably no more real than the wolf himself. Besides, at a time when his credibility was severely under strain, it probably wasn't a good idea to participate in any ceremony that involved barking.

Neely had drained half his tankard and finally started to loosen up a little.

"Governor," he said, with the wistfulness of a boy, "Tell us about what you saw out West."

"Oh, many marvelous things." Lewis cast his mind back on the journey. Could it really be three years since he'd come home? In some ways, it seemed like yesterday, and in other ways, a lifetime.

"The West is a golden country, Neelly," he said. "Clark and I passed through some of the richest and most beautiful land on the continent. They say the Spanish territory to the southwest is desert, and we saw some of that up north, too. But we also saw scenes of unbelievable beauty. Where the three rivers join, it's like paradise...all the deer and elk you can hunt, the rivers teeming with beavers and fish...really, it defies my power to describe it."

"Do tell, sir," Runion said. "You are truly a man who has seen God's wonders."

"I don't know about that." Lewis smiled. "As you've probably guessed, I'm a bit of a skeptic, Reverend. But there were times when even I felt the presence of the Creator...or at least felt I was gazing upon His work."

"Tell us," Neelly said.

"Well, the Missouri River, as you approach its headwaters, culminates in five great waterfalls. I had gone ahead of the party, as a scout...I came upon the first one at about two in the afternoon. I could hear the roar, and see enormous clouds of mist rising from the river before I saw the falls itself." Lewis shivered in the memory and blinked unexpected tears from his eyes. "It was truly the most perfect thing I've ever seen. As tall as the tallest tree you can imagine...it stretched across the expanse of the whole wide river. An enormous cataract, the water tumbling down in a veritable ocean, frothing white."

He looked at their rapt faces. "And that wasn't the end of it. There were four more just like it, not so grand but equally beautiful, over the next ten miles of the river. We had to tote everything we had, literally tons of goods, over about eighteen miles of rough and rocky country, just to get around 'em. At the time, I sometimes wished they didn't exist—Lord, they caused us an awful lot of trouble!—but to me, those waterfalls are truly the most sublime thing on this earth."

"Was there ever a time when you just thought 'To hell with it, I'm turning back'?" Neelly asked.

"I never even considered turning back, Neelly. For one thing, President Jefferson had gone to a great deal of trouble to send me out there, and he

was counting on my reaching the Western ocean and bringing back everything we'd found. Plant specimens, animals, rock and soil samples...celestial
readings...most important, information about the native people.

"But that was just me," Lewis said, taking another swig from his tankard.
"Pleasing Jefferson was my part of it. There were thirty other men with me,
and what kept them going, through unthinkable hardship, day after day...well,
sometimes I still don't know."

"They were scared of General Clark?" Pernia guessed.

Lewis laughed. "It certainly helped," he said. "Clark always knew better
than me how to inspire the men and cajole them, and jolly them along. There
were times when it took all the combined talents we had. In the Bitterroot
Mountains, for example. I think we came within a few days of starving, or
freezing to death...but we got out alive in the end. That was when we found
the Nez Perce...who are some of the finest damn people on the face of the
earth."

Neelly sighed. "Lord, I reckon a man could make a lot of money out there,
if he knew what he was doin'."

Runion grinned. "Jeremiah 12:12. For the spoilers shall come upon all high
places through the wilderness. And the sword of the Lord shall devour the
wicked, and the Israelites shall prosper."

"Indeed, sir," Lewis said. They had all emptied their tankards and had
them refilled by Emahota; Lewis was feeling pleasantly drunk on laudanum
and beer. The black wolf was nowhere around. He wished he could stay here
forever.

"Governor..." Neelly said, a little glassy-eyed, "can I ask you somethin'
else?"

"Of course." Lewis enjoyed talking about the Expedition; it reminded him
of happier times. "I've got all night. Let your questions flow freely, my
friend."

Neelly glanced at Runion. "Is it true you...you found a gold mine out
there?"

"Gold mine?" Lewis blinked, surprised. He hadn't heard that one before.
Neelly was looking at him with big, hopeful eyes. Runion leaned forward
eagerly. For a man of the cloth, he seemed awfully interested in gold all of a
sudden. Lewis suppressed a smile. This was going to be amusing.

He let his mind work for a moment. "Well...I wouldn't call it a *mine*, exactly." Beside him, Pernia snickered under his breath. He knew better than
anyone Lewis hadn't found a gold mine, but he could recognize when his

master was about to spin a fabulous lie.

"Well...what would you call it?"

Lewis paused, considering. "It...it's more like a *field*, actually. A big, open field."

Neelly and Runion exchanged glances. "A field of gold?" Neelly repeated.

"Yes...very much like it," Lewis said. "You don't even have to dig for it! Gold nuggets, big as your fist, just lying on the ground. You can pick 'em up and fill your pockets with 'em."

"And did ya?" Runion's pale eyes glinted.

"Of course! Me and General Clark both! Lord, we carted off all we could carry."

Neelly wet his lips. "Where is this gold mine, Governor?"

"Well, if I told you, it wouldn't be a secret, now would it?" Lewis leaned back in his chair. "No, gents, only General Clark and I know where it is, and we ain't tellin'."

Runion goggled at him. "Hell, you gotta have a map!"

"Oh, it's not on any map," Lewis grinned. "Well, except in code, of course. Someday we'll go back, and be as rich as Midas."

Their eyes were enormously big and round. Lewis rolled his gaze up to the ceiling; he was afraid he'd laugh and give the joke away. He didn't dare look at Pernia, who was trembling with the effort to hold back his mirth. Neelly was pale, and Runion was almost salivating.

"I must say, Reverend, for a fellow who has no doubt sworn to give up all worldly goods, you seem awfully interested in the yellow coin."

Runion looked surprised, then quickly recovered himself. "The love of money is the root of all evil, Brother."

"Really? I thought it was the lack of money." Lewis sighed; all of this tale-spinning had worn him out. He was beginning to feel the effects of the alcohol and knew if he didn't leave before Emahota came back with more beer, he'd never walk out of here. He pushed his chair away from the table; Pernia scrambled up with him.

"Gentlemen, I appreciate the companionship tonight, but I must offer my apologies—I'm not at my best. I'm going to go lie down a while. We'll be getting off early in the morning."

"It was our pleasure, Gov'ner," Runion said, giving him a quick shake of the hand. "You tell some wild tales, sir."

Neelly looked at him worriedly. "Governor, we'll see how you're doin' in the mornin', but I really think you oughter stay here and rest up at least through tomorrow."

"No, Neely." Lewis shook his head. "We've got to move on. I can't wait any longer. I'll see you in the morning. Good night."

Mon Oct 2 '09

Met an interesting gentleman tonight, a friend of Neely's. He professed to be a Methodist minister, and he allowed me to importune him with many questions about that unique and colorful faith. His name was Tom Runion, he appeared to be an educated fellow and asked me many questions as well.

I confess I had some sport at the expense of Runion and Neely tonight. They asked me about a gold mine Clark and myself were purported to have found on our late expedition. When I assured them that such a fountain of riches did indeed exist, they fairly drooled, and their eyes were as big as dinner plates. I believe I could have told the poor gullible fellows anything at that moment and they would have been inclined to believe me without question.

Their reaction put me in mind of my accursed book. Heretofore I have delayed the work, wanting to achieve the most scrupulous adherence to the truth, but these gentlemen have convinced me that if I merely filled the volume with fanciful tales and outlandish stories of the great fortune to be made, it would surely become a best seller, and perhaps even go into a second printing.

I am tolerably well with medicine but not so well without it. The black wolf continues to plague me. That creature has not quit me one moment since I left Fort Pickering and is often in sight and certainly never out of mind.

Lewis dipped his quill in the inkpot again, then paused, considering. On the Expedition, he had written scientific descriptions of more than a hundred animals and close to two hundred plants. Perhaps if he could only catalog the black wolf, it would cease to terrify him. It was worth a try.

I will now endeavor to describe that singular animal which has so long afflicted my life; his size has remained consistent relative to my own, which is to say, knee-high, but when nearer he seems larger, perhaps up to mid-thigh. His fur is a dull black, not quite running to gray, and covered with some kind of grease or oil, but for all that he has no discernible smell. The eyes are gray like stone or marble, and continuously spinning in the head; the teeth are yellow and about the size and sharpness of a typical gray wolf. The tongue is enormous, at least a foot long, sometimes pink in appearance and sometimes black, and lolls out of his mouth continuously, but it appears often to be dry, at other times I perceive saliva dripping from it. The lips are always pulled back in a disgusting and thoroughly unnerving grin; and the overall aspect of the beast is of a character to inspire feelings of the deepest hopelessness, foreboding, and dread.

I first recall making the acquaintance of this animal when I was about ten, in Georgia, and came upon him while on the hunt; at first I thought he was quite real, and attempted to shoot it, but after wasting several rounds of ammunition I realized he was something of a phantasm. It scared me much. I hesitated to confide this to my mother, for I assumed (rightly) she would be irritated with me for telling fanciful stories.

His quill flew across the page. It was some relief to him to pour out the details of his affliction, even if it was just in the form of ink on paper. If he could analyze the wolf carefully enough, surely he could defeat it.

All my years in the Army, I felt his skulking presence sometimes, indeed, he was always a bold fellow, even daring to hang about the President's house. My only consolation was that if I remained active in body and mind, he would keep his distance from me, and this is what I endeavored to do. During the Expedition, I perceived him only once, during the long winter at Fort Clatsop, on the Pacifick coast, but never actually saw the animal, and indeed had reason to hope he had left me for good.

Of course, that hope has proven in vain. He gives me a very difficult time of it at the moment, and distresses me often. There must be some way to kill it. I pray I may yet find one.

Chapter 22
Lewis

Twenty Mile Creek, Mississippi Territory
October 4, 1809

They were strung out single-file along the road. At Lewis's insistence, they'd gotten up very early that morning. He estimated they'd already been on the Trace for four or five hours and had gone maybe twenty-five miles.

Neelly seemed exceedingly jumpy this morning. He hadn't said a word at breakfast and seemed barely able to keep down his biscuit. Hung over, Lewis supposed. For all he knew Neelly had spent all night drinking with the Reverend. For once, he wasn't suffering from an excess of drink himself. He felt exhausted, and he looked like hell in his tattered green coat, but at least his mind was sound. Things always seemed better when he was on the move.

Neelly was riding about fifty yards in front of him, to better scout out the terrain ahead; Pernia was lagging about fifty yards behind. Seaman trotted in the tall grass alongside him. Lewis expected they would stop at Twenty Mile Creek to have a bite of dried beef or bacon before attempting to cross. And they'd brew some coffee. Neelly would feel better with some coffee in him—

Up ahead, he noticed something. Neelly had stopped.

From his posture, Lewis sensed something was wrong. Instead of his usual slump, Neelly was sitting fully upright in the saddle. Lewis could see the tension in his body. He was as still as a statue.

Lewis felt puzzled. Was there a wild animal in the road? He checked his pistols: both primed and ready. His rifle, resting in a sling on his saddle, was charged and ready to fire.

Seaman started to bark.

Lewis's pulse ticked up a notch. Something was happening. His horse twitched its ears and whickered. He sensed a slight vibration in the ground.

Neelly looked off to his right, towards the woods. Somebody was coming. Neelly must not be able to see them, or else he'd be pointing and shouting. Lewis twisted around in the saddle.

"Pernia!" he yelled. Pernia looked up from his sullen reverie. Lewis held up his hand, palm out, motioning Pernia to stop.

He could hear it now: the pounding of hooves. Horsemen. More than one. Riding fast. He quickly checked his ammunition pouch. Balls, powder, flints. Then he remembered something and cursed under his breath. He was packing the goddamn journals with him. If he had to run, he couldn't take them, and he couldn't risk them being lost. He stood up in the stirrups, unfastened his saddlebags, and heaved them off into the tall grass.

"Governor," Pernia called out, annoyed. "What the hell are you doing?"

Seaman was barking madly. He could see them now. Big sonsofbitches, two of them, riding out of the woods, straight for him. They had burlap sacks pulled over their heads, and sawed-off short rifles. They'd be on him in a matter of seconds.

He pulled out one of his pistols as his horse began to sidestep, its great eyes rolling in terror. Pernia started to bleat. Up ahead, Neelly wheeled his horse and started back toward him. Even at this distance, Lewis could see his eyes, wide, bulging, sick with fear—

His heart surged. He'd never felt so goddamn mad in his life. So Wilkinson thought he could take him here! Thought he'd run like a scared rabbit! *Like hell!*

Their short rifles would have longer range, but his pistol shot true. Lewis gripped the horse with his knees and reined it with one hand, backing it up, calming the animal, repeating in a low voice, "Steady. Steady." The first man, the big fat one, was riding down on him fast. He didn't know why the idiot didn't fire on him; if his rifle was any good, he could have shot Lewis off his horse from here. But instead of shooting, he was screaming like a wild Indian.

Lewis cracked his horse on the rump and spurred it into the grass, charging straight at the fat man. The tenor of the screaming changed slightly. Lewis gripped his right elbow with his left hand to steady his arm, took aim, and discharged a pistol ball straight into the man's belly.

He had the grim satisfaction of hearing the soft *pluk* of the ball tearing through flesh. The man's screaming ended in a surprised whoop as he flew off his horse and hit the ground, his rifle spinning off into the grass. He bawled incoherently, clutching at the dark stain spreading on his stomach, while another stain, lower down, appeared on the front of his trousers.

The other fellow, the taller one, yelled "Fuck!" and wheeled his horse around. He raised his rifle, took aim at Lewis, and yanked the trigger. The weapon discharged with a great boom of powder: misfire.

Now, Lewis himself screamed like a maniac. The man's face was hidden beneath his hood, but his body showed his panic. He yanked on the reins so hard the horse nearly fell. The tall fellow righted it just in time and sent it careering back into the woods.

"Neelly! Go around! We'll cut him off at the creek!" Lewis pulled his second pistol, dug his heels into his horse's flanks and spurred it into the woods. He'd be damned if he'd let the fellow get away. Send his goddamn head to Wilkinson in a box—

The forest was dense, full of tall, close-set blackjack and hickory trees, covered with dead, overhanging vines. He was conscious of nothing but adrenaline-fueled fury coursing through his body and the pounding of the horse beneath him. At this moment, he'd have given anything for a good Virginia pacer instead of this broken-down Army nag; but the little horse was giving him everything it had.

Up ahead, the sonofabitch wheeled and turned through the trees, trying to lose him, looking for a chance to reload. Lewis hoped to hell Neelly had followed his instructions and was coming around to cut him off, but he had a sinking feeling Neelly was somewhere behind him. He bent low over the horse's neck and muttered encouragement: "Come on, old fellow, just a little faster, and we'll have him..."

He was close enough to fire, but he couldn't risk wasting the ball and leaving himself with only his loaded rifle, which would be hard to manage in the underbrush and had a kick that would knock him out of the saddle. Ignoring the branches that whipped at his face and tore at the sleeves of his coat, he saw an opening and plunged the horse into a deep thicket. They emerged on the other side almost neck and neck with the man who'd tried to kill him.

The hooded man turned toward him. Lewis started to raise his pistol, but before he could take aim, the man slashed at him frantically with something metallic he was clutching in his hand. Lewis felt something plunge deep into the muscle of his left forearm.

Lewis yelped with pain. For a horrible moment, he struggled to free himself, towed along by his own pierced flesh. The weapon that had snared him was a pair of devil's claws, the hook sailors used to secure chains and anchors. The tall fellow had sharpened the prongs to two needle-sharp points. Lewis wrenched his arm loose and felt the prongs slide out just about the time a tree branch whacked him square in the middle of the forehead.

Lewis found himself lying on his back on the ground. For an agonizing span of time, he couldn't move, couldn't see, couldn't think. Then his senses returned. He was still holding his pistol. He scrabbled in the leaves and struggled back to his feet. His assailant disappeared into the woods, along with his own runaway horse. Lewis cursed and wiped blood out of his eyes. Sure enough, here was Neelly, riding just behind him instead of trying to cut the fellow off at the river.

"Oh, Gov'ner," Neelly moaned. "When I saw you fall, I thought you was kilt fer sure."

"Don't stand here jawing! Go, goddamnit!" Lewis raised his arm and pointed in the direction his assailant had gone. His left hand felt numb; little rivulets of blood were dripping down the sleeve of his coat. "You can still get him, Neelly! Kill the bastard!"

But Neelly didn't. Instead, he slid out of the saddle and dropped to the ground. "Jesus, Gov'ner, you're bad hurt—"

Lewis felt incredulous. "Why didn't you do as I say?" he raged. "You let him get away! That sonofabitch tried to blast me! I *told* you to go around and cut him off at the river—"

"I heard ye, but I guess I warn't quick enough—"

"Aren't you supposed to know this country? Weren't you supposed to be a major in the goddamned militia? Damn your eyes, Neelly!"

Neelly fell into a morose silence. Lewis glared at him and listened to the sound of his own wheezing. He could feel his strength rapidly leaking out of the holes in his arm, but he was too mad to think about it. He supposed he should be worried that Wilkinson's man would come back around and kill them both. *Frig it!* It would be a goddamn blessing just to have it over—

He wasn't aware of falling, just that he was suddenly on his knees, retching. Neelly looked scared. He said in a hollow voice, "Gov'ner, your head's busted."

"No, it's not," Lewis rasped. "It's just cut, that's all." He touched the sticky bump on his forehead and experienced another terrific jolt of pain and nausea. As he gagged and gasped for air, he felt a self-contempt so strong it almost overwhelmed him. Here he was, facing the most dire situation of his life, and what was he doing? He was down on his hands and knees in the dirt, puking his guts out.

Neelly stared at him and gulped. "Gov'ner, you're in bad shape. I gotta get you up." He reached down and took hold of Lewis's arm. "Here, lemme help ye—"

Lewis allowed Neelly to haul him to his feet. He staggered and hung on to a tree for balance. "If you really want to help me, Neelly, why don't you go round up my goddamn horse? He's got a good rifle hanging off him. I'm going to need it."

"I'll get him. I see where he is," Neelly told him. "You gonna be all right here, Gov'ner? It might take me a minute to catch him."

"I'll try and get along without your indispensable services." His sarcasm seemed lost on Neelly, who remounted and rode off pie-eyed into the woods.

Lewis leaned against the tree and closed his eyes. The black wolf was right beside him, grinning at his wounds and his blood, mocking his weakness. He gagged again. How the hell could he fight Wilkinson, Eustis, and the black wolf at once? He would kill it, that's what he would do, *he would kill it*—

Someone touched his shoulder. Lewis started violently and raised his pistol. It took a moment for his eyes to focus; when they did, he saw Neelly standing there with a shocked, pale face and upraised hands. Neelly had come back with the horse already.

"Gov'ner, I'm beggin' ya, put that thing away," Neelly pleaded. "You're awful jumpy—"

Lewis laughed a hysterical laugh. "Look at me, Neelly. Wouldn't you be?"

Neelly didn't have any answer to that. He helped boost Lewis into the saddle. With Neelly leading the way, they started back toward the road. Lewis didn't put away his pistol. The black wolf was swirling around the legs of his horse with a sickening, dizzying gait. His chest felt hollow inside. Where was Clark? When the hell was this all going to end?

He pointed his pistol at the wolf. "Get away. I mean it. I'll blast you."

Neelly stared at him, eyes wide with fear. "Gov'ner, take it easy," he said. "I'm your friend, remember? There ain't nobody else here."

"Don't you see him?" Lewis demanded, then answered himself. "No, of course not. You don't. You couldn't."

"I'm tellin' ya, *there ain't nobody*," Neelly said. Lewis shook his head. There was no way he could make Neelly, or anybody else, understand.

When they emerged from the woods, he saw Pernia cowering in the tall grass on the far side of the roadway. He was staring in horrified fascination at the fat man Lewis had shot, who was still squealing and twitching in the road. Seaman barked and ran toward Lewis, his tail aloft. His saddlebags were still in the grass where he'd thrown them; Pernia hadn't bothered to pick them up.

Pernia saw him and gave a little bleat. "*Jésus-Christ*! What happened to you? Did he shoot you?"

"Wishful thinking." Lewis had trouble forming his words. "Pernia...my head's cut, and my arm's a mess...I'm going to need your help cleaning and dressing these wounds—"

"Damned if I will!" Pernia leapt to his feet. "I'm through with you! I told you before! I'm not going to die on this goddamned trip!"

Lewis shook, sweat pouring down his face. "Let me guess, Pernia—*would you like to discuss your fucking two-hundred and forty dollars now*?" He lurched his way off the horse and stood over Pernia, trembling like a madman. "Don't you even understand what's going on? Didn't you see what just happened? Don't you realize there's not going to *be* any blasted money, not now, not ever, because that bastard Wilkinson is going to kill me?"

Pernia covered his face and blubbered like a child. Neelly goggled at them both and flapped his jaw for a moment before he blurted out: "Gov'ner, you're plumb out of your head again! I should have warned ye, there's a lot of bandits on the Trace—"

"Bandits? Those weren't any bloody bandits, Neelly! James Wilkinson wants me dead! That goddamned, beetleheaded, fat-assed *lunatic* is trying to put me in my *grave*—"

"Gov'ner, you ought not to talk that way! Gittin' yourself all upset...look, you're losin' blood." Neelly reached out for Lewis's bleeding arm. "You better let me see—"

Lewis felt suddenly, violently suspicious. What did he really know about Neelly, anyway? Neelly had led him into this! For all he knew, Neelly could be working for Wilkinson too—

"*Get back,*" he rasped, raising his pistol and pointing it in Neelly's face. Pernia shrieked and fell to the ground, throwing his arms over his head.

Neelly stopped dead in his tracks, his eyes wide. "Gov'ner...Jesus, please..."

Lewis's hand shook wildly. He couldn't steady it. "*Who the hell pays your salary?*"

"Nobody, most of the time! Look, I'm just the Chickasaw Agent! I'm tryin' my best to get you to Nashville." Neelly licked his lips wildly. "If what you say's true, maybe you oughtn't to go there! Hell, maybe you could throw 'em off a little if you turned smack around and went the other way! I could take you to Natchez—"

"Natchez?" Lewis lowered the gun. "Why would I want to go to *Natchez*? The whole reason I came this way was to escape my enemies on the river!

Hell, Wilkinson's probably got the whole goddamn army waiting for me in Natchez!"

He'd been wrong about Neelly; he could see that now. The man was too stupid to be involved in any scheme of Wilkinson's. He shoved his gun in his coat and glared at Neelly. "I'll be *God...fucking...damned*," he said, "if I will turn around, or stop, or turn back in any respect. Because *that's what he wants!* That prick thinks he can destroy me! But *he can't.*"

Lewis suddenly remembered the fat man; he was still squalling about his belly wound. Fueled by a renewed surge of adrenaline, Lewis ran across the road and snatched up the fat man's fallen rifle.

"No, Gov'ner, don't!" Neelly shouted.

Lewis had no intention of killing the bastard; a quick death would be too good for him. He dragged the man up by his shirt front. The man's eyes squirmed and popped with terror. There was no sign of intelligence in his face. "You're the sonofabitch what shot me!" he squealed.

"Damn right." Lewis pulled his lips back in a snarl. "You tell your boss in New Orleans that it'll take more than a couple of cretins to bring me down! You tell that fat fuck Wilkinson that I'll be sitting at Monticello in a couple of weeks, drinking Jefferson's wine and telling him *all about* what he offered to do for me! You tell him Meriwether Lewis'll see him hang!"

He threw the man back down in the dirt, then poked his belly wound with the butt of his rifle for good measure. The fat man wailed. Lewis tore his ammunition pouch off him and staggered back to his horse. He leaned against the horse and reloaded his pistol. Now he had two rifles and two pistols, plus a dirk, a tomahawk—and his fists.

Fuck Wilkinson! He was ready. "Let's go!" he screamed.

Neelly looked like he was going to piss his pants; Pernia already had. Neelly gaped at the weeping fat man. "We probably shouldn't ought to leave him here—"

"Don't touch him! Let the buzzards have him." Lewis dragged himself into the saddle. "Pernia, hand me up those goddamn journals." Sniveling, Pernia did as he was told.

Neelly looked at the fat man laying in the dirt, then blanched, like he was going to be sick. Finally, he got back on his horse and started them moving forward again.

Wed Oct 4 '09

Troubles mount allarmingly on every side. Wilkinson sent 2 men to cut me off at the 20 Mile Crk ... shot one, the other one escaped into the woods after inflicting injury on me with a hook. Have become very fatigued and disordered. Cannot trust Neelly nor anyone ese, My anxiety for the saftey of my papers is extreme.

I conceived I heard Clark coming on and half expected to see him at the river, I'm certain he will over take me any day. He will hear of this situation and come to my releaf, and in his usial way will set things right

Chapter 23
Wilkinson

False River, Point Coupee, Louisiana Territory
October 5, 1809

"Doctor..."
"Help me, doctor..."
"Please, water, *for the love of Christ...*"

James Wilkinson could hear the cries of the men before he even saw them. Frowning, he put the spurs to his charger until he reached a low rise overlooking the horseshoe-shaped lake called the False River, formed by the Mississippi doubling back on itself. Two army boats had drawn in close to shore, and everywhere he looked, there were soldiers lying about.

Wilkinson's chest swelled with indignation. Ever since he had left New Orleans, expecting a pleasant canter up to meet the troops at Natchez, he had been passing stragglers. A few laggards, he could understand, but this—why, there had to be at least a hundred men here! Who was going to build winter quarters up at Fort Adams, if the men were going to spend their time soaking up the sun, instead of attending to their military obligations?

Men scattered and jumped as Wilkinson came thundering into camp. "Who's in charge here?" he roared. For several stunned seconds, the men gibbered from behind dirty beard stubble. A few offered sloppy, terrified salutes. He would have thought his entrance would put the fear of God into all of these shirkers, but, incredibly, several of them continued to lie on the ground down by the river.

"All of you!" Wilkinson pointed at the men with his riding crop. "Shave, get cleaned up, and get into uniform! This camp is a disgrace! Who's your commanding officer?"

A scrawny sandy-haired officer emerged from one of the larger tents. His shirt and breeches, even his uniform coat, were stained and spattered with vomit and excrement—though to his credit, he did know how to give a crisp salute. "Lieutenant Henry Darrington, sir, at your service, sir!"

His jowls aquiver, Wilkinson bellowed, "Lieutenant, this place is a pigsty! What is the meaning of this travesty?" He shook his riding crop in the direction of the dingy river. "Why aren't these boats moving?"

Darrington said, "Sir! We had to stop and bury the dead, sir! And these men are too ill to be moved! We decided to establish a hospital here and let the rest of the troops move out to Fort Adams."

Baffled, Wilkinson looked around. By now, most of the men had realized who he was and come to their feet. One man continued to lie under a tree in his own filth, trembling.

It took Wilkinson several seconds to understand what he was seeing. "My God," he said. "What's the matter with these boys? We didn't have this kind of malingering at Valley Forge."

Darrington seemed at a loss for words, but another officer, tall, long legged, also splattered with filth, came ducking out of the hospital tent. To his surprise, Wilkinson recognized the man. "House!" he exclaimed. "What the devil are you doing here?"

"I was passing back this way after delivering your messages to Natchez," Captain House said. The corner of his mouth lifted. "Thought I'd try my hand at common decency for a change. I'm lending a hand to Darrington."

Appalled at House's indiscretion, Wilkinson snapped, "By God, House! Do not speak of our business here!"

House laughed. "Don't worry. I doubt these men are very interested in our important—er—military doings. I just couldn't help hearing your reference to Valley Forge, and I thought it might inspire these chaps to fight a little harder, if you could just tell them some stories about that terrible winter there." House smiled, an insolent gleam in his eyes. "With your friend General Washington, and all."

Wilkinson's face mottled into spots of angry color. He dismounted and grabbed House's arm, jerking him away from the group as Darrington and the others looked on in puzzlement. "Blast you, House! I should have you brought up on an insubordination charge for that! You know damn well I wasn't at Valley Forge." In fact, he'd been part of the infamous Conway Cabal, a group of officers who had schemed to remove Washington from command of the Continental Army—pity they hadn't succeeded! Through gritted teeth, he demanded, "*What—are—you—doing—here?*"

House shook off Wilkinson's hand and turned back to Darrington. "Lieutenant!" he called. "I happen to know a little secret about the general."

Wilkinson's eyes bugged. He pawed at House's sleeve—

"He trained as a doctor!" House announced. "Our prayers have been answered, men! A doctor has arrived in our midst!"

The men all exchanged confused looks. Darrington said in a quavering voice, "Is it true, sir? You were a doctor once?"

House continued to bray. "Yes, he bragged to me all about how he studied in Philadelphia under the most famous physicians of his day! Didn't you, General?"

Wilkinson's breath came in shallow gasps. Darrington and the men all stared at him, open-mouthed. House grinned. Finally Wilkinson said, "Th-that was a—a long time ago." His voice sounded unsteady—and was it any wonder? The effrontery! Without a doubt, House should be shot. It was all he could do to restrain himself from pulling out his pistol and delivering the *coup de grace* on the spot.

Instead, he crossed to his horse and struggled to mount again, his foot slipping in the stirrup. House came forward, chuckling. "Allow me, General." He gave Wilkinson's ass a heave into the saddle.

Once securely seated again on the charger's back, Wilkinson struggled to regain his composure. These men needed leadership and inspiration, now more than ever. He pointed at Darrington. "You—you are in the profession of arms, not medicine! Get this mess cleaned up and move out to rejoin the troops upriver. Understand me, boy?"

"But, sir—"

Wilkinson ignored his whining and pointed at House. "You. By God, sir, you are finished. Your behavior is a scandal! Report back to your unit in New Orleans for your court-martial."

With elaborate courtesy, House gave him a low bow.

The men seemed to be waiting for him to say something else. Wilkinson looked around and spied the man still lying under the tree by the river. He pointed his riding crop and growled, "And for god's sake someone bury that boy. He's dead."

With that, he spurred his horse in a gallop and left the terrible place behind. His mind reeled. House must have taken leave of his senses! Wilkinson felt his hands twitch on the horse's reins. The little whelp! He would crush him—*crush* him—he would pay dearly for his little joke—

He rode on for some time, blind anger consuming him. He scarcely noticed the fine day. It was all spoiled, anyway. Where was the hardihood of days gone by? Nowadays young men couldn't walk two steps without falling out from dysentery or some such nonsense. What had changed? It would be worth looking into—

But for now, he had more pressing matters on his mind. God, he hoped House had at least been telling the truth about delivering the letters. He was counting on Neelly and Runion to get those papers! With any luck, they would be waiting for him when he got to Natchez, ready to complete the deal. He could already imagine the precious journals and maps from the Expedition, safely stowed in barrels of flour and crates of apples, sailing away for Havana...

And who knew? Perhaps they'd even bring him the man himself! Privately, he doubted it—it was hard to imagine James Neelly persuading Lewis of anything. The Chickasaw agent was useful, but a born loser. And as for Runion—well, he could be a bit of a loose cannon at times. Still, the whole idea made him chuckle. Meriwether Lewis a defector to the Spanish! Wouldn't that news be a sensation?

Thus lost in thought, Wilkinson might have passed by the sugar plantation altogether if it hadn't been for the sound of the negroes singing. That morning, he'd sent his aide-de-camp ahead to make arrangements for him to stay the night at Parlange, the home of his old friend, Claude de Ternant, a wealthy sugar planter.

The sweet grass was over eight feet tall, and ready for harvest. Blacks moved amidst the graceful cane, slashing at it with big knives, the sweat pouring off their shiny dark bodies.

Wilkinson found himself unexpectedly moved. After the terrible day he'd had, it was nice to know that there was still such a beautiful thing in the world as happy darkies harvesting crops and singing in the sun. Maybe it *was* time to lay down his sword and retire out here with Celeste.

Enveloped in the warm hospitality of his friend's luxurious home, Wilkinson felt that his troubles were very far away.

After dinner, he begged off after only a short conversation—the day's events had been draining, and he was still several days ride from Natchez. A well-mannered black servant showed him to his cozy guest room and helped him undress, hanging his things up in a cedar wardrobe and taking his boots away to be blacked.

Stripped to his shirtsleeves, Wilkinson settled down uncomfortably in a big armchair. His stomach felt bloated. Probably the turtle soup. He pulled out some papers from his traveling case and looked at them, but his heart wasn't in it. His thoughts kept turning to Don Diego, Meriwether Lewis, and his big payday. What he wouldn't give to know what was happening on the Trace right now!

A soft knock came at the door and the servant poked his head in. "General Wilkinson, sir?" he said. "Master Ternant asked that I bring you these." The black man entered, carrying a small pile of newspapers and another snifter of brandy on a tray. "They came down river today with our regular mail, and he thought you might enjoy taking a look before you turn in." He laid the newspapers on the reading desk, checked on the level of the lamp oil, and turned down the bed covers. "Good night, sir."

After the servant withdrew, Wilkinson pulled the newspapers on to his lap and thumbed through them. Oh good, the *Gazette* from St. Louis. He moved the lamp closer and held the *Gazette* up to his face, tiny print dancing before his brandy-besotted eyes.

After a moment, Wilkinson read:

THRILLING SCENE

On Saturday morning a number of worthy citizens as well as other choice spirits collected in our town and for some cause, which we have not been able to clearly ascertain, rallied to arms against probable treacherous attack from the River. We wait only for the word to be to arms against rapacity, violence, and pillage from what quarter we know not where.

His Excellency the Governor and the General of the Militia being absent from the City, only fueled the wild talk of the large and excited crowd, and threats were made very freely.

Wilkinson gasped. A wheeze of laughter escaped him. "So, the rebellion of Lewis and Clark is on after all!" He felt a deeper laugh bubble up inside him. He could make people do anything he wanted, believe anything he liked.

THE GAZETTE DESIRES TO KNOW

We purposely refrain from mentioning names, or making any comments that would further excite or prejudice the swinish multitudes, but we would like to know the particulars of the posting of Messrs. Lewis & Clarke by the one who calls himself the VIRGINIAN. If tavern stories be evidence, then the pair would stand in need of the chastisement of the Virginian's cane, but thus far it appears that our explorer Governor as well as the hardy brave Kentuckian have been called lyar, rascal, villain, &c for no worthy purpose.

With a shout, Wilkinson threw the paper up in the air. Helpless laughter poured out of him in uncontrollable waves. He felt like a little boy again. Lewis and Clark *posted*--unmasked as common, cowardly rogues. Really, it was too much! Unable to stop himself, he howled and kicked his feet with unrestrained glee, heels drumming the floor.

The black servant peeked in the door. "Sir, are you all right?"

Wiping his eyes and nose with his sleeves, Wilkinson managed to pant, "Fine, fine. Just received some wonderful news about two old friends—"

The negro shook his head and quietly pulled the door to. Wilkinson stared after him for a moment, then collapsed back in the chair in another paroxysm of giggling.

The Virginian! Wilkinson held his aching stomach and tried to bring himself under some kind of control before he made himself sick with hilarity. *God bless Frederick Bates!* God, he hadn't thought about that little Virginia codpiece in months. Back in his own days as governor of Upper Louisiana, he'd always been amused by the way Bates, like a cuckolded husband, had nagged him about pinching pennies and cleaning up the territory--all while Wilkinson carried on with Aaron Burr under his very nose.

Wilkinson covered his face with his hands, his belly still shaking. *That beautiful idiot! So useful, and you don't even have to pay him! He does it all on his own!*

He bent over, wheezing, and gathered the papers up off the floor. His only regret was that Lewis hadn't been there to receive the insults in person. Perhaps he'd have the chance to tell him about it in Natchez in a few days— along with the news that the West was buzzing with talk of his rebellion.

He glanced at the paper again, suddenly struck by something he'd missed the first time.

His Excellency the Governor and the General of the Militia being absent from the City

Egad! Clark on the move too? Surely he and Lewis weren't traveling together! He skimmed the story over, but there were no further details.

No matter. There were big days ahead, and he needed to rest. He climbed into the soft downy bed and arranged the mosquito netting. To force his brain to stop cogitating, he turned his mind to pleasant visions of barrels of flour and crates of apples, bobbing across the sea to Cuba.

He imagined Meriwether Lewis walking the streets of Havana, living out his traitor's life in exile. Or perhaps rotting forgotten in a prison in Mexico City, bearded and mad. Or dead, in an unmarked grave by a lonely road...

Sleepily, he thought of Bill Clark. Clark would stay out of his way. He knew what James Wilkinson could do. And if he didn't—if he'd forgotten— well, then, he would hurt him, very badly and very permanently.

The situation thus resolved in his mind, Wilkinson turned over, let brandy and fatigue overtake him, and drifted into sleep.

Chapter 24
Clark

Fort Pickering, Tennessee
October 6, 1809

Clark smelled Fort Pickering before he saw it. He'd spent years of his life in army garrisons, and he knew well the stink a few dozen men could kick up when encamped in the pristine wilderness. Miles above the fort, his nose could already detect the deep, smoky aroma of burning wood, the sharp bite of the latrine, and the smell of animal flesh—whether smoking, cooking, or rotting, he couldn't be sure.

"Watch it, Cap'n!" York called out. They were passing the confluence of the Wolf River, where it emptied into the Mississippi from the left. The slow-flowing water had formed a large plain of sand and sludge in the riverbed. Clark pulled up on his paddle and smiled as the canoe skimmed over the surface, inches above the muddy bottom.

He noticed York looking at the right bank, where the ruins of an old Spanish fort lay in a heap in the morning sun. Decades ago, Spain had controlled this post, along with many others along the great river. "What do you think about that, York?" he said. "Mark my words, the Spanish'd be up here again in a minute if they had the chance."

York laughed. "That don't seem too likely, Cap'n."

"I'm not so sure, York," Clark said. "Plenty of things that ain't likely have a funny way of happening. Look at brother George. He was set to fight the Spanish once. Now he's about as wrecked as that old fort over there. Where once there was a fortress, now there's just a heap o' rubble."

York was silent for a moment. "I expect there's some life in Massa George yet, Cap'n. You ought not t' get so sour on him."

"Oh, I'm not." Clark grinned. "Many a man has gone to his grave waitin' for George to hang up his fiddle."

The great bluffs that commanded the Mississippi loomed over them on the left; Clark could see the American flag whipping in the air over the log stockade of Fort Pickering. "Here we are at last, York. We'll get ourselves cleaned up, have a little rest, and go see Cap'n Russell. Who knows? Maybe they can even spare a little whiskey for us, if Governor Lewis didn't already clean 'em out."

York laughed. Clark used his paddle as a rudder while York eased himself out into the thigh-high water along the base of the bluffs. They beached the canoe along a narrow sandbar, collected their baggage, and headed on up the trail to the fort.

The two soldiers guarding the gate seemed surprised to see them, but recognized Clark underneath the grime and quickly allowed him and York to enter. A rough-looking enlisted man took York off to show him where he could get cleaned up, while another boy, a beardless private, found room for Clark's baggage in the officer's quarters.

Clark was grateful for the chance to scrub off and unwind. After a while, York came back, looking marginally cleaner. He busied himself laying out some fresh clothes for Clark, but his silent, unsmiling manner told Clark he was upset.

"York," Clark said, "What's eatin' on you?"

"Nothin', Cap'n." York directed Clark to hold his arms up and pulled a fresh white linen shirt over his head, then turned him around and buttoned it up the front.

"Somebody give ya a hard time?"

York looked away, his jaw working in anger, then looked back at Clark. "Cap'n, that soldier I was with, when he found out who we were...well, he told me somethin' about what he seen when Cap'n Lewis was here."

"Well, what'd he say?"

"He said Cap'n Lewis was mighty sick...that he didn't come out of his quarters for a long time. And then when he finally did, he and Pernia weren't gittin' along too well." York swallowed. "He said Pernia was gonna take a stick to the Cap'n, but 'fo' he could, the dog damn near ate him."

Clark burst out laughing. "Lord, I hope it ain't as bad as all that! Here I was, imagining the worst possible things, but that tops anything I could dream up!"

"I don't think he was kiddin', Cap'n." York fastened Clark's cuffs. His face was dark and troubled. "I know you think Pernia's a real good darky an' all, but I'm tellin' you, Billy, he don't have no respect—"

"York, you gotta learn to tell when somebody's pullin' your leg." Clark sat down on an empty bunk and pulled on his boots. "Whatever happened, I doubt it was anywhere near so entertaining. I can't see Pernia ever takin' a hand to Lewis. He ain't suicidal, not that I've ever been able to make out."

The beardless private returned with two plates of fried, pickled salt pork and overcooked beans. He proudly pointed out a side of wild onions he'd placed on the edge of the plate. "We grow 'em in our own garden, sir."

"Thanks, Private. Makes it right homey." At that moment, he'd have given anything he had for some of Julia's cooking, rough as it was. One thing you had to say for Julia was that she tried awful hard. For a second he allowed his thoughts to wander back to his little house on Spruce and Main; Julia would be reading, or sewing, or feeding the baby...

A feeling of homesickness came on him so strong that he consciously pushed the thoughts away. He wouldn't say it to anybody, even York, but after this trip, he intended to put his roaming days behind him for good.

After they ate, York finished dressing him: cravat, waistcoat, Wayne's Legion coat. "Look 'a there, Cap'n," York said. "Ain't near as tight as it was a week ago."

"That's what paddlin' all day and starvin' all night'll do for you, York. C'mon, let's go see if we can find Russell."

They found the captain seated primly behind his desk, shuffling through a small stack of correspondence and paperwork. Russell dismissed the private, then motioned Clark to a chair. York made himself invisible just inside the doorway.

Clark got right to the point. "Russell, tell me what the hell happened here," he said. "It's important. Don't leave anything out."

Russell looked uncomfortable. "Well, first, I just want to say I have no motive for making Governor Lewis look bad—"

"Understood."

"And I don't know what the heck's going on in St. Louis—"

"Just a bunch of silly twaddle," Clark said. "Believe me, it's nothin' to pay attention to."

"Well, I don't know that I'd call rumors of armed rebellion silly twaddle," Russell said. "But I'm sure you know better than me—"

"Wait a minute. What?" Clark stared at him. "Armed rebellion in St. Louis? What are you talkin' about?"

Russell lifted his eyebrows. "We get all the news from up and down the river at Fort Pickering," he said. "From what I hear, St. Louis is in an uproar. There's been talk of declaring martial law up there. I assumed you knew about it."

"Martial law? Why? Did Indians attack the city?" It was impossible; the frontier had been quiet when he'd left just a week ago.

"I don't think so," Russell said. "But apparently, some people are afraid they might. There was even some talk of General Wilkinson sending a battalion upriver to calm things down."

Clark bristled at the mention of Wilkinson's name. *Wouldn't that conniving bastard love an excuse to send troops to St. Louis!* "Russell, who's leading this so-called rebellion?"

"Well, from what I hear, General Clark...you are."

Clark gaped at him. "Russell, that is the most unconscionable, slanderous lie I've ever heard."

"Well, *I* know that," Russell said. "I knew it had no basis in fact, because I saw Governor Lewis. Frankly, I'm relieved to see you here. I didn't know whether you would be able to come, with all the crazy talk going around."

Clark rubbed his forehead; he knew his face must be crimson. "Russell, this is a kick in the teeth, but it doesn't have anything to do with my current business," he said. "I need to get on and find the Governor, *now*. And I need to know what to expect when I do find him. So let's have it out."

Russell stared into his whiskey glass. "Well, when Governor Lewis got here—I guess it would've been about the fifteenth—he was a very sick man indeed. He couldn't walk up here, so I had to send a couple of men down to bring him up on a litter. When I saw the shape he was in, I was appalled."

Russell sighed and pulled his lower lip. "He...he had a terrible fever. And he'd obviously been drinking, *very* heavily...and between effects of the two of them, he'd taken leave of his senses."

Clark swallowed and puffed on his pipe; he doubted Lewis could hold a candle to George at his worst. "Was he raving?"

"I wouldn't call it raving, exactly. He cried, and he begged me for whiskey—which I wouldn't let him have, by the way, I've got a conscience—and then he told me all about his enemies. He was particularly concerned about Secretary Eustis. Said he'd ruined him. Why, the poor devil was so out of his head he seemed to think even General Wilkinson was out to get him."

Clark ground his jaw. The sergeant, the boy who'd brought him the letter, said Lewis was sensible and knew exactly what he was doing. To hear Russell tell it, Lewis was all but a raving lunatic. Surely they couldn't both be right—

"How long was he in that condition?"

"About five days," Russell said. "At one point I took every weapon he had out of the room, because I didn't feel I could trust him not to harm himself.

Then his fever broke, and bam! He was Meriwether Lewis again. Pale and thin, mind you—but at least recognizable."

Clark felt sick to his stomach. He'd expected the news to be bad, but he hadn't expected anything like this. He gulped down his glass of whiskey and regretted it; it churned sourly in the pit of his stomach. "So what kind of shape was he in when he left you?"

"As I said, I had my doubts about letting him go, but he was very insistent. Then Major Neelly showed up, and I felt a little more confident about sending him off over the Trace. Neelly knows that road very well—"

"Whoa, Russell." Clark wasn't sure he'd heard right. "Are you telling me Governor Lewis didn't go down the river to New Orleans?"

"No, sir," Russell said. "He decided at the last minute to take the Chickasaw Trace instead. He seemed to think it'd be quicker that way. And he was *very* adamant that I not tell anyone—anyone but you, that is."

Clark swallowed. "Damn, that's news," he said. "Who's this Major Neelly?"

"He's the federal agent at the Chickasaw Agency in Big Town. I believe his Christian name is James. A good, steady man."

Clark didn't hesitate. "Russell, I'm gonna need two horses. Best you got."

Russell looked surprised. "I already lent two horses to the Governor! I have to have enough left for my own men. You don't mean to say you're going over the Trace after him!"

"That's exactly what I mean to say," Clark said. "I intend to leave this afternoon. So, let's see what you got."

"Well..." Russell hedged. Seeing Clark's expression, he said quickly, "All right. Wait here, please, General. I'll see what I can come up with." With a little sigh of exasperation, he clomped out.

Clark looked at York. "York, I'm startin' to get nervous," he said. "We've heard an earful about Governor Lewis and his state of mind, but all I know is in the letter he wrote me, he sounded plenty clear-headed. I was hopin' we'd have some word from him here, but..."

"I think Cap'n Lewis *did* leave word," York said. "He done changed his whole direction, Cap'n. Maybe that *is* the message."

"Maybe." Clark pulled on his jaw, thinking. York had a point. Lewis said in his letter that men on the boat were plotting to kill him before he reached New Orleans. He'd already gotten off the river once to avoid them. And even if he did somehow manage to make it to New Orleans, who would be waiting for him there? Wilkinson. *He went over the Trace so he wouldn't have to have any truck with Wilkinson—*

Russell came back and called him outside. He'd rounded up a couple of old army nags. "What's the dad-blamed hurry, anyway?"

Clark got to his feet. "Russell, there's a hell of a lot going on. You probably know more than you want to already. I won't trouble you with the rest." He shook Russell's hand. "Thanks for helpin' me, and for lookin' after Governor Lewis. I won't forget it."

He strode back across the camp toward the officer's quarters to collect his things. "York! Get our stuff loaded up! Let's buy some extra rations off these folks, and take a piss or whatever you need to do, because we're goin'!"

York grinned. "Cap'n, I'm already packed and pissed and ready to go." Then his face turned serious. "You gonna write to Miss Julia? Tell 'er we're goin' down the Trace—doin' different from what you said?"

Clark thought about it for a moment. He wanted very much to write to Julia. If it were true what Russell had said about conditions in St. Louis, she'd be frantic. But he couldn't help thinking about what Lewis had said in his letter: *I trust no one now and I beg you tell no one Clark—*

"Tell you what, York—we'll write to her from Nashville, after we've found Governor Lewis. The news'll be better then. Besides, I don't have time to write letters. We got to get on."

"All right, Cap'n." York said. *He's as anxious to go as I am,* Clark thought.

There were several hours of daylight left. He and York saddled up and headed down the Trace. It was a relief to leave Fort Pickering, with its rules and its stink, behind.

Chapter 25
Neelly

Old Factor's Stand, Mississippi Territory
October 6, 1809

S*ome lamb!*

That was all James Neelly could think as he, Governor Lewis, and Pernia pelted away from the scene of the botched assassination trick. Lewis set a killing pace—they swum their horses across Twenty Mile Creek and four other streams and waded through a swamp, covering at least thirty miles from the spot where they'd left Junior Squyres for dead—that poor stupid bastard.

He will not take me, Lewis vowed again and again, even after a rain shower soaked them all to the skin in the late afternoon and he began to shake with fever, his teeth knocking together in hollowed cheeks. He held his rifle across his lap and his left arm against his chest, nursing the wound that Runion had inflicted with the devil's claws. Several times he grabbed his rifle and stumbled into the woods to be sick. Then he came back and remounted, groaning with pain, but still forcing them forward under the sheer vehemence of his willpower.

At sunset, they brought their horses and exhausted dog to a halt at the wilderness inn and trading post known as Old Factor's Stand. Neelly helped Lewis off his horse and left him shivering next to the animal. As he headed into the trading post to arrange for their lodging, Seaman whined after him. The poor dumb beast seemed to be looking to him to help his master. If he only knew...

Lem Ferbers, the old coot who ran the place, was chatting with a Chickasaw man when Neelly entered the log cabin.

"Why, if it isn't Agent Neelly!" Ferbers said. The Chickasaw recognized him too. He was dressed in the old style, his head shaven except for a fearsome crest slicked high with bear oil. "Campin' tonight? Still two bits, four bits if you want a roof." Ferbers winked. "Got some good whiskey too."

Neelly dug out his thin purse. "I reckon I'll take the lodging tonight." He put fifty cents on the table. "I got a couple of people travelin' with me. A man and his nigger. And a dog. Man's feelin' poorly. And we each got horses need seein' to."

Ferbers yelled out the back door to his black man to take care of the horses. "Well, ain't this a crowd tonight," he said. Like most of the stands along the Trace, Old Factor's provided a single log cabin for all the travelers to share. "Well, tell your friend and his nigger to come in and dry off. Hell, we got plenty a' room and plenty a' whiskey."

Just then, Ferbers' black man pushed in the front door. Neelly could hear Lewis yelling, and the black man said, "Massa, you'd better come. This fella actin' mighty strange—"

Neelly shoved his way past the slave, with Ferbers behind and the Chickasaw bringing up the rear. Pernia hurtled towards them, yelling in French. The horses milled around the clearing, ready to bolt into the woods. Lewis waved his pistol. "Get back, get back, you filthy bastard." He cursed at some unseen enemy, kicked at something that *just wasn't there*—

Seaman barked and ran to Neelly with his tail up. Ferbers and the others looked on in amazement. Neelly didn't know what to do. He tried saying, "Gov'ner, you gotta rest. You're sick. It's safe here."

The Governor stumbled, then half-sat, half-sprawled on the ground, his pistol still grasped in his right hand. He was dirty and ragged, the cut on his forehead still raw, left hand swollen, face sweat-slicked and pasty, eyes sunk in bruise-colored caves. Neelly crouched beside him and started to speak, but Lewis interrupted in a husky whisper.

"All I want is some peace, Neelly. That's all I want."

"Gov'ner, I know."

"They'll be comin' after me again. If I don't get to Nashville—" Lewis dropped his head for a moment and whispered, "God, Clark, I need you. Why don't you come? I can't fight these bastards all by myself."

The pistol was on his lap now, and Lewis stared at it for a moment as if he had never seen it before. "I think perhaps there is a way to kill it," he said suddenly. "Because I know where it comes from." He picked the pistol up and examined the barrel. "I can't be a coward."

The expression on Lewis's face was one Neelly recognized. Defeat, despair, loneliness beyond bearing. He recognized it because he'd felt it. Felt it every day since he'd come to this place, no, long before then. Felt it every day since his little daughter had died, an angel strangling in a putrid fever, his wife maddened from grief, blaming him, if he'd only made a decent living, provided like a man should, a healthy house, sunlight, good food. Nothing but a *failure*—

Neelly's hand shot out, grabbed Lewis's shaking wrist, and twisted it. He took the pistol and shoved it inside his own coat. He brushed some of the dirt off Lewis's clothes. "Gov'ner, I know something that'll help. Come on."

He helped Lewis to his feet and steered him towards Ferbers' cabin. Ferbers, his slave, and the Chickasaw stood on the porch, watching, their mouths hanging open as if to catch the swarms of gnats that buzzed around the place in the twilight. Standing apart from the rest, Pernia hugged himself and wept.

The fearsome-looking Chickasaw turned to Ferbers. "You know, I'm not feelin' much like bein' indoors tonight. If it's all the same to you, I think I'll take my two bits back and camp in the yard after all."

"Here ya go, Gov'ner. Down the hatch." Neelly lifted the heavy whiskey jug to Lewis's lips with one hand, putting his other arm around Lewis to support him. Neelly watched his Adam's apple move. One swallow...two...three....

"That's enough." Neelly took the jug back and took a swig himself. The brew burned all the way down. Neelly didn't care. All he wanted was to get drunk.

Out there in the clearing, Governor Lewis had come damn near to finishing the work that Runion had started. And he had stopped him. Why? *Because I'm stupid*, Neelly told himself. Lewis was nothing to him. Just some Virginia cake-eater, a pal of Thomas Jefferson's, for Christ's sake!

Lewis hung his head as if it had become an unsupportable burden. "These vouchers..." he whispered. "They are all legitimate. I am a man of honor."

Pernia was sitting on Lewis's other side, nursing a jug of his own; all three men had their backs to the hearth. "Don't you ever shut up?" Pernia took hold of Lewis's hair, pulled his head back, and sloshed some liquor into Lewis's mouth.

Neelly could feel Ferbers' eyes on him. "Pernia, settle down," he said. He could be on his way to Natchez right now with all the papers and journals. Wilkinson would welcome him with open arms. He'd get paid—at least the five hundred, maybe Runion's share too, and the map to that gold mine out West.

He shuddered, thinking about being rich, and took another pull on his jug. Well, who was stopping him? Certainly not Lewis. The Governor was clutching his ruined green coat around his shoulders as if he were out in a winter storm, instead of sitting two feet from a roaring fire. Shit, he could just take the papers and walk out the door. Governor Lewis wouldn't be able to stop him, most likely wouldn't even know he had done it. Sick as he was, he was probably going to die anyway—

The cabin door opened, and Lewis jerked his head up. It was Ferbers' black man.

"York, thank God you're here," Lewis pulled himself to his feet. His knees were wobbly; two tears streaked down his pale, grimy face. "Where is Clark? I have so many things to tell him." He blinked in confusion. "You're not York."

Neelly went to Lewis and handed him his whiskey jug. The last thing he wanted was for Lewis to go berserk again, looking for his friend Clark. "Here's your milk, Gov'ner," he said. "Perny's gonna put you to bed now, understand?"

In the end, Pernia refused to get Lewis ready for bed, so Neelly did it himself, spreading Lewis's buffalo robe on the floor of the cabin. Lewis insisted on having his saddlebags and trunk of papers brought to him. "Anybody who wants these things is going to have to come through me," he growled to himself, placing the items against the wall behind the bedroll. Then he propped himself up against the wall, holding the whiskey jug in both hands but not drinking from it, watching the door. Seaman settled down by his side and rested his huge head on his paws, looking worried and alert.

"You know, there won't be a damn thing I can do if someone comes through that door," Lewis said. "You took away my gun."

Neelly squatted beside him. "Gov'ner, you need to get some sleep," he said. "You're just wore out. I'll give you back your gun if'n you're feelin' better in the mornin'."

Lewis crinkled his eyes at him in a defiant smile. "I've been in worst spots than this," he said. "I'm all right. You should have been there when we were trying to find the Shoshones. Mosquitoes...eye gnats...needle grass...so many prickly pears, Clark's feet looked like blistered meat. The current was so rapid...the men were giving it everything they had, but we were all just about ready to give out, truth be told. Then, all of a sudden, the country opened up into a beautiful meadow, the place just teeming with beaver and game." He closed his eyes. "It was like paradise."

After a little while, Lewis fell asleep. Neelly watched over him for a few minutes. Again he thought of killing Lewis. Again he thought of taking the papers and leaving Lewis and Pernia to their own devices. Again he thought about the gold nuggets lying on the ground out West, just waiting to be picked up.

But he didn't kill Lewis. He didn't do anything, except take the jug of whiskey, walk outside and sit under a cypress tree, and drink it dry.

At dawn, he woke up to the strong, sonorous sound of the Chickasaw man talking to his horse. The Chickasaw was brewing coffee and frying little pieces of bread for his breakfast. When he noticed Neelly was awake, he laughed.

Neelly dragged himself into a sitting position and roughly combed his hair and beard with his fingers. Seaman was lying on the ground a few feet away. Someone—probably Pernia—must have put him out in the night. Neelly hauled himself up and staggered into the cabin to see what had become of Lewis.

Lewis lay on his side on the buffalo robe, both arms around his saddle-bags. His eyes were closed and he moaned fitfully, still asleep. Pernia knelt by his side, tugging on the bags in Lewis's arms, moving them inch by painful inch out of Lewis's protection. Nearby, the trunk stood open.

Pernia sang very quietly to Lewis, like a lullaby:

Seven long years I'm daily writing
To the Bay of Biscay-o
But cruel death brought me no answer
From my charming Willie-o

He gently removed Lewis's hand from one of the bags, then sat back, waiting to see if Lewis would react. He didn't. With another gentle tug, the bag slipped from Lewis's grasp, and Pernia began to poke through it, still singing in a soothing voice.

If I had all the gold in the Indies
And all the silver in Mexico
I'd give it all to Thomas Jefferson
If he'd send me back my Willie-o

In two strides, Neelly crossed the floor and jerked Pernia up by the back of his collar. Pernia gasped and dropped the saddlebag. Its contents tumbled out, books bound in red morocco leather, the pages covered with writing, drawings, squiggly lines that looked like the rapid current of the river Governor Lewis had told him about last night.

Lewis woke up. He noticed the books with alarm and scrambled to retrieve them and stuff them back into the saddlebags. "For Christ's sake, Pernia," he said. He didn't even seem to notice that Pernia was dangling from Neelly's meaty fist, his feet scrabbling to touch the floor.

Without a word, Neelly dragged Pernia outside, threw him up against the side of the cabin, and slapped him hard across the face. He wanted to kill the little man. He didn't know why; it wasn't really fair. Pernia was only doing what he and Runion had tried to do yesterday.

"Don't hit me!" Pernia held his hands up to protect his face. "Don't hit me! I'm only looking for what's rightfully mine!"

"Yours?" Neelly said. "You're a thief, boy! Stealing from your own master! At least have the self-respect to admit it."

"He owes me two hundred and forty dollars! I'm not a slave! He's not my master! All I want is my money. It's not his, it's mine. Mine!"

"You're crazier 'n he is. He's got all that gold! Why don't he just pay you and be done with it? God knows you're the most worthless servant I ever saw."

"Gold? Gold?" Pernia appealed to the brightening heavens. "God, please help me. Every time I think I've met the stupidest white man in the world, along comes another one!" He slapped his skinny sides and hooted at Neelly. "Oh, yes, the gold mine! *Mon Dieu, monsieur,* take a look around!" Pernia swept his arm around the clearing in a grand gesture.

Neelly blinked in surprise. "But I—"

"No!" Pernia shouted. "Really look!"

Neelly turned his head and took in the whole scene. The log cabins, the fog rising in the cypress swamp, the Chickasaw heading down the trail, Ferbers and his slave getting the trading post ready to open for the day.

"What am I s'posed to be seein'?"

"Nothing!" Pernia said. "There's nothing to see! We're in the middle of nowhere! God has forsaken us! We're dressed in rags, and hooligans are trying to kill us all! I haven't been paid in almost a year, you live in a shack, and the Governor of Upper Louisiana is lying on the floor of a log cabin making love to a bunch of old papers! Tell me, Agent Neelly, do you really think there's a gold mine?"

As Pernia stared into his eyes, Neelly felt himself flush very red. For a moment, he couldn't speak. Pernia smirked.

Finally, Neelly found his voice. "All right. All right. I'm a fool. You're right."

"At least," Pernia said, "You have the self-respect to admit it."

"Sounds like you've been done wrong," Neelly said. "So you just go ahead and keep looking for that money you say the Governor owes you. Go ahead and take it when you find it."

Pernia nodded and started back up to the cabin. Neelly pulled out his pistol. "And when you do, I'll shoot you for the traitorous little piss-ant that you are."

Pernia froze. "You wouldn't shoot me," he said. "You're a federal official."

"I would." Neelly found that he meant it.

They both jumped when Lewis came out of the cabin, slow, stiff-legged, but with his head up. He stood on the porch and took in the scene. Deliberately, he lifted his medicine bottle to his lips and took a large gulp. Neelly watched him with his heart in his throat, expecting him to collapse any second.

"For God's sake, what are you two standing around jawing about?" Lewis shouted. "The sun's up. We've got to get on! With any luck, we can make the Tennessee River tonight, or damn near. Pernia, rustle up some breakfast! And fetch me some water. Lord, I'm dirty as I've ever been in my life. Neelly, get the horses ready. I need you to help me clean up this arm. It hurts like blazes."

Lewis stepped off the porch, yelling at the old man. "Hey mister! You got any bacon?"

Neelly and Pernia glared at each other, then parted, moving to obey.

Some lamb!

Chapter 26
York

Pigeon Roost Road, Tennessee
October 6, 1809

The wild jasmine and bitterapple vines tangled around the tree trunks, climbed the branches, and leapt from one tree to the next. Together they wove a canopy so tight it was as if York and the Captain were riding under a green roof—that is, if a roof could support the weight of thousands of cooing pigeons. York was already bored with the sight, sound, and smell of those birds.

They splashed the horses across several creeks before they came to one that forced them to dismount. It wasn't much of a stream really, narrow and shallow but with steep banks coated with slick cane roots. He and Captain Clark both lost their footing on the way down and fell into the creek, slicking their clothes with mud.

"Looks like that wash at Fort Pickering was a big waste a' time." Clark swatted around his head with his hat. "Damn muskeeters!"

"Ain't bitin' me none," York said. "You the best skeeter bait there is, Cap'n. 'Long as they got you around, they leave this old black hide alone."

As the trail entered into the swamp, mosquitoes and gnats rose in clouds around them. Huge cypress trees towered over stands of cane and scrubby pawpaws. York picked some pawpaws as they passed, the ripe fruit yielding easily to his gentle tug. Tucked inside his shirt, the fruit gave off a strong but pleasant scent.

York watched the tension in Massa Billy's straight back and his hands on the reins of his black mare. It was his job to know his master's moods—he'd been Clark's manservant since he was just twelve and Clark was a reedy fourteen. Before that, they'd been playmates, not a penny's worth of difference between them in those days of playing at soldiering and exploring the wilderness. Though most everything had changed since then, York still liked it best when he and Clark were doing something together like this, hunting or fishing or riding their horses in the woods.

When the trail was wide enough to ride abreast, he pulled even with Clark. His master's face was grim and brooding.

"Frettin' on Cap'n Lewis?" York asked.

Clark didn't answer, just kept watching the road for downed trees and other obstacles.

"Ain't no situation can get the better of Cap'n Lewis," York said. "You 'member, when we was exploring that cave that time, on the Missouri, and he went up on the cliff to get a better look? And fell?" York got the shivers just thinking about it. "Quick as you please, he pulls out his knife and sticks it into that cliff face! And there he is, hangin' there hundreds of feet above our heads, but saved."

"This ain't the same," Clark said.

In his heart, York had to admit Clark was right. In many ways, it was easier to recover from falling off a cliff, ride a raging rapid or escape from a charging grizzly bear than it was to deal with all the problems back in civilization. Sometimes York wished he could talk to Lewis about it. He thought he understood some of what the Captain was going through. On the Expedition, York had discovered he was as good as any white man at most things, and among the best at some—hunting and trading with the Indians, just to name two. But under the slave code in St. Louis, he couldn't carry a gun, ride a horse, or even trade vegetables at the market without a written pass from Massa Billy.

It wasn't his place, of course, but he thought maybe he and Lewis had something in common. They both hated their lives in St. Louis, and neither one of them knew how to get free.

They made camp in a grove of pine trees near a cold stream. Clark went hunting and shot a fat beaver and two squirrels. York fried up the meat along with some mushrooms he'd found growing near the camp site. They ate the pawpaws for dessert, and washed it all down with a swallow of whiskey Clark had bought at Fort Pickering.

After they ate, York tidied up the campsite and laid out their bedrolls. Clark double-checked that the horses were tied and hobbled. York couldn't help noticing that Clark checked his pistols and their rifles, too. "Expectin' trouble, Cap'n?"

"Not tonight. Just good policy to be armed and ready."

They'd passed the worst of the pigeons, and most of the other birds had quieted down for the night. Up above their heads, though, a lone mocking-bird serenaded them with his repertoire of birdcalls. York knew the bird was just staking out his winter territory, and had too much song in his heart to be contained during the daylight hours. He put his hands on his hips and looked up. In the twilight, he could just see the little gray bird, flitting from branch to branch.

"I hope you ain't gonna holler all night," he scolded the bird. "An owl'll get ye if you ain't careful." The bird alighted and fixed York with a yellow eye, then sang again, a lilting, rapid call that York didn't recognize.

In spite of himself, York felt a chill, and over by the horses he saw Clark's back stiffen. That unrecognizable call had to be that rare thing—the mock-ingbird's own true song.

"Did'ye hear that, Cap'n?" York tried to keep his voice light. "I remember when we was little fellas, my mama used to say—"

"I heard it," Clark said, but York felt compelled to finish his thought.

"When the mockingbird sings his own true song, means somebody's gonna die."

York's voice trailed off a little at the end. Billy looked so tired, standing there in the firelight, that for a moment York was afraid he might be upset with him. Then Clark smiled; he was going to make a joke out of it instead. "York, I stopped puttin' much stock in what mockingbirds had to say after we had that one that imitated the garden gate." Clark turned his attention back to the horses. "If we get tired of him singin', we'll just sing right back. Think that's too cruel?"

"Might make his little ears bleed!"

After the chores were done, they stretched out on their bedrolls and watched the fire. Clark pulled a blade of grass and nibbled idly on the end of it, then put it in his mouth. Like most of Clark's unconscious habits, it was one York had seen and noticed a thousand times. It meant that Billy was pretty relaxed, all things considered. And why not? They were on the road, had full stomachs, and were making good time.

York poked a few little sticks into the fire. "Hey, Cap'n. Which ones did you think was prettier—the Mandan girls or the Nez Perce girls?"

Clark chewed his grass stem. "That's a tough one, York. The Nez Perce ladies were damned hospitable..."

"Well, you *was* their favorite doctor."

Clark laughed. "I was a danged fraud, is what I was. But they needed doctorin', and we'd run out of anything to trade." He tapped his temple. "A lot of what ails a person is right up here, York. If you can get people believin' in themselves a little bit, usually they can heal up on their own."

York raised his eyebrows. "So that's why you were always prescribin' body rubs for those young Indian gals? Helpin' 'em to believe in themselves?"

"Well, it worked, didn't it? 'Sides, you were the one they was all het up about. Ol' York, Mister Big Medicine."

"I can't help it I'm so pretty," York said. "I mean to tell you, Cap'n, them gals just about wore me out. But I knowed that makin' friends with the Indians was one of the things we had to do out there, so I just kep' on best I could."

Smiling to himself at the memory, York traced a pattern in the dirt with a twig. It occurred to him that, before they found Captain Lewis and got caught up in a lot of hullabaloo, now might be a good time to bring up the future.

York cleared his throat carefully. "Cap'n, Miss Julia sure is comin' along real nice at home."

"She's made me a real good wife, York."

"Seems like she takes care of you real good," York said. "Most times, maybe you don't need me quite so much as you used'ta."

"I ain't noticed that your duties overlapped that much, York."

It was suddenly difficult for York to meet Clark's eyes. "Well, Cap'n, the only reason I bring it up is—after we find Cap'n Lewis and get to the Federal City and all, I was figurin' you might could spare me for a little while. I could go ahead and ride on to Louisville, and spend a little time with my Lilely."

He forced himself to look at Clark. His master's expression was unreadable, so he kept talking, selling it. "See, you prob'ly know, her massa's fixin' to move all the way down to Mississippi territory, way South." York heard his voice catch. He couldn't help sounding desperate. "And that means I won't ever be seein' her anymore after that." His insides twisted. Never to hold her skinny little body next to his again, or feel her tender touch on his cheek. Lord, not to mention the children!

"Please, Billy—you could hire me out. You wouldn't lose nothin'."

For a long moment, Clark didn't say anything. York had no idea what he was thinking. But he leaned forward, hoping—it really didn't seem like much to ask...

Clark was silent for the longest time. Then, he shifted his blade of grass to the other side of his mouth and said slowly, "Well, York! Seein' as you're in such a travelin' mood, maybe you'd like to take a little trip down to New

Orleans instead."

York froze. For a moment, he couldn't believe his ears. *New Orleans!* For him, for any slave, that meant only one thing—the auction block.

His mind spun with horror and regret. He saw himself chained and manacled inside a pen. Men came, looked him over. One of them liked what he saw. The auctioneer made him run and dance. The man thought he looked strong—

Sold! To a stranger—

And then what? He wasn't afraid of hard work—on the Clark farm where he grew up, the whites and blacks had worked side by side to clear the fields, put up the fences and the buildings, tend the livestock, chop wood, hunt deer and turkeys. He'd always worked hard. He could hunt buffalo and elk, build fires, pole a keelboat, paddle a canoe...take care of Massa Billy when he was sick, handle a gun and protect his back when he was well...

He saw himself picking cotton, slashing cane, under the overseer's lash.

Branded—like livestock! Whipped and chained if he did wrong—

Clark watched him, still nibbling on that blade of grass. York stared at him with a rising sense of panic. Why had he said anything? Why hadn't he just left well enough alone?

"Massa Billy, I didn't mean nothin'..."

Their eyes met for several long seconds. Then, Clark made a low, rumbling chuckle in his chest and sat up. He stretched and laughed good-naturedly. "Just teasin', York. You should see the look on your face."

York felt his heart sink somewhere around his stomach. His armpits felt cold and sticky. He was limp with fear. He tried to laugh. Massa Billy liked smiling faces.

"You had me goin', Massa."

The corner of Clark's mouth lifted. "You know better'n that." He stood up and pulled out his shirttail. "Well, I'm gonna check the horses one more time, York. Then we best turn in. We got another big day ahead of us tomorrow."

York nodded. Billy wandered off for a few minutes, then came back and rolled himself up in his bedroll. York could have sworn he was still chuckling.

York couldn't sleep, even after he moved his own bedroll to the other side of the fire, so he wouldn't have to look at Massa Billy. Instead, he turned his back to the fire and stared out into the darkness.

When he tried to think of Lilely and the children, emptiness swelled up inside him. It had been six years since he'd spent much time with her. Three years gone on the Expedition, and then the move to that hateful town, St. Louis...Once she and the kids were gone away to Natchez, she would be gone forever.

He'd mentioned this before to Billy. Billy had offered to buy him a new wife.

When he tried to think about the Expedition, the greatest time in his life, bitter tears almost choked him to death. Clark had been right. The Indians had thought he was "big medicine." Most of them had never seen a black man before. All the women had wanted him. The men had thought he was so unusual, he must be the bravest warrior among them. That had been great—but it hadn't been the best part of the journey. No, the best part was the camaraderie with the other men. All of those white boys, and he'd worked alongside them, shared in all the hardships and all the triumphs. He went on important scouting missions by himself. Captain Lewis said he was the best trader.

He was almost as good as a white man. Desperately, he thought: *I was as good as a white man.*

He twisted his bedroll in his hands. Once, he and Clark had been as close as two men could be, like two crossed fingers. He'd been happy when he'd realized Clark was going to take him on the trip across the continent. Not that he'd had a choice about it—but if he had, he would have chosen to go, even though it meant leaving his wife behind for a little while. How many men got the chance to go see things no other man had ever seen?

Before the Expedition, he'd always thought that Clark could do anything. During the journey, he'd seen that he'd been right. Clark was strong—his idea of being sick was to go on a twenty-five mile scouting run. Clark was brave—he'd stood at sword point, outnumbered six to one by Teton Sioux, and the Sioux had backed down. Clark had taken their canoes over rapids so dangerous that even the Indians were afraid to attempt them. He would have followed Clark into hell.

He still would. But hell and St. Louis were two different things. At least he used to think so.

York turned on his back and blinked at the stars. For a slave, being a manservant meant he was at the top of the heap. He'd been spared many of the humiliations that were the lot of common field darkies. Not only that, he was the favorite slave of a particularly good man. Everyone thought so; he thought so as well. So maybe this was his own fault. If he hadn't pushed Billy, back in the spring, maybe things would still be good between them.

But he had pushed him, and something terrible had happened. The details were burned into his mind, as if it had happened just yesterday—

It was back in May.

York was supposed to be planting the summer vegetables. Instead, he leaned on his shovel, missing Lilely, feeling mean, smoldering. Clark came out of the house and berated him.

"York, I want to see a smile on your face and some action with that shovel!"

"Cap'n, I done told you," York said. "I want to go back to Louisville."

"We live in St. Louis now," Clark said. "I've been more'n fair, York. I've been damn lenient. For Christ's sake, you spent five months in Louisville already, and it was only supposed to be five weeks. And you sure as hell ain't been much service since you got back. You hop to, you hear?"

"You didn't have no complaints when I was totin' your stuff all over the continent," York said. "I didn't sign on for no St. Louis. I'm a Kentucky boy."

Clark growled, "You're whatever kinda boy I tell you to be."

York shook his head. "You ain't doin' right by me, Cap'n. After all I done, you oughta set me free."

Clark's face flushed red. "I can't afford to set you free." His voice twisted with sarcasm. "And I'm sick and tired of hearing about your immense services. I need you to work!"

York turned over a small amount of dirt. "Maybe I don't feel like working for you no more. I want to go back to Louisville."

In a brief instant, York realized he had gone too far, but it was too late. Clark charged at him, pulled the shovel out of his hands, and threw it aside. Clark struck him in the face, a tremendous blow that sent York reeling to the ground. He saw stars. "Billy, no—"

Clark jerked him back to his feet. He shook York, and slapped him with those big hands. Even though he was almost as tall as Clark, and heavier, York felt terrified, especially when Clark told him, his voice rough, raspy, not sounding like Billy at all: "I am the *master*. You understand? You are the *slave*. Goddamnit, I'm gonna make sure you never, *ever* forget it again."

"I won't, Billy, I won't. I'm sorry—" York heard himself babbling.

Clark dragged York out back of the house and went into the stable, picking up a length of cord and a horsewhip. Somewhere in the background, York heard the other slaves react. Nancy and Easter started to cry. Easter wailed, "No, Massa Billy, don' whip York!" Scipio hissed, "Hush up, girl!"

In all their years together, York had been the good darky. He was never bad. He never needed to be punished. Billy grabbed his shirt and tore it off his body. He seized York's hands and bound them together, his movements strong, angry, precise. York felt helpless to resist. All his life, he'd been raised to take care of Billy, to protect him. To obey him.

He'd seen men and women lashed before. His fellow blacks, of course, and the white men in the Army too, Lord, the floggings they took! Fifty lashes—one hundred—dozens of blows from the gauntlet. But never York! He wasn't any common field hand! He couldn't help struggling as Clark looped the other end of the rope around a limb of the pecan tree and hauled York's arms above his head.

"Naw, no, no Billy, please, I'll be good, I'll be happy, I swear—"

Clark came around and faced him. His hair had come loose from its queue. He looked wild. He told him, "York, I'm gonna give you a whipping you won't ever forget." He stepped back.

Twenty-five lashes. Or it might have been a thousand.

York had always thought that if he ever got whipped, he'd be brave. He wouldn't yell or cry. But oh Lord, that swish, that crack, that burn, that trickle of blood, all in the space of a single second—the pain was worse than he ever imagined. He couldn't help it. He yelled and cried. He was loud and he was scared.

The worse part was the uneven pause between the blows. If there had been some kind of rhythm, maybe it would have been easier. But after about five strikes, time seemed to stretch, longer and longer between each lash. York realized that Billy was nerving himself for the next strike. He would have screamed, "Get on with it!" if the pain wasn't so bad when the whip finally fell upon him.

He lost track. He still didn't know whether Billy had really given him twenty-five lashes. He remembered Billy cutting him down. He heard Billy say, "Nancy, take care of him." And then, his voice shaking: "Scipio, go get the doctor."

York had thought he was going to die, though of course he didn't. As whippings go, Nancy said it hadn't been a bad one. Nothing like the ones Miss Julia's father handed out back in Virginia. York was up and around again within a few days.

With a smiling face, of course.

The whipping was like another birth, into a new world in which he didn't have Billy Clark for a friend anymore. His friend was dead, replaced by this strong, harsh man who had beaten him bloody, who would not let him go home, who would not understand that he could love a woman, who no longer seemed to remember their childhood games, their youthful conspiracies, their easy companionship of young manhood, their shared suffering and success on the trail.

A man who joked about selling him out of the only life he'd ever known, to an unknown fate in New Orleans, and required him to laugh about it.

Maybe it would be easier, York thought, if Clark really were dead. At least then he wouldn't have to look at him, to see his warm smile and his easy laugh and his goddamn bravery and decency and loyalty—and feel hatred.

He had crossed the continent. He had come back to St. Louis. Everything had changed, and nothing had changed. He had left for the West, a man who knew his place. There, thanks to Billy Clark, he had tasted freedom and equality. Sometimes, York wished he had never gone on the Voyage of Discovery. Maybe if he had never learned what it was like to be a free man, he would still be a happy one.

He wiped his wet face with his sleeve and looked at the stars. Above his head, the mockingbird was still singing.

Chapter 27
Lewis

Colbert's Ferry, Tennessee River
October 8, 1809

It must have been a nightmare.

The cruel light of dawn poked through the trees, stabbing Lewis in the eyes. He winced away from it, screwing his eyes shut, trying in vain to stave off a brain-numbing headache.

They were camped in the woods somewhere near the Tennessee River, but he had no memory of getting to this place last night. What he did remember couldn't possibly be true. It was too horrible, too fantastical, to be anything other than a product of fever and exhaustion.

He tried to sit up and immediately regretted it. A wave of nausea gripped him and he rolled over on his elbows, gagging up a stream of rust-colored liquid. He scrabbled in the dirt for a minute before managing to shove himself onto his haunches and take in the scene around him.

His saddlebags were on the ground next to him. A pasty Neelly was asleep on his bedroll nearby, his breath ruffling his beard with each exhalation. Pernia was sleeping too, his coat thrown over him like a blanket, his back to the dying fire.

Seaman nuzzled Lewis's hand with a cold nose. "Jesus, Seaman, what the hell happened last night?" Lewis whispered, petting the dog's head with a shaky hand. "I barely remember anything—"

But he did remember. They'd been traveling hard since leaving Old Factor's Stand yesterday morning. Riding all day, stopping only to eat, camping in the woods. He was sick, so sick, but he wouldn't let them stop. Couldn't. Wilkinson's men were chasing him, and they'd probably catch him in the end. But at least he'd make them work for it.

And of course, the goddamn wolf besieged him. The attacks became so constant, and were mounted with such dizzying speed, that after a while he couldn't continue. He just slid off the horse and sat on the ground, desperate to stop the cacophony of violence inside his own head.

Then Neelly gave him his medicine and took him to some doggery for a drink. The place had been...what? A shack? A cave? Some half-forgotten gate of hell? In the back of his mind, he could see Jefferson in the parlor at Monticello, half-glasses perched on his nose, volume in his hand. Jefferson was reading out loud:

Through me the way into the suffering city,
Through me the way to the eternal pain,
Through me the way that runs among the lost ...
Abandon every hope, ye who enter here.

His memory resolved itself into a kaleidoscope of disturbing images. With Neelly, he walked into the wretched hole on his own power. Wisely, Pernia decided not to come. The place reeked with the smell of filth and debauchery. Twisted, fervid faces pushed close to him, a stranger. In this low den, it seemed that a gentleman, even a squandered one, was something of a curiosity.

Somebody—he supposed it was Neelly—shoved a drink down his throat, then they sat down at a table with a red-headed whore. She pressed herself on him, rousing him with a dirty hand on his trousers. Her hand was surprisingly strong. Then she pulled up her skirt and showed him something so repulsive his ardor had wilted immediately. Neelly snapped at her, doglike, and drove her off.

After that, there ensued a kind of strange hilarity. He unburdened himself to the peculiar, assembled multitudes. He told them all about Eustis and Wilkinson, and his dishonored vouchers, and how Jimmy Madison had no vision for the West except chopping it to pieces. It was all very merry and raucous. He'd felt among friends. Then, as usual, he went too far. One of his avid listeners, a large she-male, took umbrage with his politics and gave him a great wallop to the jaw. Next thing he knew, he was being tossed bodily out into the night.

Lewis groaned. It couldn't have happened that way. It was too bizarre to be real. He ran his hand along the stubble on his jaw and felt a big, painful lump. He shivered.

As he looked around the dismal clearing, he remembered something else. A man had helped him last night. At least, the creature had looked like a man, albeit a very small one. He'd had wild, dun-colored hair and beard, and a beetled brow. He spoke no language Lewis had ever heard before. The man took him to a warm, quiet place, where everything was sized in proportion to himself. He cleaned him off and let him rest for a while. Then they had a long and spirited conversation about his trip to the Pacific Ocean.

Although the man spoke a tongue unique to himself, he seemed to understand Lewis perfectly. He showed Lewis his prized possession, an extraordinary bluejay that bobbed and trilled and hopped about on his arm. Lewis knew the man's very decency belied his existence; in this place, such kindness existed only in the imagination. But still, the details were so vivid and fascinating he couldn't help wishing it were true.

Then, he remembered another detail. Sometime during the long night, he wrote a lengthy letter to Clark. He told Clark everything about Wilkinson: what Wilkinson had asked him to do and how he'd encouraged him to involve Clark in the scheme. He told him how he'd rebuffed Wilkinson, and that Wilkinson had promised to destroy him—was even now destroying him—

He told Clark other things; shameful, terrible things he had done during these last pathetic and dire weeks of his life. Deceptions, weakness, failings...things he should've told Clark long ago. For perhaps in the very act of telling, they might have disappeared. But when he'd had the chance, standing face to face with his friend, he'd been too much of a coward.

Lewis choked, despising himself, despising his own tears. None of it was real. He hadn't really written the letter—he hadn't done a goddamn thing to make things right with Clark or anyone else. He was a coward still.

He sighed and wiped his eyes roughly with the heel of his hand. He had no excuse, and there was no point crying about it. He pulled his saddlebags over and began to check through them. His journals and papers were there, and in order. Money, powder, balls, flints...

A ragged edge sticking out of one of the journals caught his eye. It was the journal he'd been writing in recently. He pulled it out of the saddlebag and examined it. Propping it open to the first blank page, he was astonished to see a number of leaves had been torn out. Confused, he flipped back to the last entry he'd written. It was there, and complete.

The first page after the torn edges was ink-stained. On the reverse page of his last written entry was a drawing. It was a picture of a bird in his own hand. A sketch of a bluejay.

Lewis stared at it, dumbfounded. Could he have written to Clark after all? If there was a letter, where on God's earth had he left it? He laughed, remembering how once during the Expedition he'd pinned a message for Clark to a tree, only to have a beaver come along and cut it down. Clark would have about as much chance of finding this one—presuming it existed at all, other than in his own disordered mind.

Neelly rolled onto his back and rubbed his face and beard with both hands, trying to wake himself up. "No 'fense, Gov'ner, but for the life of me, I can't imagine what in the Sam Hill you have to be laughin' about."

Lewis shook miserably. "Neelly...what did I do last night?"

"Oh, Christ! Don't ask!" Neelly dragged himself into a sitting position. "Man, when you get liquored up, you got a mouth on you...I felt lucky to get outta that place alive."

"But after that..."

"After that, you just disappeared! It took me forever to find you. When I did, you were walkin' your horse in the woods, happy as you please, just like you was strollin' along a Virginia fence on a summer's day."

Seaman crowded against Neelly, sniffing and licking at his beard. Neelly swore under his breath. "Gov'ner, would you please to call your dog?"

"Seaman," Lewis whispered. The dog ambled back to him. He hung onto Seaman's body for strength and warmth. He knew he'd have to get up soon. But he hurt so much, and he was so tired. He wished he could just stay here and sleep forever.

Neelly got up and pissed against a tree, then kicked Pernia into wakefulness. "Get up, you damned rascal. We ain't gonna dally all day so you can take your dang beauty sleep."

Pernia uncoiled from his bedroll like a snake. "Fuck off, cracker-boy. It's not my fault you two went on a spree last night."

Neelly flushed and brandished his fist at Pernia. "Boy, when we get to Nashville, first thing I'm gonna do is buy me a piece of big, strong rope—"

"Aw, leave off will you?" Lewis rubbed his splitting head. "You two sound like a pair of blasted old biddies. Pernia, knock it off! Cook us some goddamned breakfast! Neelly, let's get ready to break camp. I want to be across the river this afternoon."

For some reason, they did what he said. Neelly started saddling and unhobbling their horses; Pernia got out some coffee and sugar and got busy building up the fire. Lewis didn't understand how he still had the power to command them when he no longer had the power to control himself. But at least it was useful.

He left them and staggered off among the trees. He had a burning need to urinate. He steadied himself against a loblolly pine, unfastened his trousers, and managed to squeeze out a small dribble. It was less piss than blood.

Lewis sucked in air. He fastened his pants and leaned against the tree, listening to the steady pounding of his own heart. He felt numb. He was disintegrating from the inside out. There was no one to help him—

In his misery and terror, he panicked. That was when it happened. The wolf bit him.

As in a dream, he could see what was about to happen, but he couldn't stop it, for he could neither run nor scream. The beast was on him before he could make a sound. It lifted itself slowly, its greasy fur agleam, its gray eyes fixed and dead, the great tongue lolling out to curl around his arm.

He watched in slackjawed, terrified fascination, knowing what it was going to do as sure as if it had already happened. The wolf did have a smell; it stank of sulfur and nitrate. It bit down hard on his swollen arm, its foul yellow fangs fitting neatly into the holes left by the devil's claws, as if they had been made for the purpose. It gripped him, growling, the dark venom flowing into his blood—

It was agony. He sank under the horror of it. Then, suddenly, it was gone. He was on the ground, his back against the tree, his arm lying in his lap, numb. Neelly stood over him.

"Gov'ner?" Neelly waved a hand in front of his face. "Sir? You gonna be able to get up and have some breakfast? We got to get on to the river."

Lewis stared at him. He felt tears starting down his cheeks. He couldn't speak. He opened his mouth, but all that came out was a strangled whine.

"Oh, Jesus," Neelly said. "Here...lemme help ya." Lewis shrank away from him, but Neelly gripped him firmly under the armpits and hauled him to his feet. "C'mon, Gov'ner...let's go. I'm takin' you to Nashville. Move your feet, now...that's the way..."

With an arm around him for support, he allowed Neelly to half-push, half-drag him back to camp. He sat down in a heap by the fire and winced as Pernia shoved a hot cup of coffee into his hand and a plate of cornbread into his lap. Lewis couldn't eat. Instead, he stared at his ruined arm. The thing had bitten him... polluted him with its hatred...

"Poison—" he choked.

"Christ, don't think I wouldn't, if I had any," Pernia said. "Should've done it long ago, when you still had credit. Then I wouldn't be in this mess now."

Lewis turned his face away. The wolf's attack drove him deep inside himself, the only place he could retreat, where he still could find some corner of the world that seemed bearable.

He thought about it as they rode along. The West. Endless, golden hills, silver rivers running cold and clear over smooth river stones. Great pine forests...beaver, elk, deer, buffalo, enormous bears. The men singing as they poled the pirogues along. And Clark, always there, watching every bend of the river, making his calculations, writing his observations down in his field notes, much more faithfully than he did. And always, in the distance, the Shining Mountains.

Those were the best times. He would walk on shore, with his rifle and journal and Seaman, just exploring. No white man had ever seen these places before: they were the first. When he came back to the river, Clark would be there, with the red and the white pirogue, and the men would eat and dance by the firelight. He and Clark would talk over what they had done that day, and what they would do the next; he always felt smarter and stronger when they were together.

Now, he was alone. There was no Clark.

Another endless day. The sun reached its zenith and began to descend. And so here he was, at another river. It was wide, deep, dark, and swift. He had finally reached the Tennessee. The river was too big and fast-flowing to swim their horses across, so they had come to this crossing, a place where a man named George Colbert operated a ferry. Neelly said they had to cross here; it was the only ferry within fifty miles.

While Neelly haggled with Colbert, Lewis dismounted and leaned against his horse in the cold twilight. He found his medicine bottle and took a gulp of laudanum. Next to him, Pernia stamped his feet and slapped himself, trying to stay warm. His incessant bitching sounded like the whine of some nettlesome insect.

Lewis half-expected Wilkinson's man, the one who had escaped, to try to trap him here and finish the job. But the woods were quiet and still. Lewis felt almost disappointed. What the hell could he be waiting for?

Neelly talked to the ferry operator for a very long time. Lewis ground his teeth. This man Colbert was an odd-looking fellow, with white skin, but long plaited hair and Indian features. He had his arms folded across his chest, and he wasn't saying much. Colbert's ferryman stood on the flatboat, leaning on his pole and grinning.

Neelly didn't look like he thought it was too funny. He threw his hands in the air and walked a few steps away from Colbert, then turned back and said some angry words. Colbert's expression didn't change. Neelly looked back at Lewis and Pernia and let his hands fall to his sides, helplessly. The boatman laughed and let out a loud fart.

"This is *intolerable*," Lewis said. His poisoned arm throbbed. He left Pernia at the edge of the woods and strode down to the river.

"Neelly, what's the problem?"

"This fella wants eight dollars to take us all across the river," Neelly said. "A dollar each for us, a dollar each for the horses, and two dollars for the baggage. Gov'ner, that's highway robbery! I just flat out won't pay it."

Lewis looked at Colbert, then back at Neelly. "Did you tell him you're the federal agent?"

"That don't cut no ice with him. He's got the exclusive gov'ment contract in these parts."

Lewis looked at Colbert's expressionless face. "And he cannot be bargained with?"

Neelly shook his head no. Just then, Colbert's eye fell upon Seaman, who had followed Lewis down to the edge of the river. "Ah, you have a dog, too? A dollar extra for the dog. Nine dollars."

Neelly's eyes popped. The boatman laughed and farted. The sun began to slip down behind the trees.

Something sprung loose inside Lewis's head. He was fed up with these people and their goddamn games! He pulled out his pistol, cocked it, and put the muzzle against Colbert's temple.

"Maybe I'll just blow your brains out, you sonofabitch!"

"No, Gov'ner!" Neelly gasped. Colbert's face took on an actual expression: scared witless. The boatman jumped into the water, clinging to his pole. Up by the trees, Pernia hit the ground with a shriek.

"We'll pay you *four fucking dollars*, for the *whole fucking lot*." Lewis tapped the muzzle against Colbert's temple with each word. "Sound good?"

Colbert nodded, sweat shining on his upper lip. "Yes! Fine! Four dollars sounds more than fair."

"*All right.*" Lewis lowered the pistol and stuck it back in his coat. "Pay the man, Neelly! And you, get these goddamn horses loaded!"

Without looking at him, Colbert dragged his boatman out of the water and moved to obey. Neelly looked like he was going to cry. "Gov'ner...You cain't go around *doin'* that—"

"Why not?" Lewis snapped. "It worked, didn't it? You got to *deal* with these people, Neelly! You got to *deal* with 'em!"

Within minutes, Colbert led their horses onto the flatboat, hobbled them, and secured their baggage. Neelly paid Colbert his four dollars. Sniveling, Pernia followed them on board. It was a fast trip across the river.

Chapter 28
Clark

Big Town, Chickasaw Agency, Mississippi Territory
October 9, 1809

It didn't take long for Clark and York to locate the federal agent's cabin at the Chickasaw agency. It was the shabbiest one in Big Town. The front step was broken, the oiled paper was broken out of several windows, and leaves had accumulated against one side of the house. As they watched, a feeble breeze lifted more leaves onto the pile.

"This place looks deserted, Cap'n," York said.

"Naw, just our federal government, keepin' its employees in style as usual. You'd think he might fix it up a little on his own, though." Clark dismounted and jumped up on the front porch. Giving the door a sharp rap, he called, "Agent Neelly? Anybody home?" He peeked through one of the torn windows. "No sign a' life inside either."

They let themselves in and poked around, hoping for a message from Lewis. There wasn't a trace of his presence anywhere. Even Neelly didn't seem to have left much of a mark. The living quarters were musty and barely inhabited; in the office, only the stacks of paperwork gave any hint that a federal official operated out of the place.

Clark sighed and clomped back out on the porch. He swung his arms, trying to dispel some of his restless energy. Leaves swirled around the clearing. Clark watched a line of dark clouds on the horizon and silently directed them to break up before reaching the Trace. He needed to make time; they were probably still days behind. *Wait for me, Meriwether.*

"Come on, York," he said. "Let's find out where we can get a decent meal. Then we'll head out and get a few more miles under our belts before sundown."

Down the road, they found a tavern run by a woman named Emahota. With the threatening skies, the small hut had already started to fill up with travelers of all races. Clark and York found a table and soon were enjoying a meal of hot fried venison, wild greens, and a pumpkin-corn stew that York pronounced the best thing he'd ever eaten.

"Not bad," Clark said. It was pleasant to be in out of the elements and have a good woman-cooked meal. He found himself wanting to linger. York gazed at the tall tankards of home-brewed beer the woman was serving at the next table and turned to him with silent, imploring eyes. "God, York, don't tempt me." Clark pulled out his watch. "We got at least an hour and a half of daylight. Depending on the road, we could make six or eight miles. We best get going."

They pushed back from the table and ducked out of the hut. A roll of thunder sounded in the distance.

"Looks like we gonna get wet asses," York said.

"Won't be the first time," Clark replied.

As he and York untied their horses and got ready to leave, a Chickasaw family arrived on a single pony. An older man with long, loose hair dismounted and extended his hand to a very young woman clutching a baby about Lew's age. The girl, wearing a loose petticoat that showed off a pair of well-shaped calves, looked pretty and windblown. The wriggling baby had obviously discovered the sound of his own voice. He yelled good-naturedly at everything around him. The sight made Clark a little homesick. He couldn't help being reminded of another little Indian mother he'd once known—

The accident happened so quickly that for a moment Clark didn't realize what had happened. One minute, the girl was handing the baby down to the older man; the next minute, she was lying on the ground, writhing and screaming in agony. The baby wailed in the dust. Along with the Chickasaw pony, the Army horses jumped and whinnied in alarm.

Clark slid off his horse, tossed the reins into York's hands, and raced across the yard. The man was trying to control the pony before it trampled his family. Clark scooped up the baby and thrust him into the arms of Emahota, who had run out of the tavern. He turned his attention to the horse, but the man managed to lead it a short distance away, where York helped him tie the animal to a hitching post.

He crouched down by the girl. Crying with pain and distress, she had pulled herself up into a sitting position. She hunched forward, gripping her forearm and holding her upper arm away from her body.

"'S'all right, 's'all right," Clark said. "You'll be fine, sweetheart." He looked up and saw the older man loping back. Clark raised his eyebrows. "Your baby all right, mister?"

The man crouched on the other side of the sobbing girl. "Grandson. Just a little scared. I don' know what happened! Kasy was gittin' off, baby got loose, all a sudden they both fell—"

"Kasy? Your daughter?"

The man nodded. "She don' have much English."

Clark touched the girl gently on the back. "Kasy, you're gonna be feelin' right pert again in no time. I promise." To the father, he said, "Arm's either broken or dislocated. I think I can help. I know a little doctorin'."

The girl cried as Clark and her father helped her to her feet. A few fat raindrops smacked into Clark's coat; the storm clouds had paid no attention to his command to break up and leave them alone. Emahota led them to a dog run cabin. One side appeared to be her own residence; the other space she rented out to travelers. She showed them to her own side of the cabin. York followed with the baby, then went back to take the horses to Emahota's barn for the night. From the sound of the thunder in the distance, it was just as well they hadn't set out on the trail.

With the father and Emahota in attendance, Clark spoke to the girl in a quiet, fatherly voice, and with gentle hands probed her arm and shoulder. It was as he had suspected; the normal plump contour of the shoulder felt scooped out.

"Good news is, it ain't broken," Clark said.

The father looked relieved. "Then what's hurtin' her so bad?"

"Shoulder's dislocated. Hurts worse than a break. I can put it back, but it'll hurt."

The father talked to the girl in the strong tones of the Chickasaw language. The girl's replies sounded like the call of an injured songbird. She turned wide brown eyes on Clark. He smiled. "I know what I'm doin', girl," he told her. "Trust me."

She managed a brave little smile and allowed him to take her elbow. With patience, he was able to bend it and gently bring her upper arm close to the side of her chest. She let out a fierce whimper, tears running from her eyes.

"'S'all r ight, Kasy," Clark said. "You're doin' fine."

He stood up and moved behind her. He wanted to get this right the first time. He slipped his forearm between her arm and chest, and then quickly grasped her shoulder in a strong grip and heaved upwards. She screamed— he felt the resistance of her muscles fighting the movement—but he didn't flinch. The muscles gave against his pressure, and the shoulder slipped back into place. He stayed behind her, holding the shoulder firmly, while the girl cried out the rest of the pain.

After seeing to the horses, York hurried to find Massa Billy and the Chicka-saws. Emahota almost bumped into him on her way back to the tavern. She stopped York. "Your master's a good doctor."

"I know," York said. "That little gal all right? And the baby?"

"Yeah," Emahota said. "Reason I mention it, there's a feller bad hurt in my other cabin. White feller. He got shot a few days back. One of our healers took a look but there was nothing he could do. We figured he'd die. Now he's been in my cabin almost a week. Not dead, but dyin' a little bit each day."

"Ain't he got any folks?"

Emahota shrugged. "Lots of the white people around here don't have folks. They stay a little while, then they leave. Who knows why they come or where they go. I was hoping that Agent Neelly'd come back and see to him. I reckon he's in charge of the white people around here if anybody is. Anyway, maybe your master could look at him. I'm tired of having him in my cabin."

She motioned York into the tavern and handed him a jug of water and a lantern. Then, she thumbed towards a small ramshackle cabin beyond the dog run. "That's where you'll find him."

Thunder rolled in the blackening sky and raindrops bounced off his hat as York trudged across the yard. He had a sinking feeling. Usually, when people seemed especially anxious to assign him a task, it was a good indication that it wasn't going to be anything that he'd ever want to do. Take that winter at Fort Clatsop, for example. The rainy climate had made their camp on the western shore a haven for bugs, and Massa Billy had given him the special chore of turning over his bedding and killing all the fleas every day. That was one job he could have lived without—

York eased open the cabin's rough-hewn door. The smell of sweat and human filth hit him so hard that his eyes watered and his nose stung. He held out the lantern, illuminating the figure of a large man sprawled on a mat on the floor.

"Mister?" York said. "You alive?" He crept in and set the lantern to one side, then hunkered down alongside the man. He looked to be a young fellow, big and fat but scarcely more than a boy. His plump cheeks were bagged and gray; his lips were flecked with old vomit. His breath came in labored, rattling gasps.

York let his gaze travel down, looking for the gunshot wound. He winced. Right in the gut. Emahota was right. This boy was dying. There wasn't anything could be done about a wound like that.

The fat man stirred fitfully. "Water—please, water—"

York slipped one arm under his shoulders and lifted him enough to take a swallow out of the jug.

"Yer an angel of mercy," the boy choked.

"You know, that's the first time in my life anybody's ever called me an angel," York said. "What's your name, mister?"

"Junior," the boy said. "Junior Squyers."

"Well, Junior, I'm York." He tried to think what to do. He didn't think Billy had brought any opium for killing pain, but he could ask him. Clark might have some ideas about how to ease this man's passage out of this life—

"He shot me." The boy pawed at York's arm with clammy fingers. "He shot me. The sonofabitch shot me."

"Looks that way," York said. "Now you hush, don't worry. Everything'll be all right soon."

"Sonofabitch, sonofabitch, he shot me." Squyres gagged with the effort to speak. York wished he had something to wipe the boy's fevered face. He'd better go get Billy—

"Wasn't s'posed to be like this. It was s'posed to be so easy. But he shot me, man. That sonofabitch—"

"Who was this sonofabitch, Junior?"

"Meriwether Lewis."

York was so startled he fell backwards on his heels. Scrambling up on to his knees, he gripped the boy's cold arm. "What'd you say?"

"He shot me! That sonofabitch, Meriwether Lewis, shot me!"

York gaped at him for several seconds. He clasped the boy by the shoulders. "You just wait, all right? Hang on! I got somebody you gotta talk to!"

"Don't leave me," the boy whined as York jumped to his feet.

"I'll be right back," York said. He burst through the door and sprinted across the yard. The rain was coming down hard now, and he almost slipped in his haste to reach the woman's cabin.

"Cap'n! Cap'n!" York fell in the door. Clark was sitting on the bed, looking pleased with himself. He had his arm around the shoulders of the Indian girl. Her arm had been put into a makeshift sling, and she was leaning on Clark's chest and gazing up into his face with huge wet eyes. The father hovered, trying to get his daughter to take a sip from a cup of sweet-smelling tea. The baby played at Clark's feet.

Ordinarily, York would have smirked at Massa Billy's fast work, but there was no time. "Cap'n, come quick, there's a man up the hill who says Cap'n Lewis shot him!"

"*What?* Lewis *shot* him?" Clark disengaged from the girl, telling the father, "You know what to do. Just let her rest and heal up, she'll be fine." To the girl he said, "I got to go. Good luck, sweetheart."

Clark dashed out after York and followed his lantern as it bobbed ahead in the rain. They were both drenched by the time they reached the rough cabin. "You should hear this guy, Cap'n. He keeps saying—"

Clark shoved past York and into the fetid air of the fat man's sickroom. York moved in close on the boy's other side, placing the lantern near his head.

"Son," Clark said. "Son, wake up and talk to me."

"His name's Junior," York said. He gently patted Squyres' plump cheeks. "Wake up, Junior. You gotta tell Massa Billy what you told me."

In a terrible instant, York realized that something was different in the cabin. It was silent. The labored breathing had ceased.

Clark had two fingers against the boy's throat, prodding the cold flesh for a pulse. He grabbed the boy's wrist and closed his eyes, as if willing the rhythm to return. He bent over the boy and pressed his ear to Squyres' chest.

Then he sat back on his haunches and looked at York. "Goddamn," he said. "This kid's dead." He stared down at the boy, his blue eyes very dark and wide. He leaned over the boy again and slapped his cheeks. "Wake up—wake up, boy—"

"Cap'n, don't. You're right," York said. "He's dead. He ain't ever gonna wake up no more."

Clark jumped to his feet and cursed. For a moment, he got that wild look about him that York had seen back in the spring. "Goddamn puppy!" He kicked the boy's legs. "Christ, York! What the hell's going on around here?"

Then, he regained control. "All right, all right," he muttered. "Can't do nothin' about this." York stood up and came over to his side. Clark slumped against the wall for a long moment, then turned back to glower at the body of the fat boy, who remained as frustratingly dead as before. York quietly ran down the scant facts Squyres had revealed—that something had gone wrong—something that was supposed to be easy—that a sonofabitch had shot him—that the sonofabitch was Meriwether Lewis.

"And that's all, Cap'n. Then I run get you."

Clark folded his arms across his chest. His jaw worked.

"This boy bit off more'n he could chew," York suggested. "Tried to rob the Cap'n, maybe."

"Or kill him," Clark said. He stepped over Junior Squyres' gray, lifeless body and walked back out into the rain.

York followed. The thunder crashed. The rain came down in sheets.

Clark lay on his back on the hard floor. With the violence of the storm, Emahota had sold lodging to over a dozen men. There wasn't even enough space to spread out their wet clothes. York packed the soaked garments up separate from their dry things. The whole place smelled of tobacco smoke, beer, and unwashed bodies.

Clark had bought York a beer to drink while he questioned Emahota, and it seemed to have had the desired effect. York was sleeping. As for the woman, she hadn't been able to shed much light on the case of Junior Squyres. The boy was feeble-minded, she said, and of low character. If she knew anything of his friends or associates, she wouldn't admit to it. When he asked if the boy was close to Major Neelly, she shrugged.

He turned over on his side, using his arm for a pillow. She probably just didn't know; there was no reason she should. The frontier was full of people like Squyers, young men too stupid or vicious to settle down anywhere. His stomach knotted with anxiety. If Lewis had shot the boy—which he saw no reason to doubt—then he must have had a good reason. Clark just wished he knew what it was.

Clark let his hand close around the pistol he had tucked next to his body. He resisted the temptation to get up and check his other weapons. The important thing now was to rest, get on the trail early, and catch up to Lewis as soon as possible.

He needed to sleep as much as York did. He forced his thoughts away from the alarming mystery of Junior Squyers and into more pleasant channels. He thought about the little Chickasaw mother, now bunked down with her father and baby. He was glad he'd been able to help her. Pretty soon she would be good as new.

So much like Janey...

He smiled at the memory of the little Shoshone woman who had marched with the Corps of Discovery. He and Lewis had come to their first winter camp at Fort Mandan desperately in need of translators. There, they had hired Toussaint Charbonneau, a French fur trapper who had spent most of his life among the Indians. The old rascal had two young Shoshone wives, and they needed someone who could speak with the Shoshones.

Thus one wife of Charbonneau had come with them, in spite of the fact that she had given birth to her first child that winter. Every step of the way, to the Pacific Ocean and back, with the baby on her back. Even Lewis, who tended not to be as charmed by the ladies as he was, had said she showed as much determination and fortitude as anyone in the party. The same couldn't be said of Charbonneau, who proved to be damn near useless except as a cook.

He moved his lips around her name. *Sah-kah-gar-wea*. It seemed like a long name for such a little woman, so he had nicknamed her Janey from the start. And the baby, Jean Baptiste, became "my boy Pompy." The Charbonneaus shared the sleeping tent with him and Lewis, and in the evenings, as he scratched out page after page in his journal, he would raise his eyes and rest them on the sight of Janey tending to little Pomp. And when it was time for bed, he watched Janey crawl under her buffalo robe with Charbonneau. More than once he found himself resenting it.

The cabin shook with another thunderclap, and Clark realized that his arm was numb. He turned onto his back and listened to the rain sluicing off the cabin roof. It made him think of that terrible gale at the Great Falls of the Missouri. The entire party was occupied with the grueling, bone-breaking job of portaging their supplies eighteen miles around the series of five giant waterfalls. Clark left the group for what he hoped was a brief errand to reconstruct some field notes he had lost along the river. The Charbonneaus tagged along to keep him company.

They had moved up the river and were just above the largest of the falls when a tremendous storm seemed to form from nowhere. Within a matter of minutes, black and deadly clouds unleashed sheets of driving rain, lashed almost horizontal by violent wind. Hailstones as big as Clark's fists plunged from the skies. He pulled the family to shelter under a rock ledge in a deep ravine, dry and flat, where he hoped they could wait out the deluge. Janey clutched Pomp's cradleboard and clung to his arm, her body trembling against his with the sudden cold and fear.

Clark thought they would be safe, but the rain fell so hard and fast there was no chance for it to sink into the ground. Instead, a huge wave came roaring through the ravine faster than a galloping horse, driving rocks, mud, and everything before it. He didn't know which of them was clinging to him more tightly—the girl or her husband, who grasped Clark's other arm and pleaded frantically in French for Clark to save him. "*Captaine! Aidez-moi! Sauvez-moi! Nous sommes tous qui vont mourir!*"

Clark roared at the man above the storm, "Get your ass up the hill! Now!" Sobbing, Charbonneau seemed grateful for any direction, and Clark managed to get him moving up out of the ravine. Hanging on to his irreplaceable rifle with one hand, he manhandled Janey with the other, pushing her ahead of him. The water sucked at Pomp's heavy cradleboard with irresistible force; it was all she could do to tear the baby loose before the cradleboard went crashing down the river with untold tons of mud, trees, and other debris from the river. Everything in that torrent was going into the river; everything in the river was going over the Great Falls.

Clark felt his feet go out from under him. The water was already up to his waist. Somehow he pulled himself loose from the rushing water. With all his strength, he pushed the girl up the hill, rain pelting into his face. Charbonneau managed to grab her arm and pull her and the child to safety. Clark scrambled after her, heart pounding. It had been an awfully narrow escape.

Later, back at camp, Clark had his hands full tending to the injuries among the men, who had been bloodied and battered by the hailstorm. But his heart and his mind were on the girl.

That was the first time he thought of taking her away from Charbonneau. He couldn't deny it any longer. He wanted her. He was never able to read her thoughts in her face, but he was certain she would be willing. It seemed to him sometimes that all he would have to do was hold out his hand and she would come to him. God knew Charbonneau wouldn't be able to do anything about it.

Over the next days his desire for her grew so fierce that it began to disturb him. Thus far on the Expedition, he had been able to hang on to his sense of himself as William Clark of Louisville, Kentucky, a man who was part of a big, messy, loving family; an man with responsibilities and plans for the future; a man who was in love with Julia Hancock and was going to marry her when he got home. Now, this William Clark seemed to exist only inside himself. Nothing in this remote place served to remind him of that man.

If he chose, he might be quite a different William Clark out here. When Janey walked with him, he allowed himself to imagine that he already was. She was already his woman. He had made her so in his bed and by protecting her the way she deserved. And Pompy was no longer Charbonneau's son, but his.

Listening to the thunderstorm in Emahota's cabin, Clark smiled to himself. He sure had made himself miserable for a while. Good Lord, if he been dumb enough to act on his feelings, he would have had a much shorter trip. Lewis would have kicked his ass all the way back to St. Louis. And Lewis would have been right. For him to have taken up with Janey would have torn the Corps in two. For pity's sake, he was co-captain of the most important exploration ever undertaken in North America! He couldn't let his personal feelings jeopardize what they were trying to achieve.

But Lewis hadn't ever spoken to him about it, and Clark was fairly certain he'd never even noticed his feelings for the girl. If he had, he'd trusted Clark to sort it out on his own, which of course he did. His overriding sense of duty to the Expedition was a big part of his thinking, but only part. He'd had some thoughts about himself, William Clark. Janey belonged to another man. Maybe she didn't have a choice about it; maybe Charbonneau didn't deserve her. Still, was he the kind of man who would take another man's wife? And if he did take her, what then? Would he abandon her at the end of the trip? Or would he stay out here in the West, never to go back to his respectable life in Kentucky, never to enjoy the rewards of the Expedition?

For these reasons, and one other, he did not permit himself to love the intrepid little Shoshone woman, Sah-kah-gar-wea. It had gotten easier after a while just to be her friend.

Clark felt himself relax, thinking of the other good reason he'd stopped himself. All along, every rough and dangerous step of the way, he'd known that little Julia Hancock was waiting for him. Once, on the journey home, Lewis mentioned that they'd already been gone a year longer than he'd originally estimated. "I hope Mister Jefferson hasn't given up on us," he said. "Do you ever worry you'll get back and find Miss Hancock married to another man?"

Clark was startled. He could honestly say the thought had never occurred to him.

He thought with deep satisfaction of his life with Julia in St. Louis. He had come late to marriage, and it still amazed and pleased him that he seemed to be able to make Julia happy. When he granted her little wishes to buy curtains or wallpaper, she seemed so thrilled that he felt like a king. When he encouraged her about her cooking or her sewing, she glowed, and when she fussed over him, he got so tickled, he couldn't stop smiling. And she was the best mother! The day she'd put their son in his arms was the happiest of his life.

Clark couldn't help wishing she were here right now. They could have one of their little conversations. She would ease his mind about Meriwether, whom she had come to accept as a stern but loving brother. For a moment his arms felt so empty he almost groaned.

He comforted himself, as he so often had before, with the thought of her at home, waiting. Jonathan would be there soon to take her and the boy to Louisville. He would see her there when this was all over.

He wondered if it were raining in St. Louis. He closed his eyes and imagined her and Lew, warm and safe in the bedroom in the little house on Spruce and Main. "Sweet dreams, little Julia," he whispered. Then he turned over and let the rain lull him to sleep.

Chapter 29
Julia

Fort Pickering, Chickasaw Bluffs, Tennessee
October 9, 1809

Julia was as tired and wet as she'd ever been in her life. Every stitch of clothing she had, from her cloak down to her stockings, was damp and grubby with river water. She stood in the commandant's office and shifted her feet, trying not to think about the mud and gravel squelching around in her shoes. Her legs felt unsteady on land after more than a week on the river.

It had been a long trip. Who would have dreamed it would take so long to catch up with Will? In a final indignity, she'd been picked up by a dirty boatman and tossed like a sack of flour into the arms of a burly soldier on shore. She'd have bruises for weeks.

But it would all be worth it the moment she found Will. She'd come all this way, and by God, she was going to see it through. She straightened her cloak and tried her best to look dignified, ignoring the snickering soldiers blocking the doorway behind her.

Captain Russell stared at her, his eyes wide with disbelief. "You're *who?*"

Julia said, with as much authority as she could muster, "I am Mrs. General William Clark. I've come to find my husband."

"Good Lord!" Russell looked to the heavens, rubbed his eyes with his fingers, then looked back at her as if hoping she would disappear. "You came all the way down from St. Louis by *yourself?* Traveling alone on the river—a mere *child?*"

"I'm not a child, sir," Julia said, annoyed. "Besides, my servant Scipio was with me."

"Cap'n, the old uncle must be seventy if he's a day," one of the soldiers piped up. He thumbed toward Scipio, who was sitting on a chair in the corner, his chin on his chest, wheezing. "The poor old fella's plumb wore out. McGee had to tote him up here."

"Mrs. Clark...of all the irresponsible..." Captain Russell stuttered. "What on earth possessed you to leave your home?"

"I need to find my husband," Julia said. "It's very urgent that I talk to the General! I was hoping I'd see him on the river, coming back to St. Louis, but I didn't." She swallowed, gulping back tears. "I was terribly frightened something might have happened to him, but then when we tied up, one of your soldiers said he'd been here, at Fort Pickering. Captain, did you see him? Is my husband well?"

"He's fine—in the best of health! He was here just three days ago." Russell fumed and eyed her suspiciously. "Mrs. Clark, what exactly is going on in St. Louis? General Clark and I discussed the rumors, and he seemed dimly aware that something's amiss up there. But I get the impression there's some kind of armed conspiracy—"

" I don't know anything about a conspiracy." Julia tried to keep the panic out of her voice. "All I know is that I need to find General Clark! Captain Russell, please help me! If I have to go all the way to New Orleans—"

Russell dragged a hand over his face. "Mrs. Clark...General Clark didn't go to New Orleans. He went after Governor Lewis, over the Chickasaw Trace."

Julia blinked. "What's the Chickasaw Trace?"

"It's an old Indian road that stretches from Natchez to Nashville. There's a little trail from here that intersects it at the Chickasaw Agency, about a hundred miles southeast of here."

"That's where Governor Lewis went?" Julia bit her lip. She hadn't expected this. But Meriwether didn't change his plans just on a whim; if he'd taken that road, he must have had a good reason for it. She squared her shoulders and said, "Well, then *I* will go over the Chickasaw Trace."

Russell laughed, a short derisive bark. "No, Mrs. Clark. That's out of the question. It's much too dangerous." He pushed back his chair and stood up. "I'm putting you on the first boat back to St. Louis."

"You can't!" Julia cried. Her mind grasped for an argument. "General Clark sent for me. He's expecting me."

Russell shook his head. "Well, he said nothing about it to me when he was here. If he knew you were coming, surely he would have waited for you."

Julia's mouth dropped open. Was Russell calling her a liar? "My husband was just in a hurry, that's all!"

"Mrs. Clark, I don't believe you," Russell said. "For one, the General would never ask you to put yourself in jeopardy. And if he had, he would have had the decency to wait. But he didn't. Which is why I'm sending you home. Immediately!"

Tears of fury stung her eyes. She wanted to throw a screaming fit, but that wouldn't get her anywhere. "Captain Russell, I'm surprised a gentleman such as yourself would see fit to question my honesty," she said in an outraged tone. "If you choose not to help me, Scipio and I will go alone. One way or another, I'm going to find my husband, and there's not a thing you can do about it."

Russell fell back in his chair and stared at her. Enjoying their commander's predicament, the two soldiers poked each other and grinned. Scipio wheezed loudly in the corner.

"Well..." Russell struggled for words. "Would you at least agree to wait here while I send somebody after General Clark?"

Julia considered. She had missed Will by three days. That meant it would take at least that long to catch up. She was so tired from traveling. Maybe it would be better to wait—

Then, she remembered why she'd come. She saw again the look on Clark's face when he said, "Meriwether's in some trouble." Will had left in such a hurry. And then, just days later, people had been rioting in the streets, threatening to shoot her husband like a dog and yelling that the army was going to send troops to defend the city against Lewis and Clark. Julia thought about her son, who had Will's red hair, and how he would feel if he had to grow up without a father—

"No," she said. "I must find him myself. I'm willing to take the risk, Captain."

Russell got up and pushed his way around her to the door. "Fine, then. But I must say, Madam, your arrival is most inconvenient. It's unconscionable the General didn't mention it—"

"I apologize for the inconvenience," Julia interrupted coolly. "But I'll thank you not to speak that way of my husband."

Russell scowled. "Wait here." Then he motioned to his enlisted men and went out.

"Oh, Scipio!" Julia exclaimed. She felt so weak in the knees she couldn't stand up any longer. She plunked down on the floor at Scipio's feet. "I was hoping so bad we'd catch up with the General here! But he's already left without us!"

"Well, he didn' really send fo' us, Miss Julia," Scipio reminded her. "In fact, I 'spect Massa Will be in a right state, if'n he knew you was floatin' the river and hangin' around a dirty ol' army camp."

"I know! But I don't have a choice." Julia looked at Scipio's exhausted face and took his weathered hands in her own. "I'm worried about you. Especially with this Indian trail and everything. That sounds hard. And it's a long way."

"*You*, worried about *me?*" Scipio's voice lilted up. "Miss Julia, ain't neither one of us got no business on no Injun trail. Massa Will can take care of hisself. He's got York with him too, mind."

"I can't stop now, Scipio, I've got to find him before somebody else does. Captain Russell's going to give me an escort," she said with mock confidence. "But I'm sending you home. Scipio, riding this trail will be even harder than floating on the river, and I couldn't stand it if anything happened to you." She laughed a little. "We've known each other since I was born, remember?"

"Don' seem like that long ago to me, Miss Julia. You ask me, we *both* oughta go back to St. Louis."

"Well, I'm not going back without Will. That's just how it is."

Scipio sighed. "I'll swan, Miss Julia, you gets mo' like yo' father every day."

Their argument was interrupted by a loud rumble of thunder. Scipio flinched. "Ma'am, I sho' am glad we off that river. *Big* storm comin' on! I'm glad we ain't out on no Injun trail, neither."

Julia shivered. She was glad to be off the river, too, but she couldn't help thinking about Will. What was he doing right now, out on the Chickasaw Trace? She prayed he had some shelter. What if Will were out in the storm— in the thunder and the lightning and the rain—

Her thoughts were interrupted again, this time by a loud rap on the door. Julia got to her feet. A fair-haired soldier poked his head in. He looked familiar, though Julia couldn't imagine where she had seen him before.

The soldier's face lit up in a grin. "Why, Miz Clark!" he said. "Pleasure seein' you, again, ma'am! Cap'n Russell just informed me I'd have the honor of escortin' you down the Trace."

Julia couldn't forget the thick Tennessee twang. "You're the sergeant who brought the letter to our house," she said. "Sergeant Thomas, wasn't it?"

"That's right. I'm awful pleased you remember." He propped himself in the doorway. "Ma'am, we're gonna have a real good time lookin' for the General, but right now, we're fixin' to have us a sure-enough typhoon. So you'll be wantin' to get to your quarters now, 'less you want to have to swim there."

Scipio creaked to his feet and began to collect their things. Julia looked at Thomas. "I don't have a place to stay—"

"Sure you do, ma'am," Thomas said. "We've made room in the barracks for Uncle here, and Cap'n Russell said to put ya in the officer's quarters. So you'll be livin' in the lap of luxury. Plenty of room for you and your mother both."

Julia felt confused. "My mother?"

"Yeah," Thomas nodded. "You know...Mrs. Clark. Where'd your good mother get off to, anyway?"

Julia had the sudden urge to giggle. "Sergeant, *I* am Mrs. Clark."

Thomas's jaw dropped. He looked surprised, then disappointed, then finally settled on embarrassed. "Beggin' your pardon, ma'am."

"No offense taken, Sergeant." Smiling, Julia wrapped her cloak around herself. Even Scipio chuckled at the young soldier's crestfallen face.

His enthusiasm considerably dampened, Thomas led her across camp to the officer's quarters, then hurried off to scrape up some food for her. Julia lit a candle and sat alone on the bunk in the dim room, listening to the great fat raindrops splattering against the window. She hoped Scipio was making out all right. He really was too old for such strenuous travel; she felt guilty for putting him through such a trial.

Julia drew her knees up to her chin and rested her head on her knees. "Oh, Will," she whispered. "I miss Lew so much. I just want to find you and go home to St. Louis. Please, please, please wait for me."

She tried to reassure herself that Will was holed up somewhere, dry and safe. Maybe he was with Meriwether already. That would be better...unless, of course, Meriwether really was in terrible trouble. Then it would be worse. She really didn't understand any of it...it was awful not to know what was happening back home—

A loud clap of thunder made her cringe. The room was so dark and lonely, she couldn't hold back her tears any longer. She flung herself down on the bunk and sobbed.

After a few minutes, someone knocked. Sergeant Thomas hollered, "Ma'am? Here's your supper! I got some right good vittles for ya."

Julia wiped her nose on her sleeve and opened the door. Thomas stood there, soaked to the skin, water dripping off his round hat. He handed her a big wooden bowl.

"Stew," he said. "Well, soup. I forgot to cover it up on the way over here."

Julia took the vile stuff, sniffling. Thomas looked alarmed when he noticed her reddened eyes and wet face. "Law, looks like it's wetter in here than out there," he exclaimed. "You got to quit that, ma'am. Ain't no cause for tears! We ain't gonna let nothin' bad happen to ya."

"I'm sorry," Julia sniffed. "I just miss my husband, that's all."

"Don't you worry, we'll set out first thing in the mornin'," Thomas said. "We'll go down the Trace like a greased thunderbolt, and have ya to the General in no time."

"All right." Julia felt a little better. "Thank you, Sergeant. I guess I'll see you in the morning, then."

"Yes, ma'am." Thomas touched the brim of his hat and turned to leave. Then he remembered something. "Uh, ma'am? You see this bolt on the door? Well, you'll wanna throw that, and make sure it's good and fastened before you turn in. 'Cause, well, you know..." He shrugged. "...a lot of these fellas ain't seen a gal in a while."

Julia nodded, wide-eyed. After Thomas left, she bolted the door and sat at the little table to eat her cold stew. It tasted like sour meat and rainwater. She forced down a few mouthfuls, then blew out the candle and huddled on the bunk, listening to the storm raging outside. It was going to be a long, lonely night.

The morning dawned bright and clear. The brisk wind made little whitecaps on the surface of the great Mississippi that wound below Chickasaw Bluffs like a muddy snake, rushing southward towards New Orleans and the sea. Munching on her dreadful breakfast of hard biscuits and strong coffee, Julia wished she could get on a boat and get back on the river. At least the river was familiar.

She got her things and went out to look for Sergeant Thomas. She found him outside the garrison's horse paddock. Thomas had already saddled one horse and was cinching up the straps on another. Julia hung back, feeling too shy to approach. Around him, a half dozen soldiers loitered about, laughing.

"Sarge, you got all the luck!" the beefy man named McGee was saying. "First you get to go doodle the gals in St. Louis, now this! Hell, I wanna be 'lected sergeant next time!"

"You ain't pretty enough for this job," Thomas said. "Naw, boys, this ain't gonna be no romp! This gal's married to a general."

"He ain't a *real* general," a beardless private piped up. "He's just boss over some kinda half-ass militia."

"Well, he looked real enough to me. Real *mean*, that is." Thomas finished cinching up the saddle and unleashed a long stream of tobacco spit onto the muddy ground. "I'll tell ya, boys, after seein' her husband, I wouldn't fool with that gal even if she wanted me to." He paused to consider. "Well...I might, but it still wouldn't be a good idea!"

The men guffawed. Julia blushed wildly. She had never been the subject of such crude talk before. She wanted to rebuke Thomas and the other men, but she couldn't think of a thing to say.

While she was still standing there speechless, she noticed Scipio ambling toward her. She ran to meet him. "Scipio, I've written you a pass for the trip home. And I need to give you some money." She dug in her reticule and handed Scipio a few dollars. "That ought to be enough for passage back to St. Louis."

Scipio looked at the money, then at the soldiers, then at her. "Miss Julia, I sure wish you'd come home with me. If'n somethin' happens, Massa Will won' never forgive hisself, o' me neither."

"Nothing'll happen," Julia said. "Scipio, I have to go. You saw what things were like back home! Will still doesn't know what's going on."

Scipio started to say something else, but sank into worried silence as Captain Russell approached. "Mrs. Clark, I am heartily sorry you've decided to embark on this course, but I can assure you, Sergeant Thomas is the best I have," Russell said. "He knows the Trace very well, and he'll get you to General Clark as quick as anybody can." He stared at her. "There's still time to reconsider what you're doing, madam."

Julia felt frightened, but she lifted her chin and stepped forward. "My mind's made up, Captain. I'm ready to go."

She petted the nose of the big black Army horse that would carry her to find Will, then handed Thomas her meager belongings to pack in the saddlebags. She looked around for the mounting block so she could lift herself into the saddle. There was no block in sight.

She supposed one of the men would fetch it. While she waited, she ran her hand over the horse's neck, allowing the animal to get to know her. Suddenly she noticed the wide, rugged Army saddle on his back.

Julia gasped, then felt her face burn with embarrassment. Of course an Army camp wouldn't be supplied with mounting blocks and sidesaddles! She would have to ride astride, something she hadn't done since her first pony rides back when she was just a little girl. This was a complication she hadn't expected. She turned away from the men and fussed with her long riding cloak. Her ankles would show—there was no way around it. She swallowed, then reminded herself that Will's life was in jeopardy.

The horse was so tall that she couldn't reach the stirrups on her own. Sergeant Thomas had to lift her into the saddle. It was startling having his big, rough hands around her waist. He was taller and more fearsome-looking than she remembered, and it seemed like he gripped her ankles longer than necessary when adjusting the stirrups to fit her legs. She tried not to think about what her mother and father would say if they could see her now, sitting astride like a common country girl. Julia felt the great horse sway beneath her. She closed her eyes for a second and whispered a tiny prayer.

"All right, Mrs. Clark! Ya ready?" Thomas asked.

Julia nodded. Thomas swung himself onto his big yellow horse and tipped his hat to his grinning, leering fellow soldiers. "So long, gents!" he sang out. "Duty calls!"

"Behave yourself, Sarge!"

"Keep your skelp locked on tight!"

"Thomas!" Captain Russell barked, his face crimson. "This isn't any holiday! You get Mrs. Clark down the Trace and give her over to her husband, and you get your tail right back here! You understand?"

Thomas straightened up. The grin disappeared from his face. "Yessir!"

As her horse started forward, Julia turned in the saddle to look back at Scipio, her last link to home, her only protection against strangers and the wilderness. The old man waved a spidery hand. Julia watched him until she was enveloped by the trees, then turned her face forward. She followed Thomas into the woods.

Chapter 30
Lewis

Dogwood Mudhole, Tennessee
October 9, 1809

(From the journal of Meriwether Lewis)

Green River
Proceeding on at this point I believe we are about 100 miles from Nashville
I am laboring a bit. The bite I received from that creature at the Tennessee R. is a constant torment, aggravating the previous injury badly. I am poisoned by the seep of that animal and do not know how I shall ever rid myself of it now. The wound is excruciatingly tender and loathsome in appearance.

I am most anxious to see Clark and am under the greatest unease that something has befallen him. Wilkinson's reach seems illimitable and I fear Clark may have fallen prey to the same assassins W. sent to kill me. Or worse yet been waylaid in some scheme to dishonor and discredit him—for which I could never forgive myself, as it is the very thing I hoped to avoid.

Of course, there is also the possibility that he is not coming. If this is so, I cast no blame on him. That man has already rendered me more good service in my life than I had any right to expect. He received payment in deceit and lies, and my inability to keep my word, and if he has at last decided to wash his hands of the matter, where lies the fault? Wholly within myself.

Still I am desirous to see him and hope it may not be too long that fate or bad feeling will keep my friend from me, for I am by no means certain I will be returning to the western part of the country, and though tardy beyond excuse, there is much I wish to say. What my future course shall be I know not.

Lewis estimated they'd ridden about thirty-five miles from the Tennessee River when the storm hit late in the afternoon. He could see it coming—felt the wind change, tasted moisture in the air. Soon the atmosphere was heavy with the strange, metallic smell of lightning. The sky turned dark, and enormous gusts picked up great piles of leaves and swirled them around the horses' hooves.

Neelly stared at the sky, his face creased with worry. "Gov'ner, there ain't no stands along this part of the Trace...no shelter to speak of at all," he shouted above the rising wind. "We're just going to have to find a good tree to get under and ride it out."

Lewis focused on dismounting his horse without falling. Shaking with fever, he struggled to unfasten his saddlebags. The metal buckle seemed hopelessly complicated. Pernia had already made for the trees, so he wasn't any help.

"Gov'ner, come on!" Neelly hollered, as a terrifying flash of lightning burst around them. A huge limb split off a loblolly pine nearby and crashed into the road in a dazzling shower of sparks. "Lewis—leave the damn things—"

"No! Are you mad?" Lewis wrenched the saddlebags loose and snatched at the horse's bridle before it bolted off down the road. "These papers are priceless—worth far more than my own sorry life! Christ! Don't you understand?"

"I understand fine! I understand you're crazy!" Neelly grabbed Lewis's arm and pointed into the woods. "Get under that big dogwood, where Seaman and Perny are! Gimme your horse, I'll tie 'er up! Now go!"

Lewis yanked himself free and staggered into the woods. Pernia was crouched under the dogwood with the rest of the baggage, gabbling with fear. "It's just a thunderstorm!" Lewis yelled, but Pernia didn't answer. He stepped over Pernia and dug around in the baggage until he found a piece of tarred cloth.

Lewis sat down against the tree, pulled the saddlebags into his lap, and wrapped the cloth around them. The cloth would provide protection for the journals if the rain got heavier. He pushed his wet hair out of his eyes and tried to collect himself. The forest looked like an otherworldly nightmare in the hastening gloom of the storm.

By the time Neelly reached the tree, the rain was coming down in icy sheets. The wind howled over their heads, whipping the dogwood's branches in a frenzy. Seaman whined in panic and almost bolted into the woods, but Neelly shoved the dog's head under his arm and held on tight to his silver collar.

The misery was so acute all they could do was huddle together, bracing their bodies against the wind and rain, their faces screwed tight against the torrent of water crashing down from the sky. Lewis lost track of time; the storm might have lasted for an eternity. He felt this was the only part of the world left to him, his back against this tree, with Pernia wailing and Seaman whining and Neelly muttering "Goddamn!" every few seconds.

At last, the fury of the storm abated. The wind died suddenly, leaving behind a cold, steady rain. The night was so dark it was difficult even to see one another's faces, let alone make out the jumbled wreckage of downed trees and broken limbs around them. They were all shivering and half-drowned; Seaman kept shaking himself in a futile effort to shed water from his sodden coat. The ground underneath them had turned into a slippery, treacherous mess of mud and fallen leaves.

Lewis felt the fever chipping away at his self-control. Cold water trickled down the back of his neck; he jumped when Seaman's nose touched his cheek. Despite the chill, he felt unbearably warm. Sweat ran down his body inside his filthy green coat.

He unclenched his jaws long enough to ask: "N-Neelly...d-do you believe in God?"

Neelly looked out on the desolate night and laughed a little. "What would make you ask me a thing like that?"

"I don't know." Lewis shivered. "I j-just wondered."

"Oh, Gov'ner...I don't know, really. I used to." Neelly sighed. "Then I lost my little girl...and it just seemed like there was no reason for it." He picked up a wet leaf and ran it through his fingers. "After that, I didn't see much reason to believe in God anymore. I guess it's hard to believe in somebody who would take a man's child, just to be cruel."

Lewis was quiet, thinking about this for a while. Finally he said, "Neelly, I'm sincerely sorry for your pain. I haven't any children myself, so I can't imagine how that would feel." He clamped his jaws shut a while to stop the chattering, then continued, "S-sometimes I think that God deliberately puts obstacles in our path, to give us the opportunity to show Him our best selves." He snorted. "Not that I would know much about that."

"Lord, me neither," Neelly said. "I don't know why God would bother."

"I'm guess I'm the opposite of you, Neelly." Lewis didn't know why he felt the need to talk, but he kept on. "I never used to think God cared, much. He was just the architect—the impersonal Creator. At least, that's what Jefferson always said."

"Well, he oughta know," Neelly said.

"I'm not so s-sure." Lewis closed his eyes for a moment, trying desperately to ward off the return of excruciating chills. "Jefferson believes God just left us here, and that it's foolish to pray for his assistance. But N-Neelly, I can tell you, there have been times when I *did* directly ask God for help...and he helped me."

"Like what time?" Neelly asked.

"Well...at one point on the Expedition, when we finally made contact with the Shoshones, we needed to trade with them...to get horses, and a guide over the mountains. They were suspicious of me, and they wanted to leave, to go to their hunting grounds." Lewis swallowed, remembering. "Clark was bringing the canoes with all the trade goods up the river...at least, I hoped he was. But he wasn't at the rendezvous point when we got there. For all I knew, something had happened to him. He could've been stuck miles downriver, and unable to come on."

"So...what'd you do?" Neelly asked.

"I knew if we couldn't get horses, the Expedition would fall apart. I would have to go back home an utter failure. I gave the Shoshone chief my hat and my gun, and I told them they could kill me if I was lying...and then, I didn't know what else to do, so I prayed. I prayed for God to help me."

"And did he?" Neelly scratched his chin.

"Yes...one of the Shoshone braves came up the river and told us the canoes were coming. I turned around, and there was Clark! And the Indian woman we had with us—believe it or not, she turned out to be the chief's sister! How amazing is that?" Lewis choked and wiped tears out of his eyes; it was painful to remember the unbridled joy of that moment in this awful place. "I wouldn't tell Jefferson this, but Neelly, I could think of no other explanation...God didn't want me to fail."

"Ah, you beat the Dutch," Pernia crabbed, shifting his back against the tree to put some space between himself and Seaman. "Here you are, a madman in a miserable swamp, and you're talking about God and Jefferson! I always thought they were the same thing, eh, Governor?" He sniggered and wiped his nose on his sleeve. "Well, where's your divine intervention now? When's God going to show up, and help you pull out another miracle? Never, that's when! Because he's forsaken you, along with Jefferson, and your pal, handsome Willie-o! They've all had enough of your lies."

"Perny, shut yer yap!" Neelly snapped.

Lewis started to say something, but the words stuck in his throat. An awful feeling flooded through him. The black wolf was creeping up on him again, sidling through the twisted wreckage of the forest. It sat just a few feet away, grinning at him, its gray eyes pale in the darkness, its greasy fur slicked by the rain. The tongue lolled out, then twirled slowly up to lick its own fangs.

"Oh Christ," he said. "I won't let you bite me again, you sonofabitch."

Pernia edged away. Lewis fumbled for his pistol, but realized with despair that the powder was soaked; the damn thing wouldn't fire. There was no way to hold the wolf off if it decided to come after him again.

"Aw, Gov'ner, don't start that," Neelly pleaded. He noticed Lewis's violent shaking and whacked him on the arms a few times to warm him up. The force of it set every bone in Lewis's body jangling on its sinews. He shrank away. "Stop it, Neelly. Please...you can stop now."

Neelly sat back down and was quiet. Lewis stared at the wolf and lapsed into stunned, exhausted silence. He couldn't sleep, or rest, or even close his eyes. His bitten arm throbbed. He hung his head for a moment.

"Come on then," he whispered. He thought: *Just let it be over.*

But the wolf didn't come. It just sat there, grinning, watching the rain beat down on his head.

The skies cleared. A cold dawn came. Neelly got up at first light and came back with some bad news.

"Two of the horses are gone," he said glumly. "They musta got loose and run off during the night."

Seaman thumped his tail and sniffed Neelly's legs. Pernia groaned. *"Mon Dieu!* What now? We're lost in the wilderness, without even a horse."

Still sitting on the wet ground, Lewis looked dully at the Chickasaw agent. He heard the words, but his mind was somewhere else. "Shannon," he said.

"What, Gov'ner?"

"Shannon. Shannon is missing," Lewis said. "He's only a boy, really. We've got to find him. A man can't survive by himself in this wilderness." He gripped Neelly's sleeve, slurring his words. "I hope he doesn't run into any Sioux. A man alone...they'll scalp him...we've got to find him, Neelly—"

"Gov'ner..." Neelly took him by the shoulders. "It's eighteen-oh-nine! You're not on the Expedition! You're in Tennessee now." He turned Lewis's head and forced him to look around. "See? You're on the Chickasaw Trace."

Lewis gazed at the storm-swept forest, pained comprehension slowly dawning in his mind. "So I see." He licked his cracked lips. "Pity."

Neelly glared at Pernia. "Get him his medicine."

Bored, Pernia dug around in the damp baggage and came up with a bottle of laudanum. Lewis permitted Neelly to hold it to his lips and pour it down his throat, but he knew he was long past the point of it doing him any good.

He shuddered as it burned a hole in the pit of his empty stomach. The wolf was sitting very near him. "Neelly, give me back my rifle and my other pistol. And I need some fresh powder."

"No." Neelly held up the bottle of laudanum; it was almost empty. "Perny, is he fixin' to run out of this?"

"Lord, no! Governor Lewis *never* runs out of medicine."

"Or bullets," Lewis said. "I never run out of *bullets*. Eight thousand miles to the Pacific Ocean and back, and what did we have left when we got back? Nothing, but medicine and bullets." He gripped Neelly's arm. "I need my weapons, Neelly."

"I told ya no." Neelly glared at Pernia again. "Perny, I *got* to find those horses! You've gotta take the Governor and—"

"No," Pernia said. "I'm not taking him anywhere!"

"Damn you!" Neelly snarled. "So help me, you little cocksucker, I'm gonna tear you limb from limb when we get to Nashville—"

"It's all right!" Lewis grabbed Neelly's shirt and held onto it as he dragged himself to his feet. The world swayed alarmingly. "Clark'll be along."

"Oh, Clark!" Pernia laughed. "He's not coming—"

"*Fuck you, Pernia*," Lewis said. Then to Neelly: "Neelly, I can't stay here in these woods. You know I can't. I can't just sit here and wait." He choked, hating the desperation in his own voice. "I have to go on. For the love of God, give me my weapons and let me get out of here."

"Gov'ner..." Neelly's eyes darted around in an agony of indecision. "I don't feel right about lettin' you go off by yerself. But I know—I *know* you can't stay here." He looked at Lewis. "We got one horse left. I have to find the others. I'll let you go on, under one condition. You pull off at the next settlement up the road, and wait for me. All right? About twenty miles up, there's a couple of cabins run by a family named Grinder. You wait for me there! Understand?"

"I understand." Lewis looked down; the bottle green coat was falling to pieces around him. The wool felt had dissolved in the rain. He pulled it off his body. "Shoddy," he whispered. "Trottier's work. Can you believe I owe that bastard seven dollars?"

"Can you believe you owe me two-forty?" Pernia asked. Neelly silenced him with a murderous look.

They didn't have anything to eat for breakfast. Lewis found some dry tobacco in his saddlebags and smoked a pipe, letting the sweet soothing smoke drift into his lungs and calm the seething tempest in his mind and the violent chills in his body. He felt jumpy and stupid from drugs and fever. He couldn't talk anymore. He just wanted to leave this place.

But he waited. He wasn't even sure anymore what he was waiting for. He sat for a very long time and smoked and gazed down the road, just watching. A time or two he thought he heard the sound of horses coming, and familiar voices calling his name. But nobody came. The wolf sat on the edge of the road, grinning mockingly.

Finally, he got up. "Neelly, I have to go now."

Despite repeated requests, Neelly refused to give him back his rifle and his second pistol. He packed Lewis's saddlebags onto the one remaining horse and found him another coat to put on, a blue-and-white striped duster. "Gov'ner, you sure do got some fancy clothes."

"Neelly." Lewis looked at the Chickasaw agent pleadingly. "At least give me some dry powder. Please. I have to have it. My gun got wet last night. It's useless to me without it."

Neelly nodded and swallowed. Finally, reluctantly, he gave Lewis some powder. Then he boosted Lewis up and helped him onto his horse. "Remember what I said. You wait, you understand? You wait for me at Grinder's."

Lewis nodded wearily. "Perny, go with him," Neelly commanded. "Watch him, and make sure nothin' happens."

"What do you mean, 'go with him'?" Pernia said. "Thanks to your bungling, I don't even have a horse."

"So walk," Neelly said.

Lewis didn't bother staying around to see the outcome of the argument. He spurred his horse gently and called to Seaman. They set off at a slow walk down the road.

The afternoon sun streamed through the trees, heating the moist earth and raising a gentle mist from the forest floor. The horse plodded along the muddy road, picking its way around fallen tree branches. Every step sent little tendrils of pain snaking through Lewis's body. He wanted to stop and rest, but with the wolf dogging him, he couldn't hope for even a temporary respite.

Once, he stopped and looked back the way he had come. No sign of Pernia, but for all his complaining, Lewis didn't doubt he'd be along. Up ahead, a few days away, lay Nashville. His gut turned thinking about it. There were so many things he needed to do. He had to find out what, if anything,

had happened to Clark. He had to decide what he was going to say to Eustis
and Madison—what he would tell them about Wilkinson—

It started to come back to him then: Eustis' vicious letter, Madison's loss
of confidence, Jefferson's disapproval, the book, the goddamn book. The fur
company's trip up the Missouri. Eustis would accuse him of trying to profit
from his position. The sad thing was, what could he possibly say to refute it?

But none of that mattered, if he could make them understand about Wilkinson, how he meant to destroy this country, what they stood to lose.

So he would talk to them all, convince them about Wilkinson somehow.
He would show them his vouchers, make his justifications. He would snow
them yet again, and they'd let him go back to—

To what? Bates? His lonely room at Pierre Choteau's? Was that even a
possibility anymore?

A deep anger formed inside him. He watched the black wolf sidling along,
making his grinning way through the woods. "I'll kill you, you bastard. You'll
not attack me again—"

Suddenly, incredibly, he heard a faint chuckle. Seaman erupted in a mad
frenzy of barking. Lewis stared at the wolf, then realized that the noise had
come from a man on horseback, riding alongside the wolf, wending his way
through the trees.

He recognized the tall, lean form, the light hair, the shockingly pale blue
eyes. It was Neelly's friend from Big Town, the preacher, Tom Runion. He
had a rifle across his lap, and something shiny in his hand. Lewis stared at it.
It was a pair of devil's claws.

He gasped as a wave of nausea swept over him. He understood everything
now, understood it perfectly. God, how stupid he'd been! Runion was
Wilkinson's man. So was Neelly. Both of them had led him here.

"What do you want with me, you sonofabitch?" he asked.

Runion smiled. "'And I beheld another beast coming up out of the earth,
and he had two horns like a lamb, and he spake as a dragon...'"

"What have I ever done?" Lewis choked with despair. "In the name of
God, *tell me what I am guilty of.*" He was sickened by the evil grin on Runion's
face. Were the man and the wolf the same beast?

"Why don't you kill me?" Lewis demanded. "Why don't you just shoot me
now? There's no one around to see."

Runion laughed. He raised the devil's claws and tapped them against his
wrist. "That's easy, Lewis," he said. "I ain't finished with you yet."

I ain't finished with you yet. They never were, were they? Not Wilkinson, not

Jefferson, not Eustis, not Bates. No, they weren't finished by a long shot. And they never would be, not until they'd robbed him of everything he had. Of every dollar, every dime, every bit of reputation, every shred of self-respect.

I ain't finished with you yet. It was never finished. The only one who was done with him was Clark. But then, he always was the sensible one.

Sick with anger, Lewis turned away. Seaman quieted down as Runion disappeared into the trees, still chuckling. Only the wolf remained, sidling along, licking its filthy maw.

Lewis didn't give a damn anymore. The bastards always came back. They were never satisfied. Runion, the wolf. They'd bitten him, poisoned him, and yet they came back to torture him again.

Well, let them come. He would fight them to the last. Wilkinson would never have the satisfaction of taking him, ever.

The sun was hanging low in the sky when he reached a small clearing by the side of the road. In it were two dogtrot cabins, one of them smoking from the preparation of the evening meal. This was Grinder's Stand, the place Neelly had talked about. The place where he was supposed to wait.

Watching his own deep shadow, Lewis turned his horse into the clearing. Seaman padded along by his side. He called to the people in the cabin. The black wolf grinned in the gathering darkness and followed close behind.

Chapter 31
Julia

I *didn't even know thighs could get blisters,* Julia thought. Every swaying movement of the great Army horse sent stabs of agony down her legs, and this was only the first day of the ride. She thought longingly of her little sidesaddle at home. But she was ever more grateful for her long riding cloak, which not only shielded her modesty, but gave her some protection from the pigeons. In fact, with the red cloak's embroidered cuffs, her black beaver hat, and her little fringed boots, she thought she looked rather dashing.

"We're gonna eat good on this trip, ma'am," Sergeant Thomas announced. He rode a few paces ahead, leading the way along a narrow rough path through thickets of magnolias, black willows, and buckeyes, all entwined with vines and laden with staggering numbers of pigeons.

"Really?" Julia looked at him with suspicion. By no stretch of the imagination could anything she had eaten at Fort Pickering be considered *good.*

"Oh, yes, ma'am. There's all kinda game in this woods. Possum—squirrel—deer, a' course—coons—"

"Coons!" Julia exclaimed. "I've never eaten a coon."

Sergeant Thomas whipped around in the saddle to gape at her. "What?" he goggled. "Never eaten a coon?" He shook his head as if amazed that anyone could be so sheltered. "How old are you, ma'am, if you don't mind me askin'?"

"Seventeen," she said, a little defensively.

"Seventeen years old and never eaten a coon..." Thomas looked back at her again and smiled. "What *do* ye eat, then?"

"All kinds of things!" she said. "Cows...pigs...chickens...turkeys...fish..."

"Fish! What kinda fish? Trout? Perch?"

"My husband likes fried catfish," Julia said.

"Do you know why they call it a catfish?" Sergeant Thomas demanded.

When she shook her head, he told her, "It's because when you catch it, it cries like a cat." He let his mouth hang open like a fish. "Meow! Meow!"

Julia giggled. "That's not why! It's because it has whiskers!"

"Whatever you say, ma'am. I've heard it, though. It's right spooky."

Sergeant Thomas turned out to be a chatterbox. Though the pain in her thighs soon spread to her calves, her rear, her back, and even her arms, it was hard to get lonely or scared with him talking all day. She found herself telling him all about her life with Will, and she learned all about him, too: that he was from a little town in East Tennessee called Chillowee, that his parents and sister had all died of the milk sickness on the same day, and that his brother had inherited their little farm, and had, he told her, "run me off." She found out that he loved the Army, and he couldn't wait to go to war against the British.

"Aren't you scared of getting shot?" Julia asked.

"No, ma'am," Thomas said. "I aim to *do* the shootin'! I'm rarin' to get out of Fort Pickering and into a tussle with them rascals. We'll drive 'em outta this country for good. You wait, when I'm done with them, I'll go out West and whip up on the Indians!"

"My husband's been in war, and he says it's terrible. And he says we can make peace with the Indians."

"Aw, that's what old men always say, after they've had all the fun," Thomas said.

"My husband is *not* old."

"Beggin' your pardon, ma'am," Thomas said quickly. "He's a chirk and lively fella and no mistake."

The sun was very low in the sky when Sergeant Thomas located a place for them to camp for the night. Julia swung her right leg over the saddle and slowly slid down the body of the horse. Thomas caught her around the waist and lowered her the rest of the way to the ground. She stood flat-footed for a moment. She didn't trust herself not to collapse.

Thomas pointed into the trees. "We got a little stream there, ma'am, for gittin' cleaned up and such. I'll get the horses squared away and then go a-huntin' for our supper. Don't go wanderin' off, now."

"I won't." Julia's voice sounded small. If her husband could see her now, in the woods with a strange man—well, he would be furious. But it couldn't be helped. Will was in danger, and she was the only one who could save him. Nothing else mattered.

She didn't try to move until Thomas had disappeared into the woods to 'hunt. Tentatively, she made her way behind a tangle of brush. Her legs were so stiff, she couldn't walk without adopting a ridiculous gait, leaning heavily to one side, then the other. Squatting was pure agony that made tears stream out of her eyes. She stumbled over to the stream and managed to get down to wash her face and hands.

A great weariness overtook her. She hung her head and watched the water racing over the stones in the bottom of the creek. A tear slid down her cheek. What had she gotten herself into? Here she was, dead tired and saddlesore, after only one day on the road. It might take days to catch up with Will! What if she failed, and something happened to him?

Nearby, the horses cropped the grass with their big square teeth. She couldn't help but notice that when they drew their lips back, they looked just like Sergeant Thomas. The thought was so funny it made her forget to cry.

With a groan, she eased herself over onto her back and looked at the darkening sky. The sunset was splintered into many little pieces by the branches above her head. She closed her eyes, just for a minute...It seemed to her that Will was very near...Any moment she would hear the rumble of his voice and know that he was safe...

"Ma'am? Ma'am?"

Julia awoke in darkness with a little cry of fright. Sergeant Thomas was hunkered down beside her. Off to her right, she could see the orange glow of a campfire. Something was crackling and popping on a spit, and the air was filled with the mouthwatering smell of roasting meat.

"Sorry if I startled you, ma'am. Supper's 'bout ready."

Julia crept to the campfire with her new, peculiar rolling gait. She tried to seat herself daintily opposite Thomas, but ended up falling on the ground like a sack of meal. Thomas didn't even seem to notice. He just whacked off a hunk of meat and placed it in a wooden bowl. He carefully spooned in some wild mushrooms he had fried in the drippings from the animal, then handed her the bowl and two pawpaws.

Julia waited for a moment to receive a knife and fork before realizing her foolishness. She gave Thomas a grateful smile, then fell upon the food, famished. The meat was strong and gamy, but at this moment, she wouldn't have traded it for the finest ham in Virginia. When she noticed Sergeant Thomas licking his bowl, she did the same.

"Now you've officially eaten a coon," Sergeant Thomas proclaimed. "Ma'am, I'll bet you didn't know you could eat like that. That's what bein' out on the trail all day'll do for ye." He belched in contentment, then looked a little embarrassed. "Beg pardon, ma'am." He leaned over and brushed her arm with something long and fuzzy. "Here ye go. You can wear it on your hat."

Julia shrieked. "What is it?"

"The tail, ma'am."

She laughed breathlessly. "That's all right, Sergeant. You can have it."

He shrugged, took off his hat, and tied the coon's tail to the crown, then replaced the hat on his head. "Now I'm out of uniform."

"I won't tell if you won't." She smiled. "My husband says that on his expedition to the Pacific Ocean, they once ate a whale."

"Ain't that somethin', ma'am." Thomas sprawled back on his elbows. "What I wouldn't give to go out West like that, and see all them things. I guess you musta heard all kinds of stories about the West, and the Indians, and all the buffalo and such."

"Not really." Julia plucked at her skirt. "I was just thinking while we were eating the coon, I actually don't know very much about what my husband did before we got married. He tells stories, of course...but just spending one day on this road makes me realize it must have been much different from how I imagined."

"Different how?" Thomas wanted to know.

"Harder, I guess, and a lot less fun."

Thomas roared with laughter. "Thanks a lot, ma'am!"

"That's not what I meant!" Julia spluttered.

"Aw, I'm just teasin' ye." He sat up and started cleaning up around the cookfire. "I sure would like to know about it, though. All them wonders out there." He glanced over at her and cocked his head. "Is it true your husband and Gov'ner Lewis found a gold mine out west?"

"A gold mine?" She giggled. "If he did, he sure didn't tell me about it! I wish he had!"

"Well, that's what folks are sayin'."

Julia frowned. "I'm beginning to realize that folks say an awful lot of things they don't know anything about."

Thomas got up and unpacked a small tent. "Here's where you'll sleep tonight, ma'am. Ought to help keep the gallnippers off ye." He showed his big teeth. "I reckon you'll be wanting to rest up good tonight. Tomorrow'll be the same kinda travelin' as today. Late tomorrow we'll hit the swamps."

Julia's heart sank, but she tried not to show it. If the way to Will was through the swamps, then through the swamps she would go. She watched

Thomas setting up the tent and quailed inwardly. The tall and brawny soldier was her only protection, and she had to trust him, but she would have given anything if it were Will standing there instead.

"Well..." she said. "Good night, Sergeant Thomas."

"Good night, ma'am."

Muscles aching, she crawled into the tent. It was very dark and lonely. "Sergeant Thomas?" She stuck her head out. "Where are you going to be?"

Thomas looked down at her. "About a foot away, ma'am, just outside the tent." The big teeth again. "Is that close enough for ye?"

She blushed and ducked back inside. *Be brave*, she reminded herself. Would Will be frightened? No! She remembered something Will had told her once, just before they'd boarded the flatboat that took them downriver to their new home in St. Louis. He'd put his hands on her shoulders and said seriously, "Julia, if you fall in, don't panic. Panic is a useless emotion. It'll get y'killed." He'd tapped her gently on the chest, over her heart. "If you fall in, you go in here, and find the part of yourself that's brave. Stay calm, and wait for me. I'll save you."

Except this time, he wasn't there to save her. This time, he might need saving himself.

They were three days out of Fort Pickering now, and it seemed to Julia that she had always seen the world from eight feet off the ground on a giant Army horse. The odor of leather and horse had seeped into her clothes and her pores; she wondered if she would ever smell nice again.

"We'll get some news today, ma'am," Thomas told her. "We're almost to Big Town—that's where Major Neelly lives. He's the Chickasaw Agent, the fella who was travelin' with Gov'ner Lewis earlier. It's a sure bet somebody there will have seen 'em, and your husband. Who knows, maybe the Gov'ner and General Clark are still there."

"I hope so," Julia said. Her muscles had finally limbered up, but she was awfully sore and chafed. Maybe tonight she would be in Will's arms. She warmed a little. Will knew how to give body rubs. She could almost feel his strong, patient hands...

"General Clark'll be awful glad to see ye, I reckon," Thomas said.

"Yes." Julia was suddenly brought back to reality. Thomas seemed to have bought the story that Will had sent for her. She could only hope that Will wouldn't be too angry.

When they arrived at the Chickasaw Agency, they found the place deserted. Thomas went inside, and walked out almost immediately, scratching his head. "Nobody around here, ma'am. There ain't nothin' inside but a mess of old papers and unopened mail. I reckon they moved on some days ago."

Julia groaned. "They ought to call this place Big Disappointment then, instead of Big Town. Isn't there someone else we can ask?"

"Oh, yes, ma'am," Thomas said. "There's a couple of taverns here. We'll stop and get the lay of the land."

Julia cheered up a little. She envisioned a roadside tavern like the ones she and Will had stopped at on their honeymoon trip from Virginia to Kentucky. Most nights, they'd stayed with friends or relatives, but once or twice they'd lodged in one of these rustic but comfortable places. She particularly remembered one establishment that had served fried chicken, stewed tomatoes, and apple cobbler. When Sergeant Thomas stopped and dismounted again further up the road, she felt confused.

"Where's the tavern?" she asked as he helped her slide down from the horse. All she saw was a small rude hut, a couple of log cabins, and a few Indians, soldiers, and other disreputable types hanging around.

He thumbed towards the hut. "This is it, Mrs. Clark. You just wait here for a minute with the horses, and I'll go have a word with the lady who runs this place. I'll be back lickety-split, hopefully with some news about the General."

Disgruntled, Julia watched him disappear inside the hut. She couldn't help noticing the exotic smells wafting from the chimney. The smell didn't resemble fried chicken in any way, but it still made her stomach growl. She wondered what kind of food they served in a Chickasaw tavern. Probably something she would never have considered eating just a few days ago...

"Well, gents! Lookee what we got here!" A harsh, gleeful voice startled her out of her daydream. She looked up to see a stocky soldier with a dirty face standing in front of her. Before she knew it, two others had joined him, one tall and skinny with missing front teeth, the other young and baby-faced. For that matter, they were all young, barely older than Julia herself, and they were all grinning and elbowing each other.

"Hey, purty lady," the stocky one said. "What's your name, darlin'?"

Julia drew herself up. There was no reason to be frightened. These were soldiers. Will was a soldier. So was Sergeant Thomas. She would be polite but firm—

The baby-faced soldier grabbed at her arm and hooted, "She's right likely! Take a look at them fancy boots, fellas. We found ourselves some mighty high-class poozle—"

"Go away," Julia blurted. She intended to sound cold and firm, but instead her voice came out high and scared. "Let go of me!"

"Play nice," the skinny one wheedled. Without taking his eyes off her, he spit juice through the gap in his teeth, splashing the ground near her feet.

Julia gritted her teeth and tried to stare them down. "You boys stop this, right now! My husband is a general!"

All three men roared. The stocky one yelped, "A general! I've heard everything now!" He pushed Julia into the arms of the baby-faced soldier, who held her roughly against his body for a few terrifying seconds, then pushed her against the skinny one. They began to shove her among the three of them. They were laughing—it was a game to them, a cruel game—

Julia forced a scream from her throat, a high shrill sound that sounded weak and feeble in the face of these coarse men. She pushed at them frantically. "Get off of me! Leave me alone—"

"Let's take her in the woods," the skinny one said.

She screamed again and kicked as the stocky soldier tried to lift her off her feet. "No—no, put me down! *Put me down!*"

His eyes were bulging with mirth. Her feet were no longer touching the ground. His mouth stretched open wide to laugh—then, out of the corner of her eye she saw a man, running. It was Sergeant Thomas, dear God, he was unsheathing his *sword*—

Julia shrieked as Thomas pulled back the sword and struck the stocky man across the back with the flat of the weapon, catching him completely by surprise. He grunted "Ooof!" and dropped her, then slowly sank to his knees.

The baby-faced one tried to run, but Thomas was on him like a panther. He grabbed the soldier by his collar and threw him down next to his stocky friend. The skinny one held his hands up in a gesture of surrender, but Thomas kicked his legs out from under him. They all wallowed on the ground as Thomas stood over them with the sword. His hat had fallen off, and his fair hair stood out around his head. With his eyes narrowed and his lips drawn back in a snarl, he looked deadly.

Julia clung to her horse, trembling. Sergeant Thomas shouted, "On your feet, men! Now!"

The soldiers scrambled to obey. Julia watched in awe as they saluted and tried to straighten their uniforms. "What the hell's going on out here?" Thomas bellowed.

"Sorry, sir!" the skinny soldier said. "We were just funnin' with the lady—"

Thomas got right up in his face. "This here lady is married to a general! And even if she weren't, that ain't no excuse for what you boys was about to do! By God, you're all on report! I want your names and your unit, now!"

He whipped out his notebook, his quill and his ink. Faster than Julia would have thought possible, he took down all of their particulars, which they gave out meekly. The stocky one mumbled, "Sir, we didn't mean no harm—"

"The hell you didn't!" Thomas glared. "Y'all are a disgrace to the United States Army. Your commanding officer will hear about this and no mistake! Apologize to the lady and get on down the road and outta my sight!"

With their hats in their hands, the men shuffled past her, eyes glued to the ground.

"Beg pardon, ma'am..."

"Sorry..."

"Sorry we scared ya, ma'am..."

Thomas stood glowering as they hurried away from the tavern, glancing over their shoulders as if fearful that Thomas would pursue them and give them another whipping.

Julia turned her face against her horse's mane. Her legs felt rubbery. *Why did I come here?* she asked herself. *I shouldn't have. Captain Russell was right.*

Sergeant Thomas touched her shoulder. She jumped, then hunched her shoulders, feeling the tears start.

"Ma'am?" Thomas said. The fierceness was gone; his twangy voice sounded the same way as it always did. "Are you all right? Those boys didn't hurt ye none?"

"N-no. B-but they wanted to—" A choke welled up inside her and came out as an enraged sob. "I just realized something," she said. "I've never been anywhere without my husband or my father to watch over me. Is this what the world is really like, Sergeant? Full of people ready to set upon you, like animals?"

Thomas looked sad. "There's some right mean folks, ma'am. But plenty a' good ones, too." He brightened a little. "I got some good news for you. I talked to that lady in there. She said that General Clark was here on the night of the thunderstorm! So we're pickin' up a little time. We keep travelin' the way we have, we'll catch him most any day."

The thunderstorm—that was three nights ago! For a moment, Julia felt overwhelmed by the utter impossibility of what she was trying to do. Who was she to think she could catch up to William Clark and Meriwether Lewis? If it hadn't been for Sergeant Thomas, she would have been dragged into the woods just now and ravished by those men. She hugged herself and squeezed her eyes shut. If that had happened, she wouldn't want to live anymore...

"Ma'am?" Sergeant Thomas said. "What d'ye want to do now? I'll understand if you want to get off the road for a bit."

Julia bit her lip. Just as those men had tried to hurt her, there were people out there who wanted to hurt Will.

"No. I don't want to stop." She took a deep breath. "Let's go in this place and get something to eat. It smells really good. And then let's move out. I have to find my husband. And I will."

Chapter 32
Clark

Mississippi Territory, near the Tennessee River
October 13, 1809

"Watch it, York!" Clark shouted with alarm as York's horse stumbled on the rutted road. York jumped down to avoid being thrown. Panting, he took the reins and patted the gray's heaving flank as the animal struggled to right itself.

"Cap'n, he's just plumb wore out." York looked up at him. "I don't think he can go much further."

"Mine's winded too. Looks like we're gonna have to stop and rest 'em for the night." Clark surveyed the surrounding forest. It was already getting dark. "Damn! I was hoping we'd make the river tonight, but that ain't gonna happen now."

"I wouldn't mind stoppin' to rest myself," York said. "We been travelin' so hard, I keep thinkin' I'm haulin' that keelboat up the Missouri again. Only the food ain't near as good. And that's sayin' somethin'."

Clark laughed. "All right, I get the message. We'll stop. The last thing I want is for anybody to fall out."

"Well, I'm worried about you too, Cap'n. You been like a man possessed ever since we talked to that fella at Old Factor's."

"I don't mind tellin' you, what that man had to say disturbed me mightily," Clark said. "If he was even halfway tellin' the truth, Captain Lewis is in a very bad way. I'm awful anxious to catch up to him."

Thinking about it now, Clark felt a cold knot of fear in his stomach. The man Ferbers had described didn't even sound like Lewis. Sick, crazy, helpless. It galled him to think his friend could have deteriorated so badly in such a short time, but then, he'd seen it before. He wondered how George was making out in Kentucky. *Doubtless being one-legged hasn't improved his disposition any—*

He shook the thought out of his head. "York, let's get off the road for a while. We'll find a good place to water the horses, and hopefully, water ourselves. I don't know about you, but I could use a good dram." He looked at the lengthening shadows. "Then we'll bed down someplace, and set off early tomorrow."

Clark dismounted and they led their exhausted horses into the woods. The ground was still muddy and treacherous from the heavy rains a few days earlier. Twisted tree limbs seemed to reach out and pluck at their hands and faces. Clark had a disturbing feeling they weren't alone in the woods, but he couldn't see or hear anyone moving. Strange noises drifted through the forest, mingling with the soft cries of night birds.

"Cap'n, this is some place," York said. "I don't much like it here."

"Me neither." Clark sniffed the air and lifted his head. "York, do you hear that?"

"Hear what, Cap'n? You mean that music?"

"Is it music?" Clark asked. "Sounds more like a rusty gate swingin' on its hinges."

"Naw, I'm pretty sure it's somebody a-playin' on a fiddle." York gazed off into the dark woods. "It's comin' from over there, Cap'n. Through the trees. Looks like there's a fire burnin'."

"Well, let's go take a look," Clark said. "I don't much relish the thought of huntin' in the dark for our supper. Sure would be nice if we could buy a meal off somebody."

They picked their way through the trees until they came to a small clearing. A ramshackle cabin stood in the center of it, its windows alight with small flickering flames. Judging from the noise and the loutish types loitering about, the cabin was teeming with people. From its gaping door, all manner of sounds issued: laughter, shouts, groans. York had been right: somebody was playing the fiddle, though at close distance it sounded more like a injured animal than any recognizable tune.

Clark smelled the strong, telltale odors of corn liquor, vomit, and piss. "Gotta be a tavern of some sort," he whispered. "Looks like a pretty rough place."

"That's puttin' a pretty face on it, Cap'n." York gave him a worried glance. "You ain't thinkin' 'bout goin' in there, are you?"

"Well, it don't look like a high-class establishment, but some of these people might have seen Lewis. I might as well ask 'em. Besides, I can buy us some liquor and somethin' to eat." He looked at the shadowy faces of the men hanging outside the door. "York, I think you'd better skip this one."

"Billy, it don't seem real smart you goin' in there by yourself."

Clark laughed. "I can take care of m'self, York, in case you've forgot. But somethin' about this place makes me think a black man might not be too happy with the service. You go on and water the horses in that little stream yonder. Come back in a few minutes. In the meantime, I'll see if I can find anything out from these people."

"All right, Billy." York took the reins of both horses and led them off toward the stream. His voice drifted back: "Be careful."

Be careful is right, Clark thought as he stepped out into the clearing and approached the seedy cabin. The thugs hanging around the door looked at him with interest, at least those who weren't too corned out of their skulls to open their eyes. Clark felt his pulse quicken. He adjusted his stance and his facial expression to send them a message: he was strong, he was mean, and he wouldn't hesitate to kill.

He shouldered his way into the dank interior of the smoke and stink-filled cabin. People seemed to scuttle out of the way as he passed. It was a tavern, all right, but God, what a place! Clark had been in many a low roadside grog shop in his day, but this was the most abandoned and debauched scene he'd ever witnessed. In the corner nearest him, a cadaverous-looking wraith sawed on a gourd fiddle, scratching out a tinny tune while ragged men jigged and capered around him. Pox-ridden prostitutes prowled the crowd. Every soul in the place was clutching a tankard, tin cup, or gourd full of vile-smelling whiskey.

In the far corner, a big woodsman seated on a wooden chair copulated with a painted bawd, moaning rhythmically. Other men stood around elbowing each other and watching with hungry eyes. To Clark's revulsion, one of them was dressed as a minister of the cloth.

He blanched, but he couldn't let himself be deterred from his purpose. He pushed his way through the crowd to a rough plank table that served as the bar. Behind it, a large person was surveying the scene with satisfaction, grinning through a mouth of ruined brown teeth. The person's rough features gave every appearance of a man, but the dress, if you could call it that, was that of a woman. His instinct told him: *woman.* Whatever the sex, the barkeep was not kindly to strangers. She fixed Clark with a hostile glare as he approached.

He glared back and put both hands on the bar. "I'm looking for food, whiskey, and information."

The woman folded her arms across her chest. Her biceps looked like wallowing pigs. She replied in a harsh twang, "It'll cost."

Clark dug in his purse and came up with some money, which disappeared inside the barkeep's meaty fist. She put a large jug of corn whiskey in front of him. He guessed he wasn't going to get any food, or any change either, but it hardly seemed prudent to make an issue out of it.

At the sight of the cash, the men around him began to brush up against him, their fingers plucking at his coat. Clark started to sweat, but he kept his face a tough, hardened mask. He told the woman, "I'm lookin' for my friend. Meriwether Lewis. Have you seen him?"

To Clark's surprise, an explosion of raucous laughter erupted all around him. A man in a skunk fur hat slapped his back and hollered to the crowd, "Hey, boys! This gent says he's lookin' for *Meriwether Lewis!*"

"Meriwether Lewis!" A howl went up, followed by more riotous guffaws. A little fellow with a bald, greasy pate pranced in front of him. He flapped his elbows and cawed, "Who are *you* s'posed to be...William Clark?"

Men pressed around him, shoving and laughing. Clark's face flushed. He straightened his coat and snapped, "Well, did you see him or not?"

"Oh, we *saw* him, all right!" the man in the skunk-fur hat chortled. "Man, that fella was *crazy!* He closed this place *down!* He warn't cheap, neither! Treated everybody!" He wiped his nose on his sleeve and grinned toothlessly at the memory. "And Lord, he was some talker! Told us all about those sonsofbitches in St. Louis and the War Department—"

Clark's jaw tightened. Lewis had been here, all right—

"—And then Mom Murrell had to throw him right outta here, didn't ya, Mom?"

Clark turned in amazement to the big woman, who gave a curt nod, her chins jiggling. "Well, I don't cotton to anybody talkin' bad about the President." She jabbed a dirty thumb over her shoulder at a crude print of James Madison, nailed to the wall behind the bar. "I might be a lotta things, but I ain't no Fed."

"Hell, he warn't no Fed neither, Mom! That's when all the trouble started!" The skunk-fur hat man pawed at Clark's sleeve and grinned. "When Mom called him a Fed, he went plumb off his onion! Mom laid him out, she did! She's a tough old bird! Reckon that fella saw stars for a good long while!"

Clark swallowed, his face burning. He couldn't imagine Lewis spending two minutes in this filthy den, let alone acting bad enough to get thrown out of it. The standard of conduct wasn't exactly high around here—

The greasy little bald man pushed close to him, his face twisted with glee.

"If you're lookin' for your friend, mister, you're too late." His breath was rancid with the smell of whiskey and decay. "He done kilt hisself up at Grinder's Stand two days ago."

Clark fell back a step, stunned. Seeing his reaction, the man began to crow with laughter. Clark grabbed him by his greasy coat and growled, "You don't know what you're talkin' about—"

Wide-eyed, the man gabbled, "The hell I don't, mister! A couple of Chickasaws come this way and tell us all about it! Your friend done shot hisself!"

The man in the skunk fur hat slapped his knee and danced a jig step. "That ain't what I heert!" he squawked. "I heert Old Man Grinder came home and caught that fella in bed with his wife!" He mimed holding a rifle. "Shot him dead, he did!"

"That's a damnable lie!" Clark roared, backhanding the man across the face in a slap that sent him reeling. The rest of the tavern patrons jostled round as Clark jerked the man up by the front of his ragged shirt. "I ought to cut your ears off for that!"

The man's eyes bulged and his skunk-fur hat tumbled to the floor. Clark saw to his disgust that the repulsive fellow already wore the close-cropped ears of the habitual criminal. He threw him down on the rude plank floor. "I see someone's already beat me to the task."

"Aw, don't take on so." Mom Murrell extended the jug of corn whiskey. "Here, hon, have your drink."

Clark uncorked the jug and raised it to his lips, but the smell of the whiskey almost knocked him over. He suspected that if he took even a swig of the vile stuff, he would soon be out cold on the floor, devoid of his money, weapons, clothes—maybe even his life.

He replaced the cork and shoved the jug back at Mom. "Where the hell is this Grinder's Stand?"

"Cross the river, 'bout fifty miles up," Mom said. "But hell, don't rush off. It ain't too often we get a real gentleman in here."

Clark turned away, sickened. He shook off their pawing hands and pushed his way to the door. On his way out, in a final appalling indignity, a big red-headed whore groped at the front of his trousers.

The coarse men who had been loafing out front were now inside, blocking the doorway. Cursing, Clark wrenched himself free of their twisted faces and grasping hands. As he strode across the clearing, he gulped fresh air into his lungs and tried to tell himself that these people were lying, that what they'd said about Lewis wasn't true. It couldn't be.

He drew in a breath, but before he could to holler for York, darkness descended and a blinding pain cracked through his head. He realized in panic he'd been jumped from behind. Someone had thrown a blanket over his head; before he knew it he was rolling on the ground. A dizzying rain of blows and kicks descended on him. Clark cringed into a ball. He couldn't see, couldn't breathe. *Jesus Christ, is this what happened to Lewis?*

A heavy body wallowed on top of him. He felt a hot, clawing hand grasp at his money purse, trying to cut the cord with a knife—

Then, suddenly, somebody shouted, "Damn you! Let him alone!" Abruptly, the weight jerked off him, and he heard the sound of a violent struggle. Gasping for air, he fought his way out from under the blanket in time to see York grappling with one of the men he'd seen outside the tavern. York dodged the man's slashing knife, drew back his fist, and dealt him a bone-shaking blow to the jaw. The man spun around in the air and fell face-down, his tongue lolling into the dirt.

Sprawled on the ground, Clark felt warm blood trickling from a cut on his lower lip. He stared at the man and said, "Jesus, York, let's get the hell out of here."

York didn't ask any questions. Without a word, they mounted up and spurred the horses back to the road. They rode along in shaken silence for some minutes, picking their way along the rutted path in near darkness. Finally, York spoke up.

"Billy?" he asked. "Did you find out anything about Cap'n Lewis?"

Clark's jaw worked. He couldn't speak for a moment. When he finally did, his voice sounded like someone else—someone who was bitter, angry, and afraid. "Yeah," he growled. "They said he was dead." Clark spurred his horse forward so he could ride ahead alone.

York's mouth hung open in shock. *Dead!*

His ears heard the words, but his mind couldn't accept it. Captain Lewis couldn't be dead! Oh, many times on the Expedition he'd come close—why, he'd been chased by a goddamn grizzly bear! He'd almost fallen off a cliff! Hell, he'd even been shot through the ass!

Seemed like folks were always giving Captain Lewis up for dead. But it was impossible. He'd seen it with his own eyes. Captain Lewis always escaped with his life.

No, York thought. *I don't believe it! Captain Lewis is never dead!*

Chapter 33
Clark

Grinder's Stand, Tennessee
October 15, 1809

Knee-deep in cane grass, Clark narrowed his eyes and studied the Tennessee River. He desperately wanted to lead their mounts down the steep, crumbling banks and swim them across. The river flowed swiftly beneath him, the morning sun sparkling over a quarter-mile of chest-deep icy water. He could see by the velocity of the driftwood that the current was strong and erratic.

Clark cursed under his breath and clambered back up the bank to where York and the horses waited next to a hard-faced Indian. George Colbert had already told them that he had the exclusive government contract to run a ferry in the Chickasaw nation. "Only ferry within fifty miles," Colbert said. "Four dollars for the lot of you."

Clark drew a deep breath and fixed him with his fatherly smile. "We're just two men," he said. "Four dollars is too much. I'll give you two dollars."

Colbert's expression didn't change. "Four dollars. One each for the pair of you and one for each horse."

Clark kept smiling. Inside, he felt close to the breaking point. What the hell was the matter with the people along this road? All he wanted to do was cross the goddamn river and find Lewis. "Three dollars," he said. "Now that's robbery, mister."

"Get across as best you can, hoss," Colbert said. "My price is four dollars."

Clark's hands twitched with the desire to wrap them around Colbert's thick neck. He looked across the river, grinding his teeth. Lewis was on the other side. He had no time to waste dickering with this pigtailed sonofabitch. Through his teeth, he said, "York, load the horses," and forked over the outrageous fee.

Colbert didn't even bother to say thanks.

Once they crossed the Tennessee, the Trace seemed to gain in altitude, and the horses puffed and lathered even when Clark slowed the pace. A cold mist took the place of the morning sunshine. He could feel it penetrate right down to his bones.

They stopped about noon to rest the horses and eat a bit of dried beef and biscuit. It was infuriating to look back the way they had come and see the trail sloping back down toward the river, wending its way through trees and creeks they had passed hours before.

"Looks like we gone *up*, more than we gone *over*," York said as they soaked their biscuits, waiting for them to soften enough to eat.

Clark closed his eyes. He tried to ignore the painful clench of his stomach and the throb from the lump on his head. His heart was hammering. It occurred to him that he was close to panic. When he was growing up on the frontier, George had taught him that panic could get you killed.

He opened his eyes again and looked at their exhausted mounts. He loved horses; ordinarily, he would never abuse a poor beast as he was doing with these Army nags. He had driven the two so brutally that they might never recover from the ordeal. And in spite of his efforts, they were still probably forty miles from the place called Grinder's Stand.

Clark hung his head and stared down into the mush in his cup. He thought of what those loathsome people had said last night at Mom Murrell's tavern. Everything that was in him wanted to scoop the half-dissolved hardtack into his mouth, mount up again, and cruelly spur the horses through the woods. But the horses were near to giving out. So was York. So was he. Panic was his enemy now, goading him to do something stupid that would jeopardize his entire mission.

It took every bit of self-mastery he had to remain there for two hours, to let the horses eat and drink and rest, to let York rest, to pretend to rest himself, sitting with his back against a wild cherry tree and waving away the mosquitoes. As it was, the black mare pulled up lame towards the end of the day. Clark had to dismount and lead her until they found a decent campsite. While York went hunting, Clark wrapped the mare's leg and rubbed her down. He put his arms around her neck and hugged her, and put his mouth against her sensitive, quivering ear.

"You can do it, sweetheart," he whispered. "Take me to Lewis tomorrow."

They crossed a narrow creek and moved through wooded flatlands, the horses' hooves making soft clumping sounds in the moist earth. Clark found that the mare was serviceable so long as he kept the pace down to a walk.

The cold mist from the forest floor rose to meet the fog that drifted down from the sky all morning.

At length, they reached a hacked-out clearing with two log cabins standing at right angles to one another. About a hundred yards away, a rude barn and stable hulked in the gloom. "This must be the place," Clark said. His voice sounded husky; he hadn't used it all day.

"Looka there, Cap'n," York pointed. Further down the path that led to the cabin, a large black animal lay across a freshly dug plot of earth.

Clark felt all the strength drain from his body. *No,* his mind told him. *Not Seaman. It's not true—*

Then: *Yes. Seaman. Lewis is here. He'll walk out of that cabin any minute and drawl, "Clark! Where the hell have you been?"*

York dismounted and whistled. The dog lifted its square head, then got to its feet with a bark.

"Here, boy!" York called.

Tail up, the dog loped across the clearing. A flash of light on its neck—a silver collar—

Clark moaned with an almost physical pain as Seaman came to York. The dog was thin, and the hair around his collar was rubbed away. Raw skin was scabbing over. York rubbed his head roughly. "Glad to see ya, boy! Been lookin' for ya!"

Clark slid off his horse. He couldn't stop looking at the bare ground where Seaman had been crouched. The dog thrust its head into his hands and looked up at him with pleading eyes. Mechanically, Clark rubbed Seaman's muzzle and gently pulled his silky black ears. "Where's your master, dog?" he said, barely able to make his tongue form words.

A creaking hinge drew his attention to the larger cabin, where a woman stepped out onto the porch. He sized her up quickly—about his age, heavy breasted, frowsy brown hair inexpertly tucked into her cap. If this was Mrs. Grinder, then it was a sure bet that the little half-wit at the tavern had been lying about one thing. He'd been friends with Meriwether Lewis for fifteen years, and one thing he knew for certain was that the man was choosy about his women. Clark couldn't imagine him in bed with this draggle-tailed saucebox.

He strode across the yard. The woman touched her hair and smiled. "Hello there, stranger. I suppose you'll be wantin' a room."

"No," Clark said. "My name is William Clark. I've come about my friend. Meriwether Lewis. Was he here?"

The smile dropped off the woman's face, and she jerked her head towards the patch of earth by the path. "That's him yonder."

He thought he was expecting it, but the news still hit him like a blow to the gut. For several heartbeats, he couldn't think of anything to say. His hammering heart told him, *too late, too late, too late.*

Finally he said stupidly, "What happened to him?"

"How should I know?" The woman put her hands on her hips and gave him a belligerent stare.

Without taking his eyes off her, Clark stepped up on the porch. "Damn it, woman, is this your place or isn't it?"

"It is," she shot back. "You got no cause to get huffy, mister. It's not my fault some crazy man took a mind to go get himself killed at my place." She cupped a hand around her mouth and yelled towards the barn: "Robert! Robert! Someone here to see about that dead man!"

"Comin'. Hold your horses." Clark and York watched as a tall man shambled across the yard, his frame so skinny that his clothes hung on him. He ignored York, but greeted Clark with a raised hand. "Hey there. I guess you come about the feller what got hisself shot the other day." Like his wife, he put his hands on his hips and stood staring at Clark with bulging blue eyes, his mouth hanging open to reveal scattered teeth.

"You're Grinder?" Clark demanded.

The man cocked his greasy head at Clark and appraised him from head to toe with the same brazen curiosity as the yahoos last night at Mom Murrell's. Clark hardened his face, but Grinder didn't seem particularly intimidated.

"Yup. I'm Robert Grinder and this is my wife Cilla. We been runnin' this stand about a year or so. We ain't never had anybody killed afore. We run a real clean place." He sucked on the snaggle teeth. "You'll be wantin' a room?"

"For Christ's sake, man! I've come after my friend. Now you're tellin' me he's dead. I need to know what happened."

Grinder lifted his shoulders. "I couldn't rightly say. I reckon it was 'bout five nights ago, right, Cilla? I was up at my farm, 'bout twenty miles up the road. I didn't get back 'til the next mornin'. The feller'd already been shot b'then."

Mrs. Grinder nodded tightly and folded her arms across her ample chest. "My nigger girl and I were right here in this cabin, when bam! bam! We heard two shots. Your friend hollered out from the other cabin, right there. And that's all I know."

Clark heard the words, but his mind rejected them. Unconsciously, he put his hand inside his coat, where the letter from Lewis seemed to burn over his breast. He saw Grinder swallow, doubtless at the sight of his pistol and dirk. Clark felt heat spread from his chest upwards; he was lightheaded with anger. He remembered what Lewis had written:

I know not how it shall end, or where...

Shot. In this miserable place.

"Who shot him?"

They spoke up at the same time, Grinder saying, "This ain't our fault, mister," and Mrs. Grinder telling him tartly, "That man was crazy. It don't surprise me that he came to a bad end. I'm just sorry it was at our place." She glared at Clark as if Lewis's death had come as a personal affront.

Then Clark remembered something else from Lewis's letter:

I admit I suffer considerable unease about the fate of the journals and papers relative to our voyage to the Pacific Ocean...

He almost staggered. Lewis had everything with him. Clark's maps, Lewis's astronomical observations, page after page of descriptions of the animals and plants they saw, the Indians they met, everything they discovered...If the journals and the papers were gone, then they might as well have never gone on their Voyage of Discovery. Lewis might as well have never lived at all.

"His things...Where are they?"

"Still in the room." Grinder shrugged. "That feller Neelly said he'd be back for 'em. Come on, I'll show ya."

Clark followed the Grinders to the smaller cabin, with York bringing up the rear. When Seaman saw where they were going, he ran back across the yard and hugged the ground over the barren patch of earth, his ears pulled back. Clark wished Seaman could tell him what he had witnessed here. From the way the dog was acting, it must have been terrible.

Clark's eyes were watering as he stepped into the dimly lit cabin. A strange smell, acrid and medicinal, made his nostrils quiver. Laudanum. A portmanteau trunk and a pair of saddlebags were stacked in the corner. A rough bunk of bare wooden planks stood in the center of the cabin.

Grinder sniffed. "Like I said, we run a nice place. Even got a bed so's you can get up off'n the ground."

"Your friend was too good to sleep in the bed," Mrs. Grinder complained. "He was such a fine gentleman, he'd rather sleep on the floor on a dirty old buffalo robe. I told you he was an odd one."

Clark looked down. The floor was stained with a brown, irregular pattern, like something dark and viscous had seeped into the planks. He jumped. Christ, he was standing on Lewis's blood—

Mrs. Grinder pointed to the spot. "That's right where we found him. Just a-layin' there." She turned to her husband and scolded, "Robert, I scrubbed and scrubbed. That stain won't come out. You're gonna have to replace them planks."

Grinder hitched up his pants and shook his head with a snort. "Put a rug on it, woman! I ain't gonna tear up a good floor."

"Now where I am supposed to get the money for a rug?"

Grinder smirked, letting his eyes linger on his wife's chest. "You know where!"

Sickened by their low argument, Clark forced himself to shut out the sound of their voices. Lewis had died right here. His body felt hot, but inside, he could feel himself shaking. *Meriwether, why didn't you wait for me?*

Fiercely, he shoved the thought deep into another part of himself. Later. Not now. He strode across the room and unfastened the saddlebags, jerking out the contents. Books, bound in red morocco leather. A flood of relief washed over him—the journals. He pulled the trunk out of the corner. It was filled with maps, drawings, government papers, letters from Jefferson, all just as he and Lewis had packed them back in St. Louis more than a month ago.

Carefully sifting through the contents, he found some of Lewis's personal items. It broke his heart to think of Lewis fleeing for his life; at some point in these last few weeks he'd shed most of the things he'd packed in St. Louis. These were the things he couldn't bear to leave behind. An otter skin, supremely soft—Clark remembered the day Lewis had traded for it at Fort Clatsop on the Pacific coast, pronouncing it the finest fur in the world. He had been so excited at the idea of impressing Mr. Jefferson with this valuable find. A handsome tomahawk. A hefty leather medicine bag, no doubt well-stocked; Lewis was always doctoring himself for something or other. Quills and ink, of course—Lewis never went anywhere without being able to write about it—

He let his hands rest on the trunk a moment and breathed deeply, considering what was here—and what wasn't. He turned back to the Grinders. "Where's the rest of it?"

"That's all there is," Mrs. Grinder snapped. "We ain't no thieves."

"Where's his weapons, then?" Clark said, with forced patience. "Where's his clothes? Where's his watch? Where's his money?"

"All gone," she said. "That man Neelly and the little nigger divided it all up. There's nothin' left but all them all papers and books and such."

Grinder nodded. "Nothin' of any value." He sniffed and rubbed his nose. "I don't know what all he had on him. Like I said, I was up at my farm when all this happened, 'bout twenty miles up the road—"

"You said that." Clark shoved past him back on to the porch. The Grinders joined him. For a moment, he feared they were going to ask him again if he wanted to stay in the room, and he didn't think he could control himself if that happened. The rage in his chest was incandescent.

He studied Grinder for a moment. In spite of his fury, he felt a strange indifference to the man. He knew himself well enough to know that he could kill Grinder right now without a second thought. His mouth went dry. "I'll be takin' those things with me," he told the innkeeper.

"Reckon I cain't let you do that." Grinder shrugged. "That man Neelly said we weren't to let anybody take 'em but him. Said he was comin' back."

"I'll bet," Clark said. "Grinder, you can't stop me."

"Don't suppose I can." He sucked at his teeth. "Them fellas run off after buryin' the man." He chuckled and shook his head. "They took to their heels right quick, the both of 'em!"

Clark's thoughts raced ahead. His heart still hammered: *too late, too late.* Too late for anything but justice. He owed Meriwether that. In truth, he owed him much more, but now he could never repay that debt, could he? As if he could ever pay Meriwether Lewis for everything he had done for him!

But justice, he could deliver. Clark swore to himself that he would find out who had done this, and he would hang them—as many hangings as it took. It was as simple as that.

While Clark was talking with the slovenly couple, York noticed a pair of eyes peeping at them from behind the Grinders' cabin. He inched away and sidled around the cabin to get a closer look. As usual, nobody noticed him go.

Like himself, the young girl now crouched behind the cabin had mastered the art of making herself invisible to white folks. She looked up at him, trembling, her black eyes huge in her skinny brown face. York guessed her age at twelve or thirteen. She was dirty and dressed in a ragged shift of nubby brown material, much too thin for the crisp autumn air.

The girl looked frightened and very hungry. York dug in his pocket and came up with a pawpaw. He squatted down and held it out to her, but she was too scared to take it. Finally, York picked up her hand and pressed the fruit into her palm. With a tremulous smile, she closed her fingers around it, then brought it to her mouth and took a bite, oblivious to the juice rolling down her chin.

"What's your name, chile?" York asked.

"Malindy," the girl said, between bites. "Mist'ess just call me 'girl.'"

"How d'ye do, Malindy," York said. "My name's York. That red-headed fella there's my massa."

Malindy glanced around the side of the cabin, then turned her big eyes back to York. It was obvious she found Clark terrifying, and York didn't blame her. Billy was looking at Mr. Grinder with his jaw clenched tight and a strange blue light in his eyes, never a good sign. He had no doubt Billy would find out what happened here, and when he did, things could get very bad indeed. He already felt a quivery sense of dread thinking about it.

"Malindy," he said, "Do you know about that grave yonder?"

The girl's eyes filled with tears and she shook her head wildly. Dropping the pawpaw in the dirt, she hitched herself away from York, her back against the cabin. "I don' know!" she blurted. "I'm scared! That man—"

"What man?" York said, keeping his voice low and soft. "Tell me 'bout the man."

"The man who come stay here." She inclined her head a fraction of an inch toward the grave. "He in there."

York's stomach roiled. "Malindy, was your massa home that night?"

"No," she insisted, shaking her head again. "Only me and Mist'ess! We was cookin' suppah when the man came."

York ground his teeth. There was no telling what this child might have seen or heard. He decided to take a page out of Billy's book. He smiled and said in a calm, kindly tone, "Chile, I need to know what happened that night. I won't tell nobody what you said. You ain't in any trouble, and nothin' bad's gonna happen to you." He paused. "But if you don' tell the truth, the Lord'll know."

Malindy responded with a fresh flow of tears. As bad as it was to be Billy's slave, York could only imagine what kind of life she led as servant to these trashy people. It made him sad, but he couldn't let himself get all broken-hearted over it. He kept looking at her in a stern, fatherly way until she quit sobbing and started talking.

"The man came about sundown," she whispered. "He called us out and said he wanted to stay here. He was kinda scruffy and looked like he'd been in a fight, but Mist'ess was real happy, 'cause she say he a gennelman and he got money."

"Was there anybody with him?"

"No. He was 'lone, 'cept for that big black dog. I don' like that dog! I'm afraid he won't ever leave now."

York tried not to think about the dull, pleading expression he'd seen in Seaman's eyes when he and Billy first rode up. He knew what it meant, but he wasn't ready to accept it yet. "So what'd the man do? Did he say anything much?"

"He was...sick, or somethin, actin' real funny," Malindy said. "I was scared. I didn' know what to do. Mist'ess served him suppah, but he didn' hardly eat nothin', or drink nothin' neither. He kept jumpin' up and talkin', like he was arguin' with somebody. But the things he said didn't make no sense. Not to me, anyhow." She lifted her skinny shoulders and let them drop. "Then he wen' outside and smoked his pipe, and Mist'ess done bother him, and he got mad."

York frowned. "What do you mean, she bothered him? What'd he get mad about?"

"Well, Mist'ess likes to bother the gennelmans who comes." Malindy cast her eyes down. "I don' really know."

York lifted a corner of his mouth. He was beginning to get the idea that Mrs. Grinder offered male travelers more than just a meal and a room to sleep in. He shook his head. "What happened then? After he got mad?"

"Well, nothin' really. He holler at Mist'ess and say he goin' to bed. By that time, that little yaller man come. He carryin' the gennelman's things, but they not gittin' along, I guess. I don' know. I was tryin' to clean up from suppah."

York leaned forward. "How do you know they weren't gittin' along?"

"I heard cursin'," Malindy said. "Well, I stop cleanin' and give the yaller man some food. He got real bad manners, but I don' say nothin', 'cause it ain't my place." She looked at York as if he might not understand this, but of course he did. "Then we all go to bed, 'cause it real late."

"Where were you?" he asked. "And where was the yaller man?"

"He go off to sleep in the barn, and the gennelman, he go to sleep in the cabin." Malindy sniffled and wiped her eyes on her dirty brown shift. "Mist'ess and I can't sleep, 'cause the gennelman keep talkin' so loud. We can hear him! He pacin' around in his cabin, just goin' on and on, arguin' and talkin'. Mist'ess say the man's crazy."

"Who was he talkin' to?" York asked. "Was the yaller man with him? Or anybody else?"

Her eyes widened. "I don' know who he was talkin' to," she said, "but there *was* somebody else there. I know, because I looked out a chink in the wall, and I seen 'im."

"Who was it?" York's heart began to pound.

"It was that slave-catcher. That *bad man*. He roams all around the Trace, lookin' for runaways. All the black folks hate him."

York nodded and reminded himself to tell Billy: *hired gun*. "What's his name, Malindy?"

"I don't know," she said. "Some folks call him Preacher, on account of the way he dress." She stared at York. "But he weren't dressed up like a preacher that night. He was just standin' outside the window of the cabin, lookin' in at that man."

"So what then, girl?" York asked. "Did you see what happened?"

Her eyes filled with tears. "Oh, noooo—"

York leaned forward. He wasn't about to let her off the hook now. "Tell me, chile. Tell me now."

Malindy covered her mouth with her hands and stared at York with big, tearful eyes. She said through her clasped fingers, "Well, the man in the cabin, he quit talkin'. Then we heard a shot, and somebody fallin'." She gulped a breath, then continued in a rush: "It was a big bang, real loud! The Preacher, he run off in the woods. I hear that man in the cabin yell out, 'Oh, Lawd!', and I knows it's him that got shot. I was so scared, I didn't know what to do. Mist'ess was screamin', and so was I. She got up and put the bar 'cross the door and pushed the kitchen table against it."

York sighed and clenched his teeth. "So he was dead?"

"No," Malindy shook her head and hugged herself. "Wasn't but a couple minutes that we heard *another* shot."

York felt bitterness overwhelm him; the bastards had come back to finish the job. "So that was it, I guess."

"No, *suh*," Malindy repeated. Her teeth were practically chattering with terror. "That man, he wasn't dead! Mist'ess made me get away from the chink, but in a little bit, I hear the cabin door open, so I go back and look. And he come out!" she sobbed. "That poor man! He had blood all over his head, and his face, and his chest...he was all covered with it—"

"Jesus," York said. He was glad Billy wasn't hearing this. "Then what happened?"

"Well, he come over to the kitchen, and he start pullin' on the door," Malindy said. "And he's cryin' and beggin' Mist'ess to open up. He lean on the door, sayin' 'Water, water. Please, gimme some water.' So I runs to the door, and I starts to push the kitchen table away. But Mist'ess, she catch me and slap me good! She say if we open the door, whoever's out there gonna kill us too! So we don' do nothin'."

She looked at York, shadows visible in the hollows of her cheeks. "So after a while, he get up, and he start staggerin' around in the yard. I don't know why...I guess he was tryin' to find some water." Tears coursed down her face. "He fall over that stump there, and then, for a real long while, he lay up 'gainst that tree."

"Is that where he died?" York felt like something was dying within himself.

"No. He got up again." Malindy pressed her hands to her face. "This time, he goes over to the well, and he pulls up the bucket. I can hear him scrapin' and scrapin' the bucket with the gourd...but the well went dry a long time ago!" She sobbed. "There's no water in it! So I begs Mist'ess, I says, *please*, let's give that man some water! But she won't let me!" Her voice trailed off into a hollow whisper. "Mercy. Sometimes I can still hear him, just scrapin' away, and cryin' to himself."

York looked at the girl's haunted face. It was awful to think of Captain Lewis dying like that, in this place, with nobody able or willing to help. "So then what happened?"

"I couldn't stand to look no more," she said. "I went and lay down, and next thing I know it's light, and Mist' Robert come home. At first he think we're all killed, and he's bangin' on the door and yellin' for Mist'ess. But then she tell him what happened, and he say the fella's layin' in his room, and he still ain't dead."

"Lord, he was like that for *hours*?" York gasped. "Girl, tell me you helped him—"

"Well, Mist'ess tells me to go and fetch the man's nigger, which I done, but he didn't act right. I don't think he helped him much. Then that other man show up, another white man."

"Major Neelly?" York asked.

"Yassuh, I guess. After that, I don' really know what happened. I guess the man died, 'cause pretty soon they're havin' a big fight over his things, and who's gonna bury him and all." She clutched her arms and wept. "Finally, they digs a hole and puts him in the ground, and then they left. 'Cept that dog." She looked at Seaman and squeezed her eyes shut. "Now that dog ain't never gonna leave, and I'm afraid that man's ghost is gonna haunt this place forever."

York nodded. He didn't trust himself to speak. He felt a whole mess of emotions boiling around inside—grief, anger, loss. He didn't know what he was going to tell Billy, but he was certain of one thing. He would track down Pernia and kill him if it were the last thing he ever did.

"Malindy, you did good tellin' me," York said. Looking at her face, he was suddenly reminded of his own little daughter in Louisville, whom he would probably never see again. He put his hand on her head for a moment. "You're a real brave girl. And like I said, the Lord knows what's in your heart."

Malindy nodded and gave him a wan smile. York straightened up and looked for a long moment at Seaman lying on the freshly dug grave. Then he steeled himself and went back to join Clark and the others.

Clark saw York coming and stepped off the porch. The Grinders started to follow, but Clark stopped them with just a look.

"Cap'n, these folks have a little servant girl," York said. "She says that man—" he nodded toward Grinder—"wasn't here that night."

Clark raised his eyebrows skeptically. York continued, "I know. She might be too scared to tell on her massa. But she did say she heard two shots, and she saw Cap'n Lewis come outta the house." He looked away, blinking and swallowing. "He died real hard, Cap'n. She say he lived for hours after it happened."

"Jesus Christ! Did they talk to him? Did he say anything about who did this?"

"She don' know. Missus Grinder wouldn't let her help him none. They just stayed locked up in the cabin until Mister Grinder got home. That's what she says."

Clark's jaw worked. He looked murderously back at the gawking couple.

"That ain't all," York said. "She saw a slave catcher—a man called Preacher—skulking around right before the shots were fired."

Clark shook his head hard and didn't reply. He stared at Seaman. The hound was loyally guarding his master's grave. Everyone here, he thought, had reason to lie. Nothing could be accepted at face value. What had Lewis said in his letter?

I trust no one now—tell no one Clark

His jaw muscle twitched. "York, get a shovel."

York's eyes widened. "Cap'n, no—"

"I have to *see*, York!" Clark rasped at him. "I have to see for myself what happened here! Understand?"

"But, Billy, you aim to take him outta the *ground?*"

"I ain't askin' for your advice." Clark nodded towards Grinder's barn. "You heard me. Go on now."

York stared at him for a long moment, his mouth open in disbelief. Then he turned and started for the barn.

Clark waited, arms folded, brooding. It was hard to think what to do. Irrationally, he kept wishing he could talk to Lewis about the matter. Lewis was always the best man to have at your side in a crisis. He stared at Seaman, waiting.

After a few minutes, York reappeared, carrying a pick and shovel. Grinder grimaced in dismay and ambled down off the porch towards Clark. Mrs. Grinder shrieked and ran after her husband, clutching at his arm.

"Robert! Robert! They're going to dig that man up!"

"Say, mister," Grinder said. "I wouldn't be doin' that if I were you."

"It ain't decent!" Mrs. Grinder screeched. "I never heard of such a thing in my life! Robert, you have to stop him—"

"You'd better get your wife and that girl in the house, man," Clark told the innkeeper. "I aim to find out what happened here, and this is where I'm gonna start."

Grinder's eyes bulged even more than usual, then he turned back to his wife. "You heard him, Cilla. Best get inside 'til I say."

She glared at Clark. "What kind of a man are you?" She ran back towards her cabin. Clark saw a thin Negro girl dart in after her before the door slammed shut.

Grinder worked his tongue around the gaps in his teeth. "Mister, I can see you're the kind of feller who does what he wants. But I'm tellin' you right now, you ain't gonna like what ye see." He hitched up his pants. "He ain't too pretty."

Clark itched to slap Grinder hard across the chops. He had to press his hands together to keep them from acting on their own accord.

"You can take him if y'want," Grinder rambled on. "Fact is, I'd prefer it. From what Cilla said, he weren't nothin' but trouble when he was alive, and he's been a right nuisance to us dead."

"I'll keep that in mind," Clark said. "I suggest you get away from me, friend, right now."

Grinder backed off and drifted across the yard, where he busied himself chopping wood. Clark joined York, who was leaning on the shovel at the graveside, his shoulders stooped. Clark pointed at the grave with his chin and nodded at York to begin. With a queasy expression on his face, York planted his feet apart and prepared to dig.

Before he could even spear the dirt, Seaman growled and nipped at the shovel. He stood up and barked at both of them, his ears back and his lips drawn up from the teeth.

"'S'all right, dog," Clark said. "It's just us."

"He thinks we're gonna hurt the Cap'n," York said.

"Poor old beast. I'll get some rope so we can tie him up."

Clark found a length of rope in Grinder's stable. They tried to approach the dog several times, but Seaman barked and snarled and lunged, returning each time to dig in his feet and stand over the grave. Finally, Clark tackled him and wrestled him to the ground, holding Seaman down with his body weight. He wrapped both hands around Seaman's muzzle until York could tie the jaws shut. Then, they put a rope on the enraged dog and looped him to a tree some distance away. Seaman pawed the ground and stared at them with accusing eyes, crying pitifully.

Panting, Clark said, "Dog, I'm sorry. Lord knows you're the only one in this god-forsaken place who's shown any decency a'tall." He glanced at York and looked away before the tears standing in York's eyes did him in. "C'mon, York, we got work to do."

York tied a bandanna around his nose and mouth and began to dig. The ground was soft and loose, and the sickly sweet smell of recent death was present almost from the first shovelful. In spite of the chill, Clark could see the sweat soaking through York's shirt. His own body felt unbearably warm, and he shrugged off his old Army coat and threw it over a fence rail. Watching York dig and listening to Seaman's muffled howls, Clark felt his heart thumping against his rib cage. His knees were shaking.

York dug efficiently, mounding the dirt neatly to the side of the grave. He had uncovered about two feet of soil when suddenly, Clark saw him jump back as if he had been dealt a blow. He dropped the shovel and stared at the grave in horror.

Clark drew in a breath. "What is it, York?"

York turned his eyes to him. "Cap'n, I think he just right there. No box or nothing. I just felt the shovel touch somethin' *soft*—"

"Oh, Lordy." Clark swallowed hard. The smell of death was all around them now. *I have to see what they've done to him—I just have to—*

York probed at the ground again, more gently, just brushing away the dirt with the shovel's tip. Clark knelt down by the hole and began to clear the dirt away with his bare hands. York joined him on the other side. It only took a minute to uncover the form of a man, wrapped in a woven woolen army blanket that had been tied on either end with a hank of rope.

"Come on." Clark seized one end of the blanket. York took the other, and they lifted it out of the shallow grave and placed it carefully on the ground. Clark began untying the rope at one end. York stood by, gasping for air and already gagging behind his bandanna.

Clark moved swiftly to the other end and yanked away the rope. Then, he began to unfold the blanket from around the body. He wanted to flinch, to run away, but this was his duty, his obligation, he had to *see*—

Lord, it was bad. Weak sunshine had burned away the mist and now cast soft light upon the decaying corpse of a man, naked except for a shirt. Clark heard York stumble away into the nearby woods, choking. His servant was either heaving or crying—or, most likely, both. Clark wanted to do the same.

But he couldn't. Not now. Not yet. He forced his eyes to travel over the body. For a moment, he allowed himself to think that this could not be his friend. Though tall, this man was thin, not strapping like Lewis. This man was bearded; except on the most strenuous portions of the Expedition, Lewis was meticulous about shaving. Lewis could handle himself in any fight; this man was covered with cuts and bruises—

Breathing shallowly through his mouth, Clark made himself look into the face. The eyes were filmed over, the skin darkened, the features cruelly distorted by death. But even so—even so—

God, there was no use denying it! Lewis's deep-set eyes, his hawkish nose, his strong chin were as familiar to him as his own face. This was the ruin of Meriwether Lewis. In this terrible place, his soul had fled the body, alone and tortured, and left behind this wreckage.

Clark brushed the dark hair, shot with more gray than he remembered, back from Lewis's forehead. It was thickly matted with dried blood. Part of his friend's skull had been blown away.

Clark felt rivulets of sweat run down his body. *Meriwether, who did this to you?*

He pulled up the stained shirt and examined Lewis's body. Another wound, this one through the chest. As gently as he could, he pushed the body over enough to look at the back, and found the bullet's path. He closed his eyes. It was easy enough to envision the scene—Lewis shot, then someone administering the coup de grace through the forehead. Though the girl had said he lived for hours—

"God, Lewis," Clark said out loud. "I'm sorry."

He made himself look at all the rest. Someone at Mom Murrell's had said Lewis had "shot hisself." Clark examined the hands for powder burns, but they were too blistered and discolored from death's ravages for him to tell. The skin felt loose, and for a horrible moment Clark feared it would slide off in his hands. Mercifully, that didn't happen. Lewis was so strong, he had always seemed indestructible. Now, he was disintegrating—

Clark recovered himself and remembered something the man at Old Factor's Stand had told him, that Lewis's arm was a bloody mess. Clark pushed up the sleeves. Lewis's left arm bore two strange puncture wounds, all the way through the muscle.

Clark sensed a presence next to him and realized that York had come back. York's face was beaded with sweat, and his eyes were red. But he hunkered down resolutely. Clark saw determination in York's face, and he felt for the first time in a long time that he and York were united in the same cause.

Quietly, Clark pointed out what he had discovered. York had observations of his own. "That shirt's real shabby, but it ain't stained that much. Can't be the shirt he died in. That woulda been all bloody." York's eyes traversed the body, lingering on the legs and bare feet. "Whoever put him in the ground like this really hated him, Billy."

Clark could see a vein throbbing in York's temple as he explained, "If you died, Billy, I'd see to it that you went to the next world right! Like a soldier! In your best clothes, your hair clean and fixed nice, your wounds sewed or covered as best I could do..."

In spite of himself, Clark felt hot tears spill out of his eyes. "I know, York."

York clenched his fist, then pointed down at Lewis. "This is an insult," he said through his teeth. "That tells me that Pernia either did this, or he helped the man who did."

Clark blinked, overwhelmed. The Pernia he knew was a happy, smiling darky who wore nice clothes and made good cocktails. It was difficult to reconcile his memory of Lewis's manservant with the "enemies of liberty" Lewis had written about in his letter. It didn't jibe. Nothing did.

He dragged himself to his feet. He'd come too late. That was the long and the short of it. He had come to help Lewis and put everything right, and he was too late. It would never be right again.

In a strangled voice, Clark said, "York, you go get an ax, and find or make some planks, and you start making a box for the Captain, hear?"

As York jumped to his feet and headed for the barn, Clark let his feet carry him stumbling into the woods. As soon as he was out of sight of York and the terrible travesty of Lewis lying on the ground, his legs buckled. Down on his hands and knees, he retched, his gut clenching again and again until there was nothing left.

For a minute, he knelt in the damp, rotting leaves. He felt the cold creep into his bones, and his shoulders trembled. He needed to get up and help York, but something else was now being pushed up from deep inside his gut. A sob tore out of his throat, shocking him with its anger and bitterness. He coughed and choked on his own rough sobs. He bowed his head as burning tears coursed down his face.

He wrapped his arms around his chest. *Stop it—stop it, William—*

"Not now," he gasped. "Not now." With enormous effort, he forced the sobs back inside himself. Exhausted, he dragged himself on to a tree stump and sat with the heels of his hands pressed against his eyes. His loss of control shamed him. This didn't happen to him. He was the one other people depended on—the men of the Corps—George—Julia— Meriwether.

Clark rubbed the back of his hand across his mouth. Everything great that had happened to him in his life, he owed in some way to Meriwether Lewis. Way back when he and Lewis had first become friends, when they were just two junior officers, they'd spent hours talking in boyish enthusiasm about their desire to go West and explore the continent. It was something that Lewis's hero, Thomas Jefferson, had wanted to do since the United States was still under the heel of George the Third. It was something that Clark's hero, the young, swashbuckling George Rogers Clark, had volunteered to do for Jefferson as soon as the Revolution was over. For one reason and another, the dream had lain unfulfilled a long time.

When the roof had fallen in on George, Clark had left the Army and gone home to Kentucky to help. Lewis had stayed in, jumping steadily in rank and prestige. By 1803, Lewis was a captain and private secretary to the President of the United States. For his part, Clark was living in a rustic cabin at the Falls of the Ohio across from Louisville, applying all his energies to various schemes to haul himself out of poverty while preventing George from drinking himself to death.

It was a steaming day in July 1803 when the letter from Meriwether came to the little cabin where he lived with George. Lewis wrote pages of detail about his exciting plans to lead the long-awaited Western Expedition. In just a few months' time, he would be coming downriver from Pittsburgh to

Louisville, with the boat he would use to go up the Missouri. He concluded the letter with the most beautiful words Clark had ever read:

If therefore there is anything under those circumstances, in this enterprise, which would induce you to participate with me in it's fatiegues, it's dangers and it's honors, believe me there is no man on earth with whom I should feel equal pleasure in sharing them as with yourself; I make this communication to you with the privity of the President...

Lewis had concluded with the offer of a captain's commission and complete co-command of the Expedition. Sometimes, Clark still couldn't believe the gift that Lewis had placed his hands. Lord, he would have crawled on his hands and knees to go on the trip in any capacity! Naturally, he had accepted, writing back that very day.

Then, disaster. Only a few weeks before they were scheduled to leave St. Louis and begin their long trek up the Missouri River, Clark received his commission—not a captain's, but a second lieutenant's. He would not co-command the Expedition; at age thirty-three, he was a junior officer again. Official Washington had just slapped him hard in the face. He spent a long, sleepless night wondering whether to walk away.

But Lewis had stopped him. "This *absurdity* will not stand!" Lewis insisted, stabbing his finger at the commission with contempt. "On my honor, it will be replaced with your proper commission upon our return from the western sea. But as far as I am concerned, you *are* the co-captain."

"Lewis..." Clark had said. "You know it's not that I object to serving under you. There's not a man alive with whom I'd rather serve." He swallowed, his pride sticking in his throat. "It's just that the men...well, there's no way that they won't perceive this as a demotion."

Lewis crinkled his eyes defiantly. "They won't know, Clark. Because we won't tell 'em."

And they hadn't. As far as the men of the Corps of Discovery were concerned, Captain Lewis and Captain Clark were equals. And Lewis—that thorough-going military man—had never once pulled rank on him. As far as Lewis was concerned, it was always the Lewis & Clark Expedition, joined together, hand and heart. In fact, Lewis always seemed to think it was Clark who had done him a favor.

Clark sighed. They'd come back heroes. He'd gotten everything he'd ever dreamed about. His marriage to Julia Hancock, his job in St. Louis, his prospects for wealth, his happy life—it was all because of the Expedition. The ways in which he was indebted to Meriwether Lewis couldn't even be counted. It was easier just to say that he owed him everything.

Clark sifted a few leaves through his fingers. A sowbug clung to a stem. He touched the creature with his forefinger and watched it roll up in a tight ball, showing only its shining black armor. Even the humblest insects held mysteries for science. Or was this an insect at all? It looked like a tiny crustacean. He'd have to ask Lewis—

Casting the leaf aside, Clark propelled himself to his feet and strode out of the woods. As instructed, York had helped himself to some of Grinder's lumber and had already banged out a few crude planks. Clark stalked into the barn and began to rummage among Grinder's tools. He found what he needed—a handsaw, a hammer, a rasp, and a box of nails. Grinder had kept his distance since they had begun their digging, but now he sidled up to Clark and cleared his throat.

"Mister, you gonna pay me for all this? Nails is right dear in these parts."

Clark gave him an icy stare. "You'll get everything that's comin' to you."

Chastened, Grinder backed away. Clark wondered if this low man had killed Lewis. Part of him wanted to think so. It was almost exhilarating to think of killing Grinder and burning down this place, leaving his slatternly wife standing in the smoldering ruins to wail over the corpse. But as much as he wanted to slake his thirst for revenge, he couldn't. Justice required that he find Meriwether's real killers. If the innkeeper turned out to be one of them, there would be time enough for a hanging.

Working together, Clark and York took turns assembling the box, one man holding the boards while the other hammered the nails into place. At one point, their work was interrupted by a large turkey vulture flying low over the ground above Lewis's body.

"I'm gonna shoot that thing," York declared, and started for the horses to get his rifle.

Clark caught his arm. "No. Let Seaman loose. He'll protect Captain Lewis."

They untied the dog. Seaman went to sniff Lewis, then backed off, whimpering. He laid down about ten feet from the corpse and watched Clark and York, occasionally heaving his body in a great sigh. It was the loneliest sound Clark had ever heard.

Neither York nor Clark was a skilled woodworker, and their efforts took a long time. The afternoon was fading fast by the time they forced the bottom of the plain, ill-made box into place and secured it. Now only the top remained.

"Cap'n, I'd like to dress the body," York told him. "The way Cap'n Lewis is laid out...that just ain't right."

Still not looking at York, Clark rubbed his nose. "It ain't possible. He's already fallin' apart. We can't do it up right, York, no matter how much we might want to."

York dug until the sun was low in the sky, carving out a much deeper, neater grave than the shallow one in which the body had been thrown. As gently as he could, Clark tied the battered body back into the woolen blanket that would have to serve as Lewis's shroud. He jumped into the hole and had York hand the coffin down to him. Then, they carefully lowered the body into place. Their last task was to hammer down the lid of the coffin.

They clambered out of the grave and stood looking down for a long time. Clark knew he should say a prayer or some words. But his mind was blank and numb, and he didn't trust himself to speak without breaking down entirely. In the end, he just helped York fill in the hole, hating every shovelful of dirt as it fell in clumps on the lid of the coffin.

There was nothing left to do tonight. Robert Grinder was sitting on his front step, having a chew. Mrs. Grinder was sweeping off the porch and furtively eyeballing the proceedings. They watched as Clark and York loaded up Lewis's papers on the horses, the black mare taking the extra saddlebags while York's gray took the weight of the portmanteau. Clark was loath to speak with the couple again, but he had no choice.

Grinder stood up as Clark approached the porch. Clark said, "Where's the closest place to stay around here?"

Grinder let fly with a stream of tobacco juice. "Missus Dobbin runs a stand 'bout six miles up the road. It ain't as nice as our place, though."

Clark shuddered. "I'll be back to talk to you and your wife again. Don't you go anywhere."

Grinder shrugged and started to say something about his farm, but Clark cut him off. "Don't make me track you down, y'hear? And if you know anything, you best think about tellin' me. Anyone who stood by and let my friend get killed is equally guilty as far as I'm concerned."

Grinder's bulging eyes widened, and Clark said, "Save yourself, man. Think about it."

He started back for the horses, but Grinder called after him, "Hey mister!"

Clark paused as the innkeeper shambled after him. Any hopes he had of a confession were dashed when Grinder drew close with a conspiratorial grin. "You're welcome to stay here tonight." He jerked his head back towards the porch. In the twilight, Mrs. Grinder gave Clark a coquettish smile and a small wave. Her husband elbowed Clark. "My wife likes you."

"Jesus, man." Clark mounted the black mare.

York whistled for Seaman. "Here, boy! Come on, dog!"

In the last drama of that very long day, Seaman would not come. He stood his ground over Lewis's grave, barking, until York put a rope around his neck and tied him to his saddlehorn. They were in full darkness by the time they finally moved out of Grinder's Stand and back on to the Trace. It was a long six miles to the next inn. Seaman kept looking back.

Chapter 34
Wilkinson

Natchez, Mississippi Territory
October 15, 1809

James Wilkinson couldn't believe it. For days, he had been lying in wait in the old Spanish quarter at Natchez.

It had been three weeks since he had dispatched Captain House up the Trace with the letters for Major Neelly and Tom Runion. Ten days since he had encountered House at Point Coupee—dreadful place—and heard the whelp confirm that the letters had been delivered. Three days since the barrels of apples had been delivered to the docks. It remained only to fill the barrels with more precious cargo and hammer down the lids. Don Morphy and Havana were waiting.

But the trouble was, he had no cargo. No journals...no Lewis...nothing.

He paced the floor, his freshly blacked boots falling on the thick, luxurious carpet in the bedroom that Don Manuel Garcia de Texada had made available to him. The generous Spaniard had been more than hospitable in extending the use of his stately home to the commanding general of the United States Army—especially after Wilkinson had explained his latest enterprise.

He picked up speed, covering the rug in a few strides before wheeling on his heel and charging back to the other side of the room. Lamplight made the subtle pattern in the wallpaper glow golden, mirroring the ornate texture of the dark carpet. He clasped his hands together behind him, conscious of an almost unbearable tension in his arms and back.

Where were they?

He couldn't understand it. Even if Lewis proved troublesome—which undoubtedly, he had—Neelly and Runion should've reached Natchez with the journals by now! Didn't they care about getting their payoff, and the map to Lewis and Clark's fabled gold mine? Why, he had always counted on such low men for their piggishness and greed. He could hardly believe they would disappoint him in that respect—

As if in answer to his prayers, he heard a faint, distant jangle out on the street. Hardly daring to hope, he strode over and flung open the sash, letting in a rush of cold, damp air. The clip-clop of iron-shod hooves was almost eclipsed by the clattering of a wooden wagon bed. He leaned out, let his eyes adjust to the darkness, and stared as the wagon came down the street toward Texada's.

He steeled himself for disappointment. The wagon was traveling rapidly. In a few seconds, it would pass by. But no! The driver, a stout, burly man wearing a broad-brimmed round hat, called "Whoa!" The wheels creaked as the horses slowed down and brought the wagon to a stop in front of the mansion.

Wilkinson strained to make out the figures of the men entering the front courtyard. The burly driver was accompanied by a lean, fair-haired man in a dark coat. They passed just beneath him on their way up the walk, talking in low voices, their hats shading their faces from his view. Could it be? Neelly, and Runion, and between them, *oh God it couldn't be*—

Tall, broad-shouldered, with a stiff, soldierly gait—

"It *is* them! And with Lewis!"

He raced out of the room, his heart hammering so rapidly that he thought it might stop altogether. His boots drummed down the stairs as if he had wings on his feet. His journals, here at last! And Meriwether Lewis himself, worth his own weight in Spanish gold! A chuckle bubbled out of him. Speaking of gold, he supposed he'd better come up with that map to Lewis and Clark's gold mine! Neelly and Runion would want to set out for the West right away!

Giddy with anticipation, he skidded to a stop in the front hallway. At the front door, heavy raps echoed. Ever so slowly, Don Texada's liveried servant glided towards the sound. Unable to contain himself, Wilkinson shoved the astonished servant out of the way and wrenched open the door. There they stood before him, all three of them—

"My beautiful boys!" he cried.

Except they weren't. To his utter mortification, his eyes had played tricks on him. The burly chap was an army surgeon named Thurston, who had been pestering him for several days about the bad news from downriver. The lean man was not blond Tom Runion, but a gray-headed major named Backus. And the tall young soldier, whom he had wished so fervently to be Meriwether Lewis, was none other than Captain House.

Thurston and Backus blinked, no doubt surprised at being greeted so effusively by their chief. Captain House smirked, his eyes sparkling in the lamplight. Furious, Wilkinson glared at them and roared, "What the hell do you people want? It's late."

"A word, General," Thurston said.

"You'll get more than a word." Wilkinson stood aside to allow them entrance. To have expected to see Lewis, only to face yet another call from his incompetent officers, was a crushing disappointment. He gestured them into the parlor, where the fireplace glowed red with crackling warmth. As House passed him, he growled under his breath, "I hope you've come to beg my forgiveness."

House raised an eyebrow, a smile still playing about his lips. "I *have* come to beg, General—but not for your forgiveness."

Disgusted, Wilkinson took up a post in front of the glowing fire. With effort, he put aside the question of his missing journals and returned to the problem of the relocation of the Army from Terre aux Boeufs to Natchez. Even three decades of military service had not prepared him for the bungling he'd witnessed over the last several weeks. The move upriver—which Eustis had *insisted* upon, by the way—was turning into a full-fledged disaster. The overcrowded boats were still creeping like slugs up the vast gray expanse of the river, leaving filth and death in their wake.

"There is no excuse!" he announced. "In the name of God, the first boats should've reached Fort Adams already! What in blazes is taking so long?"

Major Backus exchanged glances with Thurston and House. "Sir, it ain't deliberate. The men aren't fit to travel. Every mornin' when we break camp, there's at least a dozen dead, maybe more. We're runnin' a regular burial detail, but sir, the men are exhausted. Plus, we gotta carry the dead men away from the riverbank, 'cause we don't want 'em washin' out—"

"That's absurd." Wilkinson pursed his lips. "They're corpses, what do they care? Under no circumstances should the advance of the army be delayed by affording unnecessary niceties to the dead."

Backus clenched his jaw, a little show of temper that didn't go unnoticed. Wilkinson narrowed his eyes in a silent threat. Backus licked his lips and said, "Yes, sir. I'll pass the order on to the men on burial duty that decency ain't required."

"Major, your insolence has been duly noted," Wilkinson snapped. "To put a fine point on it, I've court-martialed people for far less bumbling than you've displayed. Now what in the world do you want? You're driving me mad with these endless complaints about *trifles!*"

"Sir, speaking of trifles—" Thurston spoke up. "The officers have taken up a collection for the poor fellows we had to leave behind at the hospital at Point Coupee."

"You remember, General," House broke in, "that little spot by the False River, so reminiscent of Valley Forge."

Wilkinson gave him a murderous stare. Hadn't he ordered House back to New Orleans? What was he still doing running around loose? *And more to the point, had he heard anything about that blasted Meriwether Lewis?*

He shook himself. "What about Point Coupee, Doctor? Get to the point."

"Well, sir, they have no food down there, save for rations...but of course, they're rancid, and not fit to eat. We've raised about a hundred dollars among the officers, to buy chickens and vegetables for the sick men —"

"That's fine, Thurston, bully for you."

"Well, sir, would you care to contribute anything? Seeing as you're the commanding general and all?"

"Oh, for God's sake." Wilkinson fumed. It was just like these rascals to put all the responsibility for this shabby episode on him! Irritated, he dug around in his purse, came up with a couple of dollars, and thrust the money into Thurston's hand.

To his amazement, Thurston had the gall to say, "Sir? Is that all?"

Wilkinson choked. Surely the idiot didn't expect him to contribute more— on the salary Eustis paid him? "That's all you'll get out of me, Doctor. Now for God's sake, don't bother me any more. The only thing I want to hear from you is that the boats have been landed at Fort Adams. Is that clear? Now get out. You're dismissed."

House turned to follow the other officers out of the room. Compulsively, Wilkinson caught at his sleeve. "Captain House, a private word."

As soon as the other men were out of sight, Wilkinson drew House back to the fire. "What are you up to, Captain?" he said, doing his best to keep an icy edge in his voice. "You can't convince me you've suddenly developed a conscience."

House regarded him with the same impertinent look he'd been wearing all evening. "I do hope those two dollars won't break you, General."

"Never mind that!" Wilkinson spread his hands expansively, then rubbed them together and glared at House. "To make a long story short, I need fresh information, and I'm willing to overlook your recent, ah—transgressions— for the return of your reliable reports."

"Information about what?"

"Information about Lewis—"

"I've heard nothing aside from what's been in the newspapers." House shrugged. "Sorry."

"—and Clark. Have you heard anything of Clark? The papers say he's left St. Louis. That red-headed sonofabitch could wreck everything for me!"

House drew in a deep breath, arched his eyebrows, and studied Wilkinson for a long moment. Then he let his breath escape in a thoughtful sigh. "Wreck everything? That would be terrible, General." He looked away, and Wilkinson noticed his Adam's apple rise and fall. "I honestly don't know. I guess I've been busy with other —what did you call them? *Trifles.*"

Then, incredibly, House grinned and tapped him on the chest. "I have no earthly idea where Clark is. Hell, General, for all I know, he might even be in Natchez." With that, House clapped his hat on his head and touched the brim in a casual salute. "If that's all, General."

Wilkinson opened and closed his mouth several times before managing an enraged choke: "Dismissed."

After House left, Wilkinson stood by the fire, barely feeling the warmth. This blamed fiasco with the Army was bad enough, but that was trivial compared to his concern for Lewis's papers. Every day that passed without word from Neelly and Runion made it less likely that his gamble was going to pay off. And if they had failed—if the *awful thing* happened—

What if Lewis has escaped?

"No!" He plucked at his lower lip. "*Impossible.*"

But was it? The *Missouri Gazette* said Clark had left St. Louis days ago. What if Clark had caught up with Lewis? They had traveled over the blasted continent together—what challenge could they possibly find on the Chickasaw Trace? Banded together, good God, they could overcome anything!

"Unthinkable!" he moaned. His heart flopped into his stomach as his mind flashed back to the terrible days of the Aaron Burr trial. It was only through the grace of God that Burr hadn't dragged him down. His time on the witness stand had been so humiliating, he could hardly bear to contemplate it. What would it be like to be in the defendant's box instead? A horror, a horror! Sitting there, sweating, shaking, while Meriwether Lewis, dressed to the nines, an insufferable smirk on his proud, arrogant face, damned him from the stand—

And then what would he be? Stripped of his command? Exiled, like Burr? Or worse yet, thrown in some military prison, a despised leper, never to emerge into the light of day?

"*No.*" It wouldn't turn out that way. It couldn't. *Lewis is destroyed. I know, because I destroyed him.*

He pressed his hands together in a fervent prayer. By this time, if he had done his job properly, half the country believed Lewis had gone mad from syphilis, and the other half thought he and Clark were leading a violent rebellion in St. Louis. Even if Lewis did survive—even if he did reach Washington somehow—no one would ever believe him.

Or would they?

Well, if they did, he would just sail for Havana himself, and from thence to Spain—

Flee to Spain in poverty and disgrace, like Aaron Burr, never to return to his country—

Forlorn in his solitude, he stared at the flames dancing in the fireplace. Something had to be done, at once, to ward off disaster. He had always prided himself on his skillful handling of weapons. Sword and pistol were only the most obvious. More important to him had always been quill, paper, and ink. He clomped to his room, sat down at the exquisite writing desk Don Texada had provided for him, and gathered these weapons of war to him now.

Mentally, Wilkinson went down his list of allies. If Lewis really had broken free of the trap, he would need every one of these friends in the firestorm that would follow. Thoughtfully, he wet his lips. Then he bent over the paper and began to write:

The Honble H. Dearborn
Natchez Oct. 15th 09
Private
Dear Sir,

What a political crisis is the present! And how deeply interesting are its probable results. Thereby we must hope it may not be carried into execution.

Once again a powerful group of infamous characters threatens all we tried to build in those salutary days as Patriots of '76.

Wilkinson's pen flew across the page. Like himself, Henry Dearborn was a veteran of those terrible brave days of the Revolution. Dearborn had fought at the rail fence at Bunker Hill, starved with Benedict Arnold's force at Quebec, helped lead a dashing assault at Ticonderoga, and fought valiantly with Washington all the way to Yorktown. He had gone on to become one of the country's most influential military men. Most importantly, he'd always retained a soft spot in his heart for James Wilkinson. As secretary of war under Jefferson, Dearborn had helped save his hide during the Burr affair, and though he was out of office now—replaced by the execrable Eustis— Wilkinson knew his old friend was still a consummate political insider.

The deep, dark, and widespread conspiracy to which I refer is based in St. Louis and has strong support among the low and disaffected, who can be ever relied upon to rally to banditry. I fear the storm that may soon break upon my poor devoted head once again for being the bearer of such bad tidings, but word will soon reach you—if it has not already— that Governor Lewis has proven to be a rogue of the first order. His partner in knavery, Clark, has likewise distinguished himself, as perfect an example of the drunken obscene vandal as has ever proven the shame of that perfidious clan.

The situation in Upper Louisiana is lawless and calamitous. Should we be involved in a Rebellion (which Heaven avert), I will employ indefatigable industry, incessant vigilance, and hardy courage in demolishing same. Like yourself I glory at the thought of giving my life for the service of my country.

Wilkinson paused. Was he laying it on too thick? No, he didn't think so. In his experience, you had to lay the palaver on with a trowel before it penetrated the consciousness of those numbskulls in Washington. Dearborn, bless him, was certainly no exception. He continued:

Reports indicate that a challenge of honor was made, but that Messrs. Lewis and Clark failed to rise to the level of gentlemen and accept. Truly only the high positions mistakenly entrusted to them by our beloved trusting sage of Monticello have spared them the fate of being caned as common miscreants.

It further appears from my information that Governor Lewis has performed as a base peculator of the common good, looting the treasury for personal enrichment. As this point, it may be unnecessary to state that he is a swindler and an alien to honor.

Was this sufficient? He paused, tapping his quill gently against the blotter. Another idea came to his mind, and he wrote, chuckling:

I would be further remiss if I failed to mention that I have reason to believe his desperate enthusiasts have designs to assassinate me.

Yes, that ought to do it.

The uncertainty of human life and the instability of political affairs, induce me to lodge this information with you in its present crude State, which shall soon be improved and rendered more certain & satisfactory—

Many pressing engagements must be my apology for a short letter.

In the meantime farewell, do well, & believe me always your friend

J. W.

It was only the beginning. He would write a dozen of these letters tonight. He took a large swallow of steaming coffee brought in by Texada's servant. The rich brew scalded his tongue, but it also filled him with warmth and renewed energy—as did the thought of Lewis, arriving at the Federal City only to find every door shut, every ear closed to his eternally wagging tongue.

No matter what happened now, one thing was certain: he would survive.

Chapter 35
Julia

On the Trace, Mississippi Territory
October 16, 1809

Sergeant Thomas sat on the ground by the swollen Twenty-Mile Creek and pulled off his boots. Julia stood watching as he stripped off his socks to reveal surprisingly slender white feet with long, elegant toes.

"The trick to swimmin' with horses, ma'am, is not to try to ride 'em while they're in the water." Thomas stuffed his socks inside the boots for safekeeping. "All you hafta do is hang on to the mane and float. The horse'll do the rest." He began rolling up the legs of his white pants. "You best pack them fancy boots, ma'am, along with anything else you don't want to get wet."

Her face burning with self-consciousness, Julia slipped behind some bushes. So far, Sergeant Thomas had behaved properly towards her, but it still made her feel funny to undress knowing that he was just a few feet away. She took off her fringed boots, then hiked up her skirts and rolled down her embroidered garters and white linen stockings as quickly as she could. The ground felt cold under her feet, and rocks and sticks poked her soft soles.

Julia looked at the rapidly flowing stream. There was no sun today, and the water looked cold. "Isn't there anyplace to cross where the water's not so high?"

"I doubt it, ma'am," Thomas said. "But don't worry. Most horses like to swim."

Julia couldn't keep a plaintive note out of her voice. "We'll be wet all day."

Thomas grinned. "Well, ordinarily, I put *all* my clothes in the saddlebags, ma'am. But I figured that idea might not set too well with ye."

She felt exasperated. "No, Sergeant. That wouldn't do at all."

They mounted up and waded the horses in. The stream bed dropped off almost immediately. Julia squealed as the frigid water touched her bare feet. Thomas's horse set off for the opposite bank at once, its great head angled into the cross-current. Julia felt her horse wallowing. As the horse's feet left the ground, Julia clung to the saddle with her legs and clutched the reins, trying to maintain some kind of control. The river splashed against her skirts and filled them with water, lifting her from the saddle.

"Sergeant!" Julia panted with fear.

"Float, ma'am," Thomas yelled. "Don't ride, float!"

She grabbed the horse by the mane and hung on, her drenched clothes streaming around her. Her teeth were chattering by the time her horse pawed its way back on to dry land. Thomas lifted her down and put his Army blanket around her.

"There ye go, ma'am," he said. "Now you'll know what to do the next time."

Over the next few days, Julia wondered what her family back in Virginia would say if they could see her, swimming with her horse across wild streams and clambering out the other side, wringing water from her skirts. After what had happened at Big Town, Sergeant Thomas insisted that they keep to the woods as much as possible. At night, she and the big soldier sat close to the campfire, playing Crazy Eights and eating whatever Sergeant Thomas had caught that night.

Tonight, they were having frog legs. The meat was sweeter than she had expected, but tough. Her jaws ached from all the chewing. Sergeant Thomas reached inside his coat and pulled out his greasy pack of cards.

"You ready to play, ma'am?"

Julia shrugged and moved a little closer to the fire, trying to dry her dress. She hated to think how bedraggled she must look. "Sergeant?" she asked. "Do you think we'll ever catch up to my husband?"

"I imagine so, unless he ships out to join the Barbary Pirates or somethin'. And even then, I s'pose you'd be set on goin' after him." Thomas began to deal out two piles of cards. "I'm tellin' you, ma'am, I don't understand your husband a'tall. You'd think once he done send for ye, that he'd wait for you somewheres. I would."

Julia looked away, blinking her eyes. It was the smoke from the campfire that was making them water, she told herself. She felt a lump rise in her throat—

"Aw, ma'am," Thomas groaned. "You gone this whole day without cryin' even once." He poked her leg hopefully with her stack of cards. "Come on. How 'bout a bit o' Crazy Eights? You know you enjoy a round or two of an evenin'."

Julia turned away from him, drew up her feet, and hugged her knees. "I'm worried about Will. I miss my baby."

"Aw, no ye don't," Thomas said. "Don't you start a-talkin' that way! You'll work yourself into a cry sure as shootin', and what good'll that do either one of us?" He picked up her hand and folded her fingers around the cards, then placed the stockpile down between them and turned the top card over, starting the discard pile. "You go first, ma'am."

Julia stared at her cards in the firelight. She sniffled, selected a card to throw on the pile, and drew a new one. Sergeant Thomas responded almost instantly with his own. He whistled impatiently through his teeth while Julia studied her cards for her next play.

She wondered what Lew was doing in right now in St. Louis. Probably Easter was sitting by the fireplace, and feeding him and her own little Tom. She hoped her son was behaving. Over the last few weeks, he had developed a mind of his own, grabbing at everything and trying to put it in his mouth. He was crawling everywhere and pulling himself up on the furniture.

What if I miss his first steps? What if he says his first words, and I'm not there?

She suddenly felt Sergeant Thomas's rough fingers on hers again, gently taking her cards away. He reshuffled them and then slipped the pack back into his coat. He looked at her for a long moment. "Ma'am, how close are you to givin' out? I need to know."

Astonished, Julia stammered, "G-Giving out? Why, not close at all! My husband is in serious trouble. There are people in St. Louis threatening to kill him!" She shook her head, warm with anger. "No, Sergeant! I'm not turning back, ever. Not until I find Will."

Thomas fed a couple more sticks into the fire before speaking. "I kinda figured you'd say something like that. It's just that we haven't made up much time on the General. Which ain't that surprising, considering who he is and who *we* are."

"It's my fault. I'm holding us back."

"Now don't get down on yourself!" Thomas said. "I'm just sayin', I expect he's a-crossed the Tennessee at least two days ago, and us with some of the hardest travelin' still to go, past some of the meanest folks on the Trace."

Julia's eyes widened. "Mean enough to scare *you?* Are they Indians?"

Thomas shook his head. "Naw, just bad outlaws, white as you and me. I ain't even gonna trouble you about it, ma'am. I don't want you to wake up screamin'."

Julia wrapped her arms around her knees. "So what do we do?"

"Well..." Thomas said. "I've been in these woods a lotta times, and I happen to know a shortcut to the river."

"A shortcut? Will it save us a lot of time?"

"Half a day or more," Thomas said. "It could get us to the river and across by day after tomorrow, and I'm hopin' it'll slip us past the places where we might be spotted by any bad men. But ma'am, it ain't no easy path like what we've been travelin'. We shouldn't try it if you're close to givin' out."

Julia felt scared. In her heart, she feared Sergeant Thomas was right. But Will needed her, even if he didn't know it.

"You think I can make it?" Julia asked.

Thomas lifted one corner of his mouth. "I know I can get two horses and myself through the woods, so I guess I can take one little gal if she can keep her butt in the saddle and mind what I say." He winced to himself. "Sorry, ma'am."

"It's a deal," Julia said. Will would be waiting for her on the other side of the river. She imagined him sweeping her up into his arms—

"Get those cards back out," she told Thomas. "I want you to teach me how to play brag."

Thomas grinned. "I think Crazy Eights is more your speed, ma'am. Brag's a soldier's game. 'Sides, your husband'll skin me if he finds out I taught you how to gamble."

"We won't gamble, we'll just play. Besides, my husband doesn't have to know everything that goes on out here in these woods." She felt herself color, suddenly self-conscious again.

Thomas showed his big teeth. "What a deceitful creature is woman."

"Never mind." She edged closer to look at the suites of cards as he laid them out in the firelight. "So. Brag. How does it work?"

After a week on the Trace, Julia was coming to see the beauty in the place. The wild vines and Spanish moss tangled in the arms of the cypress trees looked soft enough to touch. But like everything around here, appearances could be deceiving. Sergeant Thomas said that some of the vines were really snakes, and that the fluffy moss was full of fleas. Even the ground itself seemed treacherous. It looked solid enough, but she could feel the horse's feet slipping with every step.

As the ground got softer, Thomas made her stop. He dismounted and put his horse on a generous lead. "We cain't risk having a horse break a leg," he told her. "I'll walk ahead and pick out a good path for us to take. You follow at a little distance. Holler if you see anything that needs my attention."

Watching him gingerly make his way through the stand of cypress, she felt nervous and she could tell the horses did too. They blew air through their big nostrils and rolled their eyes at each other. Julia leaned down and petted her horse's neck while talking softly to them both. "Don't worry, boys. We'll be out of this scary place soon."

Up ahead, she could see Thomas slogging through ankle-deep mud, holding his rifle high in the crook of his arm. Julia hoped that he didn't have a reason to use it except for shooting their supper. All the talk about outlaws had given her a shivery feeling in the base of her spine.

She saw Thomas pause, then sink down on his knees. She urged the horse a few more steps forward, trying to see what was happening. He was sinking further ...

Quicksand!

"Sergeant Thomas—Sergeant Thomas—" She heard a trill of panic in her own voice. Thomas was up to his thighs now.

"Stay back, ma'am," Thomas yelled, his voice loud but controlled. "Keep them horses back too."

Julia flung herself off her horse, falling to the ground. She picked herself up and ran forward through the mud to grab the lead line for Thomas's horse, then guided him back to stand with her own. The ground grabbed at her little boots like insistent hands.

She whirled around to watch him, expecting to see him sinking out of sight. She had heard tales of people being swallowed up in the Great Dismal Swamp in Carolina. What if that happened now? What would she do? She didn't even know where they were!

Thomas moved slowly, leaning backward with his arms spread, the rifle still raised high above the ooze. She raised her hand to her mouth to stifle the urge to scream and babble.

The next few minutes crawled by like hours. Thomas treated the quicksand more like water than earth, and with careful movements managed to position himself so that he was lying on his back. With her heart in her throat, she watched as he rolled over, then half-crawled, half-swam to drier ground, pushing the rifle ahead of him. Instinctively, she started to run to help, then stopped herself. The last thing they needed was for her to fall in the quicksand, too. She doubted she would be strong enough to lift herself out the way he had.

With a loud sucking noise, the ground finally loosened its hold on him. Thomas reached safety under a cypress tree and sat panting, covered with mud from head to toe. After a few minutes, he heaved a heavy sigh, got up, and staggered back to Julia and the horses. He laid his gun across the saddle, pulled his canteen off his horse and gulped down some water. His hands were shaking.

"Are you all right, Sergeant?" Julia asked tentatively.

Thomas leaned on the horse. "Shit," he said. "Er, I mean, p'shaw." He closed his eyes and rested his head against the horse's neck. "I didn't need that, ma'am. Most of the time, quicksand is only about knee-deep. But that patch—I couldn't even feel the bottom."

Julia didn't know what to say. It occurred to her that Sergeant Thomas could have died, and it would have been all her fault. And with him dead, she would probably perish, and Will would never even know what had happened to her.

They built a fire and had some coffee and a bit of dried beef. "Nothin' worse than wet boots full of sand," Thomas said. "Still, I was lucky. That sand coulda sucked them boots right off my feet."

Julia looked down at her own fringed boots. They were ruined, of course, and they looked laughable to her now. She wished she had a big, rugged pair that covered her legs to her knees, like soldiers wore. In fact, she wished she could just chuck the dress altogether and put on a shirt and breeches. Julia guessed such attire would be scandalous, but it would also be a lot more practical.

Thomas helped her mount up again and they resumed their march, with Thomas again leading his horse, stepping even more carefully than before. Julia couldn't stop thinking about how much nicer her legs would feel in a pair of men's breeches. "Sergeant?" she said. "Do you think I could ever pass as a boy?"

Thomas's laughter boomed through the woods, scattering the birds from the trees. "That's a good one, ma'am! You'd make a nancy boy and no mistake!"

Julia shrugged and pursed her lips. "Well, it happens in Shakespeare all the time."

"Wal..." Thomas looked back at her. "He was British, ma'am. I doubt you could fool any red-blooded American into takin' ye for a boy."

Thomas assured her they were making good time. They came upon a small but deep creek, its banks lush with cane grass. Thomas mounted up. For a while they followed the winding stream in companionable silence. Towards evening, her stomach was growling painfully when Thomas held up a hand.

"Ma'am, I'm seeing coon sign a-plenty along here. I want you to pull up and wait for just a minute." He slipped off his horse and handed her the reins to hold. "I'm gonna take care of supper. I won't be gone but two shakes of a dog's hind leg."

He slipped into the woods. Julia let herself relax a little by watching the creek. It had a good bit of clean, swift water in it. Minnows darted and dived just beneath the surface. It seemed to her that the creek was getting wider as they rode. She hoped that meant they were getting closer to the Tennessee River.

The Trace was full of strange sights, but up ahead she noticed a new one. A cloud hung about ten feet off the ground just above the water. It was fairly dense, and black. It drifted forward along the creek like a fine dark mist. She squinted at it curiously. She had never seen such an unusual phenomenon.

Without warning, the cloud engulfed her. She heard a high-pitched whine and realized with horror that it was not a cloud at all, but mosquitoes, hundreds of them, maybe thousands. She felt as if dozens of tiny needles were piercing her hands. Within seconds, they were attacking every surface, covering her face, clustering around her eyes, flying into her nose, her mouth, her ears—

She screamed and flailed at the air. The mosquitoes' whining rose to a squeal. Now they were inside her clothes, singing their mad, greedy song in her ears, biting her everywhere.

Her horse nickered and began to stamp its feet. Julia beat at the air, scratching herself in her frenzy. Her hat flew off and her hair came loose around her head. She couldn't see—she couldn't breathe—she couldn't think—

Someone grabbed her and dragged her off the horse. Julia kicked and flexed her back, screaming. She knew it was Sergeant Thomas, but somehow she couldn't stop. The mosquitoes were in her throat.

He ran down the steep bank of the creek, sliding in the cane grass, his big hands full of her hair and her dress. To her shock, she felt herself being plunged under the water. She choked and struggled, the maddening insects gone, only to be replaced with the fear of drowning. For several long, awful seconds, she didn't think he was going to let her up. She clawed at his hand as freezing water rushed over her.

His grip loosened and she flung herself upwards, seeking the air. She grabbed at Thomas for balance but succeeded only in making him lose his. His boots slipped in the mud and cane and he came crashing down, two hundred pounds of U.S. Army soldier knocking her onto her back for another noseful of cold creek water.

The next few moments were a tangle. Julia wailed. Thomas sat in the water with his head in his hands, horrified. He moaned, "By the horn spoons! General Clark's gonna kill me for sure!"

Julia dragged herself to her feet, soaked to the skin. She kicked water on Thomas, then pulled herself out of the stream by grabbing handfuls of cane grass. It left thin, painful cuts on her mosquito-bitten fingers and palms.

"It isn't fair!" Julia yelled. "I've been traveling so hard! All I want is my husband!" She stamped her foot. Tears rolled down her cheeks. She pulled at her wet, stringy, dirty hair. "I want Will!"

Sergeant Thomas stood up, dripping. His face was so red, he looked as if he might start crying himself. "I was just tryin' to help," he said plaintively. "Hope I didn't hurt ye none."

"Well, you did!" Julia shouted. "I want my husband—" She sobbed, afraid and ashamed of herself. "I want Will. I want Will." She staggered up the bank and flung herself down in the grass, crying into her cold, wet sleeves. "I want my husband. I want Will. I want Will."

She cried and cried, all of the bravery of the past two weeks exploding in her chest. She didn't want to be Mrs. General William Clark anymore. It was too hard. She just wanted to be Will's little Julia, and sit on his lap while he cuddled her and petted her and gazed into her eyes with such fondness that she felt warm and happy all over. She gasped and bit her fist. A couple of weeks ago, her biggest decision was whether to serve cabbage or peas with the roast. Now, she was in the middle of nowhere, her husband was in some kind of danger that she didn't understand, and her baby was hundreds of miles away. She hurt all over and had been wet and dirty for days on end. Three soldiers had tried to attack her in Big Town, and she was afraid outlaws or Indians might decide to scalp them at any moment.

As if that wasn't enough, now her body was on fire with ten thousand mosquito bites, and she had just screamed at the only friend she had in the world.

Julia made herself sit up. She really wouldn't have blamed Sergeant Thomas if he'd just taken the horses and left while she was throwing her screaming fit. But he hadn't. He was just sitting dejectedly under a tree, rubbing his wet head, looking as if he wished he had never been born.

Julia watched him for a minute. She felt timid about speaking to him, but someone had to break the silence.

"I'm sorry." Her voice trembled. Her throat felt sore from all the screaming.

Thomas grimaced. "Don't be, ma'am," he said. "You've actually helped me a great deal today."

"How on earth have I helped you? I've been a complete failure."

"Well, you see ma'am, I used to think I wanted a wife. But the last few days have convinced me that I don't. So you've saved me a peck o' trouble over the course of my lifetime." Thomas stood up and slapped his hat against his knee. "I gotta tell you, ma'am, when we do catch up with General Clark, I'm either gonna kiss him or punch him in the nose. I ain't decided which."

Julia stood up and limped over to her horse. Thomas lifted her up into the saddle, then crossed wordlessly to his own mount. He shook the reins. Julia shook hers. The horses plodded forward down the ever-winding creek.

Chapter 36
Clark

Dobbin's Stand, Tennessee
October 16, 1809

Clark lay on his side on the ticking mattress, his eyes open in the darkness. The growing cacophony of birds outside told him it was almost dawn. After listening for a while, he separated one song from another: the harsh cry of the bluejay, the deep-throated call of the whippoorwill, the soft morning trill of the screech owl.

He tried to picture each bird in his head, but had to push the thoughts away. Lewis loved birds. All during the Expedition, he was constantly sketching and writing about birds; he'd collected at least two dozen specimens never before seen by white men. Lewis had painstakingly described each one and lovingly packed them up to show to Mr. Jefferson. When they'd returned, Lewis had taken the birds to Philadelphia and given them to an ornithologist to be painted.

Clark sighed. Everything Lewis had ever written about birds was now sitting in a trunk in the corner of the room. Just looking at it made him feel a huge void in his chest, a great empty cavity of sadness that bordered on nothingness. He wished he could go back to not knowing. The anxiety of wondering what was happening was far better than the terrible certainty that the worst had occurred.

It was getting lighter in the room. He'd been traveling so hard for so many days that it was strange to feel no particular urgency. He could hear York shouting at somebody outside, though he didn't sound alarmed. Clark forced himself to get up, washed his hands and face in a small basin, and went outside. Seaman trotted up to him, his tail sagging at half-mast. Clark patted the dog absently. At least he hadn't gone running back to that godforsaken hole where they'd stuck Lewis in the ground.

"Well, you'll have to ask the Cap'n! There he is now!" York was shouting at the top of his lungs. He was talking to the landlady of this place. When they'd gotten here last night, the old woman had taken his four bits and unlocked the cabin without much conversation, which was just fine with him. He realized now the reason she was deaf as a post. She stood in front of her own little house with an earhorn angled toward York and a look of puzzlement on her face.

York was relieved to see him. "Cap'n, this here lady, Mrs. Dobbin...she's got breakfast for us, and she wants to know how long we're gonna be stayin'."

"Mrs. Dobbin, I expect we'll be here a couple more days," Clark hollered into the earhorn. "We got some business to take care of—I'm not sure how long it'll take. I'll pay ye in advance."

"All right—but I only take American money," Mrs. Dobbin hollered back. "It'll be a dollar. I'll get yer breakfast."

Clark paid her and gratefully accepted a tin cup of coffee and a plate of hot beans, biscuits, and bacon. Mrs. Dobbin even gave them a bone for the dog. Seaman lay on the ground at Clark's feet, gnawing away. York was quiet for once, lost in his own thoughts. Clark looked at York's tired face and felt profoundly lonely.

As he sopped up the last of the bacon juice, Clark said, "York, I intend to go back across the river. Something you said yesterday got me to thinkin'."

York looked surprised. "Somethin' *I* said?"

"You told me yesterday that that little girl at the Grinder's place told you she saw somebody standin' outside Lewis's window—a man called Preacher."

"Yessir. She said he was a slave-catcher, a real bad man, and that all the folks was afraid of him."

"Well, I think I might've run into him, two days ago. At that goddamn grog shop where I got clouted. There was a man there dressed up as a minister." Clark slung his coffee grounds in the dirt and got to his feet. "York, that's the last place anybody saw Lewis before he got to Grinder's Stand. I aim to track down this preacher, and the Chickasaw agent, too."

"Cap'n, what about Pernia? We gotta find his worthless hide! I'll be dad-blamed if Pernia didn't have somethin' to do with this."

"I doubt it," Clark said. It was painfully clear that Pernia hadn't done his job, but he didn't have the energy to waste on the little Creole right now. "I didn't think about it before, but that fella who runs the ferry must've seen Lewis. We can ask him. He might have something to tell us about Major Neelly's whereabouts."

"Yessir." York got up. They finished their breakfast and handed their plates back to Mrs. Dobbin. Clark tried to ask her to keep an eye on the trunk of papers, but communicating the request via earhorn proved impossible. He finally decided just to lash it shut and hope for the best.

The Tennessee River was running high and swift when they reached Colbert's Ferry at mid-afternoon. Colbert's flatboat was on the Mississippi side of the river when they came up, so they had to wait a while for him to cross. Clark dismounted and stood watching the river.

York said, "We cross this river too many times, we gonna be broke, Cap'n."

Clark stared at the swift current, out of habit trying to calculate its velocity and volume. It took a lot of effort to speak. "Yeah. I forgot. This fella's pretty proud of his ferry." He noticed York's eyes on him and felt annoyed. York's concern was just another unneeded weight. Maybe one of these days York would learn to mind his own goddamn business.

Within hailing distance, Colbert raised a hand and hollered out, "Five dollars."

"*Five?*" Clark shouted back. "Last time it was four, and that a damn jack-roll."

Colbert shrugged and cocked his head toward Seaman. "This time you got a dog. Dollar extra for the dog."

Clark felt his rage blooming, but when Colbert eased the flatboat over to the Tennessee shore, he swallowed his temper and put on a smile. "Friend, I know you're a tough negotiator. But before we parley, I need to ask you a few questions about a fella who came through here, about a week ago. Tall gentleman, well-dressed. He woulda been with two other people, a black man and a white man. And he had a dog with him, this dog here."

Colbert took another look at Seaman. His face suddenly darkened. "That fella a friend of yours?"

"He ain't a friend of nobody now," Clark said. "He's dead. Somebody shot him, and I'm trying to find out who it was."

"I'm not surprised to hear it, Mister. Coulda been most anybody. You ask me, that fella needed killin'."

Clark swallowed. "What makes you say that, Colbert?"

"Well, in the few minutes I knew your friend, he cussed me and held a gun to my head. Nearly blew it off. He had no cause to get huffed. I'm just trying to run a business here." Colbert frowned, still stung by the memory. "He wasn't any gentleman, either. I'm pretty sure he was drunk. He looked like a runagate, and his language was foul."

Looking at Colbert's stony face, Clark didn't know whether to laugh or cry. "What about the men he was with? How were they treating him?"

"They were scared to death of him," Colbert said. "And hell, I couldn't blame 'em. I was pretty a-scared myself. Major Neelly was one of 'em—he tried reasoning with your friend, but he wouldn't have none of it. The other fella, a little colored man, was cryin' like a woman. It was plain your friend had 'em both treed."

Clark glanced at York. If even half of what people said was true, Lewis had been violent and erratic, sometimes sick, sometimes incapacitated. He had killed a man in Big Town, brawled at Mom Murrell's tavern, threatened this man's life. And been drunk throughout.

He felt a tightness in his chest. *Just like George*, he thought with a stab of bitterness. Lewis had gone down the same terrible path as his brother. But no matter how sick, drunk, or crazy he was, in this moment he'd give everything he had to have five minutes with his friend.

He looked at Colbert. "I need to go across the river, and I'm planning on coming back tonight. Let's parley."

Colbert shrugged. "There ain't no parley, hoss. Ten round trip, including the dog."

Clark thought a moment, then fixed Colbert with a steely gaze. "Here's what. First off, my name ain't hoss. I'm a goddamn brigadier general, name of William Clark. And the man we've been talking about is—*was*—Meriwether Lewis." Colbert blinked as Clark continued, "I understand you got the exclusive government contract to run a ferry in these parts. Well, when I get done here, I just happen to be on my way to the Federal City, and I'm sure they'd be interested to hear that there needs to be a little competition out here. In other words, friend, if you won't help me, you're gonna find yourself outta business and up Salt Creek right quick."

Colbert was silent for a moment, sizing him up, weighing his words. Finally he said, in a more genial tone, "Fine, General. You shoulda said so right off. I'll pole you over for four dollars, and back for two."

"Deal." Whatever else you might want to say about Colbert, he wasn't stupid. They loaded up the horses and the dog and set off across the river.

Mom Murrell's tavern was quiet and dark, with no sign of life anywhere. The door yawned open, casting dank light on the chinked log walls and stained wooden furniture. The only souls in the place were scuttling cockroaches. Clark watched as one of them lumbered across the picture of James Madison and made its clumsy way up the wall. Bereft of his companions, Madison gazed forlornly down, as if anxious for the debauched circus to begin anew.

York said, "Lord, Cap'n, this place was packed the other night! Seems strange there ain't nobody around now."

"The woman who runs the place must've run out of liquor," Clark said. "When she gets some, she puts the word out somehow, and people come. It's amazing how fast a rumor can spread around up and down a road, or a river. These people knew about Lewis's death almost as soon as it happened."

"Cap'n, you s'pose the folks that killed Cap'n Lewis know we're here? That we're lookin' for 'em?"

"I expect they do, and that's fine with me. I want 'em to know." Clark kicked a couple of cockroaches out of his path and went outside. "York, let's double back toward the river. Lewis must've camped somewhere that night. Maybe he talked to somebody—somebody who's seen Major Neely or this fellow called Preacher. We've got to find out who this man is and where he's hiding."

With Seaman trotting along behind, they made their way through the woods toward the river. The trees were knobby and covered with tangled vines, even this late in the season. Except for birds and the soft rustle of wind through the leaves, the forest was so quiet Clark thought he could go for miles without hearing a single human voice.

But there was something there, some sign of habitation. Through a large, thorny thicket of blackberries, he saw a little shack. There were spent fires all around it, a sign that people had camped here recently.

He and York approached the place cautiously, but there was no one home. The shack was dilapidated but snug: no loose boards, no holes in the roof. As they circled around it, Clark noticed a small, hand-lettered sign above a box nailed to the door, about waist-high. He bent down and read:

CURRY'S STAND.
If I am not at home, ye may take anything ye need. Please pay here.

Beneath the sign, the small, open-topped wooden box said simply: PAY. Clark laughed. "Good Lord, here's a trusting soul. It's a cash box, York, for when he ain't here. I'm sure he makes a lotta money off of that! From what I've seen, the folks around here would dirk you for a dime."

Out of curiosity, York stuck his fingers into the box and saw them wiggling out the other side. "Ain't got no bottom to it!"

"Well, that takes care of that. Something tells me Mr. Curry's got a sense of humor." Clark tapped the door lightly and pushed it open. "I see already that people have taken him up on his offer. This place looks mighty poor."

Evidently, Curry was a diminutive fellow. The doorway was so low Clark had to stoop to avoid hitting his head on it. The interior of the shack was a shambles. For furniture, Curry had a table and chairs made out of a shabby barrel and some wooden boxes. In one corner, somebody had hacked together a little bed out of a packing crate. Everything was covered with leaves, twigs and scraps of paper, some with writing on them. Clark picked one up and studied it. It read: *How does the weather compare?*

Another read: *Ah! Too bad for the British!*

Clark shrugged in puzzlement and let them flutter to the floor. The writings were like one side of a very strange conversation; none of them made any sense. On one side of the tiny shack, a shelf holding several books hung on the wall. Clark felt surprised that no one had taken them, then remembered what Grinder had said about the journals: *Nothing of value.* The people on the Trace didn't put much stock in something as intangible as knowledge.

A sharp rasping cry made him jump; he was about to grab his pistol when he realize that the noise had been made by a bird, hanging in a rusty metal cage near the door. From what Clark could see in the dim light, it was nothing but a common bluejay. Doubtless its ordinariness explained why no one had stolen it. The bluejay stared at him with beady eyes and cocked its crested head nervously to one side.

He was about to go back outside when a piece of paper, half-buried under some leaves on the table, caught his eye. He brushed off the leaves, snatched it up and read with astonishment:

PROSPECTUS
OF
LEWIS AND CLARK'S TOUR
TO THE
PACIFIC OCEAN
THROUGH
THE INTERIOR OF THE CONTINENT OF NORTH AMERICA.

Clark gaped at it. Lewis had been carrying these advertisements around for months, trying to get people to subscribe in advance to his proposed three-volume work about the Expedition. He'd buttonholed almost every man in St. Louis. Clark studied the prospectus and noticed that next to the description of the first book, "Volume First," someone had written neatly: "Due out Spring 1810. 5 per cent discount for early subscribers. M. Lewis."

"York! Captain Lewis was here!" Clark ducked back out of the cabin and waved the paper in York's face. "He was here, he signed this. He must have talked to this man Curry. We need to find this gent."

"In a minute, Cap'n," York said, staring off into a bush. He reached in his coat for his slingshot and slowly stooped to pick up a rock.

Clark followed York's gaze and immediately saw what York was so interested in: a big, fat possum, ambling through the bushes toward the shack. The possum would make a fine supper for them both, with a scrap left over for the dog. He watched with anticipation as York swung the rock and took careful aim—

Before York could release the sling, a well-aimed rock flew out of nowhere and clipped the possum on the side of the head. The animal jumped, then fell dead in the dirt without so much as a squeak. York lowered the sling, mystified. "What—"

As they stood there watching, a man came out of the woods and hurried towards the possum. Though he was barely as tall as a boy, he was sturdy and rugged, dressed in a faded waistcoat and pants. He had a dark shock of hair, and his squarish face bore evidence of a beard. His arms were short and his stubby legs gave him a peculiar, bow-legged walk. He seemed oblivious to their presence.

Clark remembered that when he'd been a young man back in Kentucky, a woman from a nearby farm had given birth to a child that looked something like this. The unfortunate creature had lived only a year. Though small, this fellow appeared to be a full-grown man. He barely came up to Clark's waist, but judging from the swiftness with which he'd felled the possum, he could take care of himself. Caution was necessary.

Clark cleared his throat. "Sir—"

Startled, the little man jumped in the air. He grabbed up a rock from the ground, sending Seaman into a frenzy of barking. He looked like he might bolt into the woods in terror any second.

"Wait!" Clark held up his hands. "We're friendly. Are you the man that lives here? Are you Curry?"

Staring at him suspiciously, the little man lowered the rock and nodded. He blurted out a couple of syllables. York shushed Seaman and put away his slingshot. He muttered, "Don't forget, Billy, while you're busy makin' friends, they ain't too fond of strangers around here. You best tell him who ya are."

Clark nodded at York, then took a step toward the man and stuck out his hand. "I'm pleased to meet you, Curry. I think you might have met my friend, Meriwether Lewis. My name is William Clark."

Curry's whole aspect changed in an instant. He dropped the rock and burst into a gleeful cackle. Rushing forward on his tiny feet, he grabbed Clark's hand and gabbled, a long string of half-words. It sounded like the cawing of a bird: *gaw, ca, gaw*.

York chuckled and scratched his head. "He looks right glad to see you, Cap'n."

"You got that right." Clark couldn't account for it, but Curry seemed to know who they were. He could only figure Lewis must have told him.

"*Parlez vous francais?*" Clark tried, without success. "*Habla español?*" Curry shook his head. As far as Clark could tell, Curry could understand him, but the little man's palaver didn't make any sense at all. It wasn't Chickasaw, or any other language he'd heard spoken by the Five Civilized Tribes who lived in this area.

York moved closer and nudged him. "He don't have no tongue, Cap'n," he said quietly. "That's why we can't understand him. There's just a stump where his tongue should be."

Clark saw that York was right: at some point in his life, this man had been horribly mistreated. He shuddered to think about it. Unfortunately, it was going to make him devilish hard to talk to.

Curry hurried into his dark little cabin and lit a candle, then eagerly cleared the leaves and papers off the barrel that served as his table. He rummaged around and pulled out a wrinkled sheet of foolscap and a bottle of ink. Clark finally understood the little pieces of paper he'd seen lying all over the floor. This was how Curry made conversation.

Curry motioned them in and gestured for them to sit down around the barrel. Clark lowered himself onto a wooden box and propped his legs out in front of him. York perched precariously on another one nearby. Clark suppressed a smile and turned to his host. "Sir, I don't mean to cause you offense with this question, but may I ask how you came to lose your tongue?"

Curry dipped his quill in ink, scribbled a few words on a corner of the paper, tore it off and handed it to Clark. The paper read: *I'm a liar.*

Clark shook his head and smiled a little. "The fella says he's a liar, York. Somebody must've cut out his tongue for it."

"Doesn't exactly make you real confident in his word, does it, Cap'n?"

Sighing, Clark turned back to Curry. "Mr. Curry, I came here after my friend Lewis. I'm trying to find out what happened to him these last few days."

Curry scribbled away on the paper: *He was here. Fascinating man. He has a rare appreciation for beautiful things.*

Clark nodded, though he didn't see anything around here that could remotely be called beautiful. "Did he come alone?"

Yes, though he told me about his companions. He said they were dismal.

Clark laughed in spite of himself. He didn't doubt it. "What else did he say?"

We talked of botany and politics. And birds.

"I'll be damned." Leave it to Lewis to sniff out the only other educated man within a hundred miles and harangue him on his favorite subjects. "I suppose he told you all about the Expedition."

Yes, all about the needle grass and prickly pear. Sharp!

Curry put down his quill for a moment and looked at Clark with burning eyes.

He spoke of you. He's most anxious to see you. Please remember me to him when you see him.

"I will," Clark said. Obviously, this little man hadn't heard the news. "How long was he here?"

A few hours. I wish he'd stayed longer. He was desperate, and quite drunk. But then, so was I.

"What was he desperate about?"

Curry's hand flew across the page: *He didn't trust his companions. He feared people meant to do him harm. It was clear to me they already had. He had a wound on his arm*

"Yeah." Clark looked down at his hands. They were shaking. He looked up and saw that Curry had finished his sentence: *that had been made by a hook.*

"Good Lord." From what he remembered about the wound's appearance, it made sense. Who in God's name would attack another man with a hook?

Suddenly, Curry leapt up from his chair. Scattering dried leaves about, he rushed to his bookshelf, took down a book, and thrust it into Clark's hands.

Clark stared at it, confused. It appeared to be some kind of Latin botany text. He was about to hand it back when he noticed a folded letter tucked into the spine of the book.

"Is this for me? From Lewis?"

Curry nodded. Clark plucked the letter out of the book and unfolded it. It consisted of several loose sheets with ragged edges, as if the paper had been torn out of a notebook. At the sight of Lewis's handwriting, his vision started to swim, but he blinked the tears away. This was important. This was what Lewis wanted to tell him. He pulled the candle closer and began to read.

Dear Clark,

My friend I have much to tell you, and I fear time may be short, so please forgive the abruptness of this letter. This man Curry has given me respite in his home and peace enough to write, so I will take the opportunity to make this note in the hope it will find its way to you.

Clark, I have failed you in so many ways it is difficult to know where to begin. Perhaps I shall begin with the one attempt I have made to spare you pain, though I fear I have failed in that also; and that is in respect to my dealings with General Wilkinson, whom I unwittingly encountered in Cahokia last July.

Wilkinson lured me to a tavern under the anonymous guise of "an old friend." Upon my arrival, I was astonished to meet with the general himself, and at that time he made me a most extraordinary proposition, involving myself and you. He believed we could be persuaded to abandon our posts in the govt. of U. L., and enter into a corrupt alliance with the Army to take the Wstrn trirrity and Mexico.

Clark I assure you I rejected this obscene entreaty in the strongest and most unequivocal terms, and further left him with no mistake about my intentions, which were to expose him for the loathsome traitor and scoundrel that he is, and thereby ensure that he would never again jeopardize the liberty of any part of the U. States.

I should have told you then, but knowing the villainous and relentless attitude of the general, I feared the consequence to you and family should you be drawn directly into the conflict, knowing how much your family has already suffered at the hands of this miscreant.

It was my full intent to relate Genl W's offer to Pres. Madison and Secy. Eustis upon reaching the Federal City, and let them draw their own conclusions on the matter; I can only hope my credibility is not so tattered that they will disregard the intelligence.

Clark, Wilkinson is fully aware of my intentions and my whereabouts, and has already made one violent attempt on my life, which I repulsed, but I am expecting another any moment. I fear I am not at my usual strength and cannot rely with confidence upon my own bodily powers. I have been suffering from malarial ague for months, with episodes of agonizing pain and extraordinary weakness, the worst of my life, and have begun to lose all hope of ever shaking it off.

In my desperation I have done something unpardonable. In the summer I began to dose myself with opium pills, which at first had the desired effect of lessening the fever and pain; but eventually they failed to operate, so I began to drink laudanum, which initially helped a great deal. But Clark I am fully in the grip of the laudanum now and am taking two or three ounces a day, with little effect except to keep the fever at bay for a few hours. If I do not take it, I am subject to such agony of mind that I am fully out of my senses, I must have it and know not how I shall ever free myself of it now. The shame is intolerable.

In my current state I fear I will not reach Nashville. I have the Expedition journals and papers safe with me for the moment, but as I have little faith in either Pernia or Major Neelly to dispose of them properly in the event of my death, I am very uneasy over their fate should I not reach Nashville. I do fervently hope you are coming on.

Clark there is something else I must tell you regarding the manuscript of the book about our late journey to the Pacific Ocean. It pains me greatly to admit this to you, but I have been deceiving both you and Mr. Jefferson for some time about my progress on the book. In truth, I have written not a line—not a word—not a single letter. I should have been truthful with you about this from the beginning, but I continued to deceive you about this, as about many other things. I am sorry.

So Clark, now you know all. It is doubtless clear to you that the man you counted as your friend is in fact, a liar and a coward. You are too good a friend and have always been too inclined to trust; I fear I have abused that tendency in you. I shall reproach myself for it until the day I quit this earth.

I have entrusted this letter to my friend Curry, and I commend him to you. He has a tamed blue jay which is the most talented I have seen of that species; both his song and his affinity for human beings are extraordinary. Ask him to show you if you have not seen it.

Am still in great hopes of seeing you. I am not deserving of your forgiveness, but perhaps in time all can still be made right. In any event, I remain your most sincere and obdt. servt. and eternal friend—

M. LEWIS.

Clark read the letter over twice. So many emotions were seething inside him he didn't know what to feel. About Wilkinson, shock. Then rage. That sonofabitch had cost him so much. He'd ruined George's life. Now he'd taken Lewis's.

And Wilkinson would pay. He'd see to that. It was intolerable to think that that bastard could be allowed to drive just men into ruin—into their *graves*—

But the laudanum! *Oh, Lordy. I had no idea. Lewis never showed it. Or maybe he did. Maybe I just didn't want to see it—*

And the book. That hurt, like a punch in the gut. It was awful to think that Lewis would lie to him about something as important as that. The Expedition was the central event of their lives, and the whole world was waiting to learn about the scientific and geographical discoveries they had made. How could Lewis have done nothing in the past three years to get the book ready for publication? *He lied to me, even lied to Jefferson...Makes me wonder what else he's been lying about—*

Even as the thought came into his head, he dismissed it as unworthy, disloyal. This letter included, Meriwether Lewis was still the most honest man he'd ever met. He was even honest about his lying. Clark remembered when he and Lewis had discussed their respective duties on the Expedition. Lewis had asked him to handle the day-to-day discipline of the men, saying, "I'm a prick, Clark. I'm too hard on people." Whatever else you wanted to say about Lewis, the man knew his own faults. And yes, he could be hell on other people. But he was always hardest on himself.

Clark realized tears were running down his cheeks. Both Curry and York were staring at him. Curry's face was creased with concern; York's was maddened by the need to know. Clark folded the letter, put it in his coat, and gave York a small, imperceptible nod.

Clark turned back to Curry. "Thank you for saving this letter for me, Mr. Curry. It means a great deal." He paused for a moment to compose himself. "Curry, do you know anything of a man called Preacher, that travels this Trace?"

Curry grimaced, picked up his quill and scribbled on the piece of paper: *Preacher is the man with the hook.*

Clark stared at him. "What is this man's name?" he demanded. "Where can I find him?"

Curry evaded his eyes and fingered his quill pen. Clark said, anguish in his voice, "Curry, this man hurt my friend."

Curry dipped his quill in the ink again, the words spilling out of his pen onto the wrinkled foolscap: *His name is Tom Runion. He's not a preacher at all. He stays at Big Town, or across the river.*

Clark studied the words. Big Town. That meant Runion knew Major Neelly. He could see now how it must have played out. With Neelly's help, Runion and that fat fellow, Squyres, had attacked Lewis outside of Big Town. They'd gotten more than they'd bargained for; Lewis had shot Squyres and left him for dead. But the game was just beginning. This bastard Runion had stalked Lewis up the Trace, while he got sicker and sicker, and Neelly got him drunker and drunker. What had the man at Old Factor's said? *They were just pouring liquor into him.* Until he choked.

York was right. Pernia was part of it. He had to be. When Lewis was dead—after Runion had executed him—Neelly and Pernia had divided up his valuables. Then they wrapped him in a blanket and threw him in a hole to rot.

Clark breathed deeply. He felt clear-headed, almost calm. "Curry," he said, "I'm obliged. You've been a great help to me. And I appreciate the hospitality you extended to my friend. It meant a lot to him. He said so right here." He tapped the letter in his coat pocket. "I have to go, but before I do, can you do something for me? Can you show me that beautiful bird you've got?"

Curry beamed. He went over to the bluejay's cage, took it down from its hook, and carried it over to the barrel. He unlatched the door and the bluejay hopped out onto his stubby arm. Curry petted it and made his soft sounds, then laughed as the bird danced up and down on his arm.

The bird opened its throat and made a shrill trilling noise. Clark shook his head in amazement. Somehow, this little man had taught a bluejay to sing.

He smiled at Curry and thanked him. As he and York rose to leave, Clark remembered the prospectus for their book about the Expedition. He found it again among the shamble of papers on the floor and held it up to Curry. "I hope you didn't give him any money."

Curry looked surprised, then nodded vigorously. Clark shook his head. Only Lewis could sell a subscription to a man in the middle of nowhere, for a book that didn't exist. He took Curry's quill pen and started to scratch out the words Lewis had written on the prospectus: "Due out Spring 1810." Then he thought better of it. He crossed out "Spring" and wrote in "Fall." Then he signed his name: William Clark.

He and York ducked out the door and collected their horses. Night had fallen, and a soft fog rose over the Trace. York was quaking with agitation. "What do we do now, Billy?"

Clark put his hand on York's shoulder. "York, this preacher, this slave-catcher, is a man named Tom Runion. He hangs around down at Big Town, and Curry thinks he has a place upriver. I think this man killed Captain Lewis, and that Major Neelly helped him."

York seethed with outrage. Clark realized, with dawning surprise, that York cared about finding Lewis's killers as much as he did.

"We're goin' back across the river, and I'm going to find this Runion. He'll be hard to catch. I'm not worried about Major Neelly, because he can't hide.

Everybody knows him here." He looked at York. "You were right about Pernia. I think he was in on it. At the very least, he stood by and let it happen, then helped himself to his master's things."

"Cap'n, I want to get that little fucker," York's eyes were wide and pleading. "I want to track him down. There's no way Pernia could've gotten out of these woods by himself. Wherever he is, he's hidin' where the white folks won't go. Please, let me look for him. Please, Billy."

Clark considered it. He hated to divide their tiny force, but York could probably find Pernia faster than he could. "All right. But York, be careful. This fellow Runion is a slave-catcher. If he finds you alone, you can bet he won't hesitate to kill you—or worse. We'll split up at Grinder's."

They re-crossed the river at the ferry, then took to the dark woods, disdaining the road, stealthy as a pair of owls. The sky was already beginning to lighten by the time the winded horses got to Grinder's Stand. Clark looked at the dark cabins squatting in the gloom. He felt haunted. Would he ever know exactly what happened there?

York slithered down from his horse with his rifle and dirk. "York, you got enough ammunition to last you?" York nodded. "All right. I'll meet you back here tomorrow afternoon. Come whether you find him or not."

"All right, Cap'n." York grinned, a bright flash of white in the dark. He whistled softly for Seaman. "Come on, boy."

Clark watched as the two of them disappeared into the woods. He tethered York's horse to the back of his saddle and continued up to Dobbin's, his shoulders sagging with exhaustion. He would rest for a little while, clear his head, then go out and see if he could find where this man Runion lived. He'd find out what drove him...what he wanted...then he'd lay a trap.

He was almost stumbling with fatigue when he reached his cabin at Dobbin's Stand. Dawn was just beginning to break over the trees. He hobbled the horses and left them to graze, then hitched open the door of his cabin. A few hours shuteye and he'd be good as new—

He heard a strangled moan and realized it had come from his own throat. What he saw inside the cabin nearly brought him to his knees.

The cabin had been ransacked. Lewis's trunk lay upended in the middle of the room, the lid jimmied open, the contents scattered about. Piles of paper littered the floor. Their field notes from the Expedition had been dumped out of their portfolios and were now a hopeless jumble; maps and scientific notes had been shuffled in with letters, vouchers, and government documents. The bound journals lay haphazardly all over the room, along with the otter skin, the tomahawk, and whatever else was left of Lewis's things.

"Oh, Christ." He stepped inside the cabin and sank down on the floor. *Who would do something like this? And what the hell were they looking for?* There were hundreds of pieces of paper here, and no way to tell what had been taken. He didn't know how he would ever put it all back in order.

As he sifted numbly through the detritus nearest his knees, a large rolled sheet caught his eye. It was a map he had drawn at Fort Mandan, during the long winter of 1805.

Clark clutched it as if he were drowning. The map was impossibly neat and precise. He doubted anything would ever make that much sense to him again.

Chapter 37
Neelly

Nashville, Tennessee
October 18, 1809

A sharp rap came on the door. Neelly lifted his head and realized he had no idea where he was. Nothing about the dingy room seemed familiar. Floundering facedown on a stained, shapeless mattress, he raised himself on his elbows and tried to remember which roadside stand he and Governor Lewis had camped at last night.

The tavern-keeper's harsh voice cut through the door like an ax. "Major Neelly! Open up, damn you! You need to settle up, or I'll bloody well toss you out on your arse!"

Neelly peeled his eyes open and moaned. He wasn't on the Trace at all. He was in a run-down tavern on Water Street. Water Street was just far enough off Nashville's main square to be disrespectable; this part of town was known as Cheapside. Only it wasn't as cheap as he'd hoped. How long had he been here? Two, three days? Governor Lewis wasn't with him any more.

Governor Lewis is dead

"Neelly!" The tavern-keeper brayed again. "I know you're in there! Open this goddamn door—"

"I'm comin', for Christ's sake." Neelly wallowed upright and put his feet on the floor. Acrid, alcohol-tinged bile vaulted into his throat. His own odor offended him. The wash basin still had a little dingy water in it; he splashed it on his face and tried in vain to smooth down his disordered hair and beard. A man had to keep up at least an appearance of self-respect—

"For the last time, Neelly—"

Cursing, Neelly lurched to the door and wrenched it open. The tavern-keeper, Boyd, stood there, his heavy eyebrows knitted into a glowering frown. Neelly's stomach clenched; he hated the Scotch sonofabitch.

"Major, you owe me for last night's lodging, an' the night before. I've been trying to rouse you for days. I ken you've been on a spree, and that's your affair. But I will have me money."

"Fine. Jesus! Just wait for a second." Neelly staggered back from the door and looked around the room with gummy eyes. Finally he saw his bags and saddle heaped under the table by the window, where he'd thrown them the night he got here. That was after he'd bought three bottles of whiskey.

He kicked an empty bottle out of the way and sent it skittering under the bed. He rummaged through the bags until he found Governor Lewis's black leather pocketbook. "What do I owe you?"

"Six dollars, for lodging and meals, and stable and oats for the horses."

"But I haven't eaten anything since I got here."

"The meals were made and served. It's your affair whether you eat 'em or not."

Neelly sighed. He pulled out six dollars and handed it over. Governor Lewis's money.

Governor Lewis is dead

Boyd looked at him with tight, greedy eyes. "Will you be stayin' another night, then?"

Neelly looked around the bleak room, vaguely hoping to find someone he could ask. "I don't know," he said. "Can I tell ye later?"

"Fine, but if you don't pay me by sundown, I'll throw you out bag an' baggage," Boyd said. "This ain't a poorhouse, mister."

"I understand," Neelly said. Boyd continued to stare at him with beady-eyed contempt. *God, what more does he want from me?* It was almost as if he *knew*. Finally, Boyd sneered and moved off. His footfalls clattered down the rickety staircase like nails being hammered into Neelly's brain.

Neelly closed the door. He crossed unsteadily back to his saddlebags, banging his knee on the table leg and almost upsetting a pot of ink. A dark blob splashed onto the surface of the table, barely missing a crisp sheet of paper on which he'd penned the beginnings of a letter.

The sight of the letter made him feel sick. It was ridiculous, really, for a man like him to presume to write to Thomas Jefferson. But somebody had to tell him—

Sir, Nashville Tennessee 18th Octr. 1809

It is with extreme pain that I have to inform you of the death of His Excellency Meriwether Lewis, Governor of Upper Louisiana who died on the morning of the 11th Instant

"Oh, Lord." Neelly sank back on the fetid mattress. He had the money. He had the horses. What he didn't have were the very things he was supposed to take, the things that mattered most.

"Them goddamn papers." He dropped his head in his hands and fingered his greasy hair. Governor Lewis had sure thought the world of those papers. Why, on the last night they'd been together, Lewis had cradled them on his lap like a baby while icy rain poured down on their heads. He didn't care whether he lived or died, as long as the papers got delivered to the President—

Governor Lewis is dead

Only great man I ever knew—

Neely struck his knee with his balled fist. *Damn General Wilkinson anyway!* How had he ever let himself be talked into this scheme? He should have known it would end in disaster, but he could never have imagined how bad the end would be. Grinder's Stand, all those people around. Pernia, nasty and rotten to the last. The broken bottle, laudanum and blood running through the cracks in the floorboards. He'd never seen so much blood in his life. Lewis's buffalo robe had been soaked with it—God, some of it was still caked under his fingernails—

"I'm sorry," he blurted to the empty room. Truth was, he'd panicked, and in his panic, he'd managed to botch it, just like he always did.

And in the end, when it was all over, he'd run like a rabbit, without the damn journals. He'd seen them sitting there, but he couldn't bear to touch them, didn't want them in his possession, *it just seemed wrong—*

But as usual, he'd been stupid. Runion wasn't squeamish. Shit, Runion was probably halfway to Natchez with the journals by now, panting after his reward and the map to the gold mine Wilkinson had told them about. The one where there were gold nuggets as big as your fist, just lying on the ground for you to pick up. He almost wished Pernia hadn't set him straight on that one. It'd sure been nice to think about.

But those journals...that was another matter. He'd started something with Lewis back on the Trace, trying to get his hands on those papers, dreaming of the five hundred dollars Wilkinson had promised to pay him. All the mistakes he'd made...well, they couldn't be fixed. But he could still finish it.

Neely got up. He had to go back. He would leave today, this afternoon. He could be back at Grinder's in a couple of days, find the journals, find Runion. He wondered if Runion would kill him on sight. He found he didn't care. It was still worth trying to get back some of what he'd lost.

And speaking on the subject, before he left, he'd sit down and finish his letter to Jefferson. He could post it on the way out of town. What did it matter who he was? He had a right to say his piece. *I'm a man too, ain't I?*

Chapter 38
York

On the Trace, Tennessee
October 17, 1809

York whistled sharply. "Keep close, Seaman!" The dog, who was sniffing about fifty feet ahead, trotted back over the broken trail. The bare branches of withered bushes caught at his long fur. York stopped, petted the dog, and took the opportunity to sniff the air himself. The overriding scent was polecat, no doubt the object of Seaman's attention. York smiled. He had heard that some of the Indians had found a way to cook polecat like possum, complete with taters and dumplings.

"I think we can do better'n that, boy," he whispered. He pulled out the last of his grease and applied it again to his face and hands. The mosquitoes and gnats were so fierce back here in the swamps that it was difficult not to become distracted. He didn't even have Massa Billy around to act as bait for the ravenous critters.

A lapse in concentration could cost him and Seaman more than a tussle with a smelly polecat. York had already seen one big, mean iron bear trap nestled in the gravelly soil—the kind of trap that would break a man's leg or a dog's back. In a strange way, the sight of the traps was encouraging. He had seen nothing in the way of bear sign, which told him that the traps were probably intended for other large predatory animals—say, white men and their tracking dogs. Unless he was very much mistaken, he was near to finding the people who lived in this poor place.

They were called maroons. It wasn't something that white folks talked about much, but almost every place in America had its little colonies of runaway slaves and Indians who banded together and hid out in the woods or the mountains, or anyplace else that was hard to get to and easy to defend. A few years back, George Washington had tried to drain the swamps in Carolina to get rid of a huge maroon settlement that was attracting every Negro within a hundred miles.

There weren't enough blacks on the Natchez Trace for a big operation like that. Still, York was willing to bet these woods were supporting plenty of folks who had gotten tired of their white or Chickasaw masters or had somehow managed to jump free of the slave traders who marched people down from Nashville to the Mississippi Territory. So far, he hadn't heard anything that sounded like a settlement, and he didn't see anything but dark, rough woods. But he could swear he smelled venison and sweet potatoes.

They moved on, York stepping cautiously and using all his senses. Looking down, he could see Seaman's tongue dripping.

"What'd I tell ya, Seaman? Here's hopin' you and me are big and black enough that these folks'll talk to us. Or at least that maybe they won't shoot us." He straightened up. He had spotted motion in the woods. "I think we're about to find out."

York pushed his round hat back on his head so that his black face was unmistakable. He held his rifle loosely. He wanted whoever was watching him to know that he was ready to defend himself, but that he wasn't looking for a fight. "Hello!" York called, just as Seaman began to bark.

A man stepped out of the woods. York found himself looking down the barrel of an old-fashioned musket. The man who held the musket was the most impressive-looking person York had seen since they'd met up with the Nez Perce three years ago. He was taller than York, and his fully dressed crest of hair gave him at least six inches more height. His light buckskin vest revealed a powerful build, with a finely muscled chest smeared with animal grease. Below, he wore leggings that appeared to have been cut from an old pair of pants, and his feet were clad in moccasins.

But most striking of all was his color. In spite of his Indian appearance, the man, like himself, was as black as a buffalo.

York lowered his rifle to show that he wanted to be friends. The man stood watching him suspiciously, his gaze flicking between York and Seaman.

"He ain't no trackin' dog," York said. "And I ain't with no patroller. I'm by myself. Ain't nobody followed me here." He thumbed back in the direction from which he'd come. "I seen that y'all don' exactly welcome strangers."

The man's gaze remained hard. When he spoke, it was with a strong, guttural Chickasaw accent. "You don't look like no runaway. Where'd you get that Kentucky rifle?"

"Home," York said. "You're right. I ain't a runaway. My name's York. I'm from Kentucky. I'm travelin' through your country because a bad man killed a friend of mine. I'm lookin' for him." He jerked his head towards the dog. "This here's Seaman. He was my friend's dog."

The man introduced himself as Catfish. He continued to look at York skeptically. "I don't know of no black man killed 'round here. You're travelin' by yourself?"

"Only today," York said. "I'm with my massa, but he's back up on the Trace. He give me permission to come back here. I gotta meet up with him later today at the place called Grinder's Stand. And my friend, he was white." York noticed the frown on Catfish's face. "But brave. A real good man."

"We don't have much truck with white men back in here, York." Catfish startled York by taking the front of his vest between his thumb and forefinger and gently rubbing the material. "Nice clothes you got there." He flicked the fabric-covered buttons before backing off a step." Well, come on into camp, York. Least you can do while you're out here is eat a meal with some free folks before you hustle your black ass back to massa." He turned and slipped back into the woods. Feeling stung, York followed, Seaman at his heels.

The camp turned out to be a tight group of four huts. York saw about fifteen people bustling around, though he presumed there were probably more out hunting or watching for intruders. Besides Catfish, he spotted at least three other warriors in camp along with the women and children. Two young women knelt over stone mortars and ground corn with pestles. Another woman was laying out cut sweet potatoes to parch, while another, no more than a girl, stirred a pot steaming with boiling venison. A half dozen little girls and boys, clad only in fragments of blankets or ragged pantaloons and frocks, ran around the campsite, capering and playing jokes. They ranged in shade from black like York and Catfish to the light tawny skin of the Chickasaws.

Catfish instructed the girl at the cookpot to bring York a meal, then led him to a clearing near one of the huts, where some felled logs had been arranged as makeshift benches. York hunkered down with Catfish and another man, this one a Chickasaw whom Catfish introduced as Big Field. York gratefully accepted a gourd filled with venison and sweet potato stew, along with a hunk of hot, ashy bread. The children had discovered Seaman and engaged the dog in a game of chase. It did York's heart good to see the dog's tail wagging for a change.

Catfish filled Big Field in on what York had told him, and York gave them both hunks of tobacco. Big Field said, "York, what do you care if some white man kill another white man? Sounds like a good thing to me."

"This white man was special to me," York said. "I don' expect you to understand."

"Just as well," said Catfish.

"Listen, though," York said. "I think a man named Preacher killed my friend."

Both maroons stiffened and exchanged glances. Catfish said, "Preacher don' come back in here. He know that if he do, he gonna suffer the way he make other folks suffer." He pointed over to the spot where the two young women were pounding corn. "See that black girl there?"

York nodded. The girl wore a red bandanna and had a broad, appealing face, with apple cheeks and slanted dark eyes. "What about her?"

"She belong to a Chickasaw family down 'round Big Town. One day, her mist'ess send her out with a pass to go help with a baby-birthin' down the road. Preacher caught her out. She shows him her pass, but he say that the time already up, even though it ain't. He tell her he gonna punish her, and then he make her bargain with him."

York closed his eyes and swallowed. "Yeah. I can guess the rest. She have to let him have his way so he won' beat her."

"I don' know *what* he do," Catfish said. "She won' talk about it much. All I know is she say she wish now he just beat her. That woulda hurt her on the outside, 'n then heal up. 'Stead, he took her back to his cabin, and the things he do, and make her do—she say they hurt her on the inside. Her heart been broke since then." He looked down. "She been with us about two years now. She still too scared to have any doin's with men."

York watched the girl and rubbed his hands together for several moments. "Preacher's gonna die. I promise you that. The white man who was killed up on the Trace? Well, he was a real important man, not just a little girl who couldn't fight back. And my massa? Well, they was best friends. They was closer than twin brothers. Preacher won't survive this."

The men exchanged glances, and York could tell they didn't believe him. "You can help me," York said. "Reason I came here is that I'm lookin' for a man who helped Preacher. He's a little yaller fella by the name of John Pernia. He's a New Orleans boy—"

A high-pitched giggle from Big Field interrupted York. The expression on Catfish's fearsome face had changed too, and he laughed out loud. York smiled and added, "He ain't the kinda man you usually see wanderin' around in the wilderness."

Catfish grinned. "York, I guess I'm enough of an Indian now to believe in fate! We was just talkin' this mornin' about what're we gonna do with Pernia, and now here you come along!"

"Shit," Big Field said. "We ain't ones to give up runaways, but you can have 'im. We got our standards too, you know. I voted to bash his head in, but Catfish thought we oughta wait and see if he don't die on his own and save us the trouble."

Catfish explained, "That fella's been hangin' around here for days, moochin' meals and tryin' to get one of us to guide him outta of the territory. He don't have nothin' to trade but some fancy duds nobody'd ever want. And nobody much cared to spend a week or two in his company, so we passed on the trip."

He nodded towards the apple-cheeked girl at the mortar. "You say he helps Preacher? Don't tell her. She's the only one who has a soft spot for the little bastard. She's been putting out a plate for him at the edge of camp in the evenings. By morning the food's gone."

"Where can I find him?" York asked.

"After the first day we wouldn't let him stay in camp," said Big Field. "He was too fussy, and he can't do nothin' to make himself useful."

"I hear he makes a mean hangover remedy," York said.

"Oh yeah?" Catfish said. "Well, that might come in handy ever' once in a while. Anyways, York, he's stayin' in a cave we sometimes use for smokin' meat. I'll be more'n happy to take ya to 'im."

Feeling cheered, York took his empty gourd back to the women. He thanked them for their hospitality, whistled for the dog, then followed Catfish back out of camp.

The cave was only about fifty yards from the maroons' huts. Catfish showed him inside. Pernia wasn't around, but from the strong smell of unwashed body that mingled with the redolence of smoked venison, he couldn't have been gone too long.

Seaman thrust his nose into a heap of clothes on the floor and started to whine. York bent down and examined the garments. On top was a ruffled shirt of fine white linen. Underneath were a couple of pairs of yellow nankeen breeches—Captain Lewis's typical daywear. A pair of badly scuffed black hussar's boots lay nearby.

"Thanks, Catfish." York stood up and ducked out of the cave. "I'll take it from here."

Catfish shook his hand and turned back towards his camp. He didn't give

York a backwards glance. York watched the black Indian for a moment, feeling a little envious. He had no desire to live a life as a fugitive, but he admired the grit of these maroons.

He began to scout the area, Seaman by his side. Sure enough, a fair amount of human waste was heaped under a nearby bush. It was just like Pernia not to bother digging a latrine.

York widened the circle of his search. He heard a low rumbling sound coming from Seaman. The dog's black lips were drawn back; he had picked up the scent of something he didn't like.

Then, York heard the faint sound of a human voice. "Seaman!" he whispered. "Hush a minute!"

Our captain he lies dead, handsome Willie-o
Our captain he lies dead, handsome Willie-o
Our captain he lies dead
With a bullet in his head
If ever I return, handsome Willie-o

York couldn't believe it. *Still singing that goddamn song!* He swiftly rounded a brushy ridge and saw Pernia shuffling around a tree holding a round hat in one hand. The Creole's face looked dull and dirty. He was dressed in a long duster coat made of blue striped ticking. The coat was so long that it flapped around his ankles, and the sleeves had been folded up several times. His feet were covered in a pair of bright red lounge slippers. Every so often he would stoop over, pick up a pecan, and deposit it in the hat.

York cleared his throat. Pernia looked up and gave him a blank stare. It was almost funny to watch his expression change over the next few heartbeats, from puzzlement to dawning recognition to abject terror.

Pernia dropped the hat, pecans flying everywhere, and dashed headlong into the woods. "Come on, Seaman!" York sprang forward as the baying dog raced ahead. He barreled through the brush, his legs rapidly closing the distance. Pernia foiled him momentarily by skittering across a stream on a bridge made from a fallen tree, a feat of daring York wouldn't have thought him capable of back in St. Louis. Seaman didn't bother with the bridge; he just plunged into the water and bucked up the other side, almost upon his quarry.

York slowed down enough to teeter across the log, then spotted Pernia crashing into an area of thick creepers. York's thick boots tore through the vines, but they caught at Pernia's flapping slippers and billowing blue coat. As Pernia faltered, Seaman flew at him, knocking him to the ground and seizing the back of his neck in his jaws.

"No!" Pernia kicked and flailed. "*Tas de merde!* He's biting me—York, for Christ's sake, help me!"

"Seaman!" York grabbed the dog by his silver collar. "Hold off, boy. Leave a little piece for me." He flipped Pernia over and punched him in the face, drawing blood from the smaller man's nose. Pernia yowled and shielded his face with his hands. York kicked his legs. "Get up! Get up, damn you!"

Pernia struggled to his feet. "I didn't think I'd ever see you again," he gasped. "I didn't think handsome Willie-o was coming."

York shook him by the scruff of the neck. " We's both here, and I know what you done to Cap'n Lewis. We dug him up. I seen with my own eyes what you done!"

"I did nothing! I swear, I didn't kill him!" Pernia's expression hardened defiantly. "God knows I wanted to."

York threw Pernia against a chinaberry tree. "Only reason I don' kill you right now is that Cap'n Clark wants to talk to you 'fore I do. But that's all right. I'm real good at waitin' for what I want." He stabbed Pernia in the chest with a trembling finger. "You sonofabitch. Captain Lewis was my *friend.*"

Pernia stared at York and laughed. "Your friend? Oh, come on, York! Don't tell me that you're really that naïve! It isn't enough for old Yawk to have that slow-witted chawbacon for a massa, you want Lewis too? *Jésus!* You can have him! I got news for you, York—*your friend* was nothing but a drunk and a wastrel who couldn't get a woman unless he paid her!"

"Watch your smart mouth, Pernia," York said. "Bottom rail's on top now! Your so-called freedom doesn't mean shit out here in these woods." He prodded Pernia hard with his rifle butt. "You worthless little fucker. How could you put him in the ground like that?"

"Because I hated him!" Pernia shouted. "Get that through your thick head, York!"

"I know what you think a' me—just a stupid country nigger," York said. "But I seen more 'n you ever see! And I know a great man when I see one. Cap'n Lewis wasn't no massa to us men, he was more like our *father.* He save all our lives, mo' times 'n I can count! And *smart*—"

Pernia threw up his hands. "Spare me the story of the great explorer, York! And stop pretending you don't understand." He grabbed York by the front of his hunting coat. "Don't tell me you don't know about hating your master. *Because I know you do.*"

York shook his head. "Th-that ain't true."

"He's not around to hear this," Pernia said. "For God's sake, York, be honest with yourself for once in your life. We're not so different, you and I. You could get free of him anytime you want to."

Once, on a trip to the Federal City with Massa Billy, York had seen actors prancing on a stage. As Pernia began to pace and act out his own words, preposterous in the torn coat and red slippers, York was reminded of that spellbinding experience at the theater. He knew the play wasn't real, but he held his breath anyway, almost paralyzed in his anxiety to see what came next.

"You shave him, don't you?" Pernia said. "Well, cut his throat—you know you've thought about it." He mimed the motion of a slashing razor. "You could poison his food. No one would ever be the wiser. You could loosen the shoes on his horse—oops, there goes Willie-o with a broken head!"

York cringed. Pernia's antics were sickening, but the worst of it was, the things he was saying weren't just fancy words in a stage play. They were *true*—

Pernia sidled closer. "The big stupid dolt—look at how he trusts you, York. This is your chance! We're completely isolated, in the middle of nowhere. And you with that rifle! You got a pistol on you, too?"

York nodded numbly.

"A knife, too, I'll wager. What's stopping you?" He breathed into York's ear. "This doesn't have to play out Massa's way. This time, it can come out the way *you* want it."

"No, Pernia—"

"Why not?" Pernia demanded. "I'll help you! You won't have to be alone. We'll go up and meet him, just like you said. While he's distracted with me, shoot him! We'll kill him and hide his body in the woods."

York felt hot sweat trickle down his scalp into his eyes. "And then what?"

"Then we'll *both* be free. You'll help me get out of these woods and I'll be on my way back to New Orleans." Pernia held up his hand in a parody of a man taking an oath. "Never more to roam, no sir! And you—why, you'll go back out West. Stick to the back country and run, back to those Indians you're always telling me about. Remember, York? How they thought you were big medicine? And all the women wanted to fuck you?" Pernia grinned and gripped York's forearm with a cold, damp little hand. "Paradise, Lawd!

You deserve it, York. I can help you."

York's heart raced. Pernia seemed to know all of his secret thoughts. After the whipping in May, he had dreamed many times of killing Billy and running away. It was easy to imagine how they could pull it off. Once he got to Grinder's with Pernia, he would have done what Billy needed, and would thus become invisible to him until the next time he wanted something. While Pernia put on a show, he could slip around behind Clark. He could almost hear Billy's voice rumbling out now in the clearing, see the familiar tension in the shoulders and the swing of the long red queue hanging down Clark's back. How many times had he brushed and tied that thick, straight hair?

He imagined the weight of the rifle in his hands as he slammed the butt into that vulnerable spot at the base of Billy's skull. The crack of shattering bone would send Billy to his knees. It would only take another couple of blows to finish him off. Imagine Billy's shock, the feeling of betrayal that would be his last thought on earth—

York turned away, gasping for breath. "Goddamn you," he said. God help him—he loved Clark. He had been raised to love him since they were both babies. He could never kill him, could never hurt him in any way. He choked. Pernia was right—Billy trusted him. York worked hard to earn that trust, to keep it, to deserve it.

And as far as he knew, Billy would repay him by keeping him a slave the rest of his life.

"Yes, I hate him," York said hoarsely.

"Good!" Pernia said. "So do I. Lead the way, my friend. *Liberté!*"

York grabbed Pernia by the throat and punched him hard in the face, once, twice. Pernia struggled, but he was no match for York's explosive anger. He squeezed Pernia's windpipe as the little man's eyes eyes bulged in terror.

"You little yellow coward," York spat. "You didn't kill Cap'n Lewis. You don't have the guts. It's always somebody else who does the dirty work."

Pernia shook his head wildly, his face turning purple. York threw him on the ground with weary disgust. Pernia clutched his bruised throat. "You're a fool, York. You could be free."

Like you? York wanted to ask. Without another word, he prodded Pernia's legs to get him moving. Pernia dragged himself up and started tripping through the woods. Seaman harried him every step of the way, growling and nipping at his ankles.

York trudged behind. He had composed his face in a dark mask that he hoped would convince Pernia never to speak to him again. Inside, his chest hurt so much that he wondered if there was enough love and friendship in the world to keep his heart from shriveling up and dying. Watching Pernia shuffling through the leaves in the clothes he'd stolen from York's dead friend, he could only pray the answer was yes.

Chapter 39
Clark

The hardest thing about dealing with these people, Clark reflected, was keeping his self-control. He knew from experience that mental strain, hunger, and fatigue did terrible things to a man's ability to think. He'd learned this years ago as a young officer in the Indian wars; it had also been in his mind during some of the hardest days on the Expedition. It was when you got tired, when you were worn out in body and mind and soul, that you made stupid decisions. That was when you did things you regretted.

Looking at Mrs. Grinder's blowsy grin, he felt his hands ball into fists and forcibly told himself: *No. Don't do it. You've never raised a hand to a woman in your life, and this ain't the time to start.*

He clenched his teeth and repeated, "Tell me again what you heard."

"I done told you a thousand times already," Mrs. Grinder said. "I heard two shots, boom boom. Then I heard some hollerin'. Then the fella died. I don't know what happened to his money, or any of his other things. I ain't no thief."

Clark sighed and looked at the ground. He was standing in the Grinders' patchy yard next to the cabin where Lewis had died. He'd spent the whole morning winding his way through the woods between here and the river, trying to find somebody, anybody, who could tell him where this Preacher lived.

It had been an utter waste of time. Now he was back at Grinder's Stand, trying to get some information out of Mrs. Grinder that would help him find the man who killed Lewis. York had filled him in on the details he'd gotten from the slave girl, Malindy. The girl's harrowing tale only roughly matched the couple's description of what had happened. He hoped a little more interrogation would get him closer to the truth.

"Your girl said there was a man hangin' around that night," Clark said, trying to keep his voice even. "That he was standing outside *this* window, looking in on my friend."

"How would I know?" Mrs. Grinder twisted her mouth. "I was in the other cabin. Like any decent person at that time'a night, I was tryin' to sleep. Whatever that little nigger told you is all gum anyway."

"Well, did you hear anybody walkin' around out here that night? It's important, for Christ's sake." He fixed her with a stern stare. "Mrs. Grinder, if you have any information to offer me about this situation, you'd best tell me now. Because I will find out who killed my friend. And when I do, there's gonna be some Kentucky justice comin' down."

"Don't you threaten me, mister!" Her voice grew shrill. "I told you a-fore, I don't know nobody called Preacher! There wasn't nobody here that night but Malindy and me, and that colored man what brought the gentleman's trunk. Far as I know, he was in the barn. My husband was up at his farm, 'bout twenty miles up the road—"

"I know that already—"

"—and that's where he is now. You got a problem, you should take it up with Robert." She sniffed and jerked her head towards Lewis's grave. "It's bad enough we got to have that troublemaker on our property. Now all kinds of riffraff are beatin' a path to my door. Why, just this mornin' some soldier stopped and asked about you—"

"About *me*?" Clark stopped her in mid-rant. "A soldier? What did he want?"

"How would I know? He was in such a dad-blamed hurry he didn't say. Looked right disreputable to me."

Clark's stomach clenched with worry. A soldier—one of Wilkinson's men, no doubt. They'd gotten Lewis, now they were looking for him too—

"People have heard about you!" Mrs. Grinder shook her finger in his face. "Diggin' that man up—you ought to be ashamed! I never saw the beat."

Clark turned away from her and rubbed his temple. He hadn't had but a few hours of sleep in the last forty-eight, and he knew he was beginning to lose his ability to function. The wreckage inside his cabin early this morning had been the final crowning blow. He'd finally scraped the papers and journals into a pile, put it back in the trunk, and shoved the trunk into the corner. Then he'd done his best to push the whole mess to the back of his mind.

Despite his best efforts, it was eating on him terribly. *Lewis cared about those journals more than his own life—if I can't fix it—if I can't make it right—*

He shook the thought off and said, "Tell me what you did *after* you heard the shots."

Mrs. Grinder frowned. "What are you talking about? I didn't do a thing."

"That's what I'm talking about. You said my friend got shot around one in the morning. He was still alive around dawn, when your husband got home. I'm askin' what did you do all that time?"

"I was in my cabin all night," she said primly. "I was terrified. 'Fraid if I set a toe out the door, I'd be shot myself. "

"All right, first you say there was nobody around, then you say you were scared of bein' shot. So you stayed in your cabin. Your girl said Lewis came out and begged you for water, and that you wouldn't open the door. Is that true?"

"No!" Mrs. Grinder's eyes widened. "I'm gonna skin that child alive for tellin' such lies!"

"Your girl said my friend crawled around the yard all night, all shot up, cryin' and beggin' for water, and that you wouldn't give him any—"

"That's not true! We're decent people here—"

"Well, which is it, lady? Did you open the door or didn't you?"

"No. I don't know! What if I didn't?" Mrs. Grinder yapped. "Your friend was nothing to me! Just a blamed nuisance, was all he was. I ain't about to risk my life for some joe-fired traveler. I don't care for your makin' an issue out of it."

"That's what I thought. You're a real angel of mercy, *madam*," Clark said coldly, placing undue emphasis on the last word. "I'd like to see the inside of the cabin again, if you don't mind."

"Suit yourself. But I don't know what you think you're gonna find. It ain't changed any since last time."

With theatrical indignance, she marched around the side of the cabin, pulled open the door, and ushered him in. Clark looked around the room as Mrs. Grinder scuffed her toe across the stained floorboards. "This room is so lorn now," she said, with a pitiful warble in her voice. "It gets so awful lonesome here on the Trace, without my husband around."

Clark gave her a curt nod and turned away. He noticed for the first time that there were tiny remnants of broken glass on the floor. He crossed over to the window and examined it from the inside.

The window didn't have glass in it and never had. The panes were covered with sun-faded waxed paper. Clark supposed it was possible Preacher could've shot Lewis through the window, but it didn't look like it. Judging from the undisturbed paper in the windows and the grisliness of his friend's wounds, the murderer had to have been in the room with Lewis. That meant either he broke in, or Lewis let him in. Or someone else did.

He stood for a second with his hands gripping the windowsill. Behind him, Mrs. Grinder drifted around the room, making a great show of tidying up. Clark was about to turn around when he felt something press up against his back. Suddenly, Mrs. Grinder's arms were around his waist, clutching at the buttons of his waistcoat.

"Oh, Lord," she panted, pawing at his chest and grinding her belly against his backside. "It's been so long since I've had a gentleman—"

Revolted, Clark yanked her arms loose, whirled around and thrust her bodily away from him. His voice shook with outrage. "Lady, you forget yourself!"

Mrs. Grinder recovered her balance and glared back, affronted. "Damned if you're not as odd as the other one!" she exclaimed. "That's just what *he* said!"

Clark's jaw dropped. "You pulled this jig on my friend?"

"Yes, and he wouldn't have none of it either," Mrs. Grinder said scornfully. "What is it with you St. Louis men? You taken up French ways or what?"

"Lady, if you were a man, I'd slap you simple—"

"If I were a man, I s'pose there'd be no problem, would there?" she taunted. "Now it all comes clear! Lewis and Clark, out in the woods together! 'Tis the fashion amongst the savages, I suppose."

Appalled, Clark shoved her aside and pushed his way back into the yard. Mrs. Grinder's randy laughter sickened him. These people had no decency, no human feeling whatsoever. They made every noble emotion into something base and sordid. It was intolerable that Lewis had died in this place—

He heard a bark and raised his head. A black shape emerged from the woods behind the small clearing. Seaman loped towards him, his tongue hanging out and his tail waving like a flag. Clark guessed York must have found something.

Seaman jumped at his legs, then turned and stared back towards the woods. Sure enough, York had tracked down John Pernia and was now prodding him along at the point of his rifle.

Clark noticed immediately that the little Creole was all decked out in Lewis's clothes. Both the clothes and the man looked the worse for wear. Pernia's face and throat bore big purple bruises, and the blue-striped duster coat he was wearing—Lewis's coat—was dirty and torn. Even from a distance, Clark could see the glaze of anger in York's eyes.

"There he is!" Mrs. Grinder pointed. "That colored man was here on the night your friend got shot. Why don't you ask him what happened, and leave me be?" With a whirl of her skirts, she stomped over to her cabin and slammed the door.

Clark calmed himself and quietly watched them come up. As they approached, York met his eye and said in a shaky voice, "I got 'im, Cap'n." He pushed Pernia forward.

Pernia looked into his eyes and smirked. Then he unleashed a wad of spittle onto the ground at Clark's feet.

Clark swallowed, his jaw clenched white. He looked at York, who stood gripping his rifle, his lips compressed into a hard knot. Clark stepped forward and flicked open Pernia's coat to examine the rest of his clothes. White linen shirt, waistcoat, black silk breeches. Pernia even had on a pair of red velvet slippers, no doubt something Lewis had packed to lounge around in when he reached Monticello. Pernia looked ridiculous, like a boy who had raided his father's closet, but the look on his face was anything but funny. It was an expression of pure hatred.

Clark ran his tongue over his upper teeth. "Helped yourself, did you?"

"Why shouldn't I?" Pernia said. "He won't miss 'em! That sonofabitch beat me out of two-hundred and forty dollars—"

Clark backhanded Pernia across the face, almost knocking him off his feet. "Don't you talk about the Governor that way, you little animal!"

Pernia laughed, an hysterical high-pitched giggle. "What'd he ever do for me? He lied to me—he cheated me out of my salary—he tricked me into coming to this godforsaken place—"

"And you *killed* him for it!" Clark roared.

"I didn't!" Pernia shouted back. "God knows if I'd had the guts to kill him, I would've done it long before he dragged me to this shithole! I would've bashed his goddamned skull in when he was drunk—"

Clark smacked him again. Whimpering, Pernia held his hands up in front of his face. Clark's insides squirmed with contempt.

"Tell me what happened here." He jerked Pernia up by the front of the striped duster coat. "Damn you, tell me the truth."

"The truth?" Pernia said. "Oh, God, General Clark, you don't want to know the truth."

"Yes, I do. If you won't talk willingly, I'll beat it out of you. Your choice."

"Oh good. My choice." Pernia rubbed the back of his hand across his nose and drew it away, striped with blood. "All right. Fine." He staggered back a little, the battered red slippers scuffing in the dirt. "You won't believe this, but I don't even know what happened. I don't know any more than you."

"You're lying, you little piss-ant."

"I am not," Pernia moaned. "The governor was fine when I went to bed. I mean, as fine as he ever is, which is to say, *un grand pochard*. I suppose he took his medicine, yes, he wouldn't miss a dose, a couple of gallons of laudanum to help him sleep." He shrugged. "I was tired. I'd only walked twenty miles that day, carrying his blasted trunk—"

"You can skip the complainin'. I need to know what happened to the Governor—"

"Somebody shot him! I don't know who! I was asleep in the barn, all night!" Pernia shouted. "The first I heard about it was when the little nigger girl who lives here came to wake me up in the morning. I went and looked, and sure enough, Governor Lewis was full of holes."

"Was he still alive?" Clark demanded. "Did he say anything?"

"He begged me to blow his brains out, but it looked like somebody had already done a first-rate job of it without my help."

"Who, goddamn you?" Clark shouted. "Did he say who shot him?"

"No, but I confess, I wasn't really listening. I'd had enough of his blather."

Clark wanted to weep. He couldn't understand how he'd been so deceived by the cheerful face Pernia showed back in St. Louis. He hated to think that this man's hatefulness was the last thing Lewis knew on this earth. "Where was Major Neelly all this time?"

"Who knows?" Pernia shrugged to the heavens. "He showed up quickly enough when there was money to be had. *My* money. He took it all, and left me in the woods to die." He glared at Clark. "Major Neelly is an *imbécile* and a thief, General. He hasn't a brain in his head."

"Well, tell me what you know about this goddamn preacher—"

"Preacher?" Pernia stared at him in puzzlement, then started to laugh. "Is that who killed him? Neelly and the preacher? Lord, what a joke on the governor! We sat down and had dinner with that man." Pernia snickered, then his face turned vicious again. "Frankly, I don't give a tinker's damn who did it. I'm glad he's dead, and good riddance. I'm just sorry I never got my money."

Clark's fists clenched. "What the hell's the matter with you? Lewis took you off the streets and fed you for a goddamned year! Your master was shot to death! Don't you give a damn—"

"*He's not my master!* I'm a free man, damn you! And you don't know *anything* about the kind of man he was."

"Well, why don't you tell me, you little monster?" Clark shoved Pernia so hard the Creole went tumbling into the dirt. York shifted his feet and clutched at his rifle.

"You weren't there!" Pernia scrabbled backwards on his hands like an overdressed crab. "You didn't see him when he was stinking, puking drunk! You didn't hold his head while he heaved in the gutter! You didn't have to lie to people that he was out of the house, when really he was soused in bed with some whore, the two of them silly on laudanum and pills—"

"That's a lie—"

Pernia's face twisted with hate. "You didn't see! He used to go down to the levee and drag home the cheapest pieces of filth—yes, *your* friend, His Excellency, the great hero governor!" He laughed wildly. "Don't you think we black folk got eyes? Don't you think Old Yawk knows some things about *you*, that you wouldn't want the fine people of St. Louis to know about?"

York shook his head and stepped back, as if saying, *Leave me out of this.* Pernia stared at Clark, his face red and his eyes bulging. He seemed to have moved beyond fear, beyond recklessness, beyond caring whether he lived or died.

"You stupid cracker!" Pernia hissed. "You were deceived like everybody else, handsome Willie-o! He lied to you all the time! He made you look like a fool with Bates and the others! He never wrote that book! He played with you like you were just another one of his whores—"

Clark's mind snapped. He couldn't bear the outrage, the obscenity of Pernia's ranting any longer. No man, black or white, had ever spoken to him in this manner. He jerked Pernia up and began to beat him with his fists, powerful, bone-cracking blows that soon had the little man curled on the ground in a shaking, whimpering ball.

In the Army way, he was methodical in his brutality. He told himself he was in control. While Pernia cried in the dirt, he turned around and strode over to his horse. He yanked open his saddlebags and found his horsewhip. It was a fearsome thing, over four feet long, with a handle of braided leather. It was designed to move and manage unbroken horses. It could also be used to flog a man to death.

Clark walked back to where Pernia was lying on the ground. He plucked him out of the dirt and set him on his feet, then shoved him roughly over to

York. "Strip him, York. Tie him to that tree yonder."

York started to take hold of Pernia's clothes, then stopped. He looked sick, his face gray.

"What are you waiting for?" Clark said. "Hop to, dammit!"

York still hesitated, his eyes fixed on the whip in Clark's hand. Pernia whined and pawed at York's shirt. York yanked himself free of the smaller man's grabbing hands and pushed Pernia away, shaking his head slowly.

"No, Cap'n," he said. "I'd do most anything for you, you know that...and Lord knows he deserves it...but I can't. I just can't."

A terrible look passed between them. Clark felt a flood of awful emotions: rage, dismay, betrayal. York had let him down. After everything they'd been through, all the horror of the past few days, the one man he counted on the most refused to help him. This little bastard had stood by while Lewis got shot, and mocked him as he lay dying. York had tracked Pernia, had brought Pernia to him, but now that things had gotten rough, he wouldn't follow through.

Clark looked away from York. Even as the anger burned inside him, he felt something worse: shame. He was going to flog Pernia to death, viciously and brutally. The reason York wouldn't help was because he'd felt the sting of the lash on his own back, the warm blood flying with every crack of the whip. He'd whipped York for a lot less cause than this. York had just wanted to go to Louisville, to be with his family...he'd just wanted to see his wife...

"Damn you," Clark said. York's quiet refusal defeated him. He threw the whip in the dirt. With a growl of rage, he grabbed Pernia, spun him around, and tore the striped duster coat off his back, ripping it in two. Then he grabbed at Pernia's shirt. He wasn't going to let this little bastard go around wearing Lewis's clothes—

Pernia shook, his face twisted with glee and pain, his mouth a bloody grin. He rolled his eyes up at Clark. "Looks like you have a *mutinerie* on your hands, General." Then he started to sing:

You're the man that I adore, Handsome Willie-o
You're the man that I adore, Handsome Willie-o
You're the man that I adore, but your fortune is too low—

Enraged, Clark booted Pernia hard in the ass. The Creole went down on his hands and knees.

"Get the hell out of my sight, you worthless piece of shit," Clark choked.

"And *stay away*. If you ever show your face in St. Louis again, so help me God, I'll finish what I started."

Pernia laughed soundlessly. He got to his feet and staggered a few steps. When he realized Clark wasn't going to follow, he limped jerkily off towards the trees. Before he disappeared, Pernia looked back at Clark and York and yelled over his shoulder:

Bid a last farewell to handsome Willie-o!

Then he melted into the woods in back of the Grinders' cabins, leaving nothing but a deep silence behind.

Chapter 40
Clark

Neither man said a word on the ride back to Dobbin's Stand. York felt shaken to the core by his encounter with Pernia, but he had known for a long time the little Creole was treacherous and two-faced. To Massa Billy, it came as a big surprise. Slogging behind Billy and the black mare, York didn't have to see Billy's face to know his master was devastated. His back was as stiff as an iron rod, and he was holding the reins so tight his knuckles were white.

York wanted to tell Massa Billy that it didn't matter what Pernia said about Captain Lewis. Sure, Captain Lewis might have had some bad times, but it didn't erase all the good he'd done in the world. Mistakes and all, Captain Lewis was a great leader and a good friend. York knew for certain he'd counted Billy as his best friend in the world.

He wanted to tell Clark this, but he didn't say a word. He didn't dare. Since they'd left Grinder's Stand, Clark hadn't so much as glanced in his direction, though he rode slowly enough for York to keep up. He was sure Massa Billy was furious with him for refusing to help him whip Pernia. York didn't see how he could have decided any other way, but it was hard not to have mixed feelings about it. The last time he'd refused a command, he'd gotten the treatment he'd just spared Pernia. He hoped he'd made the right choice.

The sun was just dipping below the horizon when they reached Dobbin's Stand. York stepped back as Billy climbed down and stroked the black mare's neck. After a long moment, he handed York the reins and wordlessly trudged off toward Mrs. Dobbin's cabin. York felt his throat choke with unspoken words as he led the horse away to the stable.

He was surprised to see activity there. For the past several days, he and Billy had been Mrs. Dobbin's only guests, but now they had company. Two winded Army nags, similar to their own, already stood in the stable. A lanky soldier was brushing the coat of a big yellow horse and whistling to himself.

York greeted him, then took a second look. The young man looked dirty, exhausted—and familiar. "Sergeant..." York said, noticing the man's rank. "Do I know you?"

"Sure do," the soldier replied with a grin. "Sergeant John Thomas. You rode me out to Fort Bellefontaine a few weeks ago."

"That's right." York smiled. "Well, Sergeant, you sure do get around."

"Law, nothin' compared to you fellers!" Thomas said. "Me and Mrs. Clark had a heckuva time catchin' up with ye."

York's jaw dropped. He wasn't sure he'd heard right. "Mrs. Clark...are you tellin' me that Mrs. Clark is *here?*"

"Well, a'course," Thomas said. "We come as fast as we could. I 'spect the General'll be real worked up to see her."

"Yeah, I...I reckon he will." York swallowed. He felt a great and overwhelming need to make himself scarce. As quickly as he could, he wiped down the mare, watered her and his own gray, and covered them both with blankets. Then he took his leave, explaining, "Ever since we got back from the Expedition, I grown real accustomed to sleepin' outdoors."

Thomas smiled and bid him goodnight. York slipped down by the creek. Thomas didn't know what he was in for. He didn't want to be anywhere near the poor innocent fool when Billy's wrath came down.

Mrs. Dobbin's cabin was dark and quiet. Not wanting to waste a candle, the old lady had already locked up and gone to bed. Out of consideration for her guests, she'd left an iron pot of stew sitting on the porch.

The stew was lukewarm and salty, but Clark forced himself to sit down and eat it anyway. He'd never much cared for salt on his food. Lewis had craved it and complained about the lack of it all the way to the Pacific Ocean. Once there, he'd set up a special camp to extract the salt crystals from seawater. In Clark's opinion, it hadn't made their monotonous diet of boiled elk and wapato roots any tastier, but it had kept the men busy during their boring winter at Fort Clatsop.

That winter seemed a thousand years ago now. He hadn't thought of it during those long days of endless rain, but their little fort on the windblown coast near the mouth of the Columbia marked the fulfillment of a dream. In accordance with Jefferson's instructions, they had explored the Missouri River to its source and penetrated the continent to the Pacific Ocean. All that remained was to get home safely, with the maps intact and the scientific information safely recorded in the journals.

He pushed his bowl of stew away. The journals were all he had left of that triumphal time, and now they were in a shambles. There was no book, no manuscript. Lewis had done nothing, and it was left to him to try to put the scattered pieces back together. But if he couldn't, it might as well never have happened. He and Lewis might as well never have gone—

And if they hadn't gone, where would he be? Still living with George in a cabin at the Falls of the Ohio? *Maybe if I were, George would still be all right—maybe he wouldn't have lost his leg—*

Angry with himself, he rejected the thought and got to his feet. To hell with it, he thought as he walked toward his cabin. He was sick and tired of cleaning up other people's messes. To hell with George, and to hell with Lewis. *I ain't responsible for every damn thing that goes wrong in the world—*

Then, suddenly, his instinct told him to stop. Something strange caught his eye. There was a faint flickering light behind the papered windows of his cabin.

A feeling of utter rage spread through his belly. The sonofabitch had come back. He hadn't found what he was looking for the first time he rifled through Lewis's trunk. Damned if he hadn't returned for a second crack. Well, this time, it was going to turn out a little different, wasn't it?

Breathing deeply, he jerked his pistol out of his coat and made sure it was primed and ready. He shifted the pistol to his right hand and thumbed the hammer back. With his left hand, he unsheathed his dirk and held it close to his body, ready to strike.

No hesitation, he told himself. *Do what you have to do. It's him or you—*

He stepped back and kicked the door hard enough to splinter the wood, sending it crashing in on its hinges. A candle was burning on the table; somebody was lying on the bed. The person jumped up and rushed toward him—his finger tightened on the trigger—

"Will! Oh, Will!"

To his infinite astonishment, he found himself being embraced. It took him another half-second to realize that the woman who had just flung herself on his chest was his wife. Julia hugged him, babbling and crying and saying his name. In shock, he uncocked the hammer and lowered his arms, letting the pistol and dirk hang at his sides. He felt on the verge of collapse. *For the love of God, I almost shot her—*

"Oh, Will, thank God I found you, I've been traveling for ages—"

The words flowed into his ears, but he couldn't fathom what she was saying or that she could be here at all. As he stood in her embrace, his disbelief turned into outrage. Of all the damn fool things she could have done, this capped them all. The last goddamn thing he needed was for her to put herself in harm's way—

He shoved the dirk and pistol back in his coat, grabbed her roughly by the shoulders, and set her away from him. Julia looked up at him with a tear-stained smile that faded when she saw how angry he was.

"What the *hell* are you doing here?" he roared.

"I...I came to find you! I had to let you know what was happening—"

"Lord, there is no excuse for your doin' this! None! This is the stupidest goddamn thing I ever even heard of anybody doin'—"

"But you haven't even heard what—"

"—can't last a week on your own—you come runnin' after me like a goddamn child—"

"But Will, I had to—"

"Had to?" he repeated. "Had to? Julia, all you *had* to do was stay in St. Louis and wait for Jonathan to come get you, like I told you to do! But instead—"

"It was the only thing I could do, I—"

He gripped her shoulders and stared into her eyes. "Tell me you didn't bring the boy!"

"Of course not!" Julia snapped. "That would've been much too dangerous!"

"Too dangerous!" Clark shouted. "But it's not too dangerous for *you* to come trippin' down the river and prancin' through the woods for hundreds of miles? Goddamn it to hell, Julia! You shouldn't have come here! You shouldn't have come!"

Julia clenched her little hands into fists. "Well, if I'd known how awful and mean you were going to be, I wouldn't have! I had a damn good reason, William Clark! But I suppose you don't even want to know what that is!"

"No, I don't." He looked at her in cold fury, his jaw working. It occurred to him, staring into her angry, tearful eyes, that she was not one of his enlisted men. To be certain, she didn't respond in the same way to Army discipline. He noticed for the first time that her face and hands were swollen with scratches and mosquito bites. His rage and incredulity bloomed anew.

"Julia, how in all of goddamn tarnation hell did you get here?"

"I went downriver to Fort Pickering!" Julia cried. "I went with Scipio! Then I asked Captain Russell to help me. He assigned Sergeant Thomas to bring me here."

"Sergeant Thomas." Clark felt calmer; his anger channeled into another, deeper place. "Sergeant Thomas. Is he still here?"

"Yes, he's in the stable—"

"Julia." Clark put his hands on her shoulders. "I want you to *wait here*. Don't move a goddamn *toe*, do you understand?"

"But Will—"

He silenced her with a look, then strode out of the cabin toward the stable.

Sergeant Thomas was sacked out in the straw in his underclothes when Clark came upon him. His sword and pistol lay close at hand. Clark carefully nudged them away with his foot. The boy was so deeply asleep he didn't stir, not even when one of the horses, sensing danger, started to nicker.

Clark stepped back, opened his throat, and let loose a yell that sounded like a whole charging brigade.

"Sergeant Thomas!"

Thomas jerked awake as if startled out of a very pleasant dream. His eyes rolled around for a few seconds in confusion before they fixed on Clark. He scrambled up on his bare feet and tried to arrange his gangly body into some semblance of a salute.

"General Clark, sir—"

"Spare me the goddamn niceties!" Clark roared. "What the hell do you mean draggin' my wife over the Trace? Have you no brains a'tall?"

Thomas stood dumbly, straw sticking out of his hair. "Wal, sir, she said that—"

"*I don't give a damn!*" Thomas's voice trailed off as Clark unleashed a stream of invective that would make even a hardened veteran blush. Thomas flapped his jaw a couple of times as if he were going to protest his treatment, then thought better of it and stood silently, eyes squinched tight as if weathering a nasty storm.

"I'll see you busted down lower than a buck private for pullin' a stunt like this!" Clark swore. "Sergeant, I hope you like shit, because you're gonna be shovelin' out latrines for the rest of your natural life." Warming to his topic, Clark tongue-lashed Thomas up, down, and sideways until the boy quaked and his knees knocked together beneath the hem of his shirt.

With a last burst of fury, Clark wound things up by questioning Thomas's patrimony. Then he blew out as quick as he'd come, leaving the boy white and shaking. As he walked away, Thomas collapsed in the straw, holding his head. "Jesus, she hornswoggled me!"

Damn right, Clark thought as he charged through the woods. He still couldn't believe Julia was capable of doing such a silly thing. Breathing hard, he threaded his way down to the creek. He knew he'd have to go back and talk to her sometime, but right now, he was still too angry.

He guessed he'd always be a riverman at heart; the sound of the trickling stream helped soothe his nerves. He squatted down and let the cool water flow over his fingers, then cupped his hands and splashed water on his face. Under a tree nearby, York was stretched out on his back. York had his hat clamped over his face and was pretending to be asleep. Clark returned the courtesy by pretending not to notice him.

After a while, he squared his shoulders, got up and walked back up to the cabin. Julia's candle was still burning. Clark shoved his way into the cabin and shut the door, setting it back on its hinges.

Julia sat on the bed on the ticking mattress, her feet dangling over the side. Her little dress was much too thin for the cold air. She looked exhausted. Clark winced inwardly when he saw all the mosquito bites on her legs, but he kept his face a stony mask. Julia watched him with big forlorn eyes but didn't say anything.

Without speaking, Clark took hold of Lewis's trunk, dragged it to the center of the room, and propped it open. Lewis had a medicine chest, a black leather case he kept stocked with remedies for every conceivable ailment. Snatching the candle off the table, Clark held it in one hand while he rummaged through the vials of liquid and bottles of pills. Finally, he found what he was looking for: a bottle of calomine lotion, good for soothing insect bites.

There was some cotton gauze in the chest too; that would do. With quick movements, he replaced the candle on the table, sat down next to Julia on the bed, and slapped his knee with his hand.

"Put your leg up here."

Julia did as she was told. Clark uncorked the calomine and soaked a piece of gauze in it, then began to dab it roughly onto Julia's skinny leg. He could feel her studying his face and purposely kept his expression hardset, so as not to give her any quarter. He wasn't about to let her think she had gotten away with anything.

Finally she said in a small voice, "Will...are you still mad?"

"Yup."

Julia was quiet for a minute. "Are you awful, awful mad?"

He nodded. "Yup."

She sighed and dropped her shoulders in exasperation. "Well, how long you gonna *stay* mad?"

As if considering the question, he gazed across the room for a moment. "Forever, I expect. I'm never gonna not be mad again."

Julia looked so hurt and defeated he wished he hadn't said it. The poor little thing thought his heart was eternally hardened against her. In a softer voice, he admitted, "I ain't really all that mad."

With a cry of relief, Julia swung her leg down and flung herself into his arms. He wrapped his arms around her. He could feel her trembling, or maybe it was he who was trembling. The thought that something might have happened to her—that this awful place might have claimed *her, too*—was more than he could bear.

"Everything's all right, darlin'."

"Thank God," Julia stroked his hair. "Oh, Will, I was so afraid something would happen to you."

Clark gazed into her wide, pleading eyes. No one since his mother had ever worried about him in quite the same way that this little gal did. Most times in his life when somebody had been in trouble, he was the one who tried to save them. Somehow, Julia had taken it into her head that *he* was in trouble, that *he* was the one who needed to be rescued. And she'd come all this way to do it.

He caressed her face. "Julia, what could happen to me?"

"The people in St. Louis—they thought you and Meriwether had done something awful! I was scared they'd kill you, Will—"

He could not stand to hear about it. He put his fingers to her lips to silence her. "Later," he murmured. "Tell me later."

He lowered his mouth to hers and kissed her. Julia's mouth, so warm and sweet. She returned his kiss with a passion he'd never felt from her before. He cradled her head in his hands and felt her body strain closer. Julia took his queue of hair in her fist and opened her mouth for him, their tongues touching, their lips fused together in burgeoning warmth.

He felt the bonds of self-control slip away. His beautiful darling, his heart's desire, his child bride. The woman he'd thought about for three years on the Expedition, then come home to claim. He'd missed her so terribly these past few weeks he hadn't even let himself think about it, because it would keep him from doing his duty. Now, somehow, she was here. He needed her so much he thought he'd die from it.

Clark laid her down on the hard mattress, touching her, loving her with his hands and his mouth. Julia whimpered and tugged at the buttons on his clothing, pulling a few loose in her haste. Clark helped her, quickly shucking off his boots, shirt and trousers. He moved to help her with her dress, but Julia yanked it off over her head and cast it onto the floor, then squirmed out of her chemise and back into his arms.

Julia's body was leaner than he remembered: she felt strong and coltish in his arms. Even motherhood hadn't thoroughly rounded out her slender curves. Her nipples were taut against his palms, and grew tighter still when he leaned down and flicked them with his tongue. Julia moaned and pressed her face against his neck. He could feel her mouth kissing him, her hands roving over his back and rear, then sliding around to grip his swelling hardness.

"Oh, Julia." Clark rolled her onto her back. He knew he should try to go slow, give her more time, but he just couldn't wait. Julia opened her legs for him and he pushed himself into her. He wanted to lose himself inside her, to let her love wash away all the misery and hurt and pain of Lewis's death. He wanted to forget about everything but her.

Julia made a little noise and he eased off, afraid of hurting her, but she just tightened her legs around him and drew him deeper. Their bodies surged together, finding a fierce rhythm: like antelope crossing a boundless plain, a waterfall pounding against the rocks, a wave striving for a distant shore. He thought of nothing but her face and her lips and her hair, the sweet smell of her, the feel of her hands digging into the muscles of his back.

In her passion, Julia whispered his name, and he felt the last tether slip away. With a groan of release, he poured all the love he felt for her into the soft warm center of her body. Julia wept with happiness, her face salty and wet with tears. "Oh, Will," she sobbed, "I love you so much—"

He'd known she loved him, had never doubted it, but he hadn't known how much until this moment. The small miracle of her presence had proven it to him. "I love you, too, darlin'. God, I hope you know it. You're the most precious thing I got in this world," he whispered to her in the darkness. "Don't you ever do anything crazy like this again. Ever, you hear me? Say you won't."

"I won't," Julia said, but her giggle told him she'd do it again in a heartbeat.

Chapter 41
Clark

Dobbin's Stand, Tennessee
October 17, 1809

She moaned with disapproval when he slipped off the mattress and started rummaging in his traveling trunk. "Will...come back..."

"I'm right here." He came back to the bed. "I found what I was lookin' for. Sit up, darlin'. I don't want you to get cold."

Obediently, Julia sat and held up her arms, allowing Clark to pull one of his clean, soft cotton shirts over her head. Cut full to begin with, it was so big on her that it looked like she was wearing a cloud. He smoothed the shirt down the length of her mosquito-bitten body; at full length, it reached halfway down her calves. Then he flapped open his Army blanket and pulled it up over the two of them.

She folded herself back into his arms and lay pressed against his chest. Savoring her warmth and the comforting rhythm of her sighs, he stroked her hair, running his fingers slowly though the long silky curls. Then he put his forehead against hers and kissed her on the end of her nose.

"Will," she whispered. "I'm so glad you're not mad anymore."

Clark gave her a wry smile. "I wouldn't say that. You put yourself in danger, Julia. You took a very foolish risk comin' to this place." She started to protest, but he quieted her, cupping her chin in his hand and rubbing his thumb gently across her mouth.

"I know you're just bustin' to tell me why you came here," he said. "I got a funny feeling I ain't gonna like it."

"Will, I *had* to," Julia said. "Please listen. I thought I'd catch up with you—it was only two days after you left that all the trouble started. I just knew you'd hear about all the foolish talk and gossip and turn back for home to put a stop to it. In fact, I still don't understand how you didn't. I thought sure I'd meet you on the river—"

"York and I got ourselves a canoe. We were travelin' mighty fast and keepin' to ourselves. Julia, is this about the so-called armed rebellion I'm supposed to be leadin'? Captain Russell told me—"

Julia nodded, tears standing in her eyes. "People were saying that you and Meriwether had gone out west of the city and raised an army of Kentucky riflemen and wild Indians, and that you were going to attack the city and set up your own empire. I couldn't believe that grown people could be so silly as to believe such a thing—but they did!"

"They were scared, Julia. When people are afraid, they do things they wouldn't ordinarily do."

"Half the people in town were running around like chickens with their heads cut off. They were boarding up their windows, and some of them said they would *kill* you if you tried to come back to the city!" She hugged him. He could feel her tears on his chest. "I tried to get some help from Secretary Bates, but he was rude and scornful. He yelled at me and said terrible things about you and Meriwether—oh! And that wasn't the end of it. Main Street was plastered with handbills calling you and Meriwether names—"

"What kind of names?"

She hesitated. "Stupid, awful things. Something about Meriwether being a liar and a poltroon, and that you were base and villainous and not a gentleman. These things were *everywhere*—"

Clark didn't know whether to be enraged or disgusted. *Poltroon?* Christ, only Bates could dream up something like that. Small wonder he wouldn't help Julia. He would jam that little popinjay into a cocked hat as soon as he got back—

Quivering, she pressed her face against his cheek. "Will, you do understand, don't you? There wasn't anybody to help me. If you were shot, and I could have prevented it, I could never, ever forgive myself."

Clark brushed her hair back from her face and kissed the tears from her cheeks. "Lord, Julia...You risked your life to try to save mine. I would never have wanted you to do that. What if somethin' had happened to you, and me not there to protect you?"

"I felt just the same. Just exactly the same," she whispered. Their faces were close enough for another kiss, but instead Julia brought her hand to his cheek and began to stroke his face and his hair. "You're all right. That's what matters."

The tenderness of her light caress made him feel like weeping, but instead he managed to laugh. "Well, I still wish you were home safe with the little man-boy. I hope Jonathan ain't too surprised when he gets there and finds himself in charge of a ten-month old baby." He smoothed his hand across Julia's back. "When'd you get so brave, girl?"

She laughed. "I'm not brave at all. I was frightened to death the whole time."

For a few minutes, they lay without speaking, needing only to hold each other. Then, he felt an unexpected anxiety wrap itself around his heart. Though he did not move or loosen his arms, he looked away, unable to bear the intense scrutiny of her gaze. When she was still only a child, he had fallen in love with the dark sweetness of her eyes, the promise of the woman she would become. He hadn't ever considered that she might someday use those eyes against him.

He squeezed his eyes shut and swung closed the gate that would enable her to breach his feelings. She had told him about her journey, now she would expect him to tell her about his. The image came to him again of Lewis's ruined corpse. He did not want her to know about the certainty of Lewis's lonely, tortured death and unspeakable burial. Nor did he want her to share the pain and confusion of his memories of Lewis, in which everything he prized was replaced by its opposite: the iron self-discipline vanquished by whoring, the brilliant imagination addled by drink and drugs, the unwavering friendship and loyalty corrupted by lies.

She was stroking his cheek, brushing her palm over his ear and his hair, saying his name. In her innocence, she could not realize that he had the barricades up for a reason. Her hands were at his temples now, touching his eyes, and he flicked them open, just for a moment, intending to find a fatherly smile for her. He'd rumble out some nonsense, a few little jokes. Then he'd wrap her up in the blanket and call her a good girl and watch her fall asleep.

The look in her eyes slapped him with an almost physical pain. *She knew.* She said:

"Will, did you ever catch up with Meriwether?"

He tried to say, "I didn't." It came out as a choke. He drew in a deep breath. *No, William. Not now. Later.*

"We talked to that woman down the road," Julia said. Clark let his breath go and tried to concentrate on what she was saying, so he could respond in a calm and considered manner. Tears streaked from her lovely eyes. "Oh, Will, she said he was dead."

Clark swallowed and managed to nod. He tried not to think about her kindness, her relentless consideration for him. He didn't want it—

"Will, what happened?"

In spite of his good intentions, he shoved her hand away and growled, ferocious: "Somebody killed him."

Julia gasped. In spite of everything that had happened, everything that she had been through, all that she'd told him, he could see the news shocked her. He tried to sit up. He wanted to get away from her. But as he rose she did too. Her little hand on his forearm exerted no pressure at all, but it held him there beside her like a cruel iron manacle.

"Oh, Will, no! Why? Who would want to kill our darling Meriwether?"

He clenched his fist, sick, sweating, scared. *Our darling Meriwether.* "The Chickasaw Agent, and a man named Tom Runion." He felt a sob well up in his chest and almost panicked, but he was able to force it back inside before it emerged. "They were hired guns. I have to find them, Julia, and hang the bastards. Make them *pay* for what they've done—"

Julia hugged him, wiping the tears from her eyes with the floppy sleeve of the shirt. "But why, Will? He was such a good friend."

The barricades were crashing in. He couldn't defend them. "There's a man," he tried to growl, but it came out higher, out of control. "An evil, powerful man. James Wilkinson. The head of the whole goddamn Army." For a moment, he grasped at the rage. It would sustain him and keep him strong. He'd see Neelly and Runion hung—he'd *personally* break their necks, and then he would take on Wilkinson—

Julia knelt beside him and held his hand in her lap, remorselessly stroking his fingers. He stared at her. Wilkinson had killed Lewis and would probably try to kill him too. The possibility existed that he couldn't protect her, just as he hadn't been able to protect Lewis. That Wilkinson would win.

With the barest movement, Julia squeezed his hand and laid it down at his side. Then, she touched her knuckles to his cheek and whispered, with infinite gentleness: "Poor Will."

Clark felt the sob well up again in his chest. He took Julia by the shoulders and tried to set her apart from him, but she wouldn't go. Without warning, the sob tore out of him, frightening him beyond measure. He felt the tears start, another sob chasing the first, ripping out of his throat. It didn't seem to matter any more what he wanted—

Shaking, he raised his hands to his face. But she was pitiless even about that. She took his hands in hers and kissed them while he wept helplessly. He had always hated the sound of men crying, the way his father had cried when he'd had to bury two sons, the way his brother George cried when he got drunk and crazy and then became sick with the shame.

She pulled him down to lie with her on the hard narrow mattress, cradling his head against her breasts. It was terrible the way he needed her, Julia, woman, wife, mother of his son.

He knew from experience that in battle, the combat seemed to last much longer than it actually did. This battle was no different. It seemed to last for hours, but it might only have been a few minutes. When it was over, all his defenses lay breached and shattered, his positions overrun, his tactics exposed as useless, his strategy unmasked as folly. He finally admitted his utter surrender.

The prisoner and his captor slept in each other's arms all night.

By the time he felt her stirring, he had been sitting on the edge of the bed for a half-hour, watching the waxed paper covering the windows lighten with the coming dawn. The cabin was chilly in the morning air, and she crawled over to sit beside him, drawing the Army blanket close around her, then shyly offering one corner to him.

He looked inside himself and easily found the smile that had gone missing last night. He took the blanket and threw around his shoulders, then pulled her close to sit under it with him. She leaned into his chest and drowsed against him as the light in the windows grew stronger.

At length, Julia sat up and pushed long mussed curls out of her eyes. When she spoke, her voice was soft. "Will? Are you all right?"

"I am," Clark said. Somewhat to his surprise, it was true. He had dreaded facing his grief. Somehow, she had known that, had known that the heavy burden was crushing his heart, and had willingly taken it on herself. He had thought he might be embarrassed to face her, but he wasn't. Instead, he felt cleaner and stronger.

Outside, he heard the unmistakable sizzle and pop of bacon hitting an iron skillet. His mouth watered and his stomach growled. He squeezed her fingers. He couldn't remember the last time he'd had a decent meal. "I expect we'd better get dressed, girl."

He slipped off the bed to wash up, the water in the basin cold and bracing after her warmth. Still holding the blanket around her shoulders, she tiptoed to him and kissed him on the neck, then dressed herself. He sat on the bed and pulled on his boots, watching her. She slipped a simple gray dress over her chemise, then worked on brushing the rats out of her hair. "Not even a mirror," she complained. "I must look an awful fright."

"You don't, 'cept for the muskeeter bites." He forced himself to turn his attention to the immediate problem at hand. "What am I gonna do with you?"

She put the brush back in her traveling case and came to him. "Let me help you," she begged. "I came all this way. I'll do anything."

He grimaced. "Julia, this is dangerous work. There's nothin' you can help with. I'm just worried about keepin' you safe." His eye fell on Lewis's trunk, still open in the center of the room. He stepped over and started to close it, averting his eyes from the jumble of papers and journals inside.

Julia scampered after him and peered inside the trunk. "What is all that stuff?"

"Years worth of papers," Clark said. "Some of it's Meriwether's government papers. Most of it's the papers from our trip. Maps, journals, scientific field notes, letters, you name it." He dragged the trunk back into the corner of the room. "Some rascal broke in here the other night when I was out and ransacked the damn thing."

"Oh no! Did he steal anything?"

"Who knows? It was all a-jumble when I found it. I don't know what's there and what isn't, or even what they mighta been lookin' for." Clark straightened up and squeezed the bridge of his nose. Just thinking about it made his head hurt. "All I know is that everything Lewis ever had was taken from him at the end, except these papers. Julia, the folks around here are too thick to know it, but these old papers are Meriwether's real treasure. His and mine. If something happens to these papers, we might as well have stayed home."

"Will, I *can* help you!" Julia said. "Let me try to straighten it out. I'll sort everything and put it in order. It'll keep me busy, and out of trouble—"

"Saints preserve us," Clark said.

She bounced on her toes. "And it would help you later. Wouldn't it?"

Already, he felt as if another huge weight had been lifted off his shoulders. He raised his eyebrows and blew out a long whistling breath. "To be perfectly honest, darlin'—it would help me a great deal." He kissed her. "Private Clark, you've got the job. Just don't forget who's the general of this outfit."

"Hooray!" Julia hugged his neck. "You see, Will, you're going to be glad I came after all."

He lifted one corner of his mouth. "Don't push your luck, private."

She saluted him, and he burst out laughing. "Darlin', let's go get some breakfast. I got a lot of serious business to take care of today, and now, so do you." He started for the door, but Julia caught his arm.

"Will, there's one more thing I have to tell you."

He threw up his hands and rolled his eyes heavenwards. "Land sakes! What'd you do, knock over an Army paymaster on your way out here?"

"Well..." Julia dug her toe into the floor. "I didn't rob a paymaster, but I wasn't exactly honest with Sergeant Thomas. Will, you shouldn't have screamed at him last night. I kind of told a little fib...I told him you sent for me...and he believed me..."

Exasperated, Clark put his hands on his hips and stared at her, shaking his head. "Well, he shouldn't have. All right. I'll make it up to Sergeant Thomas."

Clark flung open the door of the cabin and strode out into the yard. York was sitting on a tree stump with Seaman at his side, forking in biscuits, fried eggs, and long strips of fragrant greasy bacon, occasionally throwing a small piece to the dog. Sergeant Thomas came trudging out of the barn, leading the two Army mounts that he and Julia had arrived on yesterday. Both horses were saddled and ready to go.

"Sergeant Thomas!" Clark yelled. "Where the hell do you think you're going?"

At the sound of Clark's voice, Thomas cringed. Then he straightened up, saluted, and stared straight ahead. After a slight pause during which he waited for Clark to heap more abuse on his head, he realized that Clark actually expected him to answer the question.

"Fort Pickerin', sir. I reckon I'm 'bout done here, sir."

"At ease, Sergeant." Clark put his hands behind his back and fixed Thomas with a friendly smile. Thomas flinched, a defiant set to his jaw.

"Sergeant, I got a little problem. I think you can help me out."

Thomas's eyes flicked over him, then straight ahead again. "Me, sir?"

Clark nodded. "Sergeant, you may not be aware of the reason that I came here." He put his hand on Thomas's shoulder. "You see, somebody just murdered my best friend."

Clark swallowed. The boy's expression softened and he cocked his head, intrigued in spite of himself. "There's gonna be justice done," Clark said. "There's gonna be at least two bastards hung. You get my meaning?"

"Yes, sir!" Thomas said. His sullenness and suspicion gone, he told Clark, "Sir, I would be more'n happy to help you with your hangin's, sir!"

York bent over, coughing. Clark pulled at his lower lip to keep from laughing. He really did need the boy's help for something very important.

"But like I said—I got a little problem." He jerked his head up at the porch of the cabin, where Julia stood in her little gray dress, hands clasped demurely. "Her."

When he caught sight of Julia, Thomas's eyes narrowed and he scowled. "Aw, no, sir—"

"That's right." Clark clapped him on the back. "You brought her here, and now she needs a bodyguard. That's gonna be you."

Thomas's jaw worked. He pointed a long finger at Julia. "Who's supposed to protect me from *her?*"

Clark roared with laughter, and York just about fell off his tree stump. "For that, you're on your own, boy!"

Clark slapped his hands together. He had a slave who didn't mind, a wet-behind-the-ears sergeant, a seventeen-year-old girl, and a dog. A whole goddamn army!

He jumped up on the porch, grabbed up a wooden plate, and held it out to Mrs. Dobbin, who filled it with food. He pointed at Julia and Sergeant Thomas and grinned. "You've got your orders. Breakfast, troops, breakfast! Then we march!"

Chapter 42
Wilkinson

Natchez, Mississippi Territory
October 18, 1809

"Piffle!" James Wilkinson cried. He wrapped his muffler tighter around his throat and sank deeper into the richly upholstered chair. He repeated, "Piffle!"

A violent shiver of self-pity overtook him. A few days ago, he'd caught a terrible cold. While he appreciated the generosity of his host Don Texada, this brick box was as cold as a barn. He feared he would never be warm and comfortable again. But the freezing weather wasn't the only reason he was shivering. He'd spent the evening perusing the latest newspapers. In some rag from Nashville called the *Democratic Clarion*, he'd come across a black-bordered box containing this little tidbit:

It is with extreme regret we have to record the melancholy death of his excellency Meriwether Lewis, governor general of Upper Louisiana, on his way to the city of Washington...

"Hallelujah! At last!" Wilkinson cried. Weak with excitement, he eagerly read the particulars of the story: Lewis alone and deranged at some godforsaken house along the Natchez Trace, shot twice, said to be a suicide. It was all well and good, but for the love of Jehovah, what about—

In the death of Governor Lewis, the public behold the wreck of one of the noblest men. He was a pupil of the immortal Jefferson, by him he was reared, by him he was instructed in the tour of sciences, by him he was introduced to public life...

"Oh, spare me." Wilkinson rolled his eyes heavenward, then scanned greedily down the page. His breath caught in his throat. The writer had the unmitigated gall to drag *his* name into the mess—

The territory of Upper Louisiana had been torn to pieces by party feuds. No person could be more proper to calm than he...The parties created by local circumstance and Wilkinson soon were united—the Indians were treated fairly, the laws were amended, and judicious ones adopted...

"Why, of all the brazen nerve!" Wilkinson said. "As if the mess in Louisiana were *my* fault, and Jefferson sent that whelp Lewis to clean it up! By God, I'll sue them for libel."

He read on. The writer babbled on about Lewis's tragic demise—a rash of worthless, inconsequential details. Wilkinson had almost reached the end of the column before he noticed the following heart-stopping line.

When in his best senses he spoke about a trunk of papers that he said would be of great value to our government.

Indeed! he thought, dry-mouthed. *And of great value to me, too! But where* are *they?*

The newspaper fell from his hands onto the carpeted floor. He pulled his cape around his shoulders and whimpered under his breath. "Blast!" His stomach knotted with anxiety. "My journals, my precious journals! Neelly and Runion—where are those devils? Why don't they come?"

A stab of pain flickered through his sinuses, and he pressed his face with trembling hands. The barrels of apples were rotting at the dock. In New Orleans, Don Morphy was no doubt getting impatient. And the officials in Havana—Lord, what would they think of him?

He snatched up the paper again and read the story a second time. The newspaper said Lewis had died on the eleventh. By any route, Neelly and Runion should've reached Natchez with the journals by now—

Overwhelmed by pique, he jumped to his feet and tore the newspaper to shreds, scattering the pieces around him like a snowfall. *"Where are my papers?"* he shouted in anguish to the empty room. There was no answer. On the walls, portraits of Don Texada's ancestors stared mockingly out of their frames.

As penance for his rage, a painful paroxysm of coughing gripped him. He hacked and clutched his cape around himself, trying to stop the violent jiggling of his belly. "Damn them, damn them!" Could Neelly and Runion really have cheated him? For the first time, it occurred to him that they just might be smart enough to recognize the value of Lewis and Clark's papers. After they'd killed Lewis, what if Neelly and Runion had stolen the Expedition journals for themselves? Perish the thought—what if they'd decided to cut their own deal with the Spanish, or worse yet, with *Thomas Jefferson?*

"Good Lord!" He shook his clammy fist at the frigid air. "Can no one be *trusted?*" He paced the room, his slippers falling on the thick dark carpet with soft thuds. All the money he stood to gain from Morphy...gone! All that cold, hard, Spanish gold... slipping through his fingers! And when would such opportunity *ever* come again?

Wilkinson fumed. Why did his schemes always have to be derailed by some idiot? George Rogers Clark, Aaron Burr...and now this. "Those dolts! I'll kill them! I'll wipe them from the face of the earth!" A sneezing fit overtook him and he lurched around the room, bumping into the heavy carved furniture, groping wildly for something on which to dry his face. He found a tapestry hanging on the wall—some kind of Spanish monstrosity—and buried his face in it, almost sobbing. It wasn't *right* that he should suffer such a blow—that he should be treated with such disrespect—

He dabbed his eyes and nose on the tapestry, then staggered to the window. He yanked back the brocade drapes and looked out on the cobblestone street below, serene and picturesque in the winter sunshine. There was nothing to do but brazen it out with Morphy. He had to think of some way to *save the plan*—

He started to pull the drapes closed again when his eye fell on a tall fellow standing on the street across from Don Texada's house. The gentleman was smoking a pipe and was dressed in a round hat, shiny boots, and a long military surtout with the collar turned up against the cold.

Was it Wilkinson's imagination, or was the man looking up at him through the frosted window? And was it possible—*oh, God*—he thought he caught a glimpse of long, red hair hanging down the back of the man's neck.

"Deliver me!" He backed away from the window, his heart hammering. It was Clark, it was Clark! Egad, how could he have forgotten? He raced back to his chair and scrabbled at the discarded scraps of newspaper he'd thrown on the floor. It was bad enough not to know about the journals' whereabouts, but surely the writer had mentioned *Clark*—

Lips moving, he pieced the story together and read it again. Nothing.

He pressed a fist to his lips and stifled a wheezing cough. In his concern over the fate of his journals, he'd overlooked... well, it had seemed a minor complication at the time. Clark had left St. Louis weeks ago. But why? What had Lewis told him? *Where was he now?*

Wilkinson moaned aloud. A few days ago, that smirking traitor House said that for all he knew, Clark could be in Natchez. But it was obvious to Wilkinson that Clark—that pushing, stubborn fool—had gone after his friend. Had he caught up with Lewis? Did he know what happened? If Neely and Runion should have gotten to Natchez by now, *Clark* could have—

"*No.*" He rushed back to the window and looked out. The tall man was gone. Vanished.

Wilkinson tittered. He was being absurd, really. It had not been Clark at all. No, of course not! This headcold was making him rattlebrained. Imagining things! He reached once more to pull the drapes shut—

The red-haired man was still there. He'd moved a little down the block. Wilkinson saw his eyes flick up once more toward the upper-story windows. Then he leaned to say something to a large black man who had appeared by his side. A shiver ran up Wilkinson's spine, more violent than before. Downstairs, he could hear Don Texada's servants going quietly about their tasks, oblivious that they were in grave, mortal danger.

He rushed to the top of the stairs. "Ready my carriage!" he bleated. "For pity's sake, run down to the dock and have those apple barrels loaded on the next flatboat downriver! I'm leaving for New Orleans posthaste!"

To his shock, Don Texada himself appeared at the foot of the stairs, his shiny black hair gleaming. He smiled up at Wilkinson in puzzlement. "*General*, you're still ill...in no condition to travel." Then he grinned, showing a thin line of pearly white teeth. "Does your sudden desire to depart mean you have some good news for *mi camarada* Don Morphy?"

"Oh, yes, very good news. Wonderful news! I can't delay a moment, *Señor*," Wilkinson stammered. "If you please, have the carriage pull into the alley around back."

He ran back to his room—he had no time for Spanish quizzicality—and frantically packed his things. Only the essentials, for God's sake...his red-braided uniform coat, his leopard-skin saddle cloth, his bottles of claret...hurry, man, your very *life* is at stake!

He yanked on an old greatcoat and pulled a Scotch cap down over his ears, then hollered for one of the servants to come get his trunk. Only one article remained—his pistol case, with its well-used pair of pearl-handled dueling pistols. Forget the sword. If Clark wanted to make an issue out it, well...he wasn't about to let him get close enough for hand-to-hand combat! No impudent border ruffian was going to get the better of *him*!

He skittered down the stairs on the servant's heels. His host stood in the *sala*, quietly watching the proceedings. "Don Texada, *mi amigo*," Wilkinson said, "*Muchas gracias por su hospitalidad*." He gripped Texada by the shoulders and kissed him on both cheeks. The Spaniard looked nonplussed. Oh heavens, was that a French custom only? No matter! It was high time he got back to New Orleans!

Out the door, in the alley, the warm, safe carriage beckoned. Don Texada's servants were loading his trunk. Wilkinson turned his collar high and stepped gingerly out into the alley. Thank goodness, no sign of Clark. Clutching his pistol case, he sprinted the few steps to the carriage and vaulted himself in. "To the dock—hurry, hurry!"

The dock was busy and crowded. It seemed the barges bringing the remnants of his army had finally arrived. Wilkinson wiped his raw, dripping nose and snugged his muffler around his face, pushing past the shuffling soldiers with his eyes averted. Thankfully, no one recognized him. Within a short time, he had his cargo loaded and was safely on board a swift flatboat headed downstream.

"My God...that my dreams should come to this." He looked back at Natchez as the shining bluffs receded into the distance. He turned his face away from the reeking boats filled with sick soldiers, struggling upstream in the dirty water as he floated easily past. It was of little importance now. He was headed for home. His garden, Celeste...and Morphy.

Long after the flatboat had passed the soldier's ships and swung into the broad downstream current, the sickly-sweet smell of decay hung in the air. Wilkinson couldn't understand it. Then he realized. All around him, barrels of rotten apples stank in the cold sunshine.

Chapter 43
Clark

On the Trace, Tennessee
October 18, 1809

The footpath through the woods was no more than a faint indentation where wild vines and creepers had been tramped down by the occasional passage of a horse or a man. Twisted trees crowded the horses and made them spooky. Clark felt the hairs on the back of his neck prickling, warning him of unseen dangers. Hadn't they just passed this same patch of briars a few minutes ago? Clark had a remarkable sense of direction, but now he stopped and pulled out his compass, just to make sure they hadn't doubled back on their own trail without even knowing it.

"That old Indian deerskinner seemed pretty sure Preacher lived back in these woods," York whispered. "We ain't lost, are we?"

"Naw." Clark put the compass back in his coat. "I'm just glad we finally found someone to point us in the right direction. The old man said it was a half day's ride. We're all right. Just look sharp, and keep your eye out for some limestone caves and boulders. He said Runion's cabin is near a stream just past the caves."

York's eyes roved around the dense snarls, his hands clutching his rifle. Clark watched him for a moment. The thought occurred to him that they might be heading into an ambush. After all, Runion knew these woods, and they did not. He thought of Julia back at the cabin, and little Lew...If he died out here in these woods, fighting Runion, they would wait and wait, perhaps never knowing what had happened to him. Then he thought suddenly of York's wife. He couldn't remember her name, though York had surely mentioned it many times. She too would spend her life not knowing. The idea made him feel strange and a little ashamed.

He felt his mouth go dry. Every moment he spent wondering about York or thinking about Julia, he was distracted from his mission. Quietly, he slowed his breathing and eased back his shoulders. He went inside himself and looked for his instincts, which he thought of as his animal self. He had found this self when he was a young hunter growing up in Kentucky and used it to learn to stalk large prey. He suspected Lewis had one too, though they had never talked about it. In his case, his brother George had taught him how to use it as a soldier as well as a woodsman, in case he ever needed to stalk human prey. Prey that was probably also stalking him.

He doubted he could find his animal self in St. Louis, but here in these woods it came to him easily, like a faithful wolf-dog. Once he had found it, he did not allow himself to feel pride in it, or to think about George, or Lewis, or the combat he sought with Runion. All of those thoughts were in his brain and useless at the moment. What was useful right now was in his body, this animal body that knew how to look, how to listen, how to smell, how to feel everything in its surroundings. He just got out of the way and let it happen.

They picked their way slowly through dead leaves and fallen branches. Even as alert as they were, they rode past the limestone outcropping at first, so tangled was it with holly and forsythia. It was only when they came across the small, clear, burbling creek that Clark realized that they must have reached the area that the old Chickasaw man had described.

Ordinarily, he would have told York to split off then, so they could cover more ground and search more quickly. But from what everyone had told them, Preacher was no ordinary opponent. Clark had wracked his brain, trying to recall any details of the man he had seen watching the obscene display at Mom Murrell's, but all he could remember was the long, dark, close-fitting coat that marked the man as a minister. It was a camouflage as simple and effective as any predator Clark had ever seen.

They began to scout the area, knowing that Runion's cabin couldn't be far from this source of water. They spotted one ax-felled oak, then another. As they guided their horses round, Clark had to admit Runion had chosen well the spot of his redoubt. The boulders provided a natural fortress; the caves gave him a place to store meat and other supplies; and the outcropping gave him a place to slither up and gain some height on any approaching travelers.

He was certain that his animal self would warn him if he and York were being observed from this rock. He was even more sure when he came upon the neat log cabin nestled in a small clearing at the base of the outcropping. There was no fire, no cooking smell, no ripe privy stink. Keeping their rifles at the ready, they dismounted and looped the horses' reins over a log hitching post.

"He ain't here," Clark said.

York pointed to the churned clay and mud at their feet. "No fresh droppin's. No horse has been here last coupla days."

They entered the spare cabin, and Clark could see immediately that Runion was a man who paid fanatical attention to order. The floor was made of ordinary split puncheon planks, but they had been smoothed to perfection and swept clean of every trace of mud, crumbs, or dust. The chinking between the logs of the cabin walls was solid and tight. A fireplace was swept clean of ash. Next to it sat a kettle, a skillet, and a couple of sacks of flour and dried beans.

The only furniture in the entire place was a bed covered with a straw-stuffed mattress, a split bottom chair, and a table made from a halved log, flat side up.

"This place is different from how I imagined it." York poked the sack of beans with the butt of his rifle. "I guess I thought it'd be more...evil, somehow."

"Me too." Clark examined the few items lying on the table, their edges lined up with impeccable precision. "I guess if evil were that obvious, it'd be pretty easy to avoid."

The table held a clean wooden plate and a drinking gourd; also a torn piece of paper with a message scrawled in looping, unschooled handwriting. The rough ink looked like powdered soot. Strong, dark India ink had bled through from the other side. Clark read aloud, "Never again will they hunger. Never again will they thirst. The sun will not beat upon them, nor any scorching heat—"

"Sounds like a Bible verse." York held up a long black coat that had been folded neatly and laid across the bed. "Here's his preacher coat. What's that on the back of that paper, Billy?"

Clark turned it over and blinked. It was a page torn from one of his own journals, a map depicting the confluence of the Snake and Columbia Rivers.

"This is one of my papers," Clark said. "It was Runion who ransacked my room." He felt a long deep shudder down his spine. What was Runion looking for? It had to be something that Wilkinson wanted—but if so, wouldn't it have been easier to take all of the papers and run? And if he were looking for some particular thing, then why take this one page, a page that could never be of any conceivable use to him?

Having exhausted all interest in the spartan furnishings, York ducked out of the cabin and began to scout around the clearing. Clark folded the map and began to put it in his coat. Remembering something, he unfolded it and read the rest of the inscription:

For the Lamb at the center of the throne
Will be their shepherd
He will lead them to springs of living water
And God will wipe away every tear from their eyes

He stepped out on the porch. The horses were cropping vines and weeds from the ground. They seemed calm and unaware of any danger, even though he felt his heart racing. An image had crystallized in his head of Julia, cross-legged on the bed in the little cabin at Dobbin's Stand, faithfully working on restoring order to his precious documents. And Runion, with a job still left to do...

Panic is a useless emotion, he reminded himself. He followed York down to the edge of the clearing. York was surveying an expanse of pitted, rocky ground. Thought it looked like every other place on the Trace, there was something about it that set his instinct to screaming again, his nerves raw and taut.

"Look at this place, Cap'n," York said. "All them flowers."

Across the ground, in small, discreet patches, the barren rocks were covered with stringy witch hazel. The blossoms embodied every color of yellow from lemon citrus to vibrant copper, stars of life across the earth's desolation.

"What makes 'em grow patchy like that, Cap'n? Gotta be something different about the soil—"

"Graves," Clark broke in, feeling sick. "They're growin' on graves."

York blinked, then swallowed as if bile had filled his throat too. "You're right, Cap'n. Some of 'em are sinkin' in. Lord, who are they?"

"Rob a man, York, and he'll eventually make it back to civilization and spread the word. Kill him, and nobody might ever know what became of him." Clark moved his lips silently, counting. "Jesus Christ, there's gotta be a dozen."

He folded his arms across his chest and made himself think. "York, I ain't one to run from a fight, but I'll be dad-blamed if I'm not gonna sharpen the odds in my own favor as much as I can. We need more fire-power. And we need to get Julia out of here." He turned to head back to the horses. "We'll leave tomorrow for Nashville, first light."

As he strode across the clearing, a dark shape caught the corner of his eye. He jerked his head back in the direction of the body pits—yes, there it was, on the ground, dark, straight, precise—

With several long running strides, he crossed the ground over the silent victims, the witch hazel rioting under his boots. At the edge of Tom Runion's private graveyard, he found himself standing at the edge of three freshly dug rectangles of earth, the soil heaped neatly beside each one.

"Billy!" York called behind him, catching up. "What is it? What—" He stopped. They stood looking down into three yawning holes. They were perfectly empty. A man with a passion for order had made these holes, a man who planned ahead—

Never again will they hunger
Never again will they thirst

"York, these are for us. You, me, and—" He felt his knees tremble. He would not allow himself to think that the third grave might be intended for Julia. Such a thing could not happen. He would not allow it. Their bodies thrown in these graves to nourish the witch hazel. Broken and discarded like Lewis—

"Come on, York!" he roared. "Let's go!"

The horses, sensing danger, nickered as he and York swung themselves back into the saddle and turned away from the small cabin in the woods. They had called upon the predator, and found him not at home. Instead, he was out, hunting them.

He called to the animal self again, to keep him strong and alert. Then he remembered something he hadn't thought of in many years. He was a small boy, kneeling beside his mother on a smooth plank floor. With ten children in the family, it wasn't nearly as clean as Tom Runion's. His mother was praying fervently for her sons in the Continental Army, gripping little Billy against her warm soft body. He couldn't remember the words she used, just the way he'd squirmed and offered his own secret prayer that God would find a place for him in the war too, deliver him from his terrible fate as the baby son, too young to fight and die.

No, that was wrong. He did remember something from his mother's long-ago prayer.

Defend us from all perils and dangers in this night

As he and York wound their way through the woods back to the Trace, Clark offered up these words again and again.

Chapter 44

Julia

Dobbin's Stand, Tennessee
October 19, 1809

Julia's heart sank a little as she watched Will ride away with York. It had taken so long to find him, she wished he would never be out of her sight again. But Will wasn't much for staying put. At least she could be thankful that he'd given her a way to make herself useful. She felt certain she could have Will and Meriwether's papers sorted out in a jiffy.

But first, she had some making up to do. Sergeant Thomas hadn't said a word to her all during breakfast, not even when she tried to start up a conversation by asking him didn't he think the bacon was good. He just shrugged and kept on chewing. Now he was standing with his back turned, watching Seaman romp in the woods looking for squirrels.

Julia crept up and said shyly: "Sergeant?"

Thomas hiked up his shoulders, gripped his rifle, and stared into the woods. "I ain't talkin' to you."

"You're supposed to be guarding me," Julia said. "How can you guard me if you won't even look at me?"

He turned and fixed her with a hard glare. "You got me in a peck o' trouble, ma'am," he said. "I feel dang deceived."

Julia sighed. "Aw, come on, don't be mad. I just did what I had to do."

"Wal, I jus' did what I was *ordered* to do, and your husband says he's gonna have me busted down lower than a buck private."

"He won't," Julia said.

Thomas snorted. "How do you know? He was right set on it, last I heard."

"'Cause I won't let him," Julia said. "He didn't mean it, Sergeant! He was just surprised, that's all."

"Yeh, him and me both." He unleashed a stream of spit onto the ground and looked back at the trees. "Well, what are ye botherin' me for? When the Army pays me a'tall, it ain't to stand around and talk to shifty gals."

"Oh, now you're just being mean." Julia flounced her skirt. "I thought you were going to teach me how to play brag."

"Teach ye—like I'd sit down at cards with ye after what you done!" Thomas shook his head in amazement. "'Sides, I thought you were supposed to be doing some job for your husband."

"I am." Julia traced out a few dance steps in the dust. "I'm supposed to be putting some old papers in order for him."

"Sounds borin'."

"It probably will be." Julia looked up at him with big, contrite eyes. "I could play brag for an hour, though, and then I have to get on with sorting out those papers."

"Aw..." Thomas screwed up his face, then broke into a laugh. "All right, you've tempted me. I'll teach ye for an hour." He dragged his greasy pack of cards out of his uniform coat and squinted at her. "You'll prob'ly cheat."

Julia gasped. "Sergeant, I would never!"

Grinning, Thomas sat down on the stone step outside her cabin. Julia smiled with relief as she watched him deal the cards. She knew she'd been less than truthful, but at least it wasn't going to cost her a good friend. In a place like this, she needed every friend she could get.

True to her word, Julia limited the brag lesson to an hour. Thomas rolled his eyes and made a great show of feigning relief. "Law, I surrender! Another ten minutes and you would've walloped me anyway!" She retreated into the cabin, giggling, while Thomas stuffed a fresh wad of tobacco into his mouth and lounged on the step outside, hat jammed down against the drizzling rain, rifle cradled in the crook of his arm.

With a furrowed brow, Julia pulled the trunk of papers into the middle of the room and propped it open. She really did want to fix this mess up for Will; last night he'd seemed awfully worried about it.

She decided first to empty the trunk completely: she could start by separating the written material from everything else. She heaped the papers and journals to one side and turned her attention to the other miscellaneous items that remained. There was a beautiful otter skin, thick and soft, which she couldn't resist wrapping around her shoulders; it made her feel snug against the chilly air. There were a couple of old pairs of drawers, which she set aside: it seemed strange to be handling Meriwether's underclothes. Bundled in a small flat package she found some nuts, rocks, leaves, and pressed flowers.

At the bottom of the trunk was an astonishing tomahawk. She picked it up in both hands and pretended to wave it at an imaginary enemy. It was so heavy it hurt her wrists to hold it; she didn't know how Indians possibly managed such weapons in a fight. She carefully laid the tomahawk down on the otter skin, pushed them aside, and turned back to the papers.

The journals were easy to sort out from the rest; she plucked out the red morocco leather-bound books and stacked them neatly. The maps were also easy to identify. She sat a minute and studied the deftness and precision with which Will had drawn the black squiggles marking rivers, valleys, and mountains. A silent thrill ran though her. One of these rivers was named after her.

The field notes, scattered in with the other detritus, were much harder to sort out. For one thing, she'd never known that Meriwether had such messy handwriting. And Will had the worst habit of scrawling addendums in the margins that crept around the corners of the pages! Thank goodness most of the notes had a date on them, or else she'd never be able to put them right. For several minutes, she found herself mesmerized by a sweet little drawing Will had made...it appeared to be buffaloes on a plain...but for heaven's sake, why was she daydreaming? She had a job to do. "Concentrate!"

As she sifted through receipts and chits for various expenses—a keg of nails here, a pig of iron there—she reflected that when she'd first moved to St. Louis with Will, she hadn't liked Meriwether very much. Back in Virginia, while she and Will were courting, she'd somehow gotten the mistaken impression that Meriwether was a fun-loving man with an easy laugh. How wrong she had been! She arrived in St. Louis after her honeymoon and found him utterly changed. Stiff, stern, impatient. He certainly had no time to talk with his friend's silly young wife—and Will expected them all to share a house! She found it hard not to rejoice when he moved out after a month of strain and misunderstanding.

But as time went by, her opinion of him had changed. For one thing, he was an unflagging supporter of her husband. While not garrulous and warm like Will's brothers, she'd come to see him in the same light. Loyal, reliable, steadfast. Once they became accustomed to one another, he relaxed a little, and accepted her teasing in good humor.

Meriwether was someone she could count on...and he liked Shakespeare, too! Just sitting around the house with her and Will, especially after he'd had a toddy or two, he could really be quite funny—

She held the otter skin on her lap and looked at the piles before her. She found herself crying. It seemed impossible to believe that Meriwether was really gone. Any minute, she expected him to come walking in the door and be peeved with her for touching his papers. Will had been so sad last night! How haggard he looked! Meriwether was a huge part of his life. One thing was certain—nothing would ever be the same again.

She was startled by a tap on the door. "Ma'am?" Thomas called. "You gittin' on all right in there?"

"Yes, I'm fine." Julia wiped her eyes on the otter skin and held it against her cheek.

"Wal, I just thought I heard ye snifflin', is all, and I thought we agreed you weren't gonna do that no more. 'Specially now that you found your husband."

"You're right." Julia laughed in spite of herself. "I did promise. I'm sorry."

"Why don't you come out and have somethin' to eat, ma'am? Seaman caught a passel o' squirrels, and we cain't eat 'em all by ourselves."

"All right," Julia sighed. The interruption was welcome. She was hungry, and she needed to get out of this room for a few minutes, with all its painful reminders. Sorting out her own feelings was even harder than making sense of this jumble of papers.

By the middle of the afternoon, she'd gotten a handle on the job. The bills, vouchers, and letters had been ordered and bundled; the maps carefully rolled up, the loose field notes stacked and fastened back in their respective portfolios. Julia packed them all back in the trunk.

She drew up her knees and rested her head on her arms. She wished little Lew were there to keep her company. She gave thanks that he was safe back home in St. Louis. This was no place for a baby, or for her either, for that matter. Her throat caught again, but she remembered her promise to Sergeant Thomas. "Things could be a lot worse. Got to keep busy."

She looked at the stack of journals on the floor near her feet and remembered she had still to put them in order. Those pretty red leather books were so pristine and neat, it was hard to believe they'd made the trip across the whole continent. These books were Will and Meriwether's prize possessions. The clean, copied notes were eventually going to become the book Will was always talking about.

She picked up the top journal and ran her hands over its smooth leather cover. Holding the book in her hands, she realized that beyond a few anecdotes, she knew very little about what Will had actually *done* on the

Expedition. Wasn't it about time she found out?

She opened up the journal to an entry dated October 4, 1805. Will's hand-writing! She read:

Capt. Lewis & my Self eate a Supper of roots boiled, which filled us So full of wind, that we were Scercely able to Breathe all night felt the effects of it.

Julia felt exasperated. That didn't sound very heroic! Some of the subsequent entries weren't much better. Will wrote about the men's travails with their fish and roots diet, which brought on "a heaviness at the Stomach & Lax." He wrote of passing over "bad rapids," of large black rocks, of Indians on the shore with scaffolds of drying fish. He wrote about the Indians' constant thieving from the Expedition's stores, and confessed the men were "well disposed to kill a few of them." He wrote about a series of rapids he called the Great Shute, "the water passing with great velocity forming & boiling in a most horriable manner." Julia thrilled. Will had run these rapids in his little canoe! They all had!

She put the book aside and began to look at some of the others. She could only imagine the pride with which Meriwether wrote:

Friday, November 15, 1805

Today I reached the mouth of the Columbia and beheld for the first time the great Pacifick Ocean ... On the grassy side of the Cape next to the sea is a steep hill, which ascends to a height of approx. 150 feet and extends out into the Ocean. My powers of description I confess are inadequate to render my impression of this vast vista where the deep blue of the sky meets the azure of the sea, great thunderheads roiling overhead, and the dun-colored earth of the isthmus below. I carved my name on a tree to memorialize this moment of tryumph, and proceeded seven miles up the coast ...

Besides being exciting, the journals certainly revealed the difference between the two men. Will's writing was brief and matter-of-fact, but Meriwether liked to write long, exhaustive treatises on each particular bird, animal, or plant he encountered on the trail. He often included an amazingly detailed drawing of whatever he was describing. Both Meriwether and Will seemed to have an obsession with measurements. Will rarely missed a chance to note how wide, deep, and fast was the particular section of the river they were traveling on, and Meriwether measured his animal specimens down to the last hair or feather.

Julia felt confounded. How could anyone ever put all these details together into a story? These books contained *real life*—with all its diarrhea and disappointments, aches and inconvenient facts, malarial agues and messy details. Meriwether's entries in particular included moments of astonishing self-doubt. People wanted heroism and glory. They would be surprised if they knew what the trip was really like. She found herself fearing that no one would want to read a book that depicted the true hardships that Will and Meriwether and the rest of the Corps of Discovery had experienced.

Sergeant Thomas tapped on the door and handed in a bowl: supper. "More stew," he said, looking downhearted. "I'll swan, I'm gonna hug the cook at Fort Pickerin' when I get back there. I never did appreciate his slumgullion until now."

Julia took her stew and blew on it; at least it was hot. "How's Mrs. Dobbin?"

"Who knows? It ain't like you can carry on much palaver shoutin' in her earhorn," Thomas said. "As it was, I raised so much hell just askin' if she had butter for the biscuits, I'd like to wake the dead."

"Did you get any?"

Thomas's shoulders dropped. "Naw."

Julia looked out at the dreary twilight. "I sure wish Will and York would get back."

"You and me both! These woods are kinda spooky in the dark." Thomas peered past her shoulder into the cabin. "How's yer job comin'?"

"I'm just finishing up," she said. "I'll come out in a little while. Looks like the rain's cleared off, and I can't stand to stay cooped up in here much longer."

Thomas grinned. "I'll warm up the cards for ye."

Julia gobbled down her stew, lit a candle, and went back to her task. She pulled the stack of journals toward her and began to put them in order by date: Will's first, she decided. She arranged Will's journals and lay them carefully in the trunk. Then she turned to Meriwether's. Journey down from Pittsburgh to Louisville. Setting out from St. Louis...winter at the Mandan villages...

She flipped open one book and read:

Tues Sept 26th Ft. Pickering

I have been ten days in this place, very unwell. Fever took hold in such a way that I was not myself ... suffered the most bizarre delusions I have ever experienced.

Julia frowned, confused. Fort Pickering wasn't on the Expedition, at least she didn't think so. She read a little bit more. Meriwether mentioned Captain Russell, Pernia, and Major James Neelly.

"This just happened," Julia said aloud. She realized what she was reading. It was a journal Lewis had been keeping during the last weeks of his life.

*Not knowing the intent of Clark, I have decided not to wait for him, but I am certain
he will overtake me on the Trace, at which time I will be free to abandon secrecy and take
him into my full confidence about my reasons for this journey.*

"Oh, Meriwether, you should have waited," she moaned. What *were* the
reasons? Why had he kept it a secret from Will? Will said an evil man was
after Meriwether, a man named James Wilkinson...that he hired men to kill
him—

Reading on, her heart jumped with shock. Meriwether had written:

*Met an interesting gentleman tonight, a friend of Neely's. He professed to be a Method-
ist minister, and he allowed me to importune him with many questions about that unique
and colorful faith. His name was Tom Runion.*

Tom Runion! That was the man Will was looking for! Julia felt frantic for
Will to return. In the pages of this book might be critical information about
who killed their friend. Trepidation filled her as she read down the page.
Meriwether wrote about sitting down to dinner with these men...some bit of
foolishness about a gold mine...and then—

A drawing, a very strange drawing, of a wolf. Or so it seemed. Was it...?

*I will now endeavor to describe that singular animal which has so long afflicted my life;
his size has remained consistent relative to my own, which is to say, knee-high...*

*The eyes are gray like stone or marble, and continuously spinning in the head; the teeth
are yellow and about the size and sharpness of a typical gray wolf. The tongue is enormous, at least a foot long...*

"Oh, my." Julia's mouth went dry. Meriwether had been sick back in St.
Louis, anyone could see that. And often he'd seemed sad...and so
lonely...obviously he'd needed a rest. But she hadn't expected this. She stared
at the drawing. Fantastical, intricate. The wolf was horrible.

She turned the page and found several ragged edges where pages had been
torn out, and a small, exquisite drawing of a bluejay. The next entry looked
messy and hurried. Meriwether spoke of the wolf again, how it tormented
him, bit him, poisoned him. Then:

*I am most anxious to see Clark and am under the greatest apprehension that something
may have befallen him—Wilkinson's reach seems illimitable and I fear Clark may have
fallen prey to the same assassins W. sent to kill me...*

"Will, *please* come back," Julia whispered aloud. "Where are you?"

*That man has already rendered me more good service in my life than I had any right to
expect. He received payment in deceit and lies, and my inability to keep my word, and if he
has at last decided to wash his hands of the matter, where lies the fault?*

She wiped her eyes angrily on her sleeve. "Meriwether, what in God's name are you talking about?" How could Meriwether know her husband so little? Or was he just so sick in mind, body and soul that his usual sound judgment was failing him?

She turned the page to the final written entry and read:

Oct 10 09 Grinders Stand

Day's end. This intolerable trial must be finished.

Then is it sin to rush into the secret house of death, ere death dare come to us?

Julia gasped; it was a line from Shakespeare. *Antony and Cleopatra.*

I know no other course ... The beast is taking my mind, the fever is taking my body, my enemies sucked out my soul long ago, in small pieces to worry over and show off and display. The pain is too great, it's unendurable, I will not leave Wilkinson anything more to cackle over. He's done his damage, the fellow lurks outside to finish the job. Do you suppose the vulture will take Wilkinson my poor cracked head? Maybe they could put it up in Mr. Peale's museum in Philadelphia, next to my miserable portrait.

I am no coward, please, give me the courage It must be over.

We have no friend but resolution, and the briefest end

A last scrawled sentence:

May God forgive me

"Oh, no." Julia pressed her hand to her mouth. "Oh, Meriwether." Tears squeezed out of her eyes. Will had to read this, but oh mercy, what would he say? What would he think?

The room was dark except for her candle. Out in the woods, Seaman was barking at something. She hoped fervently it was Will and York coming back. She'd been so distracted by Meriwether's journal she hadn't heard their horses ride up. Putting the journal aside, she started to pack Meriwether's other books back in the trunk.

Outside, Sergeant Thomas stirred from his place on the step, his sword clanking. She heard him pacing away from the cabin. "Seaman? What yeh got, boy? Lord, I hope it's a big, fat coon...Where are you, boy? Seaman?"

Thomas's voice trailed off. There was a brief animal shriek: a quick yelp. Seaman had caught something. She heard a man's heavy footsteps, then silence.

The door swung open. At last! Her dear husband, back safe! "Will," she cried. "Oh, Will, I found something, something you have to see—"

Her voice stuck in her throat. The man standing in the door was not Will at all. He was a pale vision, a ghost, a phantom, a monster. He was the devil himself, and in his hand, he held a knife, and the knife dripped dark, red blood.

Julia dropped a couple of the journals on the floor, then scrabbled a few feet in one direction, then the other. She was trapped. Somehow, she forced her voice from her closed throat, thin, shrill. "Sergeant Thomas!"

The man kicked the door shut behind him with a loud, decisive bang. He was bareheaded, and looked like more like some predatory forest creature than a normal human being. Part of it was the way he was dressed, bristling with weaponry and all in skins, from his dark fringed hunting coat to his leather breeches, buckskin gaiters, and moccasins. But more unnerving still was his face. Expressionless except for a faint smile, it appraised her with an icy blue stare; the irises were unnaturally pale and wide. His hair was so light in color that it seemed to catch and radiate back every flicker from her candle.

She drew in her breath to scream again, and let her friend's name rip forth so loudly it hurt her throat. "Sergeant Thomas! Sergeant Thomas!"

The loud shriek caromed around the cabin, then echoed away into silence. Seaman didn't bark; Sergeant Thomas didn't come running with his sword at the ready, the way he had at Big Town. She had the terrible feeling that she and this devil-man were the only two people in the world.

"He can't hear you, girl." Almost casually, the man extended the knife for her inspection, a dirk even larger than the long knife Will carried. She cried out and cringed from its viscous dripping. *God, no, it couldn't be.* Another scream rose in her throat. The man sheathed the knife and reached for her head in one panther-like motion. Before Julia could make another sound, his right hand was gripping the back of her skull. The left pressed firmly over her nose and mouth. Her eyes bulged; she couldn't breathe—

"I said, he can't hear you," the man hissed, the ice eyes only inches from her own. "So shut the *fuck* up." He threw her down on the hard little mattress.

She scrambled into a sitting position, gasping. "Wh-who are you? What do you want?"

He sprang forward again, cat-like, and bellowed in her face, "I want that map to the goddamn gold mine!"

Julia felt as stunned as if she had been hit on the forehead with a mallet. Was that what this was all about? That stupid rumor about the gold mine? Through her terror, her mind grasped at tangled threads. Meriwether's journal:

I confess I had some sport at the expense of Runion and Neelly tonight. ...When I assured them that such a fountain of riches did indeed exist, they fairly drooled, and their eyes were as big as dinner plates.

"Map? Map? There is no map." She grabbed at the journal still lying on the bed. The thing didn't exist! If she could only show him, maybe he would leave. Desperately, she squinted at Meriwether's disordered handwriting in the guttering candlelight. "It says so right here, I'll show you—"

The man knocked the book out of her hand and chunked it into the open trunk of papers. "Greedy bitch. Enter not into anything that defiles, or works abomination, or makes a lie of the Lamb's book of life."

"Wh-who are you? Are you Mister Runion?"

"The Reverend Tom Runion," he said. "Servant of the All-Wise."

"M-my husband's out looking for you! You still have time to run b-before he gets here!"

He drew back his lips, showing wolfish teeth. "If the good man o' the house had known when the thief would come, he woulda watched, and not suffered his house to be broke up." He laughed at her terrified expression. "I hope he comes back soon. I'd hate to think he ran into any bandits on the Trace."

Runion paced the floor, his footsteps echoing on the rough planks. Her heart thrummed wildly. She wanted to scream again for Sergeant Thomas, but *oh God the bloody knife.* Instead, she tried to force herself to think, be brave for Will—

Runion was saying, "Your gold is cankered. Its rust is a witness against you. It shall eat your flesh as fire."

This man was crazy! "S-Sir? What d-does that mean?"

He reached inside his coat and pulled out a fearsome looking instrument. It was a large, two-pronged hook, each tine sharpened to a needle-like point.

Wilkinson sent 2 men to cut me off at 20 Mile Crk … shot one, the other one escaped into the woods after inflicting injury on me with a hook.

Julia couldn't help herself. She screamed at the top of her lungs. "Will! Will! *Willllll!*"

He leaned over her. "That's right, call him," he crooned. The scream choked in her throat as he stroked her hair, then ran the devil's claws lightly over the front of her dress, flexing his wrist as if to mimic the act of digging the claws into her flesh. He let the claws linger a moment over her breast.

"Please," Julia whispered, tears stinging her eyes. "I have a baby."

"And you barely off the tit yourself!" Runion said. "Congratulations, girl. Too bad you didn't bring the babe. That would have been even better! I expect your husband thinks highly of his seed, eh?"

Her breath was coming so rapidly now she thought she might pass out. "Wh-what do you want with my husband?"

"*I want your husband.* Don't you get it, little lady? Now that I got you, he'll do *anything* I want." Still grinning, he spoke slowly, savoring the word. "*Anything.*"

Julia's heart twitched and jerked. This man had tried to kill Meriwether. Now he intended to kill her and Will. "He should be here any minute. He'll kill you!"

"I doubt it, girl." Runion wagged the devil's claws at her. "Most men are mighty sentimental about their women. I expect he'll cooperate real fine." He skinned his lips back again from slick teeth and jerked his head to one side. "Git up, I'll give you a little demonstration o' what I mean." When she didn't respond right away, he roared, "Git up, bitch! Now!"

Julia scrambled off the bed. She could barely stand. He grabbed her head again and used it to pull her against him. His arms were as strong as iron. She was helpless to put up a fight and they both knew it.

She whimpered faintly, limp with terror, and squeezed her eyes shut. She didn't even know whether to pray for Will's arrival or pray that he would not come and be spared. Runion muttered, "For example, take a woman and her accursed vanity." He held the claws against one of her cheeks. She felt the sharpened point brush past her eyelash. Slowly, lightly, he traced the tines down from her cheek to her jawline, drawing two thin trails of blood and pain. Bile rose in her throat.

With one finger, he turned her chin. "I chose wrong. This side's prettier." Quicker, but still keeping the pressure light, he raked the claws down her other cheek. Julia cried out, the moan lost against his chest. He pulled her head back by her hair. "Open your eyes."

It took all the courage she had to force her eyes open, to stare into those ice-cold beast eyes of his. "Now that you've had a little taste," he breathed, "how would you like it if I were to use these to take off the side of your deceitful face? You pick the side. Hell, I don't care." The corner of his mouth lifted. "How would old Will like you then?"

"Please, no," she heard herself beg. "Please don't hurt me like that."

He released her hair suddenly and she collapsed on the floor. At once, he kicked her legs. "Git up. Let's have a little dance. Go on. Git up and dance."

She scrambled to her feet and shuffled back and forth, her arms limp at her sides. Runion clapped his hands together to make a rhythm for her.

Dully, she tried to imagine the last time she had danced. It was in St. Louis, in Will's arms, a lively, weaving reel...

Runion clapped and called, "Leap, rogue! And jump, whore! And we'll be married forevermore!" He unleashed another stream of the harsh laughter, than ordered abruptly, "You can stop now."

She stared at him, then pushed back some of her tangled curls from her face. Blood was still dripping off her cheeks.

"You see?" Runion said. "You danced for me, whore, and I didn't even hurt you. Just imagine what your Will might do to keep you alive."

"But I still don't understand," Julia said shakily. If Meriwether's wolf had tormented him like this, it was no wonder he had been driven to do something desperate. "I don't understand what it is you want to make my husband do."

"I told you," Runion growled. "I want the map to the goddamn gold mine. It was promised me by Wilkinson, it was denied me by the Lamb. O Lamb that was slain!"

She said slowly, "I guess you didn't find the map when you were here the other night."

Runion looked aggrieved. "Oh, I found maps all right! Map after god-blasted map, each covered with black lines, little symbols, the devil's writing. None of 'em made a lick a' sense! I need your husband to decode the goddamn things and give me the right one. The one I was *promised.*"

"Reverend, sir, I'm sorry I was greedy." She darted past him to the trunk and pawed through the papers she had so carefully placed there this after-noon, before Sergeant Thomas brought the stew... *Where was Thomas? Oh Lord! Where was Will?* ... "I know where the map is. I can get it for you! My husband made it. It shows just where the gold is."

She found Will's maps, neatly rolled papers covered with drawings and notations. "Here! Here!" She thrust several of them at Runion. "Take a look!"

He made no move to take them, just regarded her with cold disgust. She threw all but one back into the trunk. She felt hysteria, true madness, creeping around the edges of her consciousness. She unrolled the map and stared at it. It was covered with squiggly lines and bumps. On one side, the word "Whale" was written next to a small arrow pointing to something. *Oh, God, he would know she was trying to trick him—*

"This isn't it!" Julia threw it back in the trunk and grabbed up another. This one was better—several rivers were shown, and the rest of the page was almost entirely covered with numbers. Julia showed it to Runion. "This is it, I remember! These numbers are all longitude and latitude and the like." She stared at a curved piece of writing. It said, "Rapid." She pushed it against his chest. "Here you go! Go find your gold!"

With that, she bolted for the door. But Runion reached out a long arm, and with a powerful motion seized the back of her dress and slung her to the floor. The map rolled away and came to a stop near her traveling trunk. Julia began to weep.

"I've already looked at all this shit!" he roared. "Damn you, woman, I will scourge you for every one of the lies of your forked tongue!" Then, to her horror, he ran his hand down the front of his own body. Her eyes widened, focusing on the growing bulge between his legs.

"No." She shook her head. Her mind was ceasing to function, all rational thought being consumed by horror. "No, please, I have a baby. Please, please..."

He cocked an eyebrow at her and grinned. "Woman, the way you carry on, I'm beginnin' to wonder how you got that kid you're always yappin' about. For Chrissakes, I'll be gentle. I gotta make sure there's something left he still wants."

He kicked her legs apart. Julia screamed. "Will! Will! *Willllll!*"

He lunged forward and drove his bloody knife into the gap between her parted legs, nailing her skirt to the floor. His face came close to hers. *Oh god no no no no.* "Another lamb," he said. "Another sweet sacrifice."

He stood up. "This time by fire."

He took a step and retrieved the map from the floor. Then he held it to the candle, turning it this way and that, until the flame caught the edge of the paper. He held it near her face, then dropped it behind her on the floor. She pulled at the knife that anchored her down. She was unable to budge it.

A small fire began to eat away at the plank floor. Runion picked up one of the journals she had dropped earlier and tore out a page. He fixed her with his icy stare, and said: "Behold the fire and the wood. But where is the Lamb for a burnt offering?" He watched the paper burn for a moment, then dropped the flaming bits on her skirt. She beat out the flames, sobbing.

He laughed at her and opened his coat to show her the devil's claws. Her mind was gone, except for the thought of wanting to live, desperately wanting to live.

To live to live to live to live Will Will Will Will Will Lew Lew Lew Lew

The pages were catching faster now. He dropped them on the floor as soon as they caught. Some of them fell out of her reach and started new fires on the rough planks. She felt the heat on her back and her arms. She clawed at the immobile knife handle. He touched another flame to her skirt and mocked her as she flailed at it, beating it into ashes.

Will Will Will

Oh god please no I have a baby! I have a baby!

Chapter 45
Clark

Clark felt dead tired as he rode up to Dobbin's Stand. York trailed behind him. The night had turned unseasonably warm and humid. He'd taken off his coat and draped it over the saddlehorn. The place seemed eerily quiet in the fog. The old lady had obviously gone to bed. Clark supposed she'd left out a meal for them, but supper was the last thing on his mind. His stomach had been roiling ever since he'd seen the freshly-dug graves behind Runion's cabin. Those bright patches of flowers...then right beside, the gaping, earthy pits, just waiting to swallow Runion's next victims.

His stomach clenched as they rode into the yard. The fog was so thick he could barely see the cabin. All he wanted to do was make sure Julia was all right—

Behind the windows of his cabin, a strange, soft glow. "Where is everybody?" he wondered aloud. Seaman did not run up to greet him.

Beside him, York suddenly started in his saddle. He sucked in a breath and started to point. But he didn't need to, because all at once, Clark *saw*. The scene resolved itself in front of his eyes in one horrible instant.

Under a tree by the edge of the woods, an inert black heap. Seaman. Motionless. The dog was dead. Fifteen feet from the cabin, Sergeant Thomas lay on his back, bareheaded, one knee jackknifed up in the air, his body surrounded by a dark pool of blood, his sightless eyes staring up at the sky. Someone had opened the boy from neck to navel, oh Lordy, his goddamn entrails were all over the place, Clark's gorge rose, his mind rebelled, *it's like a charnel house*—

Behind the flickering windows, flames. The cabin was on fire. Trapped inside with the monster, burning, was Julia. He could hear her now, screaming in mindless, mortal terror—

Oh god please no I have a baby I have a baby

He flung himself off his horse, grabbed at his pistol, his rifle, anything, his mind a blank panic, his boots made of lead; traversing the ground between his horse and the cabin seemed to take an eternity. He was conscious of York yelling behind him; one long leap over the boy's broken body, he could not stop himself from looking, the dead eyes seemed to fix on him for an agonizing moment—

And then he was there at the door, viciously kicking the brittle boards, yanking the damn thing off its hinges and throwing it aside. He was inside the cabin, only to see—

Julia, struggling and kicking on the floor near the bed. She looked demented. Her hair was wildly disordered and trails of blood trickled down her cheeks. Between them, flames. And Tom Runion, grinning.

Runion had one of the journals in his hands. In the terrible split second while he stood watching, Runion tore out a page, touched it to the candle, and dropped the flaming paper down on Julia's head.

A roar of animal rage escaped from his throat. Runion tossed the journal in the flames and rushed toward him. Clark raised the pistol, fired point blank, he couldn't miss, but somehow he did. The shot went wild, the ball caroming into the wall. Runion grabbed his outstretched arm and dragged him into the fire.

"*Will!*" Julia screamed.

He felt the flames licking at his boots as he fell against Runion. He sent the spent pistol crashing into Runion's face before Runion twisted it away, dislocating his knuckle in the process. Runion rolled his pale eyes and clamped a viselike hand down on Clark's shoulder, shoving him to the floor and bending his broken finger back on itself. "For these be the days of vengeance, that all things which are written may be fulfilled." Runion laughed wildly, his lips skinning back over his teeth. "Ol' Will, damn your eyes, I want my map!"

"Run, Julia! Run, for Christ's sake!" Clark yelped in pain as Runion fell upon him. All he wanted was for her to get out of this room, but she couldn't seem to move. Instead, she flailed on the floor, struggling to free herself, like a doomed butterfly pinned to wax.

York shoved his way into the burning room. The air was full of flaming bits of paper. The sonofabitch was on top of Billy, pounding him with huge, bony fists. Miss Julia was trapped on the floor by the bed, behind a wall of flame—

York yanked his jacket off and threw it over his head. He knew what he had to do. He bulled his way through the smoke, feeling the fire sear the flesh on his arms. His jacket was in flames; he had to beat it out on the bed when he reached her.

"Help me, York!" Julia screamed. York grabbed her under the armpits and lifted her, but she was stuck fast. At first, he couldn't see how. Then he noticed the knife, piercing the skirt of her dress between her thighs, buried almost to its hilt in the plank floorboard.

"York...York..." Julia clutched at his elbow. York grasped the knife, pulled it; it did not budge. Then he grabbed her skirt and ripped it in two. Miss Julia kicked. York looped one arm under her knees and wrenched her free, then hoisted her in his arms. She whimpered as he pressed the jacket over her face, then plunged back through the fire to the other side. He didn't stop until he was fifty feet from the cabin and his lungs had met the fresh air.

Mrs. Dobbin was in the yard, wringing her hands and sobbing. She hadn't heard a bit of the commotion, but came running when she smelled the smoke. "Help her! Take care of her!" York hollered. He pulled the jacket off Julia's face, set her on her feet, and thrust her into Mrs. Dobbin's arms.

"No!" Julia immediately turned to look back at the burning cabin. York noticed for the first time her face was streaked with blood as well as tears. "Will! Will's still in there! Oh, York, *please*—" Then she caught sight of Sergeant Thomas's butchered body, limp on the ground, silhouetted in the glow of the fire.

"Aah—aah—" She gasped, wordlessly, her mouth agape with horror. Her eyes turned up in her head and she fell like a whisper to the ground. York left her with Mrs. Dobbin and rushed back into the flames.

Until recently, William Clark had never been in a fight he thought he couldn't win. But he sure as hell was in one now. As he felt Runion's thumbs pressing his windpipe, Clark wondered if he were going to die.

"I want my map! Fat Guts Wilkinson said you had a map! Now give it over, damn you!"

Clark pried Runion's hands away from his neck enough to gasp in some hot, smoky air. "What map?" he gagged. "*What blasted map?*"

"The map to the gold mine." Runion drove his knee into Clark's stomach. "He hath swallowed down riches, and he shall vomit them up again, God shall cast them out of his belly..."

Clark dropped his throbbing right hand and pawed frantically for his dirk.

On the edge of his vision, he could see Lewis's trunk of papers, the lid gaping open, little tongues of fire licking at the outside. Runion had already set one journal on fire; he could see another lying open on the floor with some other scattered papers, inches from the flames.

If he didn't get the journals out of here, they would all be destroyed. It would be a staggering loss, a failure beyond endurance. *Everything we did, everything we saw, reduced to ashes. It might as well never have happened...Lewis might as well never have lived...*

"There is no gold mine! *It doesn't exist!* Wilkinson lied to you!" he choked.

"That's what your little whore wife said," Runion sneered. "But the Lamb spoke the truth, and lied not. *I walked in fields of gold!* he said. But the Lamb was covetous and weak, and so he perished, like the goddamn sniveling puke he was! He cried out, 'O Lord, take me away from this death—'"

Murdering sonofabitch! Clark's pawing hand found his dirk, tore it loose from his belt, and plunged it into Runion's side. Runion's pale eyes bulged. Incredibly, he grabbed at the hilt of the knife and withdrew it, staring. With a vicious motion of his arm, he tossed it away and sent it skittering under the bed. Then he reached inside his coat and drew out his devil's claws. They glittered in the firelight, the two piercing points just the width of a man's eyes.

Clark saw them descending. He drove his knee into Runion's groin, jerked his head desperately, felt the claws rake his scalp. Dark, stinging pain. Runion sucked air, coughing.

Suddenly Clark was aware of York, standing beyond the flames, hacking in the smoke. "Get the trunk!" he howled. "York! *Get the papers!*"

"Fuck the papers, Billy!" York wrapped his jacket around himself and prepared to plunge toward him.

"*Get the goddamn papers, York!*" Clark roared. "*I mean it! For the love of God, if you only mind me one more time, do it now!*" His own life was cheap compared to those papers! He gripped Runion's wrist, fighting through his own pain, trying to twist the devil's claws away before they descended on him again.

York cursed. But thank God, he obeyed. He kicked the trunk lid closed and grabbed the handle. Clark heard York yell in pain; the fire had made the metal grips white-hot. But York didn't fail him. He wrenched the trunk free of the flames, dragged it across the floor, then grabbed both handles, hauled it up against his chest and staggered out the door.

He was alone with the monster.

The claws hovered above his face. Runion's other hand gripped his throat, crushing his windpipe. His lungs burned; smoke was searing his throat and filling the air, clouding his vision. He knew he had only minutes to live. The flames were close now. They licked at his clothes, illuminating Runion's pale hair with an otherworldly glow.

His mind screamed with regret. Oh, yes, he'd been dutiful William Clark: he had done what he had to do, he had saved Julia and the papers. At least he could feel some peace about that. But he didn't want to die in this place, die like Lewis, murdered by a maniac...

A dark stain spread across Runion's flank where the dirk had gone in, but Runion seemed stronger than ever. He ranted, "Your nigger took your whore, and now he'll take your gold...what kinda man are you, Ol' Will? No better than the Lamb! The All-Wise has shown the strength of his arm...He has scattered the proud in their conceit...He has cast down the mighty from their thrones..."

Crazed with fear, desperate for air, Clark bucked his body, kicked, smashed his left fist brutally into Runion's wounded side. Runion yowled; Clark felt the death grip on his neck loosen a little. He cast Runion's hand away and gulped in smoky air. He hit Runion again in the side, in the face, finally wrenching himself loose. Runion fell on his side. Clark's boots scrabbled on the floor. This whole damn place was going to collapse. There were papers on the floor, burning...

He got up, started to stagger, had to get those papers, had to get out of here, leave the monster muttering in this lake of fire. But before he'd taken a step, a terrible stabbing pain shot through his ankle. Runion had pierced him with those goddamn claws, right through the leather of his boot, right down to the bone. He toppled onto the floor again, on his knees, struggling in agony.

It was then that he saw it. Lewis's tomahawk. It was propped against the wall, lying on an otter skin that was curling and singeing in the heat. He stretched out his hand, clawed for it, lunged for it. Oh Lordy, the tomahawk was impossibly far away, he couldn't reach it. Runion was crawling up his back, about to send those bloody claws plunging into his neck—

He would swear ever after—tears coming at the memory—that he did not know how he came to hold the tomahawk. But in that furious moment, he felt it come into his grasp as firmly as if a sure, strong hand had put it there. He thrust his left elbow back, knocked Runion off balance, then turned around, rearing up on his knees.

Runion slashed at his chest with the devil claws. "Damn you for a liar! I will tear the caul of your wicked heart—"

Clark raised the tomahawk in both hands and brought it crashing down on Runion's skull, cleaving it in two. The devil claws clattered onto the plank floor. Clark gasped, gagged. Warm blood and brains covered his hands. The tomahawk blade was buried between Runion's pale, staring eyeballs. In those eyes he saw reflected terror, fire, death. Murderous rage. His animal self.

He let go; let Runion fall. Smoke was filling his eyes and lungs. He crawled forward on his knees, feeling his way; he had to get out of here. The fire was closing in. He grasped at the papers that fluttered on the floor, burning to cinders. Oh, Lord, that journal, it was lost, he could read Lewis's words on the open page even as it was being consumed by the fire—

Today I reached the mouth of the Columbia and beheld for the first time the great Pacifick Ocean ...

Crackling, browning, burning. Gone.

Clark moaned in anguish and fell down on his elbows. He couldn't see, couldn't breathe. He was swimming through darkness, floundering, drowning in a vast violent sea.

York collapsed with the trunk outside. When he released the handles, some of the skin on his palms pulled off right along with it. He pressed his raw hands to his chest, coughed, gagged. His lungs were on fire.

Miss Julia had come awake. She was screaming. Mrs. Dobbin had her arms around Julia, but Julia was fighting her, trying to crawl back towards the fire. "No, child, no!" Mrs. Dobbin pleaded, tears running down her wrinkled cheeks.

York grabbed Julia by the shoulders. "Miss Julia, you *got* to stay here! I'm goin' back 'n get Massa Billy! Ain't no good you gittin' yourself burned up, too! Remember Lew at home—"

"Oh, God, York, hurry! Hurry!" Julia sobbed.

York turned around, Lord, there wasn't much time, maybe seconds, before the whole cabin went up. He ran on rubbery legs. The heat at the door was tremendous, driving him back a step.

York moaned. His jacket was in blackened shreds, he needed a blanket or something, *anything,* to shield his body from the fire while he went in after Billy. But there wasn't time. He was about to plunge in when he heard a man's voice behind him.

"God a'mighty, what in blazes?"

York turned, saw a burly man running toward him, with a bearded face and round, shocked eyes. "My massa's in there!" he shouted. "Some god-damn crazy preacher is tryin' to kill him!"

"Christ, I'll help you!" the man hollered. York rushed forward; the man pushed in right behind him. The flames were waist-high, the smoke billowing and thick. He couldn't see anything.

"Billy!" York screamed. "*Billy!*"

"I see 'im!" The stranger grabbed York's arm, pointed. York peered through the smoke. He caught sight of Billy lying face-down on the floor, just beyond the flickering flames.

"Let's go!" He jumped forward, feeling the fire catching at his clothes, his hair, his skin, but that didn't matter now. They had to get Billy. The other man was right beside him. They each grabbed Billy by an arm; he was unconscious, a dead weight. York thanked God the stranger was there. His strength was so exhausted, he didn't think he could have lifted Billy by himself.

As for the Preacher...York saw to his satisfaction that he would go to his fiery grave with an eternal headache.

One more plunge, one more consuming blast of heat, the two of them stumbling out, coughing, choking, Billy's boots dragging in the dirt. They staggered past Sergeant Thomas, made it twenty more feet, collapsed. York turned Billy onto his back. The stranger jerked off his coat and beat out the flames still clinging to their clothes.

York squatted on his haunches, wheezing. Miss Julia came running. "Will! Oh *please.*" She fell to her knees and put her hands on his chest. "Oh, darling, you *can't* be..."

Her plea ended in a shriek as the roof of the cabin fell in behind them, sending smoke and sparks billowing into the air. "We'd better move him away from here," the stranger hollered. "He's alive, I tell you, I felt him cough."

They lifted Billy again, moved him away, laid him down under a tree. York saw Billy's hands twitch and felt tears of gratitude streak his face. Mrs. Dobbin ran to fetch some water, while Julia wept and prayed.

The stranger turned and looked back toward the flaming cabin with dazed eyes. "We'd best go move that poor fella a-layin' in the yard, 'fore our strength gives out," he said to York. "He's like to get burned up if we don't."

York nodded. He got to his feet. He wanted to give this man his hand in friendship, but it was burned raw, and besides, he was just a slave. As they picked their way back to move what remained of Sergeant Thomas away from the flames, he rasped out, "Mister, I'm much obliged for your help, and mighty glad you came along when you did. I'm York. My massa's William Clark."

The stranger nodded. "I know." Then he introduced himself. York could not have been more astonished if it were James Wilkinson himself. The stranger gave his name as Major James Neelly.

Chapter 46
Clark

Dobbin's Stand, Tennessee
October 20, 1809

Clark fluttered sore, gritty eyelids. A log cabin. Blink. A patchwork quilt. Blink. A fireplace with a kettle hanging over glowing oak. *Where am I?*

Then, he remembered. He was supposed to be dead. A feeling of grim satisfaction came over him. Choked, slashed, punctured, and burned, but not dead. No, he had tomahawked the bastard. But what then? Nothing but fire...

Blink. A girl sleeping in a chair. *Julia.*

Relief flooded him. He whispered her name, but no sound came out. Julia dozed fitfully on the hard chair, her lips moving. She wore a plain white cotton dress that was too big in the shoulders and bosom. Her hair was pulled into a braid and tied with a white ribbon. Her face bore painful tracks of scratches and looked puffed and red, as if she had been sunburned to boot. To complete the picture, her skin was dotted with mosquito bites.

In that moment, she was the most beautiful woman he had ever seen.

Clark tried to clear his throat. It seemed to be full of ashes. "Julia."

She came awake at once. "Oh, Will." Her voice was as hoarse as his, from smoke or screaming or most likely, both. She gently touched his face with cool light fingers.

He started to lift his right hand, winced, then reached out his good left hand and took her fingers in his. Wordlessly, she held his hand to her bruised cheeks. Tears came to his eyes as she kissed his hand, then folded it open to kiss his palm. Suddenly, her lips contorted and her shoulders began to quiver.

He tried to sit up, to take her in his arms and speak soft words to her, but his lungs went wild with agitation, sending him into a fit of uncontrollable coughing. He covered his mouth and nose with his hands, gasping for air between coughs. Julia crawled on the bed with him. She gave him a handkerchief and then held his shoulders and patted him on the back until the coughing subsided. He looked down at the handkerchief. It was filled with black soot and gray phlegm. "Christ," Clark croaked, his eyes watering. "I wonder how much a' that's gotta come up."

He and Julia sat together in the quiet moment that followed, just looking at each other. He raised his hand and gently rubbed his thumb over her mouth and her puffed jawline. A deep fear gripped him, though for her sake he tried not to let it show. His precious Julia, alone with that *monster*—

He tilted her head back and gazed into her eyes. Her eyes were searching his in return, dark sweet pools of concern. He broke the gaze and took her braid carefully in his fingers. He needed to know but was desperately afraid of the answer. Lord knew you couldn't tell by looking at a woman—he'd never forgive himself if—

Julia touched his cheek and turned his head back to face her, then kissed him gently on the mouth. She stroked his hair back from his forehead. His scalp stung where Runion had raked him with the devil's claws. "Poor Will. Please don't fret. You got there in time. I'm safe." She wrapped her arms around his aching chest. He felt her trembling.

"York got burned," she whispered. "Going into the fire so many times. He saved me, and the papers, and you—"

Clark swallowed. "Is he all right?"

"He will be." Hot tears fell on his skin. She cried, "Sergeant Thomas—"

"I know." He pulled her against him, wrapping the quilt around them both. He didn't try to offer any words of wisdom. A good man was dead. Lord, what was there to say?

After a few minutes, her crying ceased and she clung to his chest. He cradled her warm body and silently thanked God for her life. Somehow, he was going to be allowed to walk out of here, with her and York and his papers and what was left of his sanity and get the hell on to Nashville—

But Jesus Christ, at what cost? Lewis was dead. That brilliant flame of a mind, that generous heart, that sharp tongue—gone forever. Sergeant Thomas was dead. That promising boy had seen his wife safely through a devilish wilderness and had died at the monster's hands for her. Now his life was over. York was burned, Julia brutalized, the papers menaced and some of them destroyed, Mrs. Dobbin's livelihood burned to the ground—

"Goddamn," Clark heard himself rasp in his low, damaged voice. Goddamn James Wilkinson and all the destruction he's wrought! *He'll pay for this if it's the last thing I ever do*—

Clark loosened his grip on Julia and looked around for his clothes. He spotted them draped over a rocking chair by the fireplace. In front of the fire, a large black puddle spread over the floor. Clark watched in puzzlement as it rose slowly and began to move towards him. To his amazement, the puddle resolved itself into the shape of a dog.

His breath caught in his throat. Seaman. He had forgotten—

Lewis's dog staggered to the edge of the mattress. Somehow, the silver collar still shone, though the long black fur was matted and dull. Seaman rolled brown eyes up to Clark with a pleading look, then thrust his muzzle into Clark's outstretched hand.

Clark swallowed the lump that had formed in his throat. "Well, I'll be damned. Seaman, boy, I'd given you up for dead." The dog whined and weakly thumped his tail. Clark ran his hands over Seaman's withers. Seaman cringed, but as soon as he stopped, the dog lolled his head on the bed and moaned for another reassuring touch.

"I don't believe it. I saw him. How—"

Julia gave him a tremulous smile as she wiped away tears. "We thought he was killed for sure. But Major Neelly said he just had broken ribs. He got him to take some broth, and then sewed him up where he'd been kicked—"

Clark goggled at her with astonishment. "Major Neelly? He's here?" He thrust the quilt aside and climbed out of bed, setting off another round of violent coughing.

"Will, no!" Julia jumped off the bed and ran after him as he limped to the rocking chair and began to sort through the clothes. "You have to rest, you were hurt—"

"Where are the papers?" Clark growled. "Where are the blasted journals?"

"Right there!" Julia pointed to the trunk, which was sitting in the corner of the room. "They're safe, I haven't let them out of my sight, oh Will, please listen—"

Clark jerked on a pair of breeches and headed for the door, the unbuttoned legs flapping around his knees. Julia grabbed a shirt and caught his arm. He pulled it out of her hands and over his head, then wrenched open the door. Julia caught his arm. "Will, for heaven's sake! Major Neelly helped York save you! He went into the fire and found you. There's something of Meriwether's you should read—"

He shook her arm off. "There can still be justice, Julia! Now you stay out a' the way, you hear?"

He charged out into the yard, trying not to favor his injured leg. The ground felt cool and rough on his calloused bare feet. To his left, the guest cabin lay in ruins, the roof collapsed, some logs still smoldering. Clark sucked in his breath and stared at it for a moment. *I almost died in there.* He forced himself to look away.

At the edge of the clearing, he saw three figures. A stocky bearded man with a shovel was plugging away at a shallow hole in the ground. Nearby, York rested on a tree stump next to a half-completed plank coffin, looking ashen and exhausted, his hands wrapped in stained strips of white linen. Angry patches of raw skin were visible on his arms and face.

The third figure was only the form of a man, prone under a blanket, the smell of death already on him. Thomas.

Too damn much grave digging lately! Clark strode across the yard, coughing. York struggled to his feet, a smile of relief sweeping over his dark features. "Massa Billy, awful glad to see you—" Clark silenced him with a look. The joyful reunion would have to wait. He still had a job to do for Meriwether Lewis.

The stocky man paused in his work and turned to face him. His shy, watery eyes were able to meet Clark's eyes for only a few seconds before he directed his gaze firmly down to his boots. "You Major James Neelly?" Clark demanded.

The stocky man nodded glumly, as if dismayed by the admission. "You're General Clark."

"I understand you saved my life," Clark said.

Neelly nodded and shrugged. "I guess. Me and your man there. 'Twas the least I could do, considerin'..."

"I'm afraid I'm going to have to take yours."

Neelly looked up with an expression of surprise. Then he sighed deeply, blowing the air out through whiskered cheeks. Looking everywhere but at Clark, he glanced into the woods, then out towards the Trace, then up at the sky itself. Not finding the answer he was looking for, he shook his head and let his gaze come back to rest on his boots.

"I don't know why you helped me," Clark continued. In spite of his pain and fatigue, anger gave him strength. "I know you're James Wilkinson's man. I know you and Tom Runion killed my friend."

Neelly stared at the shovel in his hands as if noticing it for the first time, then cast it aside. "General Wilkinson gave me my job at Big Town, a job I needed bad. Far as I know, I still work for him. Seemed like I owed that man an awful lot." He shuffled his feet in the dirt. "Tom Runion was supposed to kill the Gov'ner. I was supposed to lead him into it, and stand aside."

"That's all I need to hear," Clark said. "I'm sorry for you. I'm sorry for any man who's that weak." His voice rose, then broke. "My friend died like a dog because of you."

Tears were blinding him—Lord, would they ever cease? He searched out York's face and barked, "York, get a rope."

To his utter amazement, once again York did not obey him, just stood rooted to the spot with a sad, stricken expression. Clark drew in a deep breath, intent on putting the fear of God into his servant, but instead he found himself kicked in the chest by another wracking round of coughing. York came to him and seized him around the shoulders. To Clark's fury, York seemed intent on trying to maneuver him back towards Mrs. Dobbin's cabin. The old woman was following Julia off the porch, clutching her earhorn.

"You need to *rest*, Massa Billy," York said, "not be runnin' 'round hangin' folks." While Clark struggled to control his tortured lungs, Julia ran at him and assaulted him from the other side, pulling at his arm tenderly, making solicitous noises, and babbling about Meriwether's journal.

Clark felt like strangling them both. Were they deaf? Major Neelly had just confessed to leading Lewis to his death! He wasn't surprised at Julia's tenderheartedness, but York? He threw Julia's hand off, then shoved York. "You heard me! Hop to! Goddamn it, I need you!" Without waiting to see if York followed the order, he wheeled on Julia. "Get in that house right now, girl. And take the old lady with you. Don't come out 'til I say, hear?" To his satisfaction, Julia gasped and ran back to the cabin. Mrs. Dobbin, who had just made it out to the center of the yard, turned and started to dodder after her.

It seemed to Clark that Neelly could have ridden halfway down the Trace in the time that it was taking him to extract any cooperation from his own wife and slave. Instead he just stood watching with an air of regret and resignation, as if the hanging under discussion were not his own. "General," he interrupted softly, "I know there's no reason you should care what I say. But you oughter know, it didn't work out the way you think. I didn't kill the Gov'ner. And neither did Tom Runion, may he burn in hell."

"For Christ's sake, man!" Clark stabbed a finger in Neelly's chest, backing Neelly up almost to the edge of the shallow grave. "Have some self-respect. I won't be lied to!"

York said, "Cap'n, maybe you should hear him out. I been talkin' to him all night and—"

"York," Clark said with barely controlled fury. "Damn you, I need you to mind me. Go right now and *get the goddamn rope.*" He rolled his head to loosen his neck and cleared his throat. "Neelly, I aim to hold you responsible for what you done. But let me make one thing clear—this is justice, not murder. You got the right to say your piece before you go to your Maker. So if you got somethin' you want to get off your chest, now's the time."

Neelly's eyes widened slightly. "Gov'ner Lewis told me you'd come after him. He talked about you all the time. You're just like I imagined you'd be." He shook his head, then muttered in a soft voice. "General, you got a right to know how your friend died. That's all I want to tell you. Then, I don't reckon I got much say in what happens next."

He raised his head and managed to meet Clark's steely glare. "The last time I saw him—or the next to the last time, I should say—was the morning after the thunderstorm. I never shoulda let him go..."

He watched Governor Lewis ride away at a slow walk, Seaman at his side. Neelly had only one wish: that Lewis would survive another day. Like most of the things he hoped for in life, it seemed like a long shot. Lewis was as sick in body, mind, and soul as anyone Neelly had ever known. But when he thought about all the other things Lewis had done in his life, it didn't seem impossible.

His luck ran in its usual direction: bad. It took all day to track down the missing horses. He wasn't a fast traveler even in daylight, and in the dark, with three exhausted mounts, the going was even slower. It was close to dawn by the time he rode into the clearing that surrounded the little roadside inn.

Right away he knew that something awful had happened. At an hour when everyone should have been asleep, he heard voices, talking over each other in frantic confusion. On the porch, Priscilla Grinder and a small Negro girl were arguing. The girl tried to run off the porch, towards the guest cabin. Mrs. Grinder pulled the girl's braids and slapped her. In the bare yard, a dim pool of light emanated from a lantern clutched in the skinny hand of the innkeeper, Robert Grinder. He and Pernia were squalling at each other. Pernia's hair was mussed and full of straw, as if he had just been roused from a sound sleep. Neelly could only catch scattered words: crazy—nigger—water—that man won't die—not my responsibility—blood *everywhere*—

Above it all a wolf was baying *cry-yi-yi-yi-yi*. No, not a wolf. Seaman, straining at a rope looped around a tree.

Neelly threw himself off the horse and shoved past them. Robert Grinder recognized him and yelped, "Major Neelly! There's been shootin' here tonight—"

Neelly grabbed the lantern out of his hand with a curse and mounted the step to the guest cabin. The door yawed open, the inside of the cabin so black that it seemed to absorb what little light the lantern threw out. Neelly felt his boots stumble over something just inside the door. He waved the lantern down around his knees—

"Oh, Christ." He knelt and set the lantern to one side. Governor Lewis lay sprawled on his back on his buffalo robe. His shirt was soaked with blood. His face was dead pale, and his head was blown open—you could see his brains—

Neelly began to weep. "Oh, Governor, why? Oh Christ, why couldn't you have waited?"

Lewis's eyes fluttered open. Neelly almost fainted with shock. Slowly, Lewis moved blue lips. "Clark?"

Neelly took his hand. "No, Gov'ner. It's me, James Neelly."

"Neelly..." Then, as if he felt he owed Neelly an explanation, he murmured, "I have done the business, sir."

I have done the business sir

Clark flinched. The phrase was vintage Lewis. He had to remind himself that Neelly had spent days with Lewis. He ought to know his friend's manner of speech well enough to add a few convincing details.

"That's a damnable lie, and a convenient one for you!" Clark snapped. "Suicide? You expect me to believe that, after everything that's happened? For pity's sake, I'm not a fool. I know all about you! That old man up the road told me how you poured liquor into my friend when he was helpless! The Grinders told us how you stole all Lewis's money, his watch, his guns. Then you delivered him up to Runion—he lived for *hours* like that! Goddamn, there'll be justice here today—"

Instead of replying, Neelly just looked past him, his hangdog features softening in what could have almost been a smile. Clark whipped his head around to see what Neelly found so much more entertaining than his own life—

It was Seaman. The injured dog stumbled off the porch, then crossed the yard in a shambling crawl that in no way resembled his usual prance. But his tail was up and wagging. Neelly dropped down into a squat. The dog passed Clark and the others and went straight to Neelly. As the Chickasaw agent stroked his ears and neck, the dog rolled his golden brown eyes in ecstasy, his tail thumping on the ground.

Clark felt thunderstruck. Seaman's courage and loyalty to Lewis were beyond question. Surely if James Neelly had hurt Lewis in any way, Seaman would loathe him. Instead, he was nosing Neelly's face with his big square muzzle and licking his beard as if the two of them were old friends.

"Is that supposed to impress me?" Clark demanded, his blood roaring in his ears. "For God's sake, Seaman is just a dumb beast! Just because you patched him up last night—"

He hadn't noticed Julia creep back to his side. She was clutching a red morocco bound book—one of the journals. "Will—"

"I thought I told you to get in the cabin and stay there."

"Will, please look at this. *Please.*" She held the book open to a scrawled page. Meriwether's handwriting, even messier and more heavily blotted than usual.

"Julia, I don't have time for this," Clark took the book and tried to focus on the page, his eyes grainy and burning. He skimmed over the page, looking for familiar words. Suddenly, he realized this wasn't an Expedition journal, but something very different indeed.

Oct 10 09 Grinders Stand

Day's end. This intolerable trial must be finished...

Then is it sin to rush into the secret house of death...

The pain is too great, it's unendurable...

"No." His chest tightened again. He tried to hand the book back to Julia. "Not now, Julia. I don't have time for this." He heard his voice break. "*Later.*"

"Will," Julia pleaded. "My love, it has to be now."

He stared at the page again. Lewis's handwriting, as familiar to him as his own. A thousand days of journal entries, eight thousand miles across a continent, hundreds of thousands of words, but Good Lord, never anything like this—

...my poor cracked head...please, give me the courage. It must be over...

Clark looked up from the journal and saw Seaman leaning against Neelly's legs. He groaned, closed his eyes and squeezed the bridge of his nose hard, trying to think. Since when could a damn dog testify as to a man's guilt or innocence?

Opening his eyes, he found himself looking at four final words scrawled in the journal. The last words Meriwether Lewis ever wrote:

May God forgive me

Julia and York were watching him with scared eyes, as if they were afraid he would do something crazy at any moment. Watching Neelly pet the dog, he couldn't help remembering the way Seaman had defended Lewis's grave, even though his loyalty was no longer of any use to his poor master. Perhaps he and Seaman weren't so different after all. Maybe the loss of their friend had made them both a little crazy.

"For God's sake, Neelly," Clark said. "Finish it."

Kneeling by the bloody buffalo robe, Neelly wept in helpless anger. All his life, he'd believed that there were great men. A while back he thought he'd met one in Natchez. His name was General James Wilkinson. The handsome red uniform with spurs of polished gold, the strutting walk, the manly handshake. And to think that he—the lowly Chickasaw agent—might play a critical role in Wilkinson's big plans! "You'll see, Neelly," Wilkinson had promised. "You never know where a job like yours could take you. It's very possible that you'll end up rather wealthy, with a fine house just like this one!"

Lewis's cold fingers clutched at Neelly's sleeve. "For God's sake, please bring me some water."

Neelly stood up swiftly. He marched out the door and ordered Pernia to fetch some water for his master. Pernia began to make a speech about how the Governor was not his master and how he owed him two hundred and forty—

He smacked Pernia, just to make him stop. Then he found the pump and fetched the water himself. When he tried to give it to Lewis, most of it just ran out of his mouth, pinkish with blood in the growing light of dawn. Lewis whispered, "Thank you, Neelly."

Neelly despaired. The rising light revealed what he had already known. Lewis's situation was hopeless. He grasped at ideas, some way to lessen the horror, to give this man a decent death.

Only great man I ever knew—

He forced Grinder and Pernia to help him move Lewis off the soaked buffalo robe and on to the bed. It was a mistake. Lewis screamed in agony. Neelly didn't understand how someone could lose so much blood and still be alive. Lewis lay limply on the bed. Neelly could see the end was very near, and yet—and yet—the big heart kept beating—

Lewis's hand twitched helplessly, dark with powder burns, and Neelly took it between his own. It felt cold and already strangely stiff. Lewis said, "I have no luck at all. One would think a shot to the head would suffice to kill any man. I was forced to reload—"

Lewis plucked at his sleeve, pulling him closer. As Neelly bent over him, Lewis touched the front of his shirt and said, his voice strangling in the death that was overtaking him, "Please shoot me. If you have any decency, man—"

Clark broke into tears. Lord, what if he had been there? He had never refused Lewis anything.

Ah, he couldn't have done it!

Neelly sat with Lewis. When Pernia or the Grinders tried to enter to pick through the trunks, to steal the leavings of the Governor's life, he drove them away. He held Lewis's hand and stroked his bloody forehead. He wanted desperately to make it better, somehow. "I'm sorry, Gov'ner," he said. "I was too late. I woulda saved you."

Lewis licked his lips, his tongue swollen, and whispered, "No. I had to save myself."

Now Neelly knew that what Wilkinson had told him was all humbug. He'd only ever known one great man. This man's greatness didn't come from his tailored clothes or the fancy way he talked. It came from what he'd done. Neelly could still feel the mists from those five roaring waterfalls the Governor had told him about—and the driving will that had taken thirty-one men and tons of goods around them, and thousands more miles after that—the whole damn continent!

"You're a great man, Gov'ner," Neelly said. "I never met anybody like you. People'll remember what you done—"

"Make sure my books go to the President," Lewis said suddenly. Then, he blinked in agitation. "Neelly—Neelly—"

Neelly squeezed the cold strong hand. "What is it, Gov'ner?"

"I don't want you to think I'm a coward, Neelly."

Neelly shook his head. "I don't, Gov'ner. I would never think that."

"I'm not a coward." Lewis turned his head to the side. Neelly saw his eyes crinkle, as if at a wry joke. "I'm just so strong, that's all. It makes it hard to die."

Neelly was crying so hard, he didn't know exactly when the Governor let go of his hand. It was several minutes before he realized that Lewis had been right. God was merciful after all.

Neelly wiped sweaty hands on the front of his shirt. "Perny and the Grinders started fightin' over his things. I took the valuables—the pocketbook and the guns and his watch. I figured his family'd be wantin' those." His voice trailed off a little. "I spent a little o' the money, in Nashville. I'm sorry 'bout that."

"Tell me something, Neelly," Clark said. He found it hard to speak. "Why the hell did you come back here?"

Neelly blinked in surprise. "I guess I wanted to make things right, as far as I was able. I messed up, General. I tried to make Perny and Grinder help me get him laid out and buried, but they wouldn't." He tried to meet Clark's eyes but had to look away. "That part was terrible. I guess I panicked a little. Finally I just ran."

He squared his shoulders. "I had to come back for the books. The Gov'ner acted like his whole life was in those books. I went down to Grinder's, and they told me you were here." He let his eyes rest on the smoking remains of Dobbin's Stand. "I reckon that's it. You can hang me now if you've a mind to."

Clark closed his eyes. He supposed he could still bring down his vengeance on Major James Neelly. He wanted to punish Neelly for the incompetent burial and for almost losing the papers. He wanted to punish him for being blind about Wilkinson—for letting Lewis go off without him—for being too late. He wanted to punish him for not understanding that Lewis, the man who never ran out of bullets and medicine, had run out of other weapons—courage and pride and hope.

Clark choked bitterly. Then he thought of something else. In the end, Lewis had needed three things: water; kindness; and someone to hold his hand while he died.

He wiped his eyes on his sleeves and said brokenly, "I don't suppose I will."

Julia slipped under Clark's arm and hugged him around the waist. Clark pulled her against his side. Finally he said, "York, I guess we'd better look to getting that boy buried. Then we'll be heading out to Nashville quick as we can."

"General, it would be my honor to escort you there," Neelly said.

He almost refused, then stopped himself. Lord, they were all half-dead. He needed all the help he could get. "Seaman would like that. Hand me that shovel, man."

He made Julia go inside while they worked on the grim task, taking turns digging the grave and finishing the crude coffin. York prepared the boy's body. Major Neelly had sewn shut the terrible wounds inflicted by Runion's knife. York gently combed down the boy's fair hair and dressed the body. They had lost most of their clothes in the fire, so Thomas would have to go to the next world wearing a little something from each of them.

"Tell me something, Neelly," Clark said, resting on the tree stump while Neelly flailed away at the dirt. "The Grinders' little servant girl told York that she saw Runion skulking around Lewis's room that night. And then he came after us. He kept talking about some blasted gold mine—"

Neelly shook his head. "We thought you had a map to a gold mine out West. Wilkinson promised it to me and Runion. It was supposed to be our reward for taking your papers and delivering the Gov'ner, dead or alive. Then, the Gov'ner said he had it with him, but it was all in code—you and him were the only ones who could decode it—"

"Lewis said that?"

Neelly rubbed the back of his neck. "Perny told me later the Gov'ner was playing with us. How could Runion have known?"

Neelly's answer made his head spin. There were many more questions he wanted to ask about Wilkinson and the evil that he had unleashed on this road, but he decided to wait. There would be plenty of time to talk on the way to Nashville. Besides, however Wilkinson had begun the perverse game, Lewis had ended it. Clark suspected that he could ask questions from now until Judgment Day, and never understand.

When they were ready, Clark walked over to the cabin and called out Julia and Mrs. Dobbin. York had outdone himself. Laid out in his plain wooden box, the sergeant looked clean and composed. His eyes were closed with dollar coins. He was wearing his own boots, polished black. A white ruffled shirt from Major Neelly was tucked into a pair of white breeches of York's. But Thomas still presented a military appearance. He wore an old Army coat, its blue and red colors proudly trail-worn, that marked its owner as a veteran of Wayne's Legion. It fit perfectly.

They let Julia say good-bye. She touched his pockets, then made a strange request. "Does anybody have a pack of cards?"

"There was one on him," York said. He walked over to the small pile he'd made of Thomas' ruined things and found the worn, greasy cards. "You want these, Miss Julia?"

"No." Julia dashed away a tear. "I just thought he might want them, in his next life."

They tucked the cards in the Wayne's Legion coat, then nailed down the lid of the coffin and lowered Thomas into the grave. At Julia's insistence, his sword was placed alongside his body.

Clark swallowed. "Julia, what was his name?"

She smiled sadly. "I believe he said it was John."

Clark bowed his head. As he knew he would for the rest of his life, he wished Lewis were there to help him. He cleared his throat. "Lord, this is Sergeant John Thomas. He gave his young life away nobly, doing his duty. He lies here on this battlefield. We commend his soul to you with all the honors of the brave. May he rest in peace."

York began to fill in the grave. Julia walked up to the cabin and sat on the porch with Mrs. Dobbin and Seaman. She didn't cry. Clark guessed that for now, his little wife was all cried out. He wished he could say the same.

Neelly sighed deeply. "I hope that boy went to a beautiful place. You know, Gov'ner Lewis told me about those five waterfalls you found out West. I keep picturin' him there now. Lord, I hope he's somewhere he can have a little peace."

Clark laughed a little. "Peace? Man, you didn't know Lewis very well. If there's a heaven, he's up there tryin' to tell God how to run the place."

York snorted, blew his nose loudly, and said, "Amen."

Chapter 47

Clark

Monticello, Albemarle County, Virginia
November 25, 1809

"May I help you with your collar, sir?"

Clark stood stiffly as a tall, thin Negro named Peter fastened the black leather stock around his neck and carefully buttoned his collar down over it. He swallowed. The collar felt rigid and tight. Or maybe it was just his throat.

"Sir, if you please..."

Clark held his arms behind him as Peter helped him shrug into his vest, then turned around and waited while the servant's deft fingers flew over the buttons. He caught a glimpse of his own face in the mirror and felt irritated. He couldn't be paler if he were made of wax. It just didn't do to be so damn nervous! *It's not like I've never met Mr. Jefferson before,* he thought. But this time was different from all the others. On previous visits, Lewis had always been there.

"And your coat, sir? My, this is a fine coat," Peter murmured. "I do a little tailoring here at Monticello, and I must say this is nice workmanship indeed, sir."

"That's good to hear. It's brand new. Had it made in Nashville," Clark said.

"Well, it looks mighty fine, sir!"

Clark nodded and swallowed. Mr. Jefferson had been out riding when he'd arrived this afternoon with the journals, and his French butler, Etienne, had shown him in here. Etienne had lost no time informing him that this was the bedroom usually reserved for President and Mrs. Madison, when they sought to escape the confines of the Federal City and seek the counsel of the Old Sage of Albemarle. Clark guessed he was supposed to be flattered by the news, but instead, he found it unnerving. The small miniature of Madison that graced the dressing table looked uncannily like the picture that hung on the wall at Mom Murrell's tavern. And it didn't help any that the bedroom was shaped like a damn hatbox, with eight walls instead of four. Sometimes, a man needed corners.

Peter helped him on with his gloves, politely ignoring the scars of barely-healed burns on his hands. Clark winced slightly as the leather pulled on over the tender spots. His burns were almost healed, but his heart—that was going to take a while. That was one reason he'd sent York on to Louisville. He'd just needed the solitude. Ten days from Nashville to Washington City, riding alone in the wilderness. Nobody for company but his memories.

Peter carefully combed and tied his hair and pulled his coattails straight. One thing Clark had to say for Mr. Jefferson is that his slaves were as efficient as they were polite. But he couldn't help wishing York were there. York's joking was just what he needed to calm his nerves.

York. There was another decision he'd have to make. He'd seen York off from Nashville a fortnight ago, along with Julia and Seaman. York had wanted to come east with him, but Clark thought it was more important that someone he trusted accompany Julia to his brother's home in Louisville.

"Cap'n," York had argued, "If you gonna go get General Wilkinson, I aim to be right by your side."

Clark shook his head. "You're going to Louisville, York. After everything that's happened, I'm counting on you to make sure Miss Julia gets there all right." After a long pause, he added: "And York...when you get there...you go spend some time with your own little wife."

York had fallen into silence. He looked at Clark with an unspoken question in his face. Clark knew what York wanted him to say, and nobody could argue that he hadn't earned it. But at the same time, the issue was complicated. Things were much too unsettled to decide anything right away; he told himself he'd consider the matter when he got back to Louisville. Which, if everything went as he hoped, would be soon.

"Here you are, sir." Peter handed him his plumed beaver hat and flicked a last bit of dust off his shoulder. "If you're ready, I shall run tell Etienne, and he'll show you in to Mr. Jefferson, sir."

Clark tucked the hat under his arm and squared his shoulders. "I'm ready, thank you."

As it turned out, Etienne wasn't needed, for Mr. Jefferson himself was hovering in the entrance hall. He was still dressed in his riding costume of a long blue coat, old breeches, and a faded red waistcoat a decade out of fashion. Jefferson looked older and grayer than he remembered, but his back was as straight as ever.

"General Clark." Jefferson came toward him, his hand outstretched. His gray eyes twinkled. "Fresh from the rebellion, I see!"

Clark's face reddened. "Sir, I hope you didn't give any credence to all the talk—"

"Oh, of course not! This has been a season for rumors, I'm afraid. I have not seen such a season since the summer of '76," Jefferson chuckled. "I've been hoping to see you, sir, but I knew not when to expect you in Albemarle. I'm most gratified that you came."

Clark gripped his hand: it was big, bony, strong. "I got here as soon as I could, Mr. President."

"Oh, that title is reserved for Mr. Madison now," Jefferson said airily. "I'm happy to say he possesses both its honors *and* its trials."

"Well, I'm glad to hear retirement is agreeing with you, sir."

"Yes, indeed." A small, wistful smile played about Jefferson's lips. He took Clark's arm and gestured around the room. "You have seen my Indian Hall, then? Of course, you'll recognize many of these artifacts from your late tour to the Pacific Ocean."

Clark nodded. The room was crammed with pipes, tomahawks, a painted Mandan buffalo robe, a Clatsop hat, a carved canoe paddle, and dozens of other curios he and Lewis had brought back from the West. Jefferson led him over to a table where a large fossilized bone rested. It was part of the jawbone of a mastodon, containing several huge, yellow, squarish teeth. "You remember this, of course?"

Clark smiled. "Yes, I believe my brother George found that particular specimen near our home in Kentucky."

"Well, as you can see, this is where I keep all my treasures," Jefferson said. His tone was quiet and soft, a perfect rendition of the central Virginia accent; Clark remembered Lewis saying that even when angry, Jefferson never raised his voice. "Or almost all, I should say. The rest are in my library."

At the risk of seeming impolite, Clark felt compelled to try to hasten the business for which he had come. "Mr. Jefferson, speaking of treasures, I've brought the journals with me. I took the liberty of asking your servant to put them on the desk in the parlor."

"Of course, of course," Jefferson said. "Shall we retire there, then?"

"If you please, sir."

Jefferson led him into the parlor, the parquet floor creaking under their feet. Like the entrance hall, this room was also cluttered with things; furniture and artwork filled every available space. Clark's eye was drawn to a large painting above the fireplace of a young woman carrying the head of John the Baptist on a platter. He found her smile unnerving. In the hearth underneath the painting, a roaring fire blazed away.

"I cannot stand this cold weather," Jefferson said. "I have long held that cold is the source of more suffering to all animal nature than hunger, thirst, sickness, and all other pains of life put together."

Clark chuckled. "Sir, I confess I'm burning up in this coat. That winter I spent in the Mandan villages at forty below redefined my idea of cold forever."

"I suppose it would!" Jefferson's voice dropped slightly. "General, have you been to see Mrs. Marks?"

"Yes, sir. She's holding up as well as could be expected, under the circumstances." Lewis's elderly mother, Lucy Meriwether Lewis Marks, lived only a few miles away on the Lewis family farm. Seeing her had been an ordeal in itself. Of course she'd read the news of Lewis's death in the papers, but that didn't make Clark's visit any easier. Mrs. Marks had been quiet and composed, sitting in stoic silence while he explained the details of her son's will. Lewis's older sister Jane flitted around the room like an angry wren, full of pointed questions about what happened to her brother, but Mrs. Marks had only wanted to know one thing.

"General Clark," she asked, "Did my boy die hard?"

"Yes, ma'am...I'm sorry to say that he did."

Mrs. Marks nodded, tears in her eyes, and said simply, "I thought so, General. I thought so."

There is nothing on earth, Clark thought, more painful to see than a mother's grief. He tried to shake the memory out of his mind. It didn't do any good to think about it. If he could only get through one more sad meeting—and persuade Jefferson to take the journals and write the damn book—he could go home to his wife and son.

"Mr. Jefferson, he wanted these brought to you, sir." He pointed to twin bundles that had been set carefully on the parlor's marble-topped desk. "The field notes, and of course, the Expedition journals themselves. I regret to say that two of the Governor's journals were lost in a fire in Tennessee. It was not avoidable. But thank God, the rest survived."

"I understand." Jefferson untied the twine that bound the journals together and began to look through them. "General Clark, the nation is in your debt. It would have been an inestimable loss had these papers perished." He frowned. "I do wish Governor Lewis had completed his account of the

Expedition, so that these books could be deposited with the American Philosophical Society in Philadelphia, where they of all rights should be. It was really quite unconscionable of him to have been so careless with them."

Clark swallowed. "Sir, I have every confidence that he would have died to protect these journals."

Jefferson's frown deepened. "I received a letter from a man named Major Neelly," he said. "I understood from him that the Governor's death was a suicide."

"That's my belief as well," Clark said. "And Governor Lewis did not complete his manuscript, that's true. But it was I who was careless with the papers, sir. I confess I didn't quite realize...that someone else might recognize their worth."

"Ah, well, none of us will make that mistake again." Jefferson flipped through one of the books. "The ethnographic observations, the geography, the flora and fauna...the observations are virtually priceless. The French, the Spanish, or God forbid, the British, would kill to get their hands on these."

"Yes, sir," Clark said. He wanted to add, *And your favorite commanding general, James Wilkinson.* But he held his tongue. This wasn't the time or place. Mr. Jefferson's expression was decidedly prickly.

"And the descriptions are so complete, and so revealing." Jefferson stabbed a long, thin finger at the page. "Take this example right here, of the eulachon, or candlefish. Why, anyone reading this would be able to recognize the species, and prepare it for consumption, and—"

Jefferson paused and stared down at the journal open before him. Clark waited. Jefferson seemed absorbed in the intricate drawing of the fish that cut diagonally across the written words; Lewis had expended several pages on describing it. Clark groaned inwardly. If Jefferson went off on some tangent about the candlefish, it could last for an hour—

Jefferson coughed, pressed a fist to his mouth, then turned away from him. Clark realized with shock that the old man was crying. He felt horrified. Lewis always said Jefferson was a man of reason, that he hated strong displays of emotion of any kind.

What do I do? Clark wondered. *Tell him not to take on so? Pat him on the back?* The thought of making such a familiar gesture was unthinkable. You just didn't go up to Thomas Jefferson, put your hand on his shoulder, and say, "Buck up, man." He felt paralyzed.

Jefferson gulped and struggled for a couple of minutes while Clark stood in stiff, excruciating silence. Finally Jefferson wiped his face with a handkerchief, put his shoulders back, and turned to face him. His eyes were watery and red.

"General, I hope you'll forgive me," he said, a bit brokenly. "Meriwether was almost like a son to me."

"Not at all, sir," Clark replied. His tongue felt thick in his mouth; he couldn't think of a word to say.

Fortunately, Jefferson filled in the gap. He gently closed the cover of the journal. "Did you know that when Meriwether was my personal secretary, and I was at Monticello and he was at home at his farm, I used to signal him from the window?" When Clark smiled and nodded, Jefferson continued, "We had worked out a system of code using mirrors, you see. I would signal to him from the dome room upstairs, and sure enough, ten minutes later he'd come riding up! It was an amazingly efficient means of communication."

Clark chuckled; he'd heard the same story from Lewis. People sometimes speculated about the relationship between the president and his secretary, but to Clark it had never been a mystery. Jefferson was a father without a son; Lewis was a son without a father. They filled a hole in each other's lives. Why else in God's name would they have taken the time to dream up a code using mirrors? It was a game they played together, father and son.

"You know, it sometimes seemed to me that Nature made him, and presented him to me, simply to lead the Western Expedition," Jefferson said. He paused again, smiling wistfully. "I admit, General Clark, I tend to be a bit flibbertigibbet. My thoughts fly hither and yon on a whim. But not he! Meriwether was thoroughly single-minded. Once chosen, I knew he would either complete the Expedition successfully, or not return at all." He looked down at his hands. "I had such confidence in him that at times, I may have been guilty of ignoring...the trials of his mind and heart."

Clark stared at the parquet floor. "Sir...I don't think any of us realized..."

"No? But perhaps, maybe we should have. At least, I feel that *I* should have," Jefferson said. "He was a soldier, and never one for giving up. God only knows what battles he fought in his own mind, at the end. Evidently, his adversaries were such that even his formidable will couldn't overcome them."

Clark nodded, tasting a bitter tang in his mouth. On his way east, alone in the firelight, he'd read Lewis's last journal dozens of times. A host of real and imagined enemies—to Lewis, the black wolf was no less real than Wilkinson—had surged together and combined into a dark tide strong enough to drag his friend down. He said quietly, "Mr. Jefferson, I do believe he struggled against them to the very end."

Jefferson sighed and looked at the fire. "You know, General Clark, I wrote once that the art of life was the art of avoiding pain. Now I know it's merely the art of enduring it." His eyes flicked back to Clark's: gray, steely, resolute. "I can no longer help my beloved man, so I must think not of his lost years, so tragically and suddenly expended, but of a young life lived with great intensity and purpose. I do hope you can find similar peace in your unwavering friendship toward him, and your heroic efforts to aid him in his final extremity."

Clark nodded again, not trusting himself to speak. His own mind taunted, *You came too late.* Mr. Jefferson spoke of the art of enduring pain. That was one he'd have to practice.

"At any rate," Jefferson said, "his untimely death has left a vacancy in the governorship of Upper Louisiana. Given the state of affairs in the territory, President Madison will want to fill the job right away. I have it on the best authority, General Clark, that you will be his first choice."

"*No*, Mr. Jefferson." Clark's reply came so quickly it surprised even him. "I would decline that honor, sir."

Jefferson looked taken aback. "Really?" he said. "With your experience, you'd be ideal. I can think of no one more qualified to carry on Governor Lewis's work—"

"Sir, I am not temperamentally suited to hold that office," Clark interrupted. "With all due respect, Mr. Jefferson, that job is a man-killer. I do not think myself calculated to meet the storms which might be expected."

"General, I find that hard to believe. I'm sorry to find you so decided on the matter, and I do hope you'll reconsider." Jefferson clucked his tongue and began to bind up the journals with twine again. "But certainly, you have many unfinished tasks before you even without the pressures of the governor's office. General, the world is still waiting impatiently for the published findings from your late tour. When do you expect to complete the manuscript?"

Clark gulped. Coming so quickly on the heels of the job offer, the question had caught him off guard. "Mr. Jefferson...given your sponsorship and your interest in the project...well, I thought you might want to complete the work yourself."

"I? Oh, I couldn't possibly." Jefferson waved a dismissive hand. "I am retired now, General. A gentleman farmer, practically in his dotage! Certainly not up to taking on such a Herculean task." He tied the journals with a neat bow. "No, sir, you must do it."

"But Mr. President..." Clark said. "My spelling's pretty poor. I'm all right when it comes to jotting field notes or writing dispatches, but I'm no writer, sir. You, on the other hand—"

Jefferson looked puzzled. "These books belie you, General." He gestured to the journals. "Half of these daily accounts - nay, more than half - were composed by you. Are you saying you can't take your own words, extract the pertinent information, and fashion it into a book?"

Clark groped for an answer. Jefferson made it sound so easy! If Lewis couldn't complete the task, what chance did he have? He blurted out, "Sir, I don't have the first idea how to begin. That's why I was hoping—"

"Well," Jefferson interrupted. He thoughtfully tapped his teeth. "I can think of someone who might be of service to you. Maybe you know him! His name is Nicholas Biddle, of the Philadelphia Biddles. He's a very bright young man—something of a prodigy, I suppose you could say. The family is Federalist, but I can't see that it would make much difference in this case—"

"I'm not acquainted with the young man, sir."

"Well, I'll be happy to write you a letter of introduction," Jefferson pulled quill and paper toward him and proceeded to do just that, continuing to talk while his facile pen flew across the page. "There's no doubt in my mind Biddle would make a superior editor, though of course you'll want to oversee the bulk of the work yourself. I suggest you go see him right away, so as not to delay publication of the work a moment longer. And who knows? Young Biddle is filthy rich, so he might even be willing to do the work *gratis*."

With the air of someone who had just solved a difficult problem, Jefferson handed Clark the letter with a flourish and called for Etienne. "Take these journals and papers back to the General's room, please," he instructed. Smiling, he turned to Clark. "You'll be joining me for dinner, of course. I did so want to discuss the finer points of Mandan vocabulary."

"Of course, sir." Clark said glumly. It hadn't been a question. Julia and the boy would have to wait a few weeks longer. He'd leave for Philadelphia in the morning.

Chapter 48
Wilkinson

New Orleans, Orleans Territory
March 10, 1810

Life was all about departures, James Wilkinson reflected. As his carriage bounced along the muddy street toward the levee, the colorful scene unfolding outside the open window filled him with bittersweet emotion. In this wonderful place, he'd at last found a home for his restless and wandering spirit. Silently, he enumerated the city's charms as she rolled past his window: the wrought-iron galleries and mansard roofs, the rich aroma of coffee and confections, the lively peddlers from Saint Domingue plying their wares, the slave pens with their ebony merchandise, the buskers and hustlers, the Creoles and clowns, the decadence, the elegance, the sordidness, the *money*—

Ah! His throat caught. How long would it be before he gazed upon his beloved city again?

Beside him, Celeste pressed his hand with soft fingers and dabbed at her eyes with a handkerchief. It plucked at his heartstrings to see his young bride so upset. Married only five days, and already they'd been torn asunder. These politicians in Washington City had no shame whatsoever—

His stomach tightened a little. He'd gotten the word several weeks ago that an investigation concerning him was pending in the House of Representatives. *Two* investigations, actually. The first concerned the Army's mortality rate during its encampment at Terre aux Boeufs and the movement upriver. By the time the troops had arrived at Natchez, almost fifty percent of the men had died from disease.

Regrettable, certainly, he mused, but avoidable? Certainly not! Seeing as the move had *not* been his idea—he had that boob Secretary Eustis to thank for that—plus the fact that the congressmen who had initiated the investigation were well-known for being coarse, muckraking knaves, well...he wasn't going to lose any sleep over it.

But he had to admit that the second investigation had him a little worried.

His wretched enemies had engineered a congressional resolution asking for an inquiry into his conduct, to find out—oh, perish the thought, what were the exact words?—whether he had "received money corruptly from Spanish agents and engaged in a conspiracy for the purpose of dismembering the Union." The clumsiness of his accusers was embarrassing, but the charges were serious. If he could not defend himself, he would certainly lose his command, and perhaps face a much more dire fate—

And yet...and yet, part of him welcomed the fight.

He patted Celeste's hand. "There, there, my dear. You mustn't take all this too seriously. Your husband is a sly old fox, and I assure you I'll be quite all right. It won't do to worry and fret while I'm gone."

"But it's not fair," she wept. "Why in heaven's name are these people saying such terrible things about you? You only did your duty."

"The knowledge sustains me," he said. "Take heart, my dear. As the poet said, 'Heaven tries our virtue by affliction, and oft the cloud which wraps the present hour serves to brighten all our future days.'"

"Oh, James, you see the good in everything." Celeste dried her tears and gazed at him with dewy eyes.

Wilkinson chuckled as they rounded the corner and pulled onto Levee Street. The place was a beehive of activity. The wharves teemed with keelboats, flatboats, and tall ships of every description, all loading and unloading goods. Bales of cotton, barrels of sugar, hogsheads of tobacco and whiskey—and furs, pallets of beautiful furs from the great western wilderness. The sights, sounds, and smells of commerce. It did his heart good to see it.

And, come to think of it, there was one wretch he wouldn't be seeing in Washington—that budding fur entrepreneur himself, Governor Meriwether Lewis. In his more reflective moments, Wilkinson had to admit that as an adversary, Lewis had turned out to be a bit of a disappointment. For all his bluster at Brady's tavern, the young pup had been no match for him at all. When his back was against the wall, he'd simply fled east towards safety and Jefferson. And when his men closed in on the Chickasaw Trace, Lewis hadn't even put up a fight. Instead, he dispatched himself with all the histrionic flair of an overdramatic schoolboy.

Wilkinson snorted and shook his head. *The fool! Didn't he know it was all a game?* He chuckled again. When one embarked on the game of war, inevitably there were casualties. His adversaries in Washington would do well to look to young Lewis's fate if they thought he'd go down without a fight. After all, there were many at the highest levels who still served his cause. And, he could always count on the fact that most men had small minds and quickly grew bored with lost causes. Within a few months, they would forget about all this unpleasant business.

But there were others—one, at least—who would not forget. And that was the man he'd have to watch. James Neelly was no one, a mere dogsbody. Crushing him was hardly worth the effort. But William Clark—well, it was certain he wouldn't sit silently in St. Louis forever.

Wilkinson heaved a short sigh as the driver drew up near the gangway of the schooner *Felicity*, bound for Baltimore. He steered his bulk out of the carriage and held up a hand to stop Celeste before she alighted. "Stay seated, my dear," he said, as the driver climbed down to load his trunks aboard. "The wharves are filthy. I wouldn't want you to soil your shoes."

Celeste crowded to the window, all fair hair, powder and perfume. "*Au revoir*, darling." She pressed a moist kiss on his lips. "Hurry home, my brave cavalier."

"T'will be but a twinkling," he said with a smile. "Remember what I told you—water the obedients once a week, but not if it rains. The grapevines can get along on their own."

"Yes, James." She nodded breathlessly.

"Well." He clapped his hat on his head. "Until then." Choked with sentiment, he turned on his heel and started up the gangway. He knew all the people were watching him and feeling impressed. How could they not? In his bright red uniform coat covered with golden braid, spotless pantaloons, and shining spurs, he was the very picture of a commander. Doubtless they had all come to the levee to see him off—

As he turned to wave to his multitude of well-wishers, he noticed a lone man hurrying along Levee Street, dodging draymen and picking his way over the coiled ropes that littered the wharves. It was none other than Don Diego Morphy. When he caught sight of Wilkinson on the deck of the schooner, Morphy broke into a half-run and came huffing up the gangway.

"*General*," he panted. "*Gracias a Dios* I caught you! I understand you've been recalled to Washington."

Wilkinson smiled benignly. "A person in my position must expect spurious attacks, Don Diego. I am merely going to answer the charges that have been brought against me, and to correct the false impressions of my deluded countrymen." He winked. "Me, an agent of Spain? Why, the idea is preposterous!"

"We all have to answer to our masters, General," Don Morphy agreed, with some agitation in his voice. "For example, my superiors in Havana want to know what became of the ten thousand dollars I advanced you last fall when you returned from Natchez."

"I assure you it will be spent in the service of Spain, Don Diego." In fact, those Spanish garden tiles and casks of Madeira he'd ordered ought to be arriving any day now. He placed his hand on Don Morphy's shoulder. "*Vaya con Dios*, my friend."

"But, General, that money was for specific services! Remember our discussion, at the time of the western rebellion? How you were going to deliver Lewis Merry Wether's journals and the maps to me, and I was going to forward them on to Havana?"

"There were complications," Wilkinson said hastily. "I'm afraid Lewis Merry Wether is no more. Ah, look! The captain is signaling to his men—we will shortly pull anchor. You'd best disembark."

"I know Merry Wether is dead, but I can't write to Havana and tell them I spent their money on *complications!*" Morphy said. "What about the papers you promised me?"

"Out of reach for now, my good sir." Wilkinson took his arm and hustled him down the gangway. "Patience is all! I have not the slightest doubt that Spain will come out on top in the end." He kissed Morphy on both cheeks— oh, damn, he was getting his customs mixed up again—and left him fuming on the wharf. As the *Felicity* made ready to head for the open sea, Wilkinson gazed down from the deck and gave him a small salute.

"What about the journals?" Morphy shouted. "What about the maps? *What about the gold mine?*"

Wilkinson shrugged. "There's always a shadow in the sunshine, Don Diego. But take courage, *mi amigo!* The laurels go to those who risk all for God and country."

Don Morphy looked disgusted. As the sails puffed with wind and the ship began to heave away from the wharf, Wilkinson turned, posed, and grasped for a line with which to close the show. A-ha! "'For patriots still must fall for statesmen's safety, and perish by the country they preserve,'" he shouted. "A little ditty that's apropos for us both. *Adios*, Don Diego! I'll see you when I return."

The sailors couldn't help staring at the man in a general's uniform, holding onto the gunwale, his belly jiggling with laughter. *Another day, another game*, Wilkinson thought. How he relished it all! The cat-and-mouse pursuits, the daring wagers, the comical shock on the face of the loser—*What, me? How can this be?* Oh, there was nothing better in the world! He supposed he ought to be worried about Don Morphy revealing what he knew, but the Spaniard had his own reasons for keeping their association a secret.

Just for a moment, he turned and stared back at New Orleans. "We all have dreams, Don Diego," he murmured. His own had gone up on smoke on the Chickasaw Trace—quite literally, from what he understood. But no matter. When you played a game for high stakes, you had to expect occasional losses. This was a sad fact of life that old men knew, and young men had to learn.

Still chuckling, he turned his back on New Orleans and faced the wide blue sea.

Chapter 49
Clark

Louisville, Kentucky
January 28, 1810

On a good day, George Rogers Clark could muster what little strength remained in his arms and push his frail body around on crutches, teetering around the house on his one remaining leg. He could no longer live on his own—the stroke and the amputation had made that decision for him—but on a good day, he could move himself from his bed to the door leading to the front porch at Locust Grove, the fine home owned by his sister Lucy and her husband. Once there, he could collapse into the big, comfortable chair his sister had provided for him, and spend the day drowsing, dreaming, and watching the traffic to and from the growing city he had founded thirty years earlier.

Today was not a good day.

William Clark flapped open an enormous coat made out of a grizzly bear's fur and draped it around his older brother's shoulders. Then, he helped George poke his arms through the wide sleeves. George put his arm around Clark's back; his fingers grasped the thick material of Clark's army greatcoat. Clark could barely feel it; arthritis had robbed his brother's once-powerful hands of their grip.

"You sure you want to sit outside, George?" Clark asked. "It's just about freezing."

George nodded. "I always sit outside." The stroke caused him to swallow his words, but Clark didn't have any trouble understanding what his brother wanted.

Clark raised his eyebrows at the servant who stood on George's other side. They both stood up, eased the old general into a standing position, and carried him out to the porch. George was weak today, close to being a dead weight, and Clark felt terribly afraid he would slip out of their hands and go crashing on to the floor. But it was all right. As soon as they had lowered

George into his chair, Clark waved the servant away and tended to his brother himself, arranging the grizzly bear coat so that it enveloped George's chest.

"Don't fuss over me," George growled.

"Understood," Clark said. "I hope you don't mind if I keep y'company, though."

He pulled up another chair and placed it near to his brother's. From inside, Clark could smell cinnamon and cloves and ginger. His wife was inside with Lucy; his sister had promised to give Julia a lesson in making gingerbread. Clark looked forward to sampling the results. Feeling the pinch of the wind, he pulled the collar of his greatcoat up around his face.

"I thought you said you never got cold anymore," George said.

Clark smiled. "I've been known to exaggerate."

George blinked his eyes, as blue as the winter sky, and pursed his lips. "When are you gonna tell me 'bout your friend? I've heard you talkin' to brother Jonathan about what happened." He pulled a wry face. "I know I'm a useless old bastard now, Billy, but you can still talk to me."

Their eyes met. Clark knew how much George hated being helpless. "I didn't want to burden you with it, George. Lord knows you've got your own troubles."

George's eyes narrowed. "You think I'll come apart at the seams if you mention the name James Wilkinson in my presence?"

Clark felt his self-control slip a notch. He blurted, "I'll kill that son-ofabitch."

George pulled his coat tighter around him. "I was commander of the Kentucky militia before he came along. Indian commissioner, too. By the time he got through with me, what little bit of credibility I had was gone. And everyone thought I was a drunk." He smiled, rubbed his hands together, then stuck them back under the grizzly fur coat. "A reputation I've done my best to live up to."

Clark sat silently for a moment, anger roiling in his chest. "I haven't figured out yet how I'm going to bring him down. But God help me, I will, George. This won't stand—"

"You want to end up like me, then?"

Clark wasn't sure how to answer. "George, you know how I feel about you—"

"And Lewis," George interrupted. "I know how much you esteemed that boy, too. I'm askin' you plain, do you want to end up like either one of us?"

"George, I know Wilkinson is dangerous! Don't you think I've learned, after everything that's happened? That's all the more reason to see to it that he doesn't just walk away—"

"Walk away." George snorted. "I wish I could."

"George, I didn't mean—"

"Relax. I know what you meant." George twisted around and wagged his finger at the house. "You smell that gingerbread? You hear those gals in there talkin'? You got back everything I lost, Bill Clark. You're the Indian superintendent now, and the general of the militia. You got a fine wife who'd follow you to the ends of the earth, and a strong baby son. Everybody who knows you respects you! And the Expedition—Lord, do you know how proud I feel, whenever I think of it? And jealous, too?"

"But that's just it, George." Clark swallowed hard. "Lewis deserved all those things too, and Lord knows you did. Then Wilkinson comes along with his kiss of death, and it's all gone, just like that. The way Lewis died—I can't just accept it—"

"You want my advice? Walk away." George settled back in his chair and turned his battered face to the river. "Walk away, Billy. Because there's nothing you can do for him now."

July 16, 1810
St. Louis, Louisiana Territory

Walk away. It was easier said than done. But for now, anyway, he was taking George's advice.

Clark had set up a huge table in his office—the room that used to be Meriwether's—for his work on the book. As Jefferson had predicted, he'd hit it off with Nicholas Biddle, and the young scholar was hard at work in Philadelphia on the narrative for the book. They had decided to call it *History of the Expedition under the Command of Captains Lewis and Clark*.

Clark himself was working on the natural history section and, of course, the map. He bent over the table, surrounded by draft maps and field notes, and stroked his finger over his upper lip. He was going to make a master map of the entire Western half of the continent. The finished result would be engraved and included with the book, but he wouldn't stop there. Clark envisioned the map hung on the wall, a work continuously in progress as he got new information from traders, trappers, explorers, and Indians. It would be a reference that everyone heading west could come to St. Louis and use.

The thought of all those visitors made him feel excited, but a little sad, too. He couldn't help wishing Lewis were there to share it with him.

He'd gotten back to St. Louis just after Independence Day. The book wasn't the only job he had to keep him busy. Though he'd declined the governorship—Benjamin Howard, the former Virginia congressman, was expected to arrive any day to take over the post—his responsibilities as Superintendent of Indian Affairs had been expanded.

Not to mention the task of getting his household up and running again. He felt York's absence more than he'd expected, but he hadn't had the heart to make him return with the rest of the family. York had promised to come back when his wife and children moved down South, and Clark planned to hold him to it. Still, he felt troubled when he thought of York. It seemed like each of them expected something that the other man wasn't willing to give.

He wondered what York would say when he heard the latest news from Mr. Jefferson. Since their meeting last fall, he'd kept the former President informed about the arrangements for the book, and Jefferson had honored him with regular replies. In his most recent letter, Jefferson wrote about a surprise caller he'd recently received. Incredibly, John Pernia had survived the wilderness and turned up at Monticello, demanding his two hundred and forty dollars in back wages. "I informed him that you were overseeing the settlement of the Governor's estate, and could be applied to at St. Louis for relief," Jefferson wrote. "He appeared most distressed, poor fellow." Clark didn't doubt it.

Lewis's estate might be an awful mess, but you couldn't say the same about his popularity. Death had done wonders. Not a day had passed since he got home that he wasn't taken aside in the street by someone who wanted to whisper in his ear that he had never, ever believed those rumors about the armed rebellion, and wasn't it too bad about poor Lewis—"a learned scholar and a scientific gentleman!" About the only person who hadn't joined in the flood of crocodile tears was Frederick Bates. The little whelp had never apologized, and Clark knew he never would.

Clark set aside his quill and pushed back from the big table. Moving to his desk, he pulled out the bottom drawer and retrieved a handsome leather journal, bound in red morocco. This was one book that Thomas Jefferson would never see, and that Nicholas Biddle would not transcribe for posterity. Holding the book against his chest without opening it, Clark sank back into his chair and let his eyes rest on the painted Shoshone elk hide hanging on the wall.

James Wilkinson was in Washington, sweating out the scrutiny of a congressional investigation. From what Jonathan had written, it seemed likely that it would end in court-martial and disgrace. Clark doubted it. James Wilkinson had been intriguing at least since the Revolution, and probably since the cradle. He was a survivor. It wouldn't surprise Clark if he somehow walked away from this latest scrape without a scratch.

He opened the book and flipped through the pages. He didn't need to read it. He knew every word inside from memory, the chronicle of Lewis's pain etched forever on his heart.

He remembered how sometimes on the Expedition, when things weren't going so well, Lewis would say, *Patience, men! Patience, patience...* Even then, Clark had known the words weren't really meant for the men. They were meant for Lewis himself, a reminder to hold his restless spirit in check.

Clark needed no such reminder. He was a patient man. He could wait.

He tapped the cover of the journal and stood up. He could smell biscuits baking in the kitchen. Through the window, he saw Nancy and Easter sitting under the pecan tree shelling peas while the babies—Lew and Easter's boy Tom—babbled and played in the shade. In the garden, old Scipio tended the vegetables while Seaman sniffed at his heels.

He crouched down by the fireplace. In spite of the heat of the day, he had asked Scipio to lay in some firewood that morning. Now, he found the tinderbox and picked the flint off the hearth. He struck it once, watched it flare, then fed the fire, waiting until the logs caught.

He shucked his coat and leaned his back against the wall by the window, watching the fire build. Another voice drifted in from the yard. "Mama's home!" He turned his head just in time to see Julia running into the garden, home from the market. She took off her bonnet, shook her curls loose, and swept Lew up in her arms for a big hug.

The fire was bright and hot now. He took the journal in his hands. It held a host of enemies—fear and madness, rage and despair. Clark wished he could talk to Lewis, one last time, just to tell him that he had the same demons. Every man did. But of course, he would never talk to Lewis again. George was right. There was nothing he could do for him but go on living.

Clark laid the book on top of the burning logs. Within seconds, flames licked at the cover and began to worm their way into the pages. The guts of the book flared as the leather shriveled and curled.

The smoke stung his eyes, but even as he blinked away tears he was aware of the world outside the room. Beyond these walls, he had responsibilities.

Drays groaned in the street; dogs barked; boatmen shouted down at the levee. He smiled to himself. There were fewer Creole shouts these days, and more American twangs. His countrymen were coming on the heels of Lewis and Clark, questing, ever westering. No matter what happened, it was going to be interesting.

Clark pulled the screen across the fireplace, then leaned on the windowsill to get some fresh air. Lew was staring at the ground with a look of intense concentration on his face. Clark felt his face relax into a fond smile as he watched his little son reach for a pecan. Lew's bottom touched earth before his hands did, and he sat down hard. Still calm, the child looked around for Julia. Only when he saw her did he let out a heart-rending shriek.

"That boy's got the old Clark charm!" Clark hollered as Julia rushed to the boy's side. "Already got the ladies dancin' to his fiddle!"

Then he noticed something else. Smoke was pouring from the kitchen. The biscuits had been forgotten—

"Oh, Lordy." Clark shook his head. Turning his back on the fireplace, he trotted out of the office and through the back of the house. A typical day at the Clark household! "Scipio, get a bucket a' water. Easter, your boy's running into traffic, you best catch him. Nancy, mind them peas!"

In the fireplace, the last journal, like its author, burned with fierce intensity. The end came quickly, as the spine broke apart and the pages dissolved, one by one, into ashes.

ABOUT THE AUTHOR

Frances Hunter lives in Austin, Texas. This is her first novel. To learn more about Frances Hunter, visit www.frances-hunter.com.

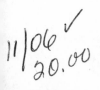

If you liked this book and would like to pass a copy on to someone else, please check with your favorite bookstore, online bookseller, or order via our web site at:

www.blindrabbitpress.com

If you prefer to order by mail, please use this form:

Name _____

Address _____

City _____ State _____ Zip _____

To the Ends of the Earth _____ copies @ $20.00 each $ _____

Texas residents, please add 8.25% sales tax $ _____

Shipping: $4.00 first copy; $2.00 each additional copy* $ _____

Total enclosed (check or money order) $ _____

*For more than five copies, please contact us for quantity rates.

Note: We do accept international orders but request that payment be made via our web site or an international money order in U.S. dollars. Residents of Canada pay the same shipping rates as U.S. customers. Please contact us for shipping rates to your location if outside the United States or Canada.

Send completed order form and your check or money order to:

Blind Rabbit Press
Order Department
P.O. Box 8136
Austin, TX 78713-8136

Fax: 815-572-8901
orders@blindrabbitpress.com